The STONE TESTAMENT

Praise for *The Stone Testament*:

"Wonderful, rich . . . breathtaking"
FINANCIAL TIMES

"A writer of Rees's calibre goes right in at the deep end. Mayan apocalypses are just the beginning . . . the book also covers shamanism, suicide cults, pterosaurs, evil gods, busking on the tube and early 20th century adventurers."
GUARDIAN

"I found this book mesmerising, multi-layered and totally absorbing."
Hilary McKay

Praise for Celia Rees:

"A major writer for teenage readers."
INDEPENDENT

"Rees' themes are those of great literature."
BOOKS FOR KEEPS

Also by Celia Rees

BLOOD SINISTER

THE WISH HOUSE

PIRATES!

SORCERESS

THE VANISHED

WITCH CHILD

THE CUNNING MAN

TRUTH OR DARE

THE BAILEY GAME

Celia Rees

The
STONE
TESTAMENT

MARION LLOYD BOOKS

First published in the UK in 2007 by Scholastic Children's Books
An imprint of Scholastic Ltd
Euston House, 24 Eversholt Street
London, NW1 1DB, UK
Registered office: Westfield Road, Southam, Warwickshire, CV47 0RA
SCHOLASTIC and associated logos are trademarks
and or registered trademarks of Scholastic Inc.

This edition published 2008 by Scholastic Ltd.

978 1407 10505 5

A CIP catalogue record for this book
is available from the British Library

Printed by CPI Bookmarque, Croydon, CR0 4TD
Papers used by Scholastic Children's Books are made
from wood grown in sustainable forests.

1 3 5 7 9 10 8 6 4 2

www.scholastic.co.uk/zone

For Roy and Owain, who both loved fantasy.

"And you believe that there are such things?"

"Oh, I think so. Yes, I believe I could give you convincing evidence on that point."

". . .but I want to know whether you seriously think that there is any foundation of fact beneath these fancies. Is it not all a department of poetry; a curious dream with which man has indulged himself?"

"I can only say that it is no doubt better for the great mass of people to dismiss it all as a dream. . ."

The White People – Arthur Machen

This might suggest that the so-called imaginary time is really the real time, and that what we call real time is just a figment of our imaginations.

A Brief History of Time – Stephen W. Hawking

Can such things be?

Can Such Things Be? – Ambrose Bierce

Contents

ELDER TIME

1   THE EYE OF THE SEA   3

TIME TO COME

2   HOPE FOR A BETTER DAY   11
3   THE ADVOCATE   28
4   10 2 NEVER   32
5   THE MOST FAMOUS GIRL IN THE WORLD   40
6   TEMPLE GREEN   43
7   IN DREAMS   57
8   VISITING TIME   65
9   THE INSPECTOR OF ANOMALIES   101
10   KA   108
11   XIBALBA BE: ROAD TO THE UNDERWORLD   118
12   INSIDE THE TEMPLE   124
13   BRICE AMBROSE STONE'S FIELD NOTES   130
14   EXTREME UNCTION   152
15   ALARM   155
16   SINGER AND THE SONG   166
17   EXEAT   173
18   UNLOOKED-FOR MEETING   179
19   11 FORFAR STREET   185
20   THE LONG ROOM   189

21 CITY DAZE 213

22 GOING UNDERGROUND 218

23 STRANGE MEETING 225

24 GHOST STATION 231

25 THE PANIC ROOM 236

26 TEA WITH FRIENDS 242

27 MIRRORS 249

28 THE GRAND MASTER'S CHAMBER 255

29 TIME PASSING 261

30 THEN THERE WERE THREE 270

ELDER TIME

I 277

II 288

III 294

IV 299

V 304

VI 312

VII 323

31 DECONSTRUCTION 326

VIII 330

IX 339

X 344

XI 347

XII 356

XIII 362

XIV 368
XV 372

32 RAID 381

XVI 386
XVII 391
XVIII 395

33 STRANGER IN A STRANGE LAND 399
34 REUNION 406
35 RAVINGS OF A MADMAN 416
37 AFTERWORD 419

Acknowledgements

ELDER TIME

1

THE EYE OF THE SEA

Mikel sang the Song of Leaving. The land was doomed to die, along with all living plants and beings. The only way to survive was to depart.

He was so intent on his lament and the task that he had been set, that he did not notice how cold it was, or how frost had formed on his hair and on his brows and lashes. He had been here for more than a day, sitting cross-legged and motionless, high on the cliff above the Cape of Souls, where three oceans met. The land fell sheer to the raging water, and then down still further to the depths of the abyss. The waves crashed against the towering cliffs, rebounding as if from the end of the world. They collapsed back into a furious chaos of white water, which turned in wide spirals, slowly at the outside, but then faster and faster, tighter and tighter, moving always towards one central pool which lay directly below the face of the cliff. Here the water was still and black, solid like glass. The Eye of the Sea.

There was something different about the bulging lens of water, something wrong. The boy was disturbed in some deep way, but knew better than to stare into the terrifying swirl of currents. To look would mean to be sucked down as surely as any ship, as surely as the spirits of the departing dead, who whispered past him on the final stage of their journey. In a late stuttering rush, the souls of men, women and children came skittering round him, like dead leaves blown on the wind.

The number of the dead had been growing. Some of those who had drawn black instead of white in the selection had elected to leave by their own hand and smoke still billowed from the funeral pyres of those taken by plague and famine. Calls for greater sacrifice meant incense choked the air above the Temple of the Beast Gods and the steps were slick with blood. The precincts rang day and night with prayer and chanting, but the Gods were not appeased.

It was not enough. It would never be enough.

There had been desperate reports even before he left the city. Weary patrols had returned from the outlying areas; hardened soldiers sickened by what they had seen. The Beast Gods were coming down from the Mountain, destroying all in their path. Stories spread quickly throughout the city. How the Gods fed on the flesh of every living thing, marking no difference between men and animals. How they had become so gorged and glutted that they only consumed the choicest, tearing out the heart and liver, breaking open the brainpan to get at the meat like a man might crack a nut. Mikel's heart became heavy with new dread. What would they do when they reached the city and discovered the betrayal that awaited them?

He would not allow these thoughts to distract him, or acknowledge the souls who passed him, or listen to their complaints and lamentations. He had been left here as part of the Great Purpose, where All must act as One. He kept his eyes fixed on the curving rim of the horizon, trying to see past it to the seas beyond these seas. His ears were attuned to the stillness below the roar of the swirling, restless, frothing surface of the water as he listened for the vast creatures of the deep ocean. He could hear them singing, calling to each other, but they were very distant. A faint sound. The grunts of hunting seals, the whistling clicks of dolphins and porpoises, the chirps of the flightless birds which darted among them, these were all much louder, but he ignored them. These creatures kept close to the coast and were not useful. Only the creatures who ranged across the vast emptiness of the open ocean could sing to him of the sea roads, the routes that ships should take across the watery wastes and what hazards they might encounter. This was what he had been put here to learn.

His head turned to the north-east. A series of stuttering notes, faint but strong, clanged inside his skull and pulsed through his brain. The sound was coming from one of the great-toothed, blunt-headed whales. The pulse received no answering chatter. A lone bull. The boy waited for him to get nearer before he sent out his own signal. There it was again, this time much stronger. He put his tongue to the roof of his mouth to approximate the clicking noise, although that was not necessary. He was sending out his thought, dressed in sounds that the creature would understand.

In return, he heard only the shrilling of the wind, the pounding surf, the roar of turning water, the scratchy scatter of snow pellets. The silence around him spread to the other animals. Seals, dolphins, porpoises, birds all fell silent.

The great beast was coming closer. They were curious creatures. Curious and intelligent. He would want to know who was summoning him from the shore. He was lying off to the east: a double stone's throwing distance from the cliffs. The boy heard the whispering hiss before he saw the white spray of the spout. The grey back just broke the surface like a rolling log. He hung there waiting, listening to the boy explaining, then with a flick of his tail he was gone in a rapid burst of sound. The boy had a quick plunging vision: a mirror shimmer of bubbles, deep indigo blue, then sickening blackness and cold. He cleared his head of that and smiled to himself. When he was given the ruler and dividers he would know where to put them, how to move them across the map.

The sounds started again, echoing against the case of his head, vibrating through the bones of his face. Loud. Soft. Loud. Soft. The voice of the largest of all. More than one individual. They drew closer, stopping further off shore. He could not see their narrow blue forms through the sleet and covering water, but he could hear their voices. They were vast, their length twice that of the tallest tree in the forest, and they ranged through many seas. He listened intently to their song. Their language was harder for him to master, but he managed to make himself understood. Their replies nearly deafened him. For such large, stately creatures, they were very talkative. His brain struggled to take in all he was being told: not only the best way to cross the trackless ocean, but of other lands: how large they were, how far. They also spoke of great changes in other places: freezings, floods, new seas forming, dry land disappearing and appearing where none had been before.

He thanked them and braced himself for the juddering coldness of their leaving. He had not been instructed to find out about other countries – merely to learn the sea roads. Nevertheless such information was useful, and could be vital. There was no point in setting sail for lands as threatened as their own. He pulled his reed cloak tighter around him. The sea was barely visible, a glitter of black through whirling snowflakes. Inland, ice was edging down from the mountains, filling the valleys like splayed fingers, pushing towards the sea. In some places the ice creep had already reached the ocean. Huge blocks fell away with great groaning crashes, pushed by the inexorable weight of the mass behind.

The chatter of the smaller sea creatures had started again. The birds on the ledges below argued and chattered. Beaks clicked and snicked as the young ones preened with long bills, working quickly to remove any remaining down from their wings. Little fuzzy feathers floated up on the wind. The birds were making ready to leave. Some had gone already. Only the hardiest would remain here. They must fly to warmer lands in the North. Even the deep ocean was preferable to this land in winter. He wondered what he could learn from them, but bird brains held little. . .

His attention shifted away from the squabbling colony. Someone was coming up the path behind him. She stepped softly, carefully, but still he could hear her feet brushing against the short frozen stalks of grass, the creaking leather soles of her shoes. He knew who his visitor was, but she had closed herself from him. One of the few who had that skill. The surface of her mind was as black and shiny as the glass of the knife she was easing from its scabbard.

She was behind him now. He could hear her breathing, light and natural despite the steepness of the climb. He'd been expecting her to come for him. He could not read her intention, but he could hear the whisper of blade against well-oiled leather. He sensed a momentary hesitation, but did nothing. Before him lay the great Eye of the Sea, behind him stood a Warrior of the Goddess, poised to kill.

TIME TO COME

2

HOPE FOR A BETTER DAY

Everyone was dead. Not just in that room, but in the next, and the next. She knew because the flies told her. One or two at first, in aimless heavy flight, buzzed and banged against the windows, but the weather had been very warm, freakishly so for the time of year, and now the sound was a constant, busy, monotonous drone as if the many had become one. She could feel the imprint of their tiny clawed feet as they crawled across her face, her hands, every part of her body that was exposed, but still she did not move. Even the flicker of an eyelid would give her away. The flies did not come alone. Baal-Zebul moved with them. This was how she knew him. He had been given many titles over the millennia, but the meaning of his name was always the same: Lord of the Flies.

The destruction would be general. The Fifth Age of the World would end in fire and flood, tempest and tumult. The Beast Gods would stalk the land and only the Children of the Sixth Dawn had been forewarned. Not just here, but in identical communities all over the

11

country, all over the world, the Children of the Sixth Dawn, C6D for short, had left early, going to another level to await the Endtime, the final setting of the sun.

She had been taken young. She did not know her age, or her true name, or the place of her birth. She had no memory of the time before they took her, but sometimes, in dreams, she saw a place that was very different from this: a place that was the colour of ashes, a land of craters and ruins where a hot wind always blew and the dust was white with stinging salts. Sometimes she saw a ruined settlement: mud huts, crumbling to dust, straggled out of a burning town. Behind them, a dried-up lake, behind that, a line of grey hills riven with black gullies. In front, lay a highway with no traffic on it. A thin dog tore and worried at a lump of something that lay beside a wreck at the roadside. She knew there were people, crouched in the corner on the mud-stamped floor of a hut half destroyed by rocket fire, but there were no people in her dreams. There were never any people in her dreams. She was always alone, tasting the bitter wind.

They had probably purchased her. When they were harvesting, they went well equipped with dollars. They went to countries which were poor to begin with, torn by war and conflict, where there was no lack of people willing to sell their children. They had given her a name: Zillah. They consulted a name book when they took in new children, working through A to Z and back again, as methodical in this as in everything else. She had no surname, no family name. She was a Truechild of the Sixth Dawn. That was seven years ago. She would have been perhaps seven or eight years old, older than their preferred age for taking children, so now she was probably fourteen or fifteen. Old enough, anyway, to be moved to the Women's House, which was where she lay now, surrounded by the only family she had ever known. She felt no sorrow or pity for the dead who lay around her. She held no affection for any one of them. Relationships of any kind had been discouraged. The children in the Kinder House were regularly rotated to discourage friendship; their carers constantly changed to prevent any kind of bonding between adult and child. All contact with the outside was, of course, strictly forbidden. To be a Child took believers beyond earthbound ties of family and friendship. Such relationships were invalid. They were formed of clay. That was what they had believed. And they had all been believers. They had obeyed the edict. Taken their lives without question. Now they were all dead and her only feelings were anger and contempt.

All love was reserved for the Divine Founder, saviour and preserver, the ineffable I AM. His was the only true religion, based on vision and visitation. The Founder had passed on to a different level years ago, but his work was carried on by another, the Advocate. All other belief was false. It was all written down in *The Meaning of the Sixth Dawn — The Book of the Law*. This was the only permitted work, but Zillah had found other books.

The Children of the Sixth Dawn had community houses, called Chapters, spread across the world, but this was the Master House. Formally called Ringmere

Hall, it was perfect for the Children: a secluded mansion set in large grounds deep in the English countryside, with electronic gates at the top of a long drive and high fences all around. The main building was very grand, fashioned from dark honey-coloured stone and built around a central courtyard. The Children only used the porticoed main building and the two wings leading off it; the eastern range over the entrance was sealed off from the rest of the house. This was the Founder's Wing, where he had lived when this was his home. It was kept as he had left it, with nothing changed, in anticipation of his possible return.

Entry was forbidden to all except the Advocate.

Zillah found a way in when she was ten or eleven. A small door at the foot of a neglected flight of steps led to the sequestered wing. She'd kept her visits infrequent, choosing her times carefully: afternoons when the younger children were supposed to be resting, or in the grounds exercising; at night when everyone was sleeping. She collected stubs of the candles used in ceremonies, stole matches from the kitchen and moved like a ghost through the shuttered rooms. It was clear that the wing had not been occupied for many years. Wallpaper peeled and tapestries gaped, the heavy fabric torn by its own weight. Dark portraits glowered down from the walls and shrouded furniture made vague shapes in the dim light. The rooms smelt of coal fires, long extinguished. Cobwebs hung like banners from the ceilings and dust lay on every other surface. Zillah was careful not to touch anything and crept from room to room, fearful that she might find the Founder's mummified form stretched out behind the drooping canopy of one of the four-poster beds, but there was no sign of him, or anyone else.

Except in one room that Zillah called the library. Books lined the walls and lay about open on tables, as if someone had just been reading them. When Zillah found this room, her heart beat harder. She stood on the threshold, gripped by fear. The small, windowless room was completely free of dust and cobwebs, which meant it *was* visited, and frequently. A leather chair was pulled up to the fire. Next to it was a small round table with an oil lamp on it, a decanter of amber liquid and a glass coated with a sweet, sticky residue. Some kind of alcohol, she guessed, although such things were against the Law. The ashes in the grate were still warm, and a large coal scuttle contained the makings of a fire. Leather trunks and suitcases lay in a row on the floor. If she was found in a forbidden area, there was no telling what would happen to her, but her curiosity overcame her. The suitcases tempted her into the room.

The battered leather cases were stamped across the corner: B. G. Wesson. A chill ran through her as she recognized the name of the Esteemed Founder before he shed his earthly persona, but she was curious. She had never thought of him as a real person with possessions. The cases were covered with old labels, half torn off, brown and brittle, from all over the world. Inside, they contained a baffling mix of things. One was full of old documents: maps and manuscripts. Another contained personal papers of some sort: curling, dog-eared letters written in the same cramped hand on small sheets of cream paper, the ink fading to sepia. Another appeared to contain bits of rock, some marked in red crayon to show where there might be an inscription. The last contained a series of small objects, their shape uncertain, worn away over time, or sucked by the sea. There was a strange, domed box, made of discoloured bone or ivory, brown and streaked, like an old man's teeth. It was covered in faint symbols, worn to mere scratches. It was empty. The inside was lined with padded green leather, ridged and gnarly, like crocodile skin. Zillah was about to close it, disappointed, when she saw something gleaming through a crack in the lining. Zilla reached in to retrieve it, using her finger and thumb like tweezers. The object was small, but made of gold. It was hard to see what it was, but Zillah thought it was a bee. The wings had broken off, the body had been smoothed by age, but there were still faint stripes on its back, and the shape tapered from a broad head to where the sting would be. It fitted exactly into the palm of her hand.

At that moment, the cobwebs in the corridor stirred and fluttered, disturbed by a draught of cold air coming from behind her. She listened and her ears seemed to move on her head as she heard the gritty scrape and tread of feet on stone. The door by which she'd entered was not the only entrance into the room. She shut the box with shaking fingers, checked that she had disturbed nothing, and crept out the way that she had come.

It was afterwards, when she was back in the dormitory, that she realized that she was still holding the golden bee. She'd never owned anything. Personal possessions were not allowed. Everything was communal, even clothes. This was the only thing she had that was different from anybody else. She had kept it ever since, making a pocket for it in the mattress of each successive bed that she occupied. Somehow, having it near her, made her feel safe. She had it now. Clutched in her hand.

The library was used by the Advocate, and only by him. Only one glass, only one comfortable chair. So she confined her visits to when he was away from the house. It was easy. He travelled extensively – tireless in his mission to take the message all over the world. They were told of his whereabouts in the announcements made at Prime, so she would know then if it was safe to go to the library. She read with a hunger. The books were strange to her because all books were banned, apart from those written by the Founder. The only one she'd heard of was the Biblos. The Holy Book. The Founder used little quotations to justify things that he said in his own writings. Now, with the whole text in front of her, Zillah could see how he had corrupted what was written, twisting the words to serve his own ends. The more she read, the more she realized that *The Meaning of the Sixth Dawn* was a crazy mass of borrowed beliefs, as flawed as a jigsaw where the pieces had been cut to fit.

She wondered how anyone could possibly believe in it, yet C6D was a worldwide movement. New Chapters were formed every day, and more and more people were wearing the multicoloured bracelets, woven from threads of brown, blue, red and gold. It was belief based on blind faith, not logic. Hope for a Better Day. The Children Will Show the Way. Slogans mixed and merged in bright, oily colours, swirling like a film on the surface of her mind. They shifted to show the truth at the heart of it. The craziness was all part of it. In the dim, dark rooms of the forbidden wing, Zillah explored rare and unusual volumes. Many were very old, with strange illustrations, written in languages she did not understand, but the sense of evil was palpable. She began to discover who they really were, and the terrifying, dark secret that lay hidden within *The Book of the Law*. Then something happened that was so far beyond her wildest, most nightmarish imaginings that her visits stopped for ever.

She had taken a wrong turning on her way into the Founder's Wing and had somehow ended up in the cellars. Attracted by a flickering purple light, she came across a small chapel, the short central nave made narrow by elaborate carving that snaked and writhed over every surface, curling round the fluted pillars and arches. The Advocate must have returned early, for he was there, standing in front of a squat stone altar, dressed in his golden robe. The violet light pulsed from a dark crystal skull in front of him. He laid his hands upon the source and the light split into rays between his fingers, playing in beams across the embossed stone ceiling. Then his whole outline had begun to blur and shimmer. As he raised his arms, the robe took on different hues and colours and seemed to solidify and stiffen into chevron patterns of rayed striations, like huge feathered wings. He seemed to expand and grow bigger, as though his human form had become engorged by something else, something differently shaped, hideous and other. He raised his head, and it seemed to be crowned by curling horns, or a pair of curving crests. The thick bulge of his neck flexed and the musculature of his back rippled with smooth, sinuous movement, like a python or anaconda. From the base of his spine, flat, bony plates seemed to broaden out, elongating and extending, tapering into something reptilian. . .

Zillah locked her fingers into the barley-sugar twists of a stone pillar, praying that it was wide enough to hide her, while all the time fearing that she might faint. She steadied herself enough to step backwards, very slowly, very carefully, one shaking leg after the other. Then she fled.

She had no reason to believe that her incursions into the Founder's Wing had ever been discovered, but what she'd seen there on that last visit made escape from the Children imperative. All her thoughts began to focus on how to get away. She was old enough now to go on "fishing expeditions" to raise funds and recruit. She'd found life outside a revelation. The streets were not filled with the drunkards and thieves that she'd been led to expect. She saw few signs that these were the End of Days. She used her time well: to watch, listen and learn. She had just begun to formulate a plan, when events decided her exit for her. They were to make ready for departure. There was no more time.

Two days ago, just before daybreak, the whole community had assembled in what was still called the Ballroom. Dressed in robes of brown and black, the colours of earth and the night sky, they had processed around the intricate maze of petallate patterns marked out on the parquet floor, painted in blue, the colour of water. A lector waited at each exit, as they did each morning, robed in red, the colour of the coming dawn. This time, instead of receiving benediction, each supplicant was given a small white capsule.

Perhaps the lectors' own eyes were already on eternity. Certainly, they were not paying much attention as the last, most junior, members of the community filed past. It was no secret what they were about to do; there had been preparations and meditations. When the process was completed it would be posted on the Internet, for the whole world to know. But not yet. To broadcast their intention too soon would invite tiresome interference from the authorities. Theirs was not the only community, and the whole thing had to be carefully coordinated from the Master House.

Zillah palmed her pill, substituting it for another, something harmless from the Infirmary that she had folded into her sleeve. First light was showing in the long panel of windows as the lectors lined up to receive their capsules from the Advocate. She took her place near the back of the large room. From the opposite wall, the portrait of the Divine Founder looked down at them: his eyes like tarnished copper coins tucked in pockets of flesh in his pockmarked face.

The Advocate turned to address them, his golden robe turned bloody by the rising sun.

"Hear, my brothers and sisters." He stared down at

them. He had always been heavy set and swarthy, but lately he had begun to bear an uncanny resemblance to the Founder. They could be father and son. "Here is your salvation." His fleshy face was shining, shining with love for them as he held up a tiny white pill between his right thumb and forefinger. He raised his hand. The heavy silk sleeve fell back. His arm was thick and muscular, covered in a spiderweb weave of fine black hairs. "Today we all attain the level above human, following the Founder to another place where the bounds of flesh and time mean nothing. There we will await the Great Cleansing and the hour of our return to a happier world."

The Advocate put the capsule into his mouth. It was seen as an act of faith and the cue for the rest of them to do the same. They swallowed a measured quantity of slow-acting poison and went obediently to their sleeping places, to wait for their eternal spirits to leave these perishable envelopes of flesh.

They died without a sound.

Zillah lay among them as if she was dead, too. She performed the Practice, a complex mixture of marshal arts and meditation, daily. This allowed her now to slow her breathing, decrease her heart rate, depress her vital functions and put her mind in another place. She'd lost any sense of real time, but judged that at least a day had passed, maybe two. Zillah had not intended to wait as long as this before making her escape, but she knew she was not the only one living and breathing. The Advocate was still here. She had heard him moving around, checking the dormitories for signs of life. He'd glided through here without a second look at her. That was on the first morning. Since then there had been no sign of him, but she had not heard him leave. She should have been shocked that he was the one still alive, but found she was not. He must have taken a harmless placebo. Sacrifice would be for others to make, not himself. Because he thought he was alone, he had revealed something of his true nature. The one she'd seen in the chapel. In the Founder's Wing. Before, she had merely been afraid. Now she was terrified.

She didn't want to risk going out of her body, but she had to do it. He might have left by a different way and she couldn't lie here for ever. She had to know.

She saw herself on the bed, looking just as if she really was dead. It gave her a cold feeling, and she was wondering how the spirit could be sensitive to physical things when she saw a movement out of the window. These rooms used to be the servants' quarters. The windows were small, the narrow panes leaded, the view further obscured by creeper, changed to its autumn colour. Down through the crimson flutter, she saw the Advocate. Just a glimpse before he disappeared out of her line of vision. He was crossing the gravel courtyard from the Founder's Wing and had swapped his robe for a suit. He had a bag with him, which he cradled close to him, as if it contained something infinitely precious, like a sleeping child. He reached down to his pocket and she heard the release of an electronic car lock. He would soon be gone. The relief left her weak. And unguarded. She was willing him to get into the car and drive away, but instead he just stood there, one hand resting on the boot lid, his head cocked to one side as if he was listening or searching in his mind for something that he had forgotten. Then he was coming back, retracing his steps, treading softly across the gravel, hardly making a sound. She took herself away from the window fast, but not fast enough. She saw him look up.

The gravel crunched hard under his determined stride. He was opening the front door and crossing the hall. He was on the stairs, taking them two at a time. He entered the Juvenile Corridor on the floor below. His progress slowed as he checked the contents of each bed, but the pause was momentary. He was back on the stairs, coming up to the Women's Quarters. She could hear his feet on the floor of the narrow corridor that led to the dormitories, the creak of the door, and everywhere the sound of the flies, getting louder and louder, rising and falling as he passed from room to room, the sound becoming more and more frenzied, until they were as loud as hornets, making ready to welcome him. . .

She lay as still as her companions, imagining herself as a little black ball getting smaller and smaller, until she was hardly there at all, hoping she would die before he found her, or at least that he would let her die quickly.

There's one in here somewhere, he thought, as he mounted the stairs. Despite his best efforts, the house contained a live one when they were all supposed to be dead. Just for a second, he'd felt her presence; the fleeting impression of a girl's face had fluttered like a butterfly trapped at a window in the upper storeys of the house. He halted at the foot of each bed, to check that the occupant was indeed dead. Where there was one, there could be others.

His first feeling had been astonishment, shock that any would have the will to disobey. Only true believers were allowed to take part in the Last Rite, invited to step from this living envelope of flesh and leave it behind like a discarded suit of clothes. Only those who did this freely, in true faith, would ascend to the next level, and by doing so attain eternal life, a reward beyond price. This was an instruction from the Divine Founder. Who would dare defy it? Their methods were thorough. None better. Most candidates came gladly, clapping and singing, begging to swap their old life for this new vision. It only took a few days, often just a weekend, and they had forgotten their old lives, who they were, that there could be any other belief, any other world but this. They would obey completely and without question, embracing death as a joyous relief. So how could this be? Who would have the power, the strength to resist? Who had the will to disobey? Or any will left at all? The tiniest of doubts registered, a little tear in his seamless certainty. With it came the faintest breath of fear. If one thing could go wrong, why not another? This was the last phase of the Grand Design. What if the whole enterprise were to be compromised, even jeopardized by something so trivial. . . He curled his fist. He was not accustomed to feelings like this. Anger flared through him, a terrible cold and a terrible heat, scorching the boards beneath his feet, smoking from his heels like a vapour trail. Some of the anger he directed at himself. He should not have slipped the mask of human flesh so soon.

Yet another reason why none should live. He strode down the Juvenile Dormitory, questing for blood warmth, listening for a heartbeat. He looked back along the beds, at the line of pathetically small bodies all lying, as instructed, sightless eyes fixed on the ceiling, hands folded on the chest. They meant less to him than the maggots beginning to hatch on their skin. He had never been a supporter of the Outreach Program. If you got them too young, they never turned into very much, too old and you risked all this. These children from the East were far more trouble than the adults who came of their own accord. There were language difficulties. They missed their families. They were all broken eventually, of course, submitting to the common good, the Will of the Founder. All except this one. He cursed the staff for not noticing, not alerting him. Too late to punish them, they were all dead.

He redirected his search to the floor above. No. 2 Women's Dormitory. The only place she could be. She would not escape him now. His fingertips itched as he felt the power in his hands. The flies buzzed around him, stirred to a fury by his presence, but he did not notice the sound they made any more than he noted his own breathing. One twitch of his fingers and her neck would break. He paused at the door of the dormitory and peered through the ribbed, strengthened glass, round like a porthole. The rubber seal sighed as he opened the double door, his fingers curling round, his long nails, like claws, biting through the brown paint into the soft wood.

He could sense her presence. His nostrils flared as he caught the scent of warm, fragrant life in the midst of so much cold, stinking death. He took a step forward, then stopped and turned. He shook his head as if the buzzing of the flies was finally annoying him, but it was not that. There was another sound. He caught the two-tone wax and wane of a wailing siren, more than one. Near, and getting nearer, the different notes weaving in and out of each other. Then, from above his head came the rhythmic, muffled thud and clatter of rotor blades.

The word had got out early. That was not supposed to happen either. The website posting signalling their departure was not due up for at least three days. He stood for a moment, frozen in uncharacteristic indecision. Someone else must have disobeyed. Someone with more enthusiasm than caution and no idea of how the bigger picture could be affected by premature release. No idea that there even *was* a bigger picture. He felt his anger flare again, but this time snuffed it out. No point in wasting energy on that. The whole world would learn soon enough, anyway. He hated to leave things unfinished, but he would find her. Eventually. Gravel crunched in the courtyard, the lead cars were already coming through the arch. She could wait.

He could not afford to be caught here, not under any circumstances. This was only the first in an intricate string of events that comprised the Last Phase and would build to coincide with the Cosmic Concurrence that would sweep away everything that had gone before and herald the New Age of the World.

3

THE ADVOCATE

He took the old servants' staircase, a narrow spiral cut into the wall. The steps descended until a fall in temperature and a new smell of earth and stone told him that he was below ground level. Still the stairs went down. The house had more than just size and isolation to recommend it for the Grand Design. It had been placed according to the ancient art of geomancy, on a site of exceptional telluric and cosmic power. The old name for it, Ringmere Hall, said it all. It lay within a ring of stone, much greater than Avebury in size and circumference, which centred on the swell of rising ground where the house stood, surrounded by lawns and gardens. The mere was now a landscaped lake, set to act as a mirror to the house's architectural glory, but deep in the silt of its murky depths lay votive offerings: twisted swords, broken spears, bones bound with leather thongs, skulls cleaved in sacrifice. Nearby, a cruel cluster of jagged stones had once formed a ritual altar. Various bumps and mounds within the grounds marked other pagan sites.

A succession of owner guardians had tended the power hidden here for well over a thousand years, making sure no church was built within the borders of the estate, maintaining a watch against other damage and interference, while feeding its appetite with offerings of various kinds. Such activities had to be protected from prying eyes and successive generations had been busy underground, building chambers and hidden passageways. A series of tunnels fanned out, leading to a wooded knoll, some distance from the house. The hill had been landscaped in the eighteenth century, and was planted with majestic evergreens: cedars skirted the lower slopes, the crown was circled by sentinel Scots pines and topped by towering wellingtonia. The tunnel emerged in an ice house, which had been built by the then owner, as was the fashion. Sir Gideon Ffulke, amateur alchemist and necromancer, had ice cut from the lake in winter and stored it deep underground, to make ice cream and sorbets for his guests in the summer, and to preserve other necessaries which he needed to be kept fresh for his purposes. It was now surrounded by fences and warnings to keep out.

The Advocate climbed the crumbling steps that took him out of the ice house. The evergreen knoll rose like a crown above the surrounding forest of conifers which had been planted by Buller Gilpin Wesson, the last owner and revered Founder, who had converted his family house into a seminary and bequeathed the Wesson Estate to the Order. The sirens had stopped now, which meant that the emergency vehicles had all probably reached the house. The thudding rotor blades still sounded above him but the canopy of dense pine needles hid him from view. He took a track leading south which would lead to the forestry estate office. There would be utility vehicles there. He would use one of these and take an unadopted road to the border of the estate. He would get out with no difficulty. The estate was too large to cordon and there were many exits.

Once he was away from here, they would not find him. He was heading for the perfect sanctuary where no one would even think to look for him. Besides, no one knew who he really was. He didn't know himself. The man that he had once been had disappeared some time ago, his original personality hollowed out entirely. He was now solely the Advocate; a walking suit of warm flesh, ready to become vehicle and conduit for the Founder himself.

He adjusted the heavy bag he was carrying, cradling it to his chest, careful not to jolt it, even though he was in a hurry. It contained an ancient ivory box, lined with crocodilian skin. The box was no longer empty. It encased a form carved from some dark crystal, gravid with the weight of harvested souls.

The helicopter banked and circled, surveying the whole estate. The pilot radioed in, reporting no movement on the ground. He selected a wide green space right in front of the house and swept in to land. He hovered for a few seconds, balancing the craft before beginning a gentle descent. The runners touched and the pilot looked up. In the late afternoon sun, the creeper made it look as though the house was drenched in blood.

4

10 2 NEVER

Adam was due in surgery at ten o'clock. He'd been given a pre-med because he didn't always react well to the anaesthetic. They must have upped the dosage, or be using another drug, because he was getting this weird floaty feeling. It wasn't unpleasant, but everything seemed slowed right down. There were big gaps between one clock tick and another, between the rain drops hitting the windowpane. They should have come to whisk him off to surgery by now, but nothing seemed to be happening. In the big space of time that seemed to yawn before him, he found himself drifting backwards through all the things that had happened so far that morning, almost as though he was living them over again. . .

He'd not been allowed any breakfast and the waiting had already seemed endless. He was wearing one of those nightie things ready for his operation and had been told under no circumstances should he get out of bed. Quite suddenly, he'd felt desperate for a pee. Nerves, probably. He'd held on as long as possible, but didn't fancy doing it in one of those bottles with a nurse hovering, or (even worse) holding it for him.

He'd swung his legs free of the covers, instinctively putting his good foot down first on to the cold floor, although he hardly limped any more. There hadn't seemed to be anyone about in the corridor, except for two guys right down the other end sitting on either side of a closed door. They were a safe distance away and the toilets were in the opposite direction. They didn't look to be nurses or doctors, or anyone likely to stop him.

They didn't give him a second glance. He was in and out and back in his room in no time. Mission accomplished.

He'd gone over to the window, his slight limp more obvious in his hospital gown. He was not scared of the operation. There was no reason to feel nervous, he knew that, he'd just wanted to see the outside world one last time before he went down. The operation on his foot was routine; the last procedure in a whole sequence. Nothing difficult or complicated, just a slight adjustment of muscle and tendon. Nothing to worry about. He wouldn't even have to stay in hospital beyond a day or maybe two. He was looking forward to it. Once that was done, he would be able to walk, run and play football without any of the difficulties that he had experienced in his life up to now.

Outside, it looked cold and grey. Everyone had been blaming global warming for the exceptionally warm weather. Well, it was over now. The season had turned from autumn to winter overnight. The sky was overcast, rain spattering, reminding him that it was the beginning of December. The trees were shedding their leaves fast now: red, brown and yellow, it didn't matter what shade, they all ended up in piles the colour of sodden cardboard. The window would not open all that much, but he'd released the catch and sniffed as a draught of cold, damp air brought the outside world into the hospital's dry stuffiness. He wasn't scared, he'd told himself again, but you could not take anything for granted. You just never knew.

He'd stood, hands braced against the window frame, looking up at the sky. He had been too taken up with his thoughts to notice what was happening right below him. A man was standing under the apron jutting out above the hospital's main entrance. He had a piece of paper in his hand and was preparing to read from it. There were people crowding in around him, taking notes and snapping pictures, even a couple of camera crews moving into position, trying to get out of the rain. Adam glanced at the TV bolted high on the wall. Sure enough, the channel, tuned to BBC News 24, was playing what he could see before him. If one of the cameras swung up, for a general view of the hospital, he'd be able to see himself. But the cameras stayed on the guy with the paper. He was just reaching for the remote to turn the sound up, when the nurse came in and caught him.

"What are you doing out of bed?"

"Something's happening outside. And it's on the telly – look!"

The nurse left off scolding and came over to the window.

"So there is! Turn up the sound, quick!"

A young woman wearing a pink suit was holding a microphone and talking to camera now.

He switched his attention to the television.

"We'll be back later if there are any developments. Now, over to Huw in the studio."

"More on that story later. After yesterday's gruesome discoveries at Ringmere Hall, Warwickshire, further shocking reports are coming in from various locations in Europe and America. . ."

The anchorman swung in his chair. The picture dissolved from emergency workers in masks and overalls, trudging about, removing body bags from some big house, to red spots pulsing on a map of the world. A list of different countries appeared, running along the banner at the bottom of the screen.

"I've missed what it was all about!"

He stood with his weight on one leg, unconsciously resting his bad foot, which had curled up, only the toes resting on the ground. He's a lucky lad. Born in any other time and he would have been very lame indeed, the nurse thought as she looked at him. His notes said that he'd suffered a hip displacement at birth, as well as what they used to call a club foot. He would have had all sorts of difficulties even walking, not to mention the names some would have called him. It's good that he's living now when we can do something about it, she told herself.

"I know what the story is about," she said.

"What, then?"

"Not saying until you get back into bed."

He obeyed immediately.

"You like this kind of thing?" She picked up the well-creased paperback book on the bedside cabinet. He'd got it from the lady with the trolley. "Fantasy?"

"Yeah," he sat up in bed, arms folded; she was deliberately spinning this out. "Sometimes."

"Me, too. This guy is supposed to be good. Haven't read this one, though." She turned the book over to read the back.

"You can have it after me, if you want. Now come on. Tell."

He grinned at her teasing and she smiled back. He liked her. She was pretty and young, and always seemed up for a chat. Not like the other one who shared her shift. *She* hardly said a word and was always frowning, like she had a permanent headache and you were the cause of it.

"OK," her eyes sparked with the excitement of the news she was about to impart, "last night a girl was brought in. She'd been mixed up with this cult thing."

"What cult thing?"

The nurse rolled her eyes. "They've been on about it non-stop since it happened. Don't you ever watch the TV?"

"Not generally. There are always bad things happening." Unless you had a Pay-TV card, which he didn't have, the TV was permanently tuned to the news channel. It was controlled from the nurses' station. You couldn't turn it off, so he kept the sound right down. The news was never good: wars, global warming, people being bombed in desert places, ice shelf the size of Wales falling into the South Atlantic. "I have enough to worry about when I'm in here."

"Well, there's – was – this cult, the Children of the Sixth Dawn?"

"Oh, I've heard of them." He sat up straighter. "What's happened?"

"They've topped themselves."

"What? All of them?"

"Seems so. Although they don't know exactly. They are still finding more centres, but it was a worldwide thing. So far. . ." She folded her arms and stared at him. ". . .they've only found one survivor. She was brought in last night by air ambulance. She's down the corridor."

"The room with two guys outside the door?"

The nurse nodded.

"Wow!"

No wonder all those cameras were outside. He'd never been this close to a major news story. Like knowing a celebrity. He felt awed.

"How do you know there's two guys out there?"

Adam coloured. "Is she going to die?" he asked, shifting her focus back to the girl.

"Not if we can help it!" The nurse sounded indignant. "She's dehydrated, more than anything. The rest of them took poison. She didn't."

"How do you know?"

"Because she's not dead."

"Will she be OK?"

"No medical reason why not," the nurse said, "but after an experience like that, who knows? Now, come on, I've got a busy morning."

37

There were no white rabbits consulting watches, but he'd begun to get this really freaky feeling, like he was outside himself. Now, he seemed to be looking down from somewhere high up on the ceiling. He could see the anaesthetist, hear him counting backwards. Normally, Adam never got to seven. He could see the nurse talking to the guy in scrubs, see him nodding, like he wasn't really listening, as the rain hammered on the window. He was aware of one of the trolley wheels squeaking as he watched himself being moved into the corridor. He slipped through the doors just in time to see this girl coming towards him. Maybe he *was* out, and dreaming, even though that was not supposed to happen, because he was suddenly in his body again and the girl was looking down at him.

She was the girl from the cult poisoning. Somehow, he knew. She was about his age, maybe older, wearing a hospital gown, pulling a drip behind her. Her hair was a kind of dark tawny: brown in some places, light in others, long and thick, falling across her face; the colour reminded him of an Asian lion he had seen once in the zoo. She pushed a hank of it back as she drew level. Her skin was kind of tawny coloured, too. Her eyes contrasted with her dark complexion; their shade lay somewhere between blue and green, a kind of milky aquamarine rimmed with black. She frowned as she looked at him, her thick black brows contracting, as though she recognized but could not place him. He'd never seen *her*, he knew that. Not in this life, anyway.

She had the kind of face you would not forget. Still, there was something about her, something familiar. . .

He was just puzzling about what that might be, when he heard the anaesthetist's voice again. He never got to number five.

5

THE MOST FAMOUS
GIRL IN THE WORLD

The boy on the trolley was about the same size as her, maybe a bit shorter. She walked alongside him, using his bed and the porters to block the sight line of the policemen whom they had put on her door. She'd told them that she wanted to use the toilet. They'd looked at each other, unsure. One of them got up to call a nurse, but there had been none around and she'd told him that her need was urgent. It wasn't far, he would be able to see her the whole way, or he could come with her if he wanted. He didn't take her up on the offer.

She'd been taking her time, trying to figure a way to get out of here, when this boy had come out, reversing into her path. She walked alongside him for a little way, then dodged back and into his room. There was a long cupboard against one wall. She opened the doors and found what she was looking for: jeans, hooded sweat top, T-shirt, spare underwear and pyjamas all neatly stacked. Even a pair of trainers on a rack at the bottom. These would do just fine. She ripped the drip from her hand and grabbed a wad of tissue from the bedside table to staunch the blood flow. It wouldn't do to stain her nice new clothes.

There was something slightly odd about the trainers. One was built up more than the other, which made her limp slightly, otherwise they fitted OK. The jeans were a bit short in the leg, she must be taller than him, but she was hardly in a position to be choosy. Money. She would need money. She checked the bedside chest and found a wallet. Perfect. Not much, but enough. It wasn't really right to take his stuff, but she had no one, nothing, and he must have people at home, a family who cared for him. There were no pictures in his wallet, but she imagined Mum, Dad, sister, brother, even a dog. They'd bring in more things for him and replace the money she had taken. She folded the notes, stuffing them in her pocket, and replaced the wallet in the drawer. It was stealing, but her need was the greater.

She pulled up the hood on the top and slipped from the room, any further concern about him going out of her mind. She had to get out of the hospital, and quickly. Her location was not exactly a secret and the Advocate would come after her, that was sure. He would not be acting alone. She did not hurry. She'd only been away a couple of minutes, not long enough for the policemen to get nervous and they weren't looking out for some kid in a hoodie. They barely glanced up from their newspapers as she walked past. *Death Cult: Latest*, the headline shouted. The rest of the front page carried a grainy image of her blown up from a group photograph which had been taken when she was about ten. The cops might even belong to them, for all she knew. Not all the Children lived in Chapter Houses. A large number were VWs: Viral Workers who operated out in the community and were spread through every walk of life, every profession.

She set off, head down, walking purposefully. It helped to look as if you knew where you were going, what you were doing. She would be out of the hospital in no time. She could have been an outpatient, a relative, a visitor, any of the hundreds of people constantly coming and going in and out of the big hospital.

There were still reporters and photographers outside, along with a camera crew. This was a big story and likely to get bigger. So far she was sole survivor. No one was moving on just yet. She might get well enough to make a statement; she might even snuff it. They were sitting in cars, the backs of vans, or standing around huddled under umbrellas. None of them gave her a second look, or took the slightest notice. They were too busy smoking, chatting, munching on chocolate bars and sandwiches. They waited for events to unfold and ignored the most famous girl in the world.

6

TEMPLE GREEN

Kris sat watching Temple Green, listening to the rain falling down on Bram's makeshift shelter. The only other shelter was the crypt, and that was half full of water. Besides, it only leaked a little bit. Bram had done a pretty good job with plastic sacks and tarps. Kris didn't know Bram's full name. Everyone went by nicknames down here, so he was just Bram. *His* real name was Christophe, but no one ever called him that, except Mamma Celestine. He wiped drops from his face, shifted his position, pulled his hood further over. Mamma Celestine was his grandma and she didn't like the rain.

She told him, "Christophe, this city is too cold! Rainin' all the time!"

Like it was his fault! It might be warm where she came from, but they had powerful storms. He'd seen it on TV. Palm trees parallel to the ground, mud slides smothering whole villages. It had been bad there lately. She didn't talk about going back any more.

He'd told her to call him Kris, right from the start, but she took no notice.

"It's who you are, boy. Named for the God Child. Why you ashamed about that?"

He shrugged, no one said it right. Not after Mom died. They called him Christopher and he took objection. They'd called him that in the children's hostel, and called him lippy for correcting them. He hadn't stayed there long. They'd called him that in the foster homes. How did they care about him, when they couldn't get his name right? He'd run away from them, too, finally finding refuge here on Temple Green. It was the nearest thing he'd had to a home until Mamma Celestine came along. She had taken him away to live with her, but he still came down, now and again. The place was full of bad types, so he came to check the old man was all right, that no one was taxing or troubling him.

The old man sat next to him, sunk like a turtle inside his layers of clothes. They didn't talk much, but that was OK. The silence was companionable; the rain pattering down was a peaceful sound. Bram's world was the Green. He lived in the churchyard. All he had was stowed under the bench in two black plastic sacks. He hardly ever shifted from this spot, but he didn't really have to. People brought him things. The priest from the church, the people who came to worship. Now the building was being converted, but the guys on the site made sure he was all right, slipping him a few coins, keeping him supplied with mugs of tea and bacon butties. They were off the site right now. Because of the rain.

They both stared out at the world beyond the gate.

Temple Green. Must have been grass one time but now it was a patch of mostly mud: bald like a worn pool table, with just a haze of green here and there. The Green was shaded by buildings on either side. Roads soared overhead, gridlocked with traffic. Every few minutes, a voice on the loudspeaker in Temple Station announced cancellations and delays because of the rain, because of stuff on the tracks, in between instructions to be on the lookout and not to do this, or that.

All kinds of people ended up here, like floating trash caught in lagoons created by the constant flow of the city. They found shelter under the flyover, in the disused tunnels and railway sheds of the station. They all had their places. Homeless under the road and in the tunnels. Some even building in flimsy cardboard and plastic against the dark, high stone wall of the Temple itself. Not advisable. Those structures were always torn down. Dealers and their customers, pimps and their whores hung around the Green. They were keeping out of the rain right now, sheltering in the empty shop doorways, leaning against the rucked and peeling fly posters that covered the broken glass of the empty offices by the station. The Green saw plenty of traffic, but they all kept out of the churchyard. This was the old man's place.

No one out there knew his rightful name, or cared who he was, but that was normal for down here. No names. No history. It was the rule. Even if someone gave a name, it was liable to be false, so there was no point in asking. As for identities, there were rock stars, doctors, millionaire bankers, lawyers and prophets.

Everyone had been someone before bad luck and hard times dumped them here. No one hassled each other all that much; the Green might be trampled mud, but it was a place of business. That did not mean it was safe. There were real bad turf fights and some of the homeless would kill for a blanket. Walk-ins from the streets above took risks coming here. But they did. There were a few out there now: nervous under black umbrellas, driven down here by some need – for girls, boys, their drug of choice.

Kris had first found his way here when he was twelve years old. Greedy eyes had been watching him, but he had not been aware of it then. He'd left the warmth of the station when he felt the prowling rail cops were noticing him too much and wandered down looking for somewhere to sleep. He'd run away from his last foster home. Sixth? Seventh? He'd lost count how many. Some of them had been nice to him, some not. He never stayed long, however they treated him. He didn't belong. Most were only doing it for the money. Even when they said different, they didn't really care. It was always the same, worse than the hostel. At least no one pretended in there. Usually the police caught him and he got sent somewhere else, but he was getting older, the child of an illegal. This time they didn't come looking. The services had better things to do.

The old man had looked after him until Mamma Celestine turned up. Kris lived with her now.

"I lose my only daughter and I ain't losing you. So don't you think about running."

She'd come from the Sugar Isles, from Tainos, where

she lived, especially to find him. She'd been born in Jamaica, so had a British passport, which allowed her to come and claim him. Kris's mom had been born on Tainos, which had been independent by then. Mamma Celestine had not found out for a long time that her daughter was dead. Kris knew the story well enough. How she'd been in her local shop and the shopkeeper had a paper from Britain, *The Clarion*, read by Sugar Islanders. The shopkeeper had tacked a page on the wall, yellowing now, a picture of his granddaughter's wedding. One of the tacks had come loose. The doors were open, front and back, to keep the shop cool, and a little breeze was blowing in from the sea. Grandma was waiting in line, fanning herself, feeling thankful for the little breeze, when she noticed a story on the back of the page. The paper had grown crisp in the sun, so she had to be careful when she folded it back; a tear in the granddaughter's dress would not be popular. The report was of a shooting. A gunfight between rival gangs. "Innocent Victim", were the words. An innocent victim caught up in some other folk's war. Her daughter's name was mentioned in the second to last paragraph.

Kris had been looking out of the window of their flat, waiting for his mother. She was in the country illegally, but had got a job, cleaning offices. She came home late every night and Kris knew she'd be tired. He'd cooked chicken curry and rice, her favourite meal. He couldn't stand it now, even the smell of it made him want to throw up. He watched for her every night, and was thinking about the happiness that lit her face when she saw him, when there she was, walking from the bus stop in Orchard Road. He'd been going to wave, had his hand in place on the glass, just in case she looked up at him. She sometimes looked up. She was walking by some boys off the estate. They were sitting on the wall in front of the flats. They had their hoods up and were smoking a bit of weed, passing it between them. She smiled and nodded as she went past. They nodded back, a bit reluctant, but she probably knew their mothers, so they acknowledged her.

What happened was so fast that it was over in a blink of an eye. So slow, Kris thought that he had time to get down to street level and push her out of the way. His hand had balled into a tight fist to hammer on the window. But she couldn't hear. He couldn't warn her. A silver car came round the corner. A black window glided down, a hand came out, with rings on every finger, he remembered that, and bracelets, gold and silver. The hand was holding a gun. A heavy automatic. Dull, not shiny like the bracelets. The hand jerked up as the bullet left the barrel, once, twice, the shots sounded pock, pock, not as loud as on the telly. The car disappeared in a squealing burn of rubber. The brothers melted into the estate. His mother was down on her knees, alone in the street. She held her hands to her stomach with this surprised look on her face, then she fell over. Or Kris thought she did, he could never quite unravel what he thought he'd seen that night from what had really happened. Maybe he didn't see any of it, but that didn't matter. Each image was sharp in his head, ready to be replayed again and again.

He hadn't told anyone that he'd seen the whole thing. Not the police. What were they going to do about it? Or the social workers and counsellors, because he didn't want them seeing inside his head. Only Mamma Celestine and the old man. He'd told them that he saw what happened. The old man had nodded and looked even sadder than he did before. Grandma's mouth had tightened and twitched a little bit. She'd groped for his hand and held it. He didn't pull away, although ordinarily he did not like to be touched. Her fingers were as thin as birds' bones and her skin felt dry, papery against his. There were tears in her dark eyes as she held his hand in her narrow grip. They didn't say anything, just stayed like that for a little bit.

"She wouldn't let me see her." Her old face twisted even more. "I couldn't get through, you know?"

Kris didn't know. How *could* she see from so far away? How did she mean, get through? Like on the phone? He wanted to ask, but something told him not to. She could act exclusive sometimes. Secretive, as though she knew things that couldn't be shared with him, because he was young. So he didn't say anything. He had wanted the moment to last longer, not for it to finish with sharp words: *Not for you to know*.

Mamma Celestine was big on people sent to help you and things meant to be. She regarded Bram as Kris's saviour, kind of like his guardian angel, however unlikely he was for the part. She was forever sending down little gifts for him. Sometimes food: a slice of her spicy meat loaf, a few salt fish cakes, a portion of jerk chicken wrapped in a roti; or else something sweet, like coconut drops, or a wedge of molasses cake. Other times she'd send a few toiletries: toothpaste, shaving cream, little tablets of the lavender soap she favoured herself. Bram stowed these items away carefully, but he never seemed to use them. On balance, Kris thought he preferred the food option. Sometimes, she even wrote him notes in the neat looping writing she'd learnt from the nuns. Bram would read the letter without comment, fold it carefully away into one of his many pockets. Sometimes he'd send a message back: tell her this, or tell her that. These messages made no sense to Kris. He could not imagine what they had to communicate with each other.

Kris gave his companion on the bench a sidelong glance. Maybe he ought to make a real effort to get them together. The old man would need scrubbing up. Make it look like he was using some of the products Mamma Celestine had been sending to him. A haircut would be good. Kris sniffed. Fresh clothes, for sure. He could keep the 'tache, but it would need trimming back. And teeth. He'd need new false ones. He would be OK looking, given all that. He needed caring for and a place of shelter. Grandma liked looking after people and she lived in a flat. Kris was out a lot of the time and stretched her caring capacity hardly at all. Bram might like it. Kris glanced down at the old man's dark corded forearms sticking out from his fraying coat, the cuffs stiff and sharp with dirt. His wrists were really thin. Thick blue veins snaked under the skin. He needed fattening. He already appreciated Grandma's cooking, and she would love to feed him.

Kris was just thinking how he might hook the two of

them up when he felt the old man go tense. Something was happening. Kris looked round. Years on the streets had taught the old man to stay alert, keep his eyes open even if it looked like he was sleeping. Kris cursed himself for being lulled like that. A regular home life was making him soft. He surveyed the scene carefully, without being too obvious. Nothing alarmed him. A girl had wandered down from the station. No umbrella. She was not even wearing a jacket. She was soaked. The rain was pouring off her. Her hair hung like strings outside her hood; the thin fabric was moulded to her body. She was attracting some attention, but that really wasn't his problem, the old man's neither, unless he knew her. That could prove trickier. She was good-looking, with a warm, tan tint to her skin, but not a sister. There were men circling in on her and they had pretty bad reputations. Muscovite pimps, some of them carrying. He could see the telltale bulge under their cheap leather jackets. They leered, flashing gold at her, beckoning her over, but she was not taken in by them. She didn't look scared. The opposite. Her greeny blue eyes blazed straight at them and she had a look on her face like a squadron of roaches was coming towards her. She held herself like a fighter, weight evenly balanced. Kris grinned, half hoping that one of 'em would get too close, so she'd chunk him. That girl could take care of herself.

He was just about to remark that, when the old man grabbed his arm.

"Hey, man! You're hurting!"

Kris tried to pull away, but the old man just hung on

tighter. He might be ancient and stringy but he certainly had a grip on him and his jagged black fingernails were digging in.

"That girl. . ."

"Yeah! I see her! What about her?" Kris tried to pull away again, but the old man tugged him closer, pointing with the bent forefinger of his other hand.

"It's her."

"It's who? You ain't making any sense, man."

"You, you've got to. . ."

The old man turned to him, brows right down, his pale grey eyes intense, even desperate, but even while Kris was looking at him, a film seemed to grow over them, making the irises cloudy, the pupils unfocused, dilated differently. His head fell sideways, jaw slack, his tongue lolling, as if suddenly too big for his mouth. The old man tried to speak, but couldn't. His head swung forward. A string of drool hung suspended for a second, then began spooling down on to his lap.

"What's up?" The grip on his arm had slackened; Kris pulled away from him. The old man slumped right over. The muscles in the boy's legs tensed, the girl forgotten. There was something bad wrong with him. Kris stood, ready to run, but something stopped him. The old man had been good to him. Kris was in his debt.

"Hey, man. . ."

Kris looked down. The old man's face had collapsed further, crumpling like all the life was being sucked out of him. He was retching, being sick.

"Yerch!"

Kris jumped back, his own face creased with distaste.

Some of that could have got on his jeans, or his All Stars. He hated illness, all the messy stuff that went along with it, but he knew enough to lay the old man on his side, so he didn't choke.

He grabbed for his phone, jabbing in the number for the emergency services. He got a message and music. They would like to help him, but due to unusual levels of demand his call was being held in a queue. He tried texting. Same thing. They would probably refuse to come anyway. They didn't like sending ambulances down here, in case they got attacked, and the crews didn't like picking up tramps because they stank up the vans. He shut his phone reluctantly. Bram didn't look good. He'd gone a weird colour and was breathing funny. Kris didn't know what to do. He looked around. People from the Green were gathering, life on the street was boring, so any diversion. But none of them would want to help.

"What are you all looking at? Fuck off," Kris snarled at them and turned back to Bram.

"Never mind me." Kris bent to hear the old man's hoarse whisper, each word a labour. "Go after *her*! You must. . ."

"OK, OK, take it easy, man," Kris said.

But Bram was gone again, his eyes rolled back in his head. Leaving him here was not an option. He would die. Kris had to get help. There *was* one man, used to be a doctor, got kicked out for using. Kris looked around but didn't see him. Then there he was.

"Hey, mate! Over here."

Kris grabbed him by the arm of his greasy parka. His

pupils were like pin holes, but he wasn't totally wasted.

He wiped his hands on his torn tracksuit bottoms and bent to examine Bram. He looked into the old man's eyes, lifting one lid, then the other.

"Looks like he's had a stroke." He loosened the clothes around the old man's neck.

The onlookers were wandering off now. They had seen people dying before. It wasn't going to be very interesting, after all. The doc would have wandered off with them, if Kris hadn't kept hold of him.

"That all we can do?"

"Pretty much. Make sure nothing is restricting his breathing. Make him comfortable." He recited the words as if from some half-forgotten script. "Pray the ambulance comes soon." He cocked his head, as if listening for the siren.

"The ambulance ain't coming. I couldn't get through."

"Oh, well. . ." The doctor stood up and sighed. "He's had it. Nothing we can do."

"There is. Has to be."

Kris stood thinking. The Green had emptied. Even the girl who had started the trouble wasn't there any more. The old man had been perfectly fine before she showed up. What was she to him to cause such a reaction? Maybe one of the Muscovite pimps had got her. Kris's anger flared. Serve her right for making the old man sick like that. He could 'jack a car, but that would take too long. Anyway, the roads were gridded. The nearest hospital was St Anne's. Just the other side of the station. He began tearing down the shelter.

"What are you doing?"

"Grab the other end of the tarp. We're going to wrap him in this, and carry him. It ain't far."

The doctor was about to laugh, but the look in the boy's eyes told him not to do that. He might be skinny, undersize for his age, but these street kids were tough. And mean. Not helping might have consequences. He lifted the inert body on to the tarpaulin. The old man was tall, but not very heavy. It was not all that much of a burden. Besides, he had been a doctor. Once. Hadn't he taken oaths?

Others came to help them once word was out that the victim was Bram. The old man was sound, always ready to share what he had. Men each took a corner. He was worth getting a soaking for.

"We can manage, kid," the doctor said. "You go ahead. Warn 'em — he's had a brain haemorrhage and it looks bad."

"Wait up!" Kris reached under the bench. There was a little leather case Bram always had with him. It was wrapped in a plastic carrier to keep out the rain. Nothing inside except a big old battered notebook and some papers, but he was always checking the contents. He'd fret if he woke and it wasn't with him. Kris poked the case under the old man's coat. *If* he woke. . .

"Anything else while you're at it?" one of the bearers complained.

"Nah." Kris tapped him on the back. "You're good to go."

"Cheeky little bugger," the bearer muttered. "We ain't doin' it for you, you know."

"See you there."

The men steadied their load and slipped and slithered across the Green with their makeshift body bag. Apart from them, the space was deserted. And the girl? No sign. It was as if she had never been there at all. He had made a kind of promise to Bram, but he'd have to try and track her later. Right now, he had other business. Kris grabbed his bike and peddled off, legs pumping. He gained the upper street and wove through the traffic waiting at the junction. He was off as soon as the lights began to change. He never saw the taxi in the bus lane, coming through on red.

7

IN DREAMS

There was someone in the room with Adam. He didn't have to open his eyes to know who it was. Brother Zachariah, known as Brother Zack, but not to his face. Adam could smell the expensive aftershave. Besides, Brother Zack was the only visitor he ever had. His presence was enough to make Adam want to go back to the warm, dark place he had just left. But that place was receding with every second. He had no choice but to wake up.

He did not open his eyes, not straight away, no reason for Brother Z to know he was awake. The dark place had not been empty. There had been echoes of other things. He'd had the strangest dreams.

Now, a series of images flashed before him, as if his eyes were open, but they were not. Tears sliding down a face of plaster, dripping on to the head of a child. Blood sprang from a wound like a tear in skin stretched tight over curving ribs, welled up and soaked into the wood around square-headed nails. Milk drops formed on the curled trunk of an elephant.

Letters he couldn't read were spelt out in little black seeds.

There was a commentary:

. . .reports of miraculous phenomena are coming in. . .

It was the TV. The commentary faded to almost nothing.

He opened his eyes. Brother Zack sat in the chair by the window, his hand on the remote control. His other thin hand twitched at the long skirt of his dark green surplice. A tiny frown quirked the smooth skin of his brow as he stared, distracted, out of the window. The TV was turned right down, but the commentary continued. All over the world, the faithful and the faithless were visiting makeshift places of pilgrimage. *Was this it?* Brother Zack's face was free of any expression now, but Adam could feel his powerful surge of excitement. *A global series of bizarre and unusual happenings. Was this what was promised?* He was accessing Brother Zack's mind! Experiencing emotions that he was feeling! Adam was so busy denying any such possibility that he lost the rest of the thought.

"I see you are awake."

The room was darkening, the light outside fading towards evening. The white cross, each arm deeply incised so it looked like a starburst, glowed on Brother Zack's breast. He flicked his black hair back from his colourless eyes and regarded the boy in the bed. His thin mouth pursed slightly as his gaze rested on the cage over Adam's leg. Adam sensed revulsion so strong that it burst in his mouth like something rotten, making him retch.

"Nurse. Nurse!"

Brother Zack was out of his seat in an instant, shouting down the corridor. Then the nurse was there, holding a bowl for him.

"Just the anaesthetic. You'll be all right in a minute."

She glanced over at Brother Zack, who was at the window now, his back to them. Then she looked down at Adam. Her pity washed over him, tepid as summer rain. The nurse left, taking the covered bowl and her pity with her. Brother Zack turned back into the room. Adam could feel his hostility, as rasping and harsh as a file on the skin.

"We have, ah, received information. . ."

No, "How are you feeling? How's the foot?" Nothing. But he wouldn't expect that, would he? Brother Zack had never liked him. Not that Brother Z liked anybody, but he had a particular dislike of disability. That was the source of his revulsion. He couldn't stop staring, imagining what was under the caged cover. Adam felt like heaving the foot out with its surgical dressing and saying, "There, have a good look." He knew that to Brother Zack he would always be disabled. Even when he was well again, Brother Zack would stare at the thin pale scars and make Adam want to hide his foot from him, like a wounded animal.

"An individual is claiming you as next of kin."

"What?"

Adam was fully alert; any lingering fog from the anaesthetic blown away by this news. That was the last thing he'd been expecting to hear. He felt deep surprise, then elation as his mind scrambled to take in the implications. Up to this moment, he had been all alone in the world. An orphan with no close relatives. That's why he had to spend his life, term time and holidays at Temple School. When he was old enough, he would enter the Temple proper and wear the green, like Brother Zack. That was the plan, anyway. The life pattern set out for him. Not that it was going to happen. He would rather die.

"Yes. You have a relative, apparently. At least, you are cited as next of kin."

"Where is this relative?"

"Here. In the hospital."

That was even more amazing. Shock, curiosity, excitement: a whole sequence of intense emotions bunched and jostled inside him. Adam's eyes filled with sudden tears of relief. He was no longer on his own. While he'd been in here, he'd sometimes fantasized about what it would be like to have a regular family: flowers in his room, yellow roses, they'd be, and the bare notice board studded with get-well cards and greetings instead of a scattering of drawing pins. He had little conscious memory of his mother and remembered his father not at all, but he saw a couple, the woman was pretty, with red hair, the man older, distinguished looking. They were hovering about him, faces creased with concern, quizzing the doctors about his well being. . .

He knew it was stupid, and didn't expect Brother Zack to reveal anything of that nature, but any relation was better than none. He would have liked a bit of time to savour his relief and elation, but his euphoria was going to be short-lived. Better to show nothing. He bit down on his feelings. Bad news was following, and Brother Z couldn't wait to tell him. His thin mouth was twitching as if he could barely smother the smile.

"He was brought in off the street. A derelict. He's in a coma. Not expected to live."

There it was. He'd been part of a family for seven seconds. Six.

"How do you know, then? That he's my relative?"

"He had papers on him. Certain documents. . ." Brother Zack cleared his throat. "As he is not likely to survive, and as you are his only known relative, at some point they will need your permission."

"Permission for what?"

"To turn off the life support."

Brother Zack could hardly get the words out, he wanted it so much. There was an excitement about him; different from the kick he got tormenting Adam. That was just an idle pastime, like pulling the wings off flies. No. It was more like when he was thinking about all those weird miracles. Why did he want this so badly? Brother Zack turned to him and Adam could smell his need, taste it in his mouth like a hot copper coin.

"But he's not dead yet. You said."

"No. . . but. . ."

"What if I refuse to give it?"

"Why would you?"

Brother Zack's patience was beginning to crack. The boy would be novitiate next year. He lived by the Rule, as they all did in the Order. It was not his place to question a superior. He had already demonstrated, on more than one occasion, that he was *not* suitable material. In Brother Zack's opinion, he should be thrown out, but the New Master insisted on protecting him for some reason. "He's an *orphan*, Zachariah. We are a charitable foundation. Ergo we must be *charitable*," he'd say, his hands held high in benediction. "Where would he go?"

Who cared? As far as Brother Zack was concerned, the little bastard could live on the streets, like the rest of the rats that infested the Green. The Temple was extremely hierarchical and he was not privy to the workings of the Abracax, the secret Inner Order, but he fully intended to be. Brother Zack had risen far for one so young, and was intensely ambitious. Knowledge is power and he knew more than they thought. He knew, for example, that there had been intense interest in the suicide cult and now these signs and portents. These events presaged great changes but how, and why, remained privy to the Inner Order.

Progression to Abracax would depend upon his giving every appearance of continuing and absolute obedience. If the New Master took an especial interest in this boy, he would not question why. The boy had been an orphan. The father surfacing had caused some disturbance. Again, Brother Zack sensed that there was more to it, another Abracax matter, but the New Master's orders had been simple and clear. Find out what he has, and then have him dispatched. He had discovered nothing yet. The wretched nurse on intensive care had been surprisingly draconian about the old man's personal effects. Short of going in and pulling the plug himself, which might bring the Order into disrepute, getting the boy's consent seemed the best way to proceed. For now. If he continued with this stubbornness, then things might change.

"He's not dead." The boy spoke from the bed. "Like you said."

"Not *now*. Obviously. In the long run. . ." Brother Zack couldn't believe he was even reasoning with him. He just about held his cold fury in check; it was like grasping a bar of freezing metal. "In the long run, it would be an act of mercy. . ."

Adam leant over, making retching noises. "Can you call the nurse? I think I'm going to be sick again."

Brother Zack was out of there, surplice flying. The guy was such a hypocrite, Adam thought he really was going to vomit.

The nurse told Brother Zack to leave.

"Can you bring some more clothes in for him?" she asked as he was going out.

"He has his uniform." He meant his surplice. It was like Brother Zack's but blue. The nurse gave him a look.

"Proper ones. He needs them here."

"What happened to the ones he had?"

"Stolen."

"Stolen? Don't you people have any security?"

"It happens. One of the other patients. . ."

Her voice dropped as she showed Brother Zack out. His attention moved from the boy in the bed and Adam caught another flare of excitement as the nurse told him what had happened. Something about the breaking-news story penetrated deep into Brother Zack's dark, ferocious focus and was absorbed. Adam sank back. That girl he saw, the one in the corridor, had taken his stuff, and then just walked on out and disappeared. Good luck to her. Hope she got right away and they never found her. Ever.

He was glad to be on his own, at least for a while. What did Brother Zack want? Why was he desperate for Adam to pull the plug on his new relative? Or throw the switch, or whatever it was you did. The TV played with no sound; the remote was over the other side of the room where Brother Zack had left it. Bad news again. An update on mud slides and flooding. Pictures from somewhere in the world showed villages washed away like so much sodden straw, children swimming like rats through milk-brown water. Adam closed his eyes against the images. He was feeling sick enough.

He was trying to get used to the idea of having a relative, any kind of relative. Who was he? What kin? Brother Zack hadn't said. He'd just wanted him dead.

8

VISITING TIME

By the next visiting time, Adam had decided that he would not sign the paper. Not now. Not ever. If he did, then he would be alone in the world again. Maybe that's what they wanted, or more likely they wanted to get their hands on some of the money that he would inherit on his relative's death. The man had lived like a tramp, but papers in his possession revealed that he was a very wealthy man.

"Can I go and see him?"

"I suppose so." Brother Zack examined his pale fingernails, gently easing an encroaching cuticle from a violet half-moon. "Not much point, though. He's comatose. I told you."

Nevertheless, after Brother Zack had gone, Adam asked if he might visit his new relative. The nurse said that she'd have to check. She came back to say it was a bit late now, Doctor would be doing his afternoon rounds. Maybe tomorrow, but no one seemed to have any real objection.

The next day, a porter came and loaded him into a wheelchair and took him to the intensive care ward.

"Friend of yours, is he?" he asked as he wheeled Adam along. "Relative?"

"Relative," Adam confirmed.

"Oh yes. What kind of relative?"

"Um," Adam stalled. No one had told him exactly what kind. "Uncle," he said after a bit. "I think."

"Ain't you sure?"

"No. We'd, er, lost touch."

"Don't yer mum know? Ain't she told you?"

"I haven't got a mother. I'm an orphan. No living relatives, or none till now."

"Well, here we are." The porter stopped at the nurse's station and was directed towards a side room off the main ward. "By the looks of him, must be yer great-uncle," he remarked as he glanced through the glass.

"Before you go in," the nurse came to open the door, "a word of warning. His physical condition is stable now, but he is unlikely to recognize you, or react to your presence at all."

"'Specially as he's never seen you before," the porter added. "Don't look like he's gonna be reacting to anybody, any time, son."

"Some relatives have rather high expectations," she went on, ignoring the porter. "Talk to him. Hold his hand. You'd be surprised what a difference it makes. A little human contact can work miracles."

66

"OK, sunshine." The porter wheeled him close to the bed. "See what you can do." He stood for a moment looking down at the patient, and then he shook his head. "Take more than a miracle. Looks like a goner and I've seen a few, believe me."

Adam found it hard to disagree. He found himself checking the machines for vital signs. The face on the pillow was yellowish grey, gaunt and drawn. The eyes were sunk right into their sockets; the lids gaped a bit, deeply wrinkled purple pits. The flesh fell away from the high cheekbones; the skin stretched taut and white over the sharp hook of a nose. Stubble silvered his cheeks, which looked odd, but Adam supposed whatever state you were in, your hair kept growing. He was nothing like his fantasy parent, that was for sure.

"You can go closer. Hold his hand," the nurse said, bright and encouraging.

Adam didn't want to do that. The hands lay over the covers, fingers curled like claws, nails discoloured, thick and ridged, veins lay like fat blue worms under yellowish chicken skin. He overcame his reluctance and reached out. The skin felt dry and rough, but his hand was warm. He snatched his own hand back. That was a shock.

"You his grandson?" the nurse asked.

"Son," Adam said. He didn't know how, but he suddenly knew.

"Oh," the nurse sounded surprised, "he looks. . ."

"Too old. Yeah. . ." Adam said. How *did* he know? To hide his own confusion, he wheeled himself to look at the notes hooked over the foot of the bed. "I was thinking that myself. Same name on the notes, though. Abraham Black," he read. "Same surname."

"In that case. . ." she came closer. "Something's been worrying me. You know that priest?"

"Brother Zack. In the long green—"

"Yeah, him." She looked at the figure on the bed. "I found him in here, poking about in the cupboard by the bed, going through the personal effects."

"Really?" Adam was interested now. "Looking for what, d'you think?"

"Your old man hasn't got much, bless him, but when he was brought in, he had a little case with him. Nothing much in it, as far as I can see, just an old book and some papers and that, but —" her face flushed slightly, indignant at the memory — "Brother Whatsisface was making off with it. I wasn't having that. Patients' personals are my responsibility."

"What did you do?"

"Took it off him, what do you think? I'd be grateful, though, if you'd look after it."

"Well, that's a bit hard." Adam didn't want to tell her that he'd be even less secure than an unlocked cupboard on an open ward. "Maybe you could keep it at the nurses' station for now. I wouldn't mind having a look, though."

"Right, ho. I'll go and get it. When you've finished, I'll keep it in my locker. No way is that priest going to get a look in there!"

She came back with a small, battered valise, not much bigger than two shoe boxes put together. It was not locked. He opened the scuffed leather lid and found a cracked brown wallet containing personal papers. There was a dog-eared old passport in the name of Abraham Black, out of date and much stamped. There was an envelope, worn and torn along the edges, tucked in the back. Inside were photographs, faded and creased, darkened and dented with finger marks, as if they had been endlessly handled and shuffled like a pack of well-used playing cards. A woman with long red hair, laughing, smiling, sometimes alone, sometimes with a fair-haired little boy squinting into the sun. Adam held them up near his eyes, turning them to the light, examining them closely for a long time. When he had seen enough, he blinked away tears and returned the photos reverently with shaking fingers. Although he had no conscious memory of her, he knew that this woman was his mother. He'd conjured her image to feed his fantasy of a happy family. The little boy was the child that he had once been.

He turned over another envelope marked:

In the event of death or accident.

The envelope had been opened. Inside was the address of a firm of solicitors: *Skidmore, Punter, Moody and Stansfield, London.* An account number at *Coutts Bank, the Strand*; and a separate slip of paper with Adam's name printed in black letters: *Next of Kin: Adam Black, c/o Temple College, Temple Green, London.*

Adam replaced the papers carefully. No secret as to how the Temple knew about his father, then. But why did they want him dead? And why was Brother Zack so interested in the contents of this case? Adam looked at the body on the bed, tethered to all those life-giving machines. His father's grip on life was so slight; any tampering with any one of the lines could make all the difference. Would Brother Zack dare do anything like that? Adam couldn't be sure, but he didn't trust him; he trusted the Order still less. He suddenly felt fiercely protective. This man might be a stranger, but he was also his father. No one was going to take him away just yet.

This room was a two-hander. There was another bed to the side, unoccupied. Adam had an idea, and it just might work. He settled down then, to examine the rest of the contents of the case. Under the wallet was a dark blue leather-bound notebook, the pages edged with wavy lines of rainbow colours. The name *Aurel Lockwood* was inscribed on the front and then again in a black double-bordered box on the marbled frontispiece.

He took the book from the case carefully. Perhaps there was a clue here as to why the Brothers were so interested. He opened it at the first section. The paper crackled as he turned it, the pages made stiff and rigid by the letters pasted there. They were written in long, looping copperplate, the blue ink fading. The accompanying annotations were in black: small, neat, sharp italic writing, which he took to be his father's hand.

LOCKWOOD[1] # 1

11 Forfar Street,
London

Friday, 6 January, 1906

My Dear Stone[2],

It seems an age since you deserted our foggy old London for the more clement climes of your beloved California. Indeed, as I write, a squall batters my window, leaving it all streaked and smutted with soot. At least the rain has fetched the snow away, but a listless, resentful fire spits in my grate and the sullen coals resist all my attempts to stoke them to any semblance of cheeriness. I must speak to Thompson (again) about the rather careless delivery habits of the coal merchant, who tends to dump the entire load in the area instead of down the chute into the relative dryness of the cellar. I did not, however, begin this letter with the intention of complaining about the inadequacies of tradesmen, my domestic arrangements, or the universally

---

[1]*AUREL LOCKWOOD (1880–1975), writer of weird fiction. His brief success in the 1890s was eclipsed by the notoriety surrounding the series of trials involving members of the Decadent Movement. He enjoyed something of a revival among writers in a similar genre in the 1920s, especially in America, before falling into obscurity. At the present date most of his work is out of print.*

[2]*STONE, BRICE AMBROSE (1872–1919?), American author, journalist and adventurer. Native of San Francisco. Moved to London, 1895. Returned to San Francisco, 1905. Accomplished writer of short stories on death, horror and the occult. Went into Mexico, 1906, and disappeared. Last seen, 1919. Presumed to have died there, although unconfirmed later sightings as far south as Brazil.*

acknowledged unpleasantness of British winter weather (even if that is among our major preoccupations and provides a tireless and often, I fear, tedious topic of conversation, as you frequently had occasion to comment).

I have been considerably perturbed, of late, by certain developments within the Circle and you are the only person whom I trust enough to share my fear. We have both, at various times, claimed membership of the group, attracted by a common interest in the occult and a fascination with "all things weird". We both suffered a similar disillusionment, although I think that this had little to do with the belief itself – I know your interest to be as strong as mine – and rather more to do with the other members. You went your own way, pursuing an altogether more scientific mode of enquiry. I have stayed a member, having a greater toleration for human folly, as you have often said. I well remember that last explosive meeting at Madame T's[3] when you asked her _why_ her spirit guide was _always_ an American Indian (your point lost on them, I fear). A heated argument broke out, if I remember rightly, and ended with you calling them "a bunch of charlatans and self-regarding mountebanks, devoted to dressing up".

I do not disagree with your summation. Although I have remained in the group, I eschew dressing up, and attend meetings rarely. They have become far too

---

[3]MADAME T – ELENA NIKOLAYEVNA TELENSKY (1842–1910), born Helena Beren of German parents in present-day Ukraine. Founder member of the Circle of the New Dawn, claimed to be one of the Illuminati, as such, in constant touch with the spirits of air and earth.

<u>ritualistic</u> for me, but harmless enough. Or so I thought. Until a recent occurrence filled me with the most hideous disquiet.

I have kept up acquaintance with one or two. I still meet M[4] at my club for dinner now and again and this involves him, though indirectly, and two other members of the Circle. The first is the one I will call the Poet.[5] You will know him as the Dark Young Man with Spectacles. I hope you will forgive me, Stone, you know it is not like me to be so cloak and dagger, but once you have read the following you will understand my nervousness about naming any of them, even in my own study. Perhaps especially here.

M and I were due to dine at the club and I have to confess to being somewhat late. It was one of those dead days between Christmas and New Year and the members' room was almost empty. I found M sunk deep in an armchair, and rather deeper in thought, the evening paper unread before him. He finished his whisky soda and ordered another and one for me. We chatted about this and that, and then he mentioned that he'd been coming across the park when he met the Poet, who'd seemed frightfully down on his luck.

"Pitiful. Practically in rags. Almost starving, I'd say."

---

[4]LORD ALGENON MOUNTJOY (1876–1944), member of the Circle from 1898–1910. Eccentric aristocrat, best known for designing the Mountjoy Tarot Pack.

[5]Y. A. CONNORS (1865–1906), promising Irish poet known to be a member of the Circle of the New Dawn 1897–1906. Death by drowning, March, 1906. Verdict: suicide. Fragments of verse left by him have led some to compare him to Thomas Chatterton (1752–1770), only published work: Unfinished Life, collected by Aurel Lockwood, pub. 1908, Yellow Book Press.

Those were his words to me. "So thin and no colour. I hardly recognized the fellow."

M managed to recall his name, and addressed him with all civility, but the young man said almost nothing.

"He mumbled something unintelligible. Truly, Lockwood," M said, "I feared that he might have lost his wits. Perhaps I should have insisted that he come along with me, but really, the state he was in," M gestured a hopeless case, "he would never have been allowed in this place. Besides, I was going to be late, and you know what a stickler I am." He gave me a disapproving frown. "I pressed a few notes on him, which he did not refuse, and then I hurried on. . ."

After a few steps, he felt further guilt at leaving a chap in that kind of plight, but when he turned round, our Poet friend was nowhere to be seen.

"Here's the thing of it, Lockwood. We were quite out in the open. One minute he's too weak to even speak. The next, he's disappeared."

The encounter had clearly perturbed him, but there seemed little more to say upon the subject. Our talk moved on to other matters, and presently we went in to dinner. We dined well, I must confess, they do a particularly good roast beef, and a pudding of the sticky kind of which I'm rather fond. We had a brandy or two, and a cigar. When I left, he was in rather better spirits.

The night was clear and cold, with a suggestion of snow dusting the ground. There are precious few nights when one can see the stars above London, so I refused the offer of a lift in M's hansom and decided to walk instead. I set off across the park, but I had barely reached the other side when it had begun to snow. At first I did not mind, I remember thinking that it seemed as though the very stars were whirling down through the trees. I made a note to the effect (I always keep a notebook about me. One never knows when it could come in useful, a phrase like that, in a snowy story, say, but unless one notes it, when one comes to recall it, the bally thing has gone right out of one's head). The snow came on, thicker and thicker until, while crossing Trafalgar, I began to change my mind and by the time I was at the Strand I was searching for a cab. But you know how it is, they are queuing up when one decides to walk, but undergo a change of mind and there is nothing to be had for neither love nor money.

I was in a snowstorm, my dear Stone, such as might be experienced in your own Rockies. And quite alone. The blizzard had driven all off the streets, pedestrian and cabby alike. I had no choice but to battle onward, in the teeth of a fierce wind blowing from the east. Past St Paul's, I turned off the main thoroughfare, hoping to gain shelter from the closeness of the buildings.

It was then that I first became aware of it. Despite the muffling fall of the snow, I fancied that I was being followed. The usually populous streets were deserted. The inclement weather, the strength of the storm, had forced all but the hardiest indoors, or I never would have heard it. I was accompanied by the slither and thud of an uneven, shuffling gait, and a tap-tapping as in someone feeling his way by means of a stick rapped against wall and drawn across railings. I thought my pursuer might be the Poet, but I was quick to dismiss the thought. I was being followed by something big and blind. . .

The thought came to me suddenly and made me turn, but I could make out nothing through the white whirl of flakes. Nothing _human_ that is. Nothing except, perhaps, a black, shapeless mass, which could have been anything, or nothing. My eyes were playing tricks, but I had a feeling of malice, quite distinct, and something else mixed with it. A very great sorrow. And an emptiness. A yearning to be filled.

As you know, my house is quite tucked away deep within a neighbourhood that is rather down at heel. It is an area that normally teems with life and has attracted a great many people from all parts of the earth. They have come to our great metropolis to seek a better life, or to escape persecution in their own country: Indians, Afghanis, Turks, Muscovite Jews and others of their race from Central Europe, Arabs from the Middle East, Egyptian and Chinese. There are great scholars among their numbers who have been reduced to humble circumstance. I have learnt a deal from them and number many friends among them. These peoples are regarded with fear and suspicion because of their foreignness, but I have never felt the slightest apprehension when walking these streets. Until now.

The public houses splashed a sickly yellow light across the swirling chaos of white and offered the possibility of human conference, but even they were singularly lacking in customers. Nevertheless, I was tempted to call in. I don't scare easy, you know that, but the relentless tap-tap was fairly unstringing me and I still had some way to go. A whisky or two might calm me. Not only that, the detour might tempt him into

76

the light, so I could get a good look, but I was not at all sure I wanted that. Such a detour would slow me down, allow him to catch up.

I hurried on. The tap-tap, the shuffling step, never faltered. I was matched stride for stride. When I stopped, it stopped. When I went on again, so did my unseen companion. Deserted streets are not the safest. M's talk in the club had brought all that business back to me. "Dangerous dabbling", you called it. What if it was more than that? What if . . . I must admit to growing more and more nervous, not to say terrified. Even so, I found my own steps slowing. I was overcome with an overwhelming temptation to turn about. Hail the fellow and have done. Though I knew. That is what he wanted me to do. He was sapping my resolve. Even the thought makes my blood run cold. Thank the angels I didn't. You will see why in a minute.

The Poet was waiting for me on the steps of my area. He was quite covered in snow, and for a moment I thought it was that dratted coal man again, for the huddled mass looked for all the world like a sack of coal covered in snow. Then he stirred. I did not have pause to think who in the blazes might have been out there with us, I was too busy shaking the snow from his coat. He had a cut on his head above the right eye.

"You're bleeding, man!"

I ushered him into the house, but he brushed my attentions aside. He just wanted to know if I had been followed.

When I said I thought I might have been he went whiter than the snow in the street; the gash on his forehead stood out in ghastly relief. I thought he might faint and helped him to a chair near the hearth. It was then that I realized: whatever was out there was after him, not me at all.

"Your head, my dear chap." I offered my handkerchief, but he waved it away.

"It is nothing." He touched the place, and then regarded the blood on his fingers with some surprise. "I slipped in the snow."

Nevertheless, I ordered Thompson to bring iodine and dry clothing. For once, there was a good fire going in the parlour and the room was cosy and warm. We were both in need of the restorative properties of a hot toddy, which I prepared myself. I took heavy tumblers from the cupboard, poured a good slug of whisky and a squeeze of lemon over a couple of sugar lumps, and topped the mixture up with water from the kettle over the fire.

The poor fellow was in a sorry state, just as M had said, but the toddy seemed to be doing the trick, he seemed to be thawing a bit. Then as the wind howled outside, his agitation seemed to grow.

"He will still be out there, you know," he said.

I poured him another toddy. He had gulped the last one in double-quick time. He was shaking so much he had to hold the glass with two hands and still succeeded in spilling half of it. I thought that the second toddy would settle him down, but he continued to be much agitated, pacing the room and testing the shutters.

I tried to assure him that all was secure. The doors were locked and bolted, shutters barred. But he laughed, a tinny hollow sound, with no mirth in it.

"My dear Lockwood," he said, "do you really think that such things will keep him out?"

I was about to enquire as to the identity of his pursuer, but just then Mrs Abbott came in with food and interrupted our conversation. He would not settle to eat, or explain, or even put on the dry clothes Thompson had provided until I had performed rituals of protection. I know what you think of those, Stone, and I am normally of the same persuasion – a waste of good salt, is my usual opinion – but on this night, I did as he asked. I informed Thompson that he and Mrs Abbott would no longer be required for the evening (goodness knows what they would think – there is only so far one can go with natural spillage as an explanation). I found my small stock of holy water, and performed both banishing and protection rituals at the thresholds and in the parlour. Only then would the Poet relax and sit down to eat.

He hardly ate a thing, but helped himself to a large glass of my best brandy. Thus fortified, he began to tell his story.

I will not deny that what he had to tell alarmed me more than somewhat, and I began to be glad that we had made certain observances, even though I believe in them no more than you do. When you read of what he had to tell me, you will perhaps share my precautions. But I fear that is a letter for another day. The forces that he feared have strengthened. Night is coming on, and I am reluctant to commit his story to paper during the hours of darkness.

The Poet is still with me, somewhat recovered, although he sleeps within the pentacle and insists that we observe the rituals every night. He will not leave the house, and I have found him some employ with me, cataloguing my books and sorting and labelling my collection, which you know is something of a jumble and *Mrs Abbott* is forever grumbling about the room it takes up and the difficulty of dusting. So we go on.

More anon.

Yours in Brotherhood,

Aurel Lockwood

The writing in the next letter was smaller and sloped markedly to the right, the words almost running into each other, as though the writer had trouble keeping up with his thoughts.

STONE # 1

> c/o Tribune Office,
> Market Street,
> San Francisco,
> California,
> USA
> Thursday, 18 January, 1906

My Dear Lockwood,

Your letter read like one of your stories. I can hardly wait for the next enthralling instalment. More of the same, and soon, please!

Joking apart – I know I said that the Circle were all fools and charlatans, but I have cause to believe that one among their number is genuinely dangerous. Before I set sail for the States, I stopped off in Paris. Your Poet was there along with another, Buller Gilpin Wesson, the one you used to call the Young Man with the Staring Eyes.[6] I have no squeamishness about naming him, and urge you to be as open. Creatures such as he feed on fear. Wesson and Connors were working away on some secret endeavor[7] and were as thick as thieves. I saw them in Les Deux Magots on more than one occasion. The Poet was pretty stewed on absinthe, but t'other fellow sharp as ever. I doubt he knew me, but I'd recognize our friend anywhere. I've never seen anyone with eyes like that; they seem to give out almost no light. And that scar like a hole in his cheek. Caused by an assegai, isn't that what they say? Or was it the rapier of an Austrian count? He's even had his canine teeth filed, in some nameless native rite. Can you believe it?

Anyway, the pair were in cahoots, like I say. There _may_ have been some falling out since then, but have a care, my friend. The stary-eyed one is not to be underestimated, especially if he has been wading in forbidden waters. He will be behind your Poet's troubles, I'll stand warrant. I would not trust him for a minute. So watch your backside, as they say

---

[6]BULLER GILPIN WESSON (1880–1969?), occultist, traveller, mountaineer, some would say con man and shameless self-publicist. He adopted a variety of pseudonyms, ranging from the jokey – Leo De Vincey – to the chilling – Lord of Dead Souls – and attracted considerable notoriety before renouncing the occult and all related practices for ever.

[7]Translation of "Claves Angelicae" – Liber Mysteriorum – variously owned by Elias Ashmole and Dr Dee. An Alchemaic text supposedly in Enochian. Considered by some in the Circle to be extremely dangerous.

over here. I do not know if the further instalment involves him. If it does, then you be careful and keep an eye upon our young friend.

Sincerely,
Your friend,

Brice Ambrose Stone

LOCKWOOD # 2

11 Forfar Street,
London

Sunday, 28 January, 1906

My Dear Stone,

Your letter has added to my fears and makes me hasten to complete my Poet's tale. We have always set great store by intuition, and yours was as finely tuned as ever when you ventured to guess in your letter that the one we call the Young Man with the Staring Eyes, and I <u>will</u> name him – Buller Gilpin Wesson – is behind all this. I have learnt from the Poet that they indeed met up in Paris, and for a time the two were close. Wesson can be both charming and beguiling, particularly after a glass or two of absinthe. The Poet was short of funds, as usual, and Wesson generosity itself. His father, the Midlands brewer, left him as rich as Croesus. Wesson père bought some crumbling pile in Warwickshire, Ringmere Hall, and spent a fortune restoring it. I attended a house party there once when Wesson first joined the Circle. There was a seance, I remember. Madame T detected horrors both past and future and wouldn't stay a minute longer. The party broke up in some disarray. But a story for another day. Back to our pair in Paris. Both having a deep and abiding interest in all things occultish, they got along famously. For a while. It was not long before Wesson made his wishes known. The Poet has made precocious progress through the Levels for one so young. Madame T once opined that his youthful face was "a mere mask for a spirit both wise and ancient" (she always had a bit of a soft spot for him). On the other hand, she was the one who named Wesson "the Beast". "An old soul," I remember her pronouncing, "and not a good one." She insisted he loiter at Thadis,[9] to atone for his previous lives. She blocked any further progress. That's why he left the Circle. He has joined another sect, the Cult of Abramelin. They are rumoured to be following a decidedly left-hand path, engaged in the pursuit of knowledge that the Circle, rightly in my opinion, has placed under an absolute prohibition.

Anyway, to return to the story in hand. The long and short of it was: he wanted the Poet to take part in a certain ceremony from the Forbidden Book. He said he had acquired a copy (you know how rare they are) in the Prague ghetto, spent a fortune getting it, thousands and thousands, but he needed the help of another Adept. As

---

[9]Level One

far as the Poet knew, Wesson was not of that rank. Not so, Wesson crowed, showing off his Abramelin regalia and badges of office. The Poet refused, quite rightly, pointing out that the ceremonies were as the name of the Book suggests, Forbidden. For anyone else to even try them would be both dangerous and foolish, risking death, or worse. Wesson cursed him for a coward and swore to get others to help him. It was a ceremony of _possession_. A foul business. Once the ceremony was completed, he would have the power to watch over anyone he wanted. He would have the key to some sulphurous transmigration and be able to project into another, taking them over like some vile parasite of the ether.

The Poet left Paris, but when he got to London, he felt _pursued_. He had used all the psychic strength he possessed to resist, but now he felt that he was being _overtaken_. It was as if a crack was opening and a darkness was creeping towards him, ready to seep into his soul. As a last resort, he sought the help of those sworn to the Knowledge, and knew that we must freely give it. That is why he came to me.

To make matters worse, if that were possible, I have had a letter from J. W. D.[10] He is a pompous old windbag and much given to exaggeration, but he, and Madame T, have detected much astral agitation. They are deeply worried that someone _has_ somehow acquired powers that are forbidden and will use his new-found knowledge to attempt a Summoning. They were truly troubled when I

---

[10]DR JONOTHON WITHERS DUNWOODY (1845–1916), founder member of the Order and Coroner for the South Eastern District.

84

told them what Wesson had been up to. As you know, his ambition is boundless. Not only that, he is reckless and without fear.

Enough. I will write more anon.

Yours in Brotherhood,

Aurel Lockwood

STONE #2

c/o Tribune Office,
Market Street,
San Francisco,
California,
USA
Saturday, 10 February, 1906

My Dear Lockwood,

I share your concerns, vis-à-vis Wesson and your poor Poet, and agree that Wesson is up to something very dark and deep. I would not trust him for a moment. He is ruthless and daring, capable of anything. He is a danger and could become a very great force for evil. I believe he has set out on a journey, call it <u>astral</u>, if you will, and his intentions are sinister, but I don't believe he has progressed very far. I will lend what help I can but from here, all these Old World doings seem very distant and foreign, laced with the musty whiff of incense and the stultifying stench of the opium pipe. I feel that those paths are all too trammeled, the seams of wisdom exhausted. I don't think the answer, if answer there be, lies there at all.

Lately, I have been beset by a growing restlessness. I came back to find my city changed from how I remembered, my work more tedious, the downtown streets more crowded with people. The blue skies of memory have been blotted by sullen gray cloud; my fond recollection thoroughly dowsed by quantities of cold rain and chilled by a constant wind from the sea.

I guess this often happens after long absence, but I don't have to put up with it! As a country man of mine once said:

". . .whenever it is damp, drizzly November in my soul . . . and especially whenever my hypos get such an upper hand of me, that it requires a strong moral principle to prevent me from deliberately stepping into the street, and methodically knocking people's hats off – then, I account it high time to get to sea as soon as I can. . ."[11]

That's how I feel right now. <u>He</u> was a sea-faring man, and found his release that way. You have the hills of your beloved Gwalia to wander. When I feel like this, I saddle up and head for the High Sierras. I plan to follow the old Indian trails south, perhaps even to Mexico, who knows? I will wander to no fixed purpose, following my horse's nose. I'm going to open myself to coincidence. Some might consider that a very small magic, but even after all those hours spent at gatherings and seances, humble serendipity is the only <u>real</u> magic that I can recall. I'm not abandoning you, Lockwood, and your trouble is ever in my mind, but I am setting out on my own journey, in search of other wisdoms, in other places, and who knows? I may find answers there.

---

[11] HERMAN MELVILLE, Moby Dick, Harper & Brothers, New York, 1851.

I aim to set off within the next day or two. After that, correspondence will, perforce, be somewhat erratic, but when I have a clearer idea of where I'm heading, I will make arrangements for mail to be forwarded. I aim to keep a notebook, so eventually you will have a full account.

Sincerely,
Your friend,

Brice Ambrose Stone

LOCKWOOD # 3

Trellech House,
Castell Newydd,
Gwent

Friday, 2 March, 1906

My Dear Stone,

As you can see from the above address, I began this letter in Wales and continue it on the train to London. I did not want to leave Forfar Street with things in such a state, but was called back on urgent business which could only be dealt with by myself. I had hoped to conclude the matter with all haste, but some things cannot be hurried. Winter is at last in retreat and I was not altogether sorry to be forced to spend time visiting my native heath, where the daffodils thicken towards budding and snowdrops stud verge and woodland like spilled beads. I was thinking of you as I took one last walk in my beloved hills and returned to find your letter waiting on the hall table. Such, as you remind me, is the serendipitous way of things. I also found an urgent summons from Thompson. His note is brief (neither T nor Mrs A being much in the writing department) and does not explain the exact nature of the trouble, but I have an ominous feeling that this has to do with the Poet.

Before I forget, a safe trip to you, and a happy one, but do hurry back. You are one of the few whom I can truly trust and I will be in need of your counsel.

Sunday, 4 March, 1906

I was forced to break off my letter to you by our imminent arrival at Paddington. I have left off the continuation for a day or so while I tried to make sense of what has happened, but if I don't unburden myself to someone, I feel as though I shall go mad.

I hope and pray that this reaches you before you begin your trip.

I arrived home to find my house in turmoil. I felt a deep – disturbance – even before I entered the house. Indeed, I mounted the steps with a sense of <u>psychic dread</u>. I was not alone in sensing something. As soon as we entered the street, the horse of the hansom grew unsettled and would not be quieted; the boy engaged to carry the bags was scarcely less tiresome. He had to be offered another penny to carry the luggage from the kerb to the top of the steps.

The house is old, older than it looks, the bones of a much older structure being cased inside a more modern skin. The house is more robust than its elegant exterior might suggest. It is strong enough to resist storms of all kinds; not just the howling wind and snow of midwinter, but other onslaughts. Its history is what first attracted me.[12] *I know you do not believe in presences in quite the way I do, but it makes sense to me to live and work within these walls. It nestles close within the shadow of Nicholas's*[13] *great church, which I count a double blessing since I am grateful for the protection thus afforded and I think we can claim him as* <u>*one of us*</u>*.*

I had scarcely entered the house before being confronted by Mr Thompson, who was wearing his most doleful expression and informing me that Mrs Abbott was packing her bags. I found her in her parlour and calmed her sufficiently to assent to drinking a cup of tea with me. My enquiry as to what could be the matter was met with an anguished expression.

"'Im upstairs. I can't stands it no longer. It's bringing on me condition." She fanned her face vigorously and shifted her bulk in the chair (if you recall, she is generously built). "That's why I told Mr Thompson to write to you. It's more than a soul can bear."

"What is, Mrs Abbott? You have to tell me exactly."

---

[12]DR ARNOLD BRUM(E) (1574–1637), *a celebrated alchemist who had a house built "without the citye" as the site of his secret laboratory, "a place where my most secrete worke can take place and not attract attention by way of noxious smells and such explosions as might occurr all unexpected and of a sudden". Exact location unknown – oral history names Forfar Street.*

[13]HAWKSMOOR, NICHOLAS (1661–1736).

"First, it was the offence, sir. Since you bin away, we've hardly seen 'im." She drew up her ample bosom and pursed her mouth in perceived insult. "And I ain't used to having me food refused, sir. Little delicacies I done for 'im. A sliver of cold tongue. It melts in the mouth, sir. You know that. Me own potted beef, made to me secret recipe, but he wouldn't touch a thing. Meat or drink. Mr Thompson would take his meals up for him. Had to be left outside his room. He could not be disturbed. He was most particular. . ."

"How long has this been going on?"

"Since you left, sir." Her plump fingers were clutching each other in a wringing motion. "If 'e does go out, must be at the dead of night, that's what Mr Thompson thinks, but that ain't the worst of it, sir. Not by a long chalk. It's. . ." She looked round nervously and lowered her voice, almost to a whisper. "It's the noises."

"Noises?" I was growing increasingly alarmed by what I was hearing. "What noises?"

"Tell 'im, Mr Thompson, my voice ain't up to it. Me throat's gone that tight." Mrs Abbott clutched her neck and Thompson's tall thin form unfolded from the shadows.

"'Ere, Mrs A," he unscrewed the top of a silver flask, "don't take on, now. 'Ave some of this in yer tea."

Mrs Abbott is sometimes prone to what she calls "the hysterics". Thompson's offer of strong spirits seemed to ward off an imminent attack, although her hand was shaking as she lifted the cup. Having drunk, she nodded her thanks and sat back, ready for him to take up the narrative.

"It's like Mrs A says. We ain't hardly seen 'im. He's kept to his room, took books and I don't know what up there from the Long Room, even though I told 'im you wouldn't like it. Says he can't work nowhere else."

"Are you sure he's still there?"

A look passed between them.

"Oh yes, sir. We <u>hear</u> 'im. At night. You can't miss it when the house is quiet. Pacing and shouting, as if he was arguing with someone, followed by shrieking and crashing about. Mrs A was all for calling you back, but then it seemed to die down. There was moaning and groaning, but soft, like. And crying enough to break your heart. I've even ventured to knock on the door, to see if he's all right, like. I either get no reply, or he tells me to 'go away' in no uncertain fashion. Sometimes there's laughing and quiet talking, as if he has someone with 'im, although no one has entered the house 'cept us and the trades people, since the time you went." He paused in his narration and glanced at Mrs Abbott. "It's been a few nights now, but his voice has changed."

"Changed in what way?"

"Gone deeper. More coarse and rasping. It don't sound like 'im at all."

"Has he left the house?"

Thompson nodded.

"I've 'eard 'im coming and going just lately. Mrs A never, on account of her taking her drops."

"Can't get a wink without them, sir," Mrs Abbott said as if by way of apology.

"He leaves in the early hours of the morning," Thompson took up the story, "and comes back just before first light. At least I _assumed_ it was 'im. Heavy steps dragging on the stairs, like he was all wore out."

"Is he still up there?"

"He don't seem to go out in the daytime, does he, Mrs A?"

This needed investigating. I told Thompson to come with me and, armed with a stout poker (ready for any eventuality), proceeded to the upper floors. Mrs Abbott insisted on accompanying us, but stayed at the base of the stairs.

I don't know if you recall, but the house is tall and narrow, built on four storeys. My own rooms are on the first floor. Abbott and Thompson have quarters on the third at the rear of the house. The Poet had moved from a room near to mine and chosen to occupy the top-most attic, which offered him a suite of rooms where he could stay undisturbed, distant from the rest of the house.

All was silent as we came to the last turn of the stairs, but there was a distinct chilling of the atmosphere. A sense of uneasiness affected us both. Thompson went first, knocking on the door, politely enquiring as to how the gentleman might be. I pushed him out of the way.

I rapped loudly, but got no response.

"For God's sake, man. Let us in! You've got my household scared to death!" I gave the door a good thump and told Thompson to put his shoulder to it.

The hinges gave way with a rending shriek and a tearing of wood and we both fairly fell into the room. To find. . .

Nothing.

There was no one there and the room was in some disorder.

"I'm ever so sorry, sir." Mrs Abbott had come puffing up the stairs. She made to enter the room with purpose, as though to take broom and duster to it then and there. "Like I said, 'e wouldn't let me in."

"That's quite all right, Mrs Abbott. You can leave it now."

I barred the way, bidding them come no further than the door. There was a mystery here. I didn't want either of them blundering about, obliterating any evidence that there might be.

Thompson scratched his head. "Well, I call it very queer. I could 'ave swore he was 'ere."

Mrs Abbott nodded. "We both been up since first light. I never seen or 'eard him leave. You, Mr T? Maybe he went out the window!" She brightened, as if this could solve the mystery.

Thompson shook his head, staring past me at the bent and snagged nails. "Them's bin nailed up. A clumsy job. Why'd he do that?"

"I have no idea."

I did not know everything that had happened, but even from the doorway I could smell the stale incense, and the acrid stench of something else; read the titles on the spines of the books scattered about; see the trickle of pale dust on the floor, the traces of a pentacle erased, the sigils of Summoning, the empty suit of clothes on the bed. Speculation and explanations came thick and fast, each one more dreadful than the last. The sooner I was alone, the better.

I sent them downstairs and sat down on the bed, suddenly weak with dread. My precious volumes lay strewn about the room as if they were tuppenny shockers. Among the debris I found a clipping from a Paris newspaper concerning an artefact, a stone sarcophagus, which had been stolen from the Louvre Museum. I was immediately beset with the most hideous fears. On its own it is just a chunk of stone; put with something else and it just might become the most awe-inspiring object in history, more terrible than the lost Ark of the Covenant. As if to confirm my worst fears, on the floor before me lay the trickle of buff clay dust.

I roused myself enough to go downstairs to the Long Room. Sure enough, my collection had been plundered. There was quite considerable evidence of disturbance but the chaos was localized. The bookcases containing my collection on the occult had been opened, the lock forced. Rare and priceless volumes lay open and discarded. The Poet had known what he wanted. As for the collections, most of the glass cases were untouched. Only that containing the clay tablets from Mesopotamia had been opened and the contents removed.

I returned to the attic, to see what further clues I might find there. I will consult Matthews,[14] if, indeed, he is back from the Middle East. Between us, we may be able to establish just what the danger is. After all, it was his expedition that discovered the tablet in the first place. I don't know if you are familiar with the story, but the

---

[14] J. R. MATTHEWS, *Archaeologist and Middle Eastern Scholar, sometime member of the Circle.*

Louvre artefact was found by the French archaeologist, Emile Chaidec,[15] in the upper level of what he thought might be a royal tomb outside Nineveh. It was never properly excavated; Chaidec was too eager for gold. He found that and plenty of it, but also something far more sinister. Instead of one or two bodies, he found many. A death pit. Dozens of bodies scattered where they had fallen. There were no marks of violence upon them. Small clay cups about their necks suggested that they might have taken poison, but whether voluntarily, or under duress, it is impossible to say. Such wholesale slaughter had been found before and marked the site of a royal tomb. The team found the gold they were searching for, but if there was an accompanying grave of a king, or queen, they didn't find it. They didn't bother to dig much more. The expedition was experiencing problems in the form of accidents, sandstorms and all manner of other difficulties. Eventually, Chaidec abandoned the enterprise, and took his booty back to the Louvre. Among the finds was a plain black stone sarcophagus.

This is what has been stolen so recently from the museum.

It had been gathering dust in a storage room for many years with nobody recognizing its significance. Forty years passed by before Matthews turned up and asked permission to examine the Chaidec finds. He had been sifting the spoil heaps of Chaidec's expedition and, based on certain other inscriptions, he had come up with a

---

[15]EMILE CHAIDEC (1816–1854), French consul and amateur archaeologist, excavated sites near the modern city of Mosul. Died an untimely death.

theory. If he was right, the French archaeologist had made the most momentous discovery, perhaps one of the greatest in history. He had discovered the tomb not of a man, but of a god. And not just any god, but one hitherto unknown: a ferocious griffinlike creature, a hideous thing with huge fangs and talons, a snarling mix of cruel eagle and scaly serpent. Matthews tentatively identified him as a manifestation of Mimma Lemnu – All That is Evil. One of the elder gods, he was demoted to a demon for stealing the Tablet of Destinies. Even in this form he proved an enemy to man and god alike. He was slain by Ninurta, for these ancient gods could die.

These gods can be killed all right, but they can also be brought back to life. A deep chill ran through me, turning me as cold as that black basalt sarcophagus. There could be only one conclusion: this must be what Wesson is seeking to do.

Emile Chaidec is, of course, long dead. So are all the other members of the expedition. None of them made old bones, but that's another story. Let me say this: many of these tomb openings are associated with curses – this time there might be some truth in it.

The French authorities would have none of it. They regarded Matthews as some kind of crackpot and dismissed his theory as tommyrot. Matthews went back to his work at the museum. He had found a mountain of shattered clay tablets, a whole library of them. Now they had to be sorted. That is where I came in. I had more than a passing acquaintance with the subject and a certain knowledge of ancient languages. We met at meetings of the Circle and I expressed an interest. He invited me to view the collection, which contained some fascinating and curious finds: tiny beads of lapis and carnelian in the shape of flies. In myth, flies were associated with the floating dead left by the Flood – and the Lord who governed them. And then there were the tablets. We worked for many months fitting the shattered pieces together. The oldest were covered with an ancient cuneiform writing and appeared to be sealing stones: warnings not to enter. There was another tablet, again in the same ancient form, but different from the others. It seemed to carry an incantation, rather than an admonition, but it was broken. We only had a tantalizing fragment. Matthews decided to go back to Mesopotamia, to Nineveh, to see if he could find the rest of it. I never thought he would, of course. It was truly most extraordinary. What would the odds be? But he did. He brought it back with him. We fitted it together with shaking fingers. The Rite of Re-Generation: a ritual incantation to bring a god back from the dead. Matthews went back to the dusty tells to see if he could find more. Meanwhile, I would keep the pieces we had safe with me.

Safe? I looked at the trail of clay dust on the floor. Hardly.

Wesson had found out about the incantation, probably via a process of deduction from the Louvre museum, to Matthews, to me. Or Matthews might have told him directly. He is a fellow enthusiast, after all. Once Wesson knew the tablet was in my possession, he had sent the Poet to steal it from me.

I continued with my detective work, searching the room, trying to piece together what else might have been happening here.

My mood did not lighten. The discarded sheets and balls of screwed-up paper showed that the Poet had successfully translated the cuneiform writing from the tablets. Then I discovered something that sent my heart plummeting directly to my boots. A clay tablet, but fresh; the reddish-brown surface was still soft. I could press my thumbnail into it. The clay had been used to take the impression from a cylinder seal. These were small cylinders about an inch or so high and made of some semi-precious stone – rock crystal, chalcedony, lapis lazuli. The stone was carved with miniature figures, sometimes writing, and fashioned "back-to-front" so that the design would come out the right way round.

The impression was made by rolling the seal across soft clay. The design came out as one long picture. I went to get my glass to study the result. This was not part of my collection. I had no such seal in my possession. I had never seen what was depicted in my life, or anything like it. It was obviously astronomical. I recognized the symbol for the moon and the rising sun. A figure with outstretched wings could be the constellation of the Phoenix and other figures could be the gods who were associated with various constellations, but some I didn't recognize while others were extremely stylized. There was a tree of life symbol growing from a sacred mound covered with curved markings. Could it be water? Or scales? Or feathers? Above this level were symbols associated with the planets, the Wanderers, strung like beads in a line. But it was strange: I counted more than five. Griffin gods, a fearsome mix of bird and serpent, with finely etched feathers, scaly skin, clawed hands and feet, stood in profile, one with his foot on the sacred mound, the other with his muscled arm held out towards the sun disc, his curled fist grasping what looked like a knife, or was it an extended talon. . .

Is this Mimma Lemnu?

I've often wondered what caused the images of these repulsive reptilian hybrids to come to the forefront of men's minds. Belief in them seems to be impossibly ancient and they appear in many different religions and cultures. They are generally considered to be evil. Satan takes the form of a snake in the Garden of Eden. The Babylonians' Mimma Lemnu would belong to this tradition. The miniature image is as sharp as the day it was cut and it certainly resembles him, but as to the planetary significance? I'm no expert in Sumerian cosmology. I hope that Wrightson will know.

Meanwhile, I went in search of Thompson to see if he could shed any light on how this came to be here. Sure enough, a parcel had come for Mr Connors, bearing foreign stamps upon it, Thompson thought from the Middle East, probably Mesopotamia. Thompson is a bit of a collector and knows his stamps. Mr Connors had seemed very agitated when Thompson delivered the package. Later that morning, he had made one of his rare appearances to demand modelling clay.

One mystery solved, but I am set about by others. All the time, I fear, I fear.

Yours in Brotherhood and much perturbation,

Aurel Lockwood

9

THE INSPECTOR OF ANOMALIES

Adam looked up from his reading. An eye was watching him.

"When's that idiot of a porter coming back for you?"

The words came straight into his head. Adam was so surprised that he just shrugged.

"What about that creep of a priest? He's not out in the corridor somewhere eyeing up the nurses?"

Adam shook his head.

"Good. Time you and I got acquainted. Talk out loud if you want." The voice sounded in the speechless silence that fell between them. "That way it won't seem so strange. If the nurse looks in, it'll seem like you're doing what you're supposed to do, not just staring like we're already in the funeral parlour."

"What shall I talk about?"

"I don't know. Tell me about yourself. Your life."

After a stumbling start, Adam found it wasn't so hard.

He recounted what he knew of his life so far. He remembered nothing before the age of seven, when he had been orphaned in a terrible fire. He had been rescued. His mother had dropped him out through a window to a passer-by who had seen the flames and raised the alarm. She had managed to save her son, but not herself. So he had been told. He had no memory of the fire or his life before. The shock and trauma had wiped that time from his mind. Glimpses came back in dreams sometimes, or when he least expected them, but he did not know if they were true visions, or if he was making them up. He did not know who his father was, and had no other relatives, so he had been taken in by the Order. He had been with it ever since.

"Did you ever think why?"

Yes, he had, many times.

"Ever think to ask?"

Of course he'd asked, but the Brothers weren't big on explaining things, especially to small boys. "You are here to make a new start," that's what they had told him. "It is not for you to question. You must accept what fate befalls you." They were big on accepting things inside the dark, forbidding walls, along the echoing stone-flagged corridors, in the cold dormitories and cavernous refectory, where the meagre meals were taken in silence. It was part of the Discipline. The Rule. Every part of their life was set down, and everyone had to live by it, even a seven-year-old boy.

He had nothing of his old life left to him, not even any photographs. Everything had been destroyed in the fire. All he had in his narrow bed at night were fragments of dreams, splinters of memory. Sometimes he saw a rough-haired dog, felt the warmth of him, the coarse hair against his skin. Other times he saw a woman whom he thought was his mother. She came to his mind when he wanted to imagine belonging to a real family. She was very beautiful, but then he was bound to think that.

"She *was* beautiful. Very beautiful."

Adam saw again the woman whose image he had examined in the creased and faded photograph, but now it was as if she was alive again, laughing, saying something, pushing back her long, thick, rich red hair. She had green eyes, like his, and luminous pale skin. She wore red lipstick, and red nail polish. The vision lasted just a few seconds, but it hurt like a physical pain and brought the tears back to his eyes, even though he hardly ever cried. Until now. Adam sat silent and willed his father to go on. His heart beat heavy in his chest.

"I hadn't thought to marry," his father said. "All my life I had avoided such an encumbrance. A wife, a child, could not be part of my life. Not in my line of business. I travelled a lot, you see, never in one place for long, and what I did was dangerous – not just for me, for other people. Not good to have anyone close to me."

"What were you?" Adam asked. "A spy?"

He laughed. "Something like that, although my official title was Inspector of Anomalies. I worked for a consortium of museums. Perfectly respectable. My job was to search the auction houses, private collections, the museums of the world, looking for anomalies. Objects, artefacts that didn't fit the archaeological record. Some of the things I sought were highly coveted, or had cult, even mythic status. People would kill to get hold of them, to protect their provenance, or prove that they were fakes.

"That was only part of my job. I was also an archaeologist and freelance curator. That's how I met your mother. She was at a conference in Vienna. I was giving a paper there. She came up to me afterwards."

The picture of a young woman, carrying a notepad, smiling up at him, was almost too much for either of them to bear.

"She said that she'd enjoyed my lecture. We had coffee, cakes – and that was it. I was in love with her. Lost. I knew it was a mistake. I was much older. My job might put her in danger. I had often been alternatively bribed and threatened by ruthless men. I could look after myself, but somebody else? I should have heeded my own warning voice but I had never known such happiness. Then you came along, and my happiness doubled. It seemed to work, for a while, but it was borrowed time. I was gaining knowledge, you see. I thought that I could see a pattern emerging. The anomalies I was collecting, they were from all over the world, but they had certain things in common. They were old, for one thing. Far older than anyone would possibly credit. The older they were, the more points they had in common, no matter where they came from, as if they had been cherished, preserved from an elder world. I was getting close to something. The arson attack was meant as a warning. To me. But. . ."

The words stopped, but Adam stayed quiet. What words were there to say?

"I was away at the time. Came home to find. . . It took me a while to get over it. I'm afraid I was not myself. They put me somewhere and you were taken into care. Into the care of the Order."

"Why them?"

"Because they could. They are very powerful. Their motivation is murky at best, often impossible to penetrate. And they are great opportunists. The arson attack might have been staged as a warning, but they were quick to seize you. All I can say is that, by the time I was released, they would not let me have you. Not a fit person. So I retreated to the street."

Adam felt his father's emotion, like a thick, black wave breaking over them. There was silence between them. There was so much Adam wanted to ask him, about his mother, about their life together when they *were* a family. His mind jumped to a different track. Why had he chosen to live on the streets, like a tramp?

"At first I didn't care what happened to me. It was the only place I could live with my guilt." His father's thought came into Adam's head. "Once I got over that. . ."

Adam waited.

Abraham Black lapsed into silence. He didn't want to be shamed in front of his child, so he found it impossible to explain how the guilt, the fear he felt, had led to a terrible lethargy, an irresistible desire to hide from reality. And yet there was something else. Sometimes it is necessary for a sane man to retreat into insanity. Rapoport to his room, Stone on his southern journeying. They had followed the path Merlin took, into the wild wood to gain wisdom. The streets had been his wilderness.

"There are reasons why the street was a good place to be," he said after a while. "It allowed me the freedom I needed to get things ready."

"For what?" Adam asked. He'd caught a fragment of the thought and wondered: who was Rapoport?

"For what is happening now." His father settled back into his pillows. "Rapoport was a man I knew. He's in there, too." He nodded towards the notebook on Adam's lap.

Adam frowned. He did not fully understand the significance of the letters. Who *were* Lockwood and Stone? Why did his father have this book?

Again, Abraham Black found this hard to explain to the boy. Just as a medieval flagellant carried a whip to scourge himself, so he'd kept this with him, until it had become a talisman. To be parted from it, would mean the end of everything. All hope departed.

"To remind me of my duty," was all he could say. "As for Lockwood and Stone . . . all in good time. I'm tired now."

Adam's mind was filled with a grey blankness. He felt a sudden, complete exhaustion, as though they had both come to the end of their strength.

"Everything all right?" The nurse popped her head round the door, making him jump. She checked the watch she wore pinned to her chest. "I think that's probably long enough and I hear that you are due off. Any sign?"

"His eyes move under the lids," Adam said. "And his hand gripped mine."

"Are you sure?"

"Certain."

"That's good." She gave him a big smile. "That's *very* good. You wait till I tell the doctors about this! Like I always say, a bit of human contact from someone close can make *all* the difference."

She hurried over to her patient.

"That priest was here again," she said as she checked the readings on the machines.

"Brother Zack? What did he want?"

"I don't know, exactly. I caught him hanging about outside the door. When he saw me, he said he was making a visit."

"What did you say?" Adam had not been aware of this at all.

"I said: 'No, you're not, matey. Only one visitor at a time.'"

Adam stared at the inert figure on the bed. He looked so vulnerable lying there, so helpless and frail.

"I've had an idea," he said.

It was not just intuition. He didn't want to leave his father on his own. Not with Brother Zack on the prowl.

10

KA

The hospital authorities were surprisingly sympathetic. Patient welfare was always their paramount consideration and even after one short visit Adam's father was showing significant improvement. He had opened his eyes and was breathing on his own. By the time Adam was installed in the next bed, Abraham Black was sitting up and taking liquids. The doctors were very pleased, although his condition baffled them. He had not had a stroke, more some species of *grand mal*, a temporary abnormal disturbance to the brain. Now that the episode appeared to be over, his recovery should be rapid.

Although his father slept quite a lot of the time, Adam found it comforting just being here with him. He lay back listening to the steady breathing, the measured beep of the machines. His mind slipped back to Lockwood and Stone. He opened the book to read some more.

11 Forfar Street,
Spitalfields,
London

Saturday, 17 March, 1906

My Dear Stone,

I have not heard from you, so am assuming that you have begun your journeying. No matter. I will write anyway, rather in the form of a diary, as a way of relieving my feelings and in the hope that my missive may reach you eventually.

It makes a change to have some good news to report. I have been to see Wrightson,[16] spun him a yarn about some paper I was working on, and asked him in an offhand manner about the bringing of Chaldean gods back to life.

He told me that a clay effigy of the god had to be placed in the sarcophagus and the right rituals of incantation made to the Seven Sages.[17] That much I knew – and my blood ran cold. He must have seen my look of horror, for he laughed.

"The Rite of Re-Generation is lost! Even if it was not, the ritual can only be successfully enacted when the signs

---

[16]DENVERS WRIGHTSON 1840–1910 – pioneering work in Egypt and the Middle East. Recognized as the founder of modern archaeology.

[17]Wise men who lived before the Flood.

in the sky say it is right to do so. Once in a blue moon, in other words. Even rarer than that."

He could tell by my face I had something else. I showed him the clay impression.

He squinted at it.

I nodded. "It's some sort of sky chart."

"Linked to bringing this god back to life?"

"Could be," I said. Then decided to come clean. "Almost certainly."

He picked up a glass to examine the tablet more carefully. "I recognize the constellations: there's the Winged Sun Disc and a second solar disc below it, symbolizing the Place Devoid of Stars. The knife is a symbol for the implement used in the Opening of the Mouth Ceremony. The winged sun disc seems to be passing through a portal into the next Age. . ."

"What about the planets strung out in alignment?"

"Umm, definitely planets, but I count nine! Impossible!" Wrightson shook his head. "Thing has to be a fake, old chap. Everyone knows there are eight planets, and the Ancients knew of only five! Still. . ." Despite pronouncing the seal counterfeit, he examined the tablet again. Then he took a tome down from his shelves and began flicking through it. At last, he found the page he wanted. "Curious. If we discount the extra planet, and look at the constellations, an alignment is predicted at the time of these precise positionings!"

"What does it mean?"

"It marks the end of the present age of the world."

He saw my face change.

"Fear not!" He grinned at my apprehension. "It's not

110

due to happen for another hundred years or so. That should see us both safely underground. Food for worms and all that!"

I generally find Wrightson's humour rather wearying, but I laughed uproariously. A hundred years! The next millennium! If Wesson <u>was</u> behind it, all his elaborate scheming would be for nothing.

My happiness was short lived. When I asked after Matthews, our mutual friend, his face grew sad and grave.

"Didn't you know? But then, why would you?" He sighed. "I've only just received the news myself. He's dead. Murdered and robbed in some foul souk where he'd gone to trade for artefacts."

<u>A week later:</u>
One trouble piles upon another. My burdens have increased a hundredfold since I last put pen to paper.

Yesterday, there was a message from JWD, asking me to go to the morgue attached to Rotherhithe police station. I was needed to make the necessary identifications. It seemed that my erstwhile lodger had been found.

I made my way along grey rain-washed streets to an ugly red-brick building near the Thames. Inside it was all brown and bile-green tiles. A dismal place, dank from the day and clammy from the river. Despite the coldness and all-pervading carbolic, there was a distinct sweetish smell of decay. The stench of death grew stronger as we wound our way down iron stairs.

Our unfortunate friend was one among several bodies

lying on slabs. Each was covered in a sheet. JWD moved from one to another, reading the labels tied to the big toes as if he was finding the correct luggage. I hung back, bracing myself. Bodies dredged from the river are often unpleasant to the eye.

JWD had evidently found the right one, for he flung the sheet back with the flourish of a chambermaid changing a bed. He beckoned me over somewhat impatiently.

"Hurry up, man! He won't bite you!"

He guffawed and I took this to be an example of the gallows humour no doubt indulged in by his fellow coroners and others who deal with death every day.

I went over smartly enough after that, and steadied myself for a quick look, but I found myself staring in fascination, not at all tempted to turn away. It was the Poet all right. Of that there could be no doubt. A slight cut, half healed, above the right eye was the only visible sign of injury. His face was darkened with the contusion of death, and there was green weed wound in his hair, otherwise he could have been sleeping.

"Anything appear odd to you?"

JWD offered snuff against the cloying odour. I declined, but he took two big snootfuls and sneezed copiously, adding to the yellow-brown staining of his large moustache. He glared at me, his beady boot-button brown eyes watering under bushy eyebrows. Silver-haired, clad in tweed, small and stocky in stature, he looks like a badly kept West Highland white terrier.

I shrugged, not sure what I was supposed to be seeing.

"Wentworth, tell him."

112

The police surgeon stepped forward.

"Excellent man." JWD proceeded to talk about him as if he wasn't there. "Highly experienced. Assisted Bond, the coroner on the Ripper murders. Now foremost in his field. He'll tell you—"

"If you'll allow me, Dr Dunwoody," Wentworth interrupted. Bearded, his dark hair tinged with grey at the temples, he was a smart-looking fellow and sharp. Knew how to deal with JWD, anyway.

"He was not in the water long. Tipped into the river a night or so ago and found almost immediately. And he didn't die by drowning. In my opinion he has been dead for some weeks and kept somewhere cold. A cellar perhaps or basement. The weather has been chilly for the time of year."

"How did he die?" I asked.

"There are no signs of violence on the body, apart from that slight cut above the right eye. I have not completed my autopsy, but my guess is we will find he died of heart failure."

JWD snorted. "And that tells us precisely nothing. We all die of heart failure in the end."

An attendant stepped forward. "Finished, gents?"

Wentworth nodded. The attendant drew the sheet up over the body, shielding it from our further gaze and leaving the poor Poet to his final sleep. All that could be seen of him now was his mop of untidy curls.

We left Wentworth to go about his gruesome trade. Once outside, JW offered me a swig from his flask, which I was glad to accept.

"I thought you said the blighter was at your place."

"He was," I replied, my mind struggling to accept the

significance of what I'd just seen.

"You know what this means?" He scowled at me ferociously.

Of course I did, but the implications were so horrible I could not reply. I put my hands to my face and turned away. Horror of horrors, ghastliness of ghastliness. That which I saw, that which I had harboured within my walls, had not been human at all, but a fetch, a ka, an approximation of the young man in life, sweated from the very ether in I know not what hideous ceremony.

"It will be hushed up, o' course." JW fished his watch from his pocket. "Accidental death, I'll make sure of that. Preferable to suicide. Relatives less likely to kick up a fuss. As for the other matter, I'll talk to Madame T. We need to take action. It will take the whole Circle, those we can trust. Come to my rooms this evening. No time like the present. By the by," he dug into his waistcoat, "the attendant found this in the lining of his jacket. Must have slipped through a hole in his pocket. I know you collect this sort of thing. Thought he might have filched it." He held out his hand to show me. A cylindrical seal, carved from blue chalcedony and about an inch or so long, lay in the cushions of his pink, fleshy palm. "One of yours?"

I accepted it from him and deposited it safely in my own waistcoat pocket. It suddenly seemed doubly precious. I did not even need to examine it to know that this cylinder had made the clay impression that I'd just shown to Wrightson. It had been delivered to the Poet in a package with Middle Eastern stamps upon it. Some rogue intuition told me that Matthews had paid for it with his life.

I accepted JWD's offer of a lift as far as Tower Bridge and then got out. My house is not far and I had much to think about. It was chill by the river and dusk was falling as I walked in the shadow of the outer ward of the Tower and followed the line of the old city wall. A mist followed me up from the river, muffling the constant noise of the streets around me, making even the traffic seem quite distant. I must admit that it gave me a shiver and put me in mind of that snowy evening, it seems long ago now, when I found the Poet huddled on the area steps. Had he even then been some foul projection, or real flesh and blood? My intuition tells me the latter. I remembered how he had said that he felt <u>overlooked</u>, <u>pursued</u>. I remembered the presence that I had felt following us that night. It is clear to me now that the possession had been far from complete when he came to seek my help. I felt an even greater chill of horror. The young man had been undergoing a battle for his very soul and I had deserted him at his time of greatest need.

<u>Some time later:</u>
I have been reflecting further on what might have happened to the Poet and consulted others in the Circle more learned than I in this arcane area of the occult. There seem to be two possible explanations as to what may have happened. The first is that the possession was gradual. As the Poet weakened in body and spirit, then his enemy, who can only be Wesson, took him over completely and used him to plunder my collection and my knowledge.

The other theory is hardly less disturbing. Dead for some weeks, the police surgeon said, kept somewhere cold, _or in some state of suspended animation_. For at least part of the time, the creature living in my house could have been some kind of undead projection. Something akin to Stoker's vampyre, without the blood-sucking aspect. At some point, the Poet left my house as one thing and came back as something entirely other, devoid of all human will and purpose save that of doing his master's bidding. In this state he could have continued to pass as a human being. This theory does not explain everything, but it accounts for the seal found inside his clothes.

It is a tiny consolation but JWD has been true to his word and recorded a verdict of death by drowning. On the balance of probability, Connors tumbled into the river, either drunk, or as the result of some other mishap. His family are satisfied. Being of the Catholic persuasion, anything else would be hard for them to take. They have taken his body for burial in Ireland. May the poor young man now rest in peace.

It has taken the whole Circle many nights working together (one reason I've been unable to finish this letter). Our powers are all but exhausted, but I think the tide against Wesson has finally turned.

I find it is a month since I started this letter. April has come already. I don't want to speak too soon, but I really do feel as though we have turned a corner. Even the weather has improved. Today was a lovely day, balmy blue skies and the streets bright with blossom. Wesson routed, and no ancient Chaldean gods to be brought back to life until the next millennium. Despite my great sadness at the fate of the Poet, and my guilt that I did so little to prevent it, I take these things as small sources of cheer.

I hope that this reaches you, wherever you are, and that you remain well and safe.

Yours in perpetual Brotherhood,

Aurel Lockwood

11

XIBALBA BE: ROAD TO THE UNDERWORLD

"Ha!"

Adam had been falling asleep. He jerked his head up, startled by his father's sudden, harsh bark of a laugh.

"Turned a corner, eh? If only it were that simple."

"What do you mean?"

His voice came out of the darkness. Adam could not tell if he was hearing it, or if it was in his head. "Probably did seem like that to Lockwood."

"These two men, Lockwood and Stone, did you know them?"

"Never met the American, except through his letters and writings, but I knew Lockwood. He was very old by then. I got to know him through Rapoport, who looked after him. Rapoport was a refugee from Czechoslovakia, came here after the war. He had something I wanted."

"One of your anomalies?"

"Yes. Stolen from the National Museum. I went after him and came upon Lockwood. Turned out he had a house full of them. Anomalies, I mean. Not Czech refugees. Lockwood kept them in what he called his Long Room. He had a better collection than most museums. I should have turned them both in to my employers at the Temple."

"You worked for *them*?"

"Yes, I did. I could say for my sins, but it was mostly for money. In the beginning. But by the time I came across Rapoport, I was forming my own suspicions about the Order's *real* mission and purpose. What Lockwood and Rapoport had to tell me went a long way beyond my most paranoid fears. I had no idea how far their network spread, how dangerous they were, or how devious. As clever and devious as the mind behind it. Lockwood was by no means a fool, but he learnt to his cost that he'd been wrong to dismiss Wesson so soon."

"What do you mean? What has the Temple to do with him?"

"What do you know about your fabled Grand Master?

"Not much. . ." Adam paused to think. He was a bit of a mystery figure. He had rescued the Order from obscurity, fashioned it into a powerful international faith organization. He was still Head of the Order, each of his successors was known as the *New* Master, no matter how long he'd been in office. Adam thought that was just one of their quirks, of which there were many. He'd assumed that the real Grand Master had snuffed it years and years ago.

"Well, think again."

"But how can he be the same person? He'd be well over a hundred!"

"It's all in there." His father gestured towards the notebook. "To really understand you'll have to read the whole lot. Suffice it to say, that where once he only had that poor sod of a Poet now he has the might of the Temple to do his bidding."

"What's their ultimate intention?"

"Beyond imagining. Very few know. Even within their organization. As for outside? Lockwood. But he's dead. Rapoport. Dead. Which leaves me and one other. Whose existence must be a secret."

"Even from me?"

"For the moment. What you don't know can't harm you. She seems to have slipped beneath his awareness. I want to keep it that way."

There was a lull in the conversation. The hospital was growing quieter. The last visitors had left. Their relieved chatter and the patter of their footsteps out in the corridor had been replaced by a single muffled footfall and the squeaking of a trolley wheel as the staff nurse set out on her final rounds. There was the distant buzz of someone's alarm going off, then a muffled cough. Adam's mind wandered back to Lockwood's seal thing and the prophecy, or whatever it was. A hundred years ago would bring them up to. . .

"Now?" His father's voice cut in. "Precisely so. The cosmic event along with the planetary alignment, involving the exact number of planets shown on the carving, is due now. So not much comfort in it for us."

"What's supposed to happen?"

"The Cosmic Concurrence describes an alignment between the galactic plane and the solstice meridian.

There is a dark rift in the Milky Way, a place devoid of stars. At midday on December 12th, the date of the winter solstice by the old Julian Calender, the sun will cross this precise location, a place known to the Mayans as Xibalba Be. The road to the underworld. This is an event of extreme significance. It is the End Date. The last day of the Long Count that began 25,000 years ago. The end of the world. Such an event has been anticipated by many different peoples: Hopi Indians, Egyptians, Kabbalists, Essenes, Incas, the Navajo, Cherokee, Apache, Iroquois Confederacy, the Dogon tribe and Aborigines, to name but a few. Their number includes the Sumerians. It is the event shown on Lockwood's seal."

"But nobody truly believes in those things, surely?" Adam replied, to reassure himself more than anything; to stop the uncomfortable feeling creeping through him. "That the world can end just like that?"

"Not *end*, exactly. That gives the wrong impression. Change, more like. Quickly and rapidly. Mass extinction. It has happened before. It could happen again. The world would go on, but not necessarily with us in charge."

It still did not seem real to Adam. He couldn't imagine it. Every familiar thing just not there any more. Gone in the wink of a cosmic eye.

"Wesson has not stood still in the intervening time. He has gathered other knowledge from many different sources. It is this dark skein that I have been following. If he can perform the Rite of Re-generation at the precise moment of the Concurrence then he will transform himself into a god and Lockwood's worst imaginings will be as nothing. The world as we know it will be snuffed out, transformed into a place of unimaginable horror. Most of mankind will be destroyed; those who remain will be ruled over by fiends from the Abyss."

His father nodded towards the screen flickering above them, at the images appearing on BBC News 24: miracles and wonders, the usual procession of disasters.

"Some would say that the end has already begun."

The final story was on the cult suicides: an aerial view of Ringmere Hall with emergency vehicles strewn everywhere, the lake as still as a steel mirror; cut to the front of their very own hospital while the newsreader appealed for sightings of the, so far, sole survivor who had disappeared two days before. A blurry photo of her flashed up above a contact number.

Adam looked up at the face filling the screen. "She doesn't look at all like that."

"You've seen her?" His father was suddenly attentive. Until now, he had remembered nothing from his episode in the graveyard, but at seeing the face on the screen, a shard of memory pierced through his consciousness, as sharp as buried shrapnel breaking through the skin.

"Yes," Adam replied. "She was down the corridor from me. On the same ward. She nicked my clothes."

"Ah." His father's voice sounded different. Just that syllable sounded more hopeful. "It doesn't have to be that way. Of course! There are other myths, other legends. . ."

His voice faded as this new thought struck him. The surface of his mind split like a screen into multiple images, more adding by the moment. The pictures took different forms: wall paintings, drawings, classical sculptures, and were from many contrasting times and cultures. Each contained two figures, male and female. Sometimes separate, sometimes together, they all had two things in common: they were young and they all looked like Adam and the girl.

When Abraham spoke again, his voice was no longer an exhausted whisper.

"The Concurrence *could* mark a new beginning!" he said with fresh vigour. "It depends. . ."

"On what?"

"On us!"

12

INSIDE THE TEMPLE

The New Master sat behind his desk. The surface of the desk was remarkably clear, except for a brass bell, a blotter, an inkwell and an old-fashioned dipping pen. He used this now and again to add a note or a signature to the papers that were engaging him. When he had finished, he gathered them together, squaring the edges with painstaking care, and rang the bell. A lay brother secretary appeared instantly, his long black robe sweeping the floor, and took them from the New Master's hand. Only then did he give Brother Zack his attention.

Brother Zack knew that all this was a controlling device, designed to keep one in one's place, and to wind the nerves to screaming pitch. In this the New Master had succeeded admirably. The younger man had to fight a temptation to bite his fist. He hated this descent into his own nervousness. Hated this feeling of being a novice again. Someone would pay, and he knew just who that would be.

As the New Master looked up, he paused for a

moment to brush a hand over his thick, carefully barbered silver hair as he registered his appearance in the highly polished surface of the desk. He adjusted the blotter slightly and then regarded his junior over steepled fingers. A smile creased his broad, handsome face. Anyone who didn't know him well might think it a pleasant countenance, even benign. He knew how to use his large, blue eyes and ready smile to great effect, but the eyes could turn to ice in less than an instant; the smile fade and compress to a thin pale line.

"The boy won't give his permission. He is proving stubborn."

"Then you'll have to find other means of getting rid of the old man."

The New Master sighed. Abraham Black was an oversight who should have been eliminated a long time ago. He had been useful, for a time, but had turned out to be a mole within their organization. Black had escaped the arson attack but it had turned his mind. He'd become a gibbering idiot and a derelict, deemed by the Marshal as no longer a threat. Indeed, it was almost as good as killing him. Better in some ways, because he was still suffering and direct intervention always carried a risk to the Order, however slight. The Marshal was responsible for matters of discipline. At the time, the New Master had concurred with his colleague's decision and had rather dismissed Black as a problem. This had turned out to be an error. The Marshal had paid for his mistake.

"And the boy? Shall I get rid of him, too?"

"No. He still serves a purpose, but I want him back

here as soon as possible. Now, what about the other matter. This girl." The older man swung round in his chair and gazed out of the window. Raindrops crawled down the little diamond panes. "Any news of her?"

"There have been sightings. Here in the capital. She appears to be living on the streets. . ."

"So?"

"She moves about. Never in the same place. These people are difficult to trace. . ." She'd disappeared from view completely was the truth of it, but Brother Zack was not about to tell him that. "The photograph you gave us. . ."

"I know." The New Master opened a drawer and took out a glossy print. It showed a girl, smiling and demure, in her dark robe. The image had been cropped from a larger group. The quality was poor. "Worse than useless. There is, however, someone who might be able to help you with her. He will join your patrols. First thing in the morning. Meanwhile, I want the old man dealt with, and sooner, rather than later."

"I thought he had information. . ."

"You are not here to think, Brother Zachariah. Only obey. What about the other one? The boy who was with Black when he collapsed."

"Still no sign, Monsignor. We believe he's. . ."

"Believe he's what? Do I have to drag every word out of you?"

"Being protected."

"By whom, might I ask? By what?"

"We don't know. . ." Brother Zack's voice had dried to a husky whisper. It trailed away as he leant forward, his hands gripping on to each other to stop them from shaking.

"There's a lot you don't know." The New Master swung back to face him. "I am tired, so tired of all these excuses."

The New Master never shouted. His voice dropped when he became angry, became silky soft in its quietness, so it was difficult to hear him. His anger could be hideous. The consequences protracted. And terminal. When a novice joined, they gave themselves to the Order, body and soul. They gave up their names; all previous identity. They no longer existed. They were lost to the world. Brother Zack had been taken in as an orphan, just like Adam. No one in the outside would even know he was missing. He did not need to be reminded of that.

"We need these individuals secured," the New Master continued. "I'm sure you do not need reminding that as Under Marshal, human resources are your responsibility." The New Master tapped the desk lightly. Emphasizing each word with a perfectly manicured fingernail. "You have done well, until now. Indeed, I was thinking, since the more senior position is still open. . ." Brother Zack's heart beat faster. The Marshalcy was vacant. "But perhaps you are not ready for such responsibility."

The New Master brushed his palms together in a vaguely dismissive gesture, as if already distancing himself from his subordinate.

"Monsignor, I. . ." Brother Zack lowered his eyes in deference and tried to keep the whining, pleading tone out of his voice as he stumbled through a further catalogue of excuses.

The New Master seemed not to hear. He swung away to stare out of the window and watched the darkness gather in the quadrangle outside. It was all mess they didn't need. The boy going into hospital. Then the old man surfacing from nowhere, like an old infection flaring. Now they were in the same place together. Coincidence? Perhaps. But the New Master did not believe in coincidence. Then there was the matter of the girl. She'd been in the power of the Advocate, and he hadn't even noticed. The New Master and the Advocate were equals, but the organizations they headed were entirely different. Completely separate. The Advocate had grown far too arrogant. The New Master blamed the nature of the cult; the way the Children of the Sixth Dawn had been set up. The unthinking devotion of all those stupid followers, the absolute power he had over them, had turned his head, made him blind to the obvious. He had held her in his power, but he'd had no idea who she was. The shake of his head was imperceptible. Unbelievable. But perhaps there was a pattern in it. Some other factor at work. Their enemies appeared weak. Helpless. But their very weakness, their anonymity, might be their strength. Things were not going exactly as planned. It was time to act. He cut into the younger man's self-justifying monologue.

"Prove it to me." He indicated with a shooing motion that the audience was over. "Well? What are you waiting for? Off you go!"

Brother Zachariah stood up and, bowing deeply, retreated from the desk.

They could remain hidden, but at the last they would be forced to reveal themselves. And then? The New Master felt a surge of excitement.

"They will have been eliminated," he said to himself, "or they will be in our power."

His mind turned to the matter of the Advocate. He was in the Temple. His true identity known only to the Inner Order. To the rest, including Brother Zachariah, he was just an important visitor, and as such to be treated with all respect and deference. The Temple's absent Grand Master was the same person as the Children of the Sixth Dawn's revered Founder, but very few people in either organization knew that. The two orders had always been kept scrupulously separate. On pain of death. The Grand Master had willed it so. Now the Children were gone. The sacrifice had been made. The first part of the Grand Master's purpose had been fulfilled. Soon he would return in person. All must be ready. The Advocate would accompany the patrols tomorrow when they went looking for the girl. Meanwhile. . .

The New Master took out a sheet of paper and wrote. He folded the paper carefully, sealing it with red wax. Orders for Brother Zachariah. Nothing, nobody would be allowed to stand in their way.

13

BRICE AMBROSE STONE'S FIELD NOTES

There was silence in the room. Adam had more things
to ask his father, but the old man had drifted off again.
There was no way Adam could sleep. His mind was a
maze of questions and puzzles. He opened the thick
pages of the blue notebook. Maybe he would find his
answers here.

A telegram, brown with age, had been pasted in after
Lockwood's last letter.

TELEGRAM – 20 April, 1906 – Santa Fey
Brice Ambrose Stone – Aurel Lockwood
SURE YOU WILL HAVE HEARD OF TERRIBLE
EVENTS STOP DO NOT CONCERN YOURSELF
STOP AM SAFE STOP AM SENDING
NOTEBOOKS AND SEALED BOX CONTAINING
ARTEFACTS OF UNKNOWN PROVENANCE
STOP TAKE TO MCKENDRICK AT MUSEUM OF
SCIENCE STOP ON NO ACCOUNT TELL HIM
WHEN OR WHERE FOUND STOP AM SET ON
TRAVELING MORE WILL BE IN TOUCH STOP

Following this, came pages cut from a small notebook. Adam recognized the American's neat, hurried script. The notes were illustrated here and there by quick, skilful sketches executed in pen and ink.

Brice Ambrose Stone's Field Notes

Frisco to Fresno:

I went by railroad to the home of my old friend, MK, who presently lives outside Fresno. We were at Yale together and I haven't seen him in an age. I figured a visit with him would be a good start to my journey. I have stayed on for a few days, enjoying the last of civilized company, while I acquire a horse, a pack mule, and the necessary supplies for my wilderness ride.

Starting Out

I set out with the sun smiling down upon me. Any doubts that I might have harbored about this project soon disappeared in the freshness of the day. I was impatient to get into the hills. Down in the valley, every foot of usable land is being put under cultivation. Wild flowers: the lupines, poppies and their Californian cousins, which once blazed across the grassland here, are now confined to the margins and the waysides as acre after acre is turned by the plough. MK was telling me that the latest scheme is to grow fruit and vegetables to be shipped in refrigerated carriages to the cities back east. He's thinking of moving to up around Santa Rosa and planting vines. Folk need feeding, I guess, and good wines too, but I prefer the wildness.

Pretty soon, I was leaving the lowlands behind me. I rode all day through black oak and white flowering manzanita, up toward the tall stands of sweet-smelling pine. Although I carry supplies, including my one luxury – a box of fine Havana cigars – I intended to forage for myself as much as possible and, finding small game abundant, bagged myself a half a dozen or so quail.

Toward evening, I crested the first of two ridges and saw below me an abandoned mining encampment. The sun was disappearing, casting the narrow ravine in shadow, and the remnants of human habitation gave the valley a decidedly dismal air. The remains of rotting cabins were strung out either side of a winding gulch. Flumes had collapsed into the stream in splintered lengths of broken planking; heaps of spoil, still bare of vegetation, rose in uneven hummocks along the valley floor. The trail led me downward and I found myself picking my way through a litter of sodden Bibles, rusting cans and broken tools. I followed the track up the steep slope toward the other ridge. It was slow going through well nigh impenetrable manzanita thicket. Then the ground leveled out. The light was going fast and I thought that this might be a good place to set up camp. The land had been cleared for some purpose, and the vegetation had not had time to reclaim it. Spongy, worm-eaten planks rose from the ground at drunken angles. I thought them the remains of some kind of dwelling. It was not until I leant close and saw the remnants of lettering that I realized I had stumbled upon a graveyard. I mounted and urged my tired horse onward. Although not overly superstitious, or fearful of spirits, this did not strike me as a happy place. I wanted to put some distance between me and the mining camp.

Strange Meeting

Sudden cloud coming down made it foolhardy to continue and although I had thought to camp out, the night was growing exceedingly chill. I began looking about for some kind of shelter, and even thought to go back to the mining camp, all other fears forgotten in anticipated discomfort. Then I came across another clearing, surrounded by broken fencing. In its centre stood a rough pine-log cabin in a sorry state of disrepair. The windows were gone, as was the door, but it had been built soundly, chimney still standing. I had a good look around and, finding the place deserted, I decided to make this my dwelling for the night.

It suited my purposes admirably. There was even a well to water my horse. I gathered fodder for him, and pine branches and grasses to put under my blanket, and settled myself in for the night. I cleared the grate and gathered kindling and soon had a good enough fire going to thread my birds on sticks and set them to roast. The fire gave plenty of light to write this journal and offered welcome warmth. I lit a cigar from the embers and a slug or two from the flask of excellent plum brandy provided by MK's housekeeper gave me added heart.

I was about to unstring my birds, the aroma of roasting meat having set my stomach growling, when I suddenly felt distinctly uncomfortable. I could sense another presence in the room. The feeling grew so strong that I found myself looking to the empty space of the doorway, almost expecting to see someone standing there. There was nothing but impenetrable blackness. This merely added to my unease. I turned back to the fire, scolding myself for being so skittish and nervous. I do not usually spook so easily but I could not help speculating on what dreadful events might have occurred in such an isolated dwelling as this. Indeed, it would have made the perfect setting for one of those stories of haunting which we used to find so entertaining, but it is one thing to be telling such a tale in your cozy sitting room, quite another to be living it.

133

The sense of being watched grew ever stronger. At first, I thought it must be some kind of bird, an owl perhaps, regarding me with large, impassive yellow eyes. . . In the end, the feeling became so intolerable that I was forced to take a blazing brand from the fire and search every corner of the place.

It was then that I saw him. He was sitting in an alcove, slightly recessed from the central room, a space that I could have sworn was empty when I first entered the dwelling. He stared, as impassive as the owl of my imagination, while I stammered my amazement, and then came to join me by the fire. He was an Indian male, about six feet in height, of middle years judging by the silver threading in his dark hair. He was not dressed in any way like the Indians of popular imagining, with no feathers in his hair. He wore sturdy twill pants and his worn chambray shirt was clean enough and neatly patched. Only his moccasins and braided hair betrayed his origins. I thought that all the Indians left hereabouts had been chased off by the miners, or rounded up by Indian agents and put on reservations. He smiled.

"We are here. If you know where to look."

He was not from these parts. He pointed to the south. I asked about his tribe.

"I am of the people," was all he would say.

He clearly offered me no threat so, in the way of travelers thrown together, I invited him to join me by the fire and to share in my supper. He squatted on his heels and ate with the fastidious relish of a mannerly man breaking a long fast. We did not speak further until all the little birds had been picked quite clean. I offered him a swig from my flask, but he declined it, saying he never partook of strong drink, but he happily accepted one of my cigars. We smoked for a while in silence, and then I asked him what had brought him so far from his homeland. He stared into

134

the dying fire and said a dream had brought him here. He did not explain further, but I know that dreams are important to these people. They hold them in high importance, and were interpreting them, attributing meaning and significance long before modern alienists[18] made their recent discoveries. I asked him what the dream was about. He said he had dreamt of me. With that he cast his butt into the embers, spread his blanket in front of the dying fire and seemed instantly to fall asleep.

I lay on my bed of sweet-smelling pine branches, but for a long time sleep evaded me. I had a sudden feeling that I was in a story of my own making, but it was somehow much bigger than any that I have ever dared to imagine.

In the morning, we broke our fast in silence. He rose in one fluid movement and went to the open door of the cabin. A horse was grazing nearby, a fine Appaloosa. He whistled the beast to him, fashioned a bridle from rope, and threw a blanket over her back. He mounted and it was clear that we were to travel on together. I made no objection. I'd set out with no stated intention, other than to rely on serendipity, but now I felt as if I'd had my guide picked out for me and was setting out on the journey that I had been destined to take all my life.

The Journey

We have spent many days together. He is a man of few words, but I've never met a wiser individual, or one more knowledgeable in matters spiritual. His knack of calling creatures to him is only the tiniest part of it. He is a master of the uncanny but he is as

---

[18]psychiatrists

distant from Madame T's "Indian Guide" as he is from a tobacco-store statue.

I do not intend to record every turn of the trail, every place we stopped, every landscape we crossed. We took roads less traveled,[19] as a poet friend of mine once said, and they led us through great forests, across trackless snowfields and rocky places, through high passes where the air was thin and left me gasping for breath. Alone, I would have perished, as many had before me. We found traces of others who had become lost in the cruel high country. In the upper passes, we came upon abandoned goods and heaps of clothing leading like a trail back to broken wagons, their iron hoops sticking up like gaunt rusting ribs. We found the remains of horses, bullock and cattle. Men, and women, too. Sometimes there was a lonely grave marker, more often we discovered them lying where they had fallen, perished from cold and hunger, their skeletons still clothed in rotting garments.

A Hostile Land

We have crossed the great mountain divide and have descended into desert country. No less cruel, and no less beautiful. I would have died within a day of my canteen running dry, two at most, but my companion always knows where to find springs of sweet water, plants that readily give up their moisture, rocky places to shelter us from the bitter cold of the night, or when fierce winds make further progress impossible. It is early in the year and the days are not as hot as I thought that they would be, but we often travel at night, guided by a moon close enough for us to see her mountain ranges and seas. Our way is lighted by a spangled mass of stars that seem to float, like celestial Chinese lanterns, just out of reach.

---

[19] ROBERT FROST

The desert is a hard country, but a place of great beauty. A beauty made terrible by its hostility to humankind. We skirt salt pans that shine with a white of startling purity, and sparkle as though the ground is crusted with diamonds, but where every breath is poison and the very air can leach the moisture from a man, sucking his life away in hours. The constant wind can blind and choke, flay a man's skin from him, but it has shaped the rocks into forms beyond any sculptor's skill.

In this place, life and death are a hair's width from each other. Beauty and danger are mixed together, each complimenting the other. In that lies one of life's great secrets, according to my companion. He does reverence at the beginning of each day, bowing his head in humble prayer as dawn appears in exquisite shades of pastel that herald a rising sun which glares like brass through the saffron clouds. A promise of pitiless power to come. Nothing can be trusted. Above us wheel great raptors, uttering strange mewing cries. They follow us as we ride, weaving the sky with beautiful, spiraling patterns of flight. They keep their distance, but if man or horse went down, they would collect in a great ravening hoard and be on us in a minute, tearing with claw and beak. Sometimes, it seems that there is no life at all in this dry, desiccated landscape, nor could there ever be. Yet even after the slightest pattering shower, the whole desert blooms with a hectic short-lived beauty, as though the flowers know that their chance will not come again. I guess there's a lesson in that, too.

The desert is not devoid of life, far from it, but it seems to me the beasts that lived here are as hostile to us as the place they inhabit. Like many people, I can't abide snakes and am careful at each stopping place, searching for any sign of the loathsome reptiles. When it came, I never saw it, just heard the dry whirring tick of its rattle and there it was, advancing across the sand toward me with a hideous squirming that I cannot find words to describe. I drew my pistol, ready to blast the vermin into oblivion, but my companion stayed my hand. He picked up the creature, seizing it behind the big, blunt head, and held it helpless. Ignoring the heaving of its muscular body, he bade me feel the silky dryness, invited me to see beauty in the shades of grey, white, brown, black and cream that made up the diamond-patterned scales. He showed me the delicate ingenuity of the hollow fluted teeth, even while the creature was spitting venom. Still holding the thrashing creature, he took a little pot of polished stone from out of the bag he always carries over his shoulder. He had me hold the vessel while he carefully and expertly milked the venom from the creature's fangs, just as a maid might milk a cow. He left the venom to dry and then scraped up the residue to keep as a powder. It has many uses, so he tells me. When he'd finished milking the snake, he cut its head off with his bowie knife. We ate well that night. He's kept the skin, promising to fashion it into a belt for me.

He collects all kind of plants, flowers, leaves, roots, bark, even salts from the rocks, stowing them in the bag that he's got. My guess is that he's some kind of medicine man, what our anthropologist friends call a shaman.

The Tracks of the Little Deer

It was a great journey, an epic journey, but one as much of the mind and spirit, as of horse and rider. Just as my companion has re-educated my senses to appreciate the beauty and complexity that exists all around me, so he is steadily revealing a world hidden from normal view.

At first, his actions seemed incomprehensible, so foolish that I was considering revising my estimation of him as a wise man altogether. With no warning, he dismounted from his horse and set off across the rock-strewn desert floor. When I called out, enquiring as to what the Devil he might be doing, he replied:

"Following the tracks of the little deer."

I could see no tracks of any kind in the soft sandy surface of the ground, but I followed. We went some way, zigzagging in this direction and that, until he stopped in front of a patch of woolly looking cactus plants. I stared at the pimpled, green blue bulbs of flesh lying squat to the ground, looking for signs of trampling, or damage. I could see none. The plants looked pretty poor specimens to me, unspectacular as cacti go, certainly nothing like the majestic saguaro, that can stand very much taller than a man, or the weirdly shaped organ pipe, or even the fat-bodied barrel cactus with its beautiful orange flowers. I was just about to remark as much when my companion drew an arrow and shot the plant, just as if it was an animal! He then knelt before it, chanting and making offerings. I truly thought that he had taken leave of his senses and cursed myself for being so trusting, for now I was stuck in the desert with a mad man.

Then I realized. This was no ordinary cactus. This was peyotl, the sacred one. I had heard whisperings about its power, but had never seen the plant, and knew nothing about the associated rites. I watched with a kind of fascinated excitement as he took a knife and cut the whole plant off at the root. He did this with gentle reverence, as if the plant might shriek, or cry out, as the mandrake root is said to do. He handled the severed plant with gentleness, as if it were indeed living, and placed it with great care into his bag.

He went from patch to patch until he had gathered quite a few specimens, and that night he left me to set up camp while he took a couple of the bulbous plants from his bag and ground them to a pulp, catching the juice and carefully scraping every last bit of flesh into a gourd. Then he built the fire with especial care. When he had a strong blaze going, he set two arrows to point in the four directions and bade me sit opposite him west of the fire. He took out deer-hoof rattles from his bag and commenced to chant. Then he took up the gourd, passed it three times, sun-wise round the cross, and invited me to drink the dark green liquid.

It had a taste that is impossible to describe and a strange texture, slightly jellified. I had heard great things about this plant and its magical properties. Far greater, so I'd heard, than sense-dulling opium, or so-called sacred mushrooms. I sat cross-legged, with my toes going numb and my knees beginning to ache. I seemed to wait for a long time, quite disappointed that nothing was happening to me, while the rattles rasped and shook and the high, whining, moaning chant rose and fell in cadence. I was suddenly aware that there were other figures dancing round the fire. I was just asking myself where they had come from, when I woke in the cold of early dawn. The fire had burned to ashes, the figures were all gone. My companion helped me to my feet, smiled a welcome and took me into his arms like a brother. He smelt of sage brush and wood smoke. That morning I joined him as he welcomed the dawn, for I had passed the Gateway of the Clashing Clouds, and visited the Other Place, and I was changed for ever.

We rode on and I welcomed my companion's usual silence (I've never known a less talkative man), for I needed time to reflect upon what had happened to me. Try as I might, I could not persuade my conscious mind to discover the experience, but I felt it was unlike any other. I have tried many ways to reach the other side in my time, but had never been convinced that any of them worked, or indeed, that there was another side to be reached. I have remained a sceptic, until this moment. I remembered an old soldier I met who had served in the conflict between the North and South. He wore a scarf to hide a deep scar on his neck, but he was not shy about describing how he came by it. He'd been hit in the neck by a sharp shooter. He knew the wound was bad and could feel his lifeblood seeping out of him at a steady rate. Suddenly the scene around him, the smoke and roar of the cannons, the crackle of small fire, the cries and screams of the wounded, even his own pain, faded and he seemed to be in another place that was in many ways the same, yet different from this. He sensed other worlds besides, that he could easily enter, and it seemed that he had an infinity of time to do just that, but then he was back in the mud, smothered in blood, his agony renewed, and he wept. The medic tending him thought he cried because of the pain, or the dread of death. Not at all, he said, he cried because he knew that he would go on living.

This is common enough knowledge among soldiers who have been taken to the brink of death and survived against all odds. Common enough to be true. I had never experienced it, but now I felt as though I, too, had found a way to the infinite. It was full of creatures and things I could not recall, let alone describe, but I felt as though I had walked with the gods.

Transformations

Something within me had changed. I began to see with new eyes. The landscape itself began to speak to me in ways it had not done so before. We rode under formidable cliffs, stratified with the entire world's history. Fossils jutted from the ground; the remains of a petrified forest. Before, I would have jumped down

141

from my horse intent on collecting samples, but now I found that these things no longer interested me. They spoke of a past waiting to be rediscovered, but what do you learn about a man when you dig his bones up out of the ground? I had begun to see differently. For me, the land was suddenly a sentient being. Impossibly old, but living still. All around, I could feel the pulse of it, sense the spirit.

We were entering a different country, riven with great canyons of pale red sandstone.[20] I began to see things on the flat valley floor, a great serpent shape that I would have previously dismissed as random marks in the dust. It seemed to point a direction, although we had entered what appeared to be a box canyon. There was no way out. Previously, this would have troubled me with fears of ambush, either from hostiles, who had left their reservations, or desperadoes, a few of whom I knew to roam this last wilderness. My companion signed that we should dismount. He led me up a slippery scree-covered slope toward a rock face that seemed too sheer to be scaled at all, let alone be climbed by a man and a horse. The petroglyphs I saw pecked out on the rocks held new meaning for me. I puzzled over the strange markings, as though this was a language I had once known, but could no longer call to memory. I could discern paintings on the side of the cliff. Depictions of awesome creatures, many feet tall, somewhere between bird and man and lizard, with scaly jaws and long curling claws. A shiver ran through my soul, for I felt that these were beings I had somehow encountered in dreams or visions I could not recall.

---

[20]Anderson's Canyon. Now within Area 51. Formerly a nuclear test zone and still a restricted area, controlled by the USAF. Has become focus of UFO conspiracy theories related to reverse engineering and alien contact.

I asked who had made the marks on the rocks. What were they for?

"The Hohokam. The people who came before. They show what is to be feared; what is to be revered."

I told him that images seemed weirdly familiar to me.

"Sometimes we dream of what has happened," my companion replied. "Sometimes we see what is to come."

He said nothing more.

The climb was hard and precipitous. At certain points the way became so narrow, the incline so steep, that my horse had to be blindfolded before he would move another step. Many times, I wished that my companion would do the same for me. I do not have much of a head for heights and one false step, the slightest slip, would have sent me tumbling to oblivion.

At last we reached the top. Here, the narrow wall of rock was pierced by twin archways. The rock between them seemed to be shaped like an eagle's head, the arches made by the swell of his wings, as though a great bird had been petrified, caught for all time in the very moment of flight. I did not express this fancy to my friend, but he smiled, as though he understood, and nodded as if to say that was indeed the case.

He bade me look through, for the arches acted as the lenses of two great eyes. Far below, I could see a rich and verdant valley, and I knew that we had, at last, reached our destination.

Arrival

The bottom of the valley was washed by a wide, meandering, glittering stream of milky aquamarine. We led our animals to water there and my companion has made camp under the spreading shade of a cottonwood while I find time to catch up with my notebook.

There is much to wonder at in this wild, rugged landscape. Eagles circle high above the crags, like specks of ash against the clear blue of the sky. All around us there is a line of beauty in the sculpted forms which quite takes one's breath away. I gaze upward and find my imagination ignited still further for some of these are man-made formations. They are built in what seems to be the most inaccessible places, halfway up sheer cliff faces, and are not easy to see, they fit the natural landscape so perfectly. They have a grandeur that I have not hitherto associated with the dwellings of native peoples and I cannot wait to explore the square-cut towers and solid-looking buildings that are several storeys in height. How did such things come to be here, out in the middle of this pristine wilderness? I got the same reply that I had received about my earlier enquires.

The people who came before.

I thought to collect some artefacts, for surely there was evidence here of an unknown people of some sophistication. There seemed to be no lack. The floor of the valley was marked with low stone walls and pocked with deep-lined pits called kivas. A casual scuffing of the foot revealed exquisitely patterned pottery, carefully worked stone implements and finely woven basketware buried in the sand.

The Womb of the World
I have spent the afternoon doing some collecting while my companion rested under a tree.

He rose just as the shadows fell over the floor of the canyon. He indicated that it was time to go and I followed him.

We made our way up the sloping side of the canyon through a

pygmy forest of piñon and juniper. I thought that we were climbing toward the mysterious buildings that I had seen perched high on the cliff face, built within the shelter of a great open-mouthed cave, but these he ignored. He led me away from the dwellings by way of an ancient path, a narrow groove worn deep into the rocks. We followed the contours of the cliff for some time, and then he indicated that we must climb by means of footholds and handholds carved into the sheer rock face.

Having no love of heights, I climbed with dogged determination, my attention fixed upon the square of stone before my eyes. Fearing to look down, I could not tell how high we were climbing, but the eagles' screaming calls seemed very near, and although the valley floor had been exceedingly still, here the wind whined in my ears and tugged at me so hard I feared for my footing.

We climbed on until we came to a great split in the side of the cliff, a crooked, vertical aperture. My companion squeezed himself into this narrow space and indicated that I should follow him.

We entered a dark interior dimly lit by windows cut high into the rocks. We sat for a while in a circular chamber, like a kiva. This was the <u>crack in the world</u>, he explained, a word the people also used for the birth canal. He gave me buttons from the peyotl cactus to chew and explained that this was the place from where the children of the gods first emerged into the world, bringing their gifts and showing the people how to live like human beings.

"Who were these first people?" I asked him.

He shrugged, as if it was not a question to be answered. They just <u>were</u>. That was all. They had come here on a strange boat, brought on a flood which had washed them into the mountain for them to be. . . He struggled to find the right word here, there seeming to be no equivalent in English, the nearest he could find was _reborn_. The whole mountain was sacred. Holy. It was. . . Again, he could find no equivalent, _the body of the Mother_, it seemed to be, but I divined it meant more than corporal presence. The Mother in spirit and essence. As we sat together in that cool, quiet place, I felt such warmth and grace, peace and calmness that he did not need to explain further. It was as though she was there, with us. He told me stories of those first times, when great animals ruled the earth and walked the plains, free of hunters. I do not know how much time passed but, when I looked up, the high windows were marked by bright pepper points of stars.

He rose to his feet and, lighting a torch to illuminate our way, led me on down narrow paths deep into the sacred mountain.

As we went deeper, the rocks grew warm to the touch and white vapour wisped from the walls. This was the breath of the serpent who circles the earth. He had been caught by Atar, a child of the gods, and forced to swallow his own tail, but he fights always to be free; his struggles shake the earth and heat the rocks about him.

We were nearing the heart of the mountain. The narrow ways opened out and we entered a circular chamber. It was hot here and my companion stripped off his clothes. I followed his example without prompting. It felt in no way strange. A ledge had been cut into the wall, circling a deep pool that reflected our torches in perfect stillness. White vapour writhed up from the surface and he indicated that we should bathe here in some kind of ritual of purification. The water was above blood heat and so syrupy with minerals that we floated. We emerged dripping, as from some amniotic liquid. We collected our things and he led me still deeper into yet another chamber. The Place of the Mother. The Womb of the World.

The chamber rose into a curved dome high above our heads. Every sound was amplified. The slightest tap on a drum resonated out and came back very loud, as if the earth had gained a heartbeat. When he played on his pipe, it was a most eerie sound, as though the wind had been captured and kept underground. I caught the scent of copal, tobacco and sage coming from a row of vessels burnt black from many offerings. The walls were darkened by smoke, but markings showed through the patina of time. They seemed to me to be very different from those that I had hitherto encountered. These are often simple pictographs, their meanings easy to guess, taking the shape, as they often do, of man, woman, sun, stars, trees, birds and animals. The glyphs I saw were more abstract. They sprang out at me in deep black, and ochre as red and vibrant as blood. One of the effects of the drug, I guess, but they seemed to dance before my eyes, rippling over the rock, as if writing themselves on to the walls in some unknown language. The meaning seemed just outside my grasp. I saw them for days, every time I closed my eyes, as clear as in the cave. Clear enough for me to transcribe them as best I can, copying them into my notebook.

A line of spirit beings, Kachina, were watching us. They stood on legs, like men, but some wore feather crests, or pairs of horns, and all wore masks with the features of some grotesque creature. My companion sprinkled copal and tobacco into soot-blackened offering bowls. He touched fire to them and the smoke rose in clouds. These beings were fierce and dangerous and to be placated.

Two very different figures occupied niches carved into the rocks. They stood almost life size, totally human and wholly naked. The man stood with one foot raised, as if lamed in some way. Both were young, barely out of adolescence.

"First man. First woman." He bowed his head and offered corn to them, laying the ears reverently in front of their feet. "Our father. Our mother. They were accompanied by another," he pointed to the figure of a humpbacked flute player. "Kokopelli. The restless one. He left them to wander, making the land fertile. Everywhere he went, he gave food to the people, spreading seeds from the pack that he wore on his back."

There were other strange objects. Artefacts bearing witness to a long history from the earliest times to now. Offerings brought here over millennia: beautifully worked stone blades, crafted from jade or some other semi-precious stone, were laid in a fan in front of a rusting cuirass, the property, no doubt, of some unfortunate Spanish soldier sent to fry inside his armor in the fruitless search for gold. He was accompanied by the religion he brought with him, the Virgin and the Baptist positioned looking inward as if set to comfort him. No similar courtesies had been afforded the union officer's hat or the pairs of cavalrymen's spurs.

My companion did reverence before each of the relics, made his own offerings and lit the copal burners, but this was not our final destination. There was another chamber to visit. The Holy of Holies.

The Chamber of the Ship

This was the innermost crypt. I will call it the Chamber of the Ship. This room was small. There was hardly room for two of us standing, and it contained the holiest relic of all, and to my eyes the most curious. It stood on a rough stone altar. The skeletal remnants of a boat, but a boat such as I had never seen, a boat made of bone and skin.

"A boat of the first people," my companion explained reverently. "The ones who came from far away, borne on a flood."

He told me the story, half singing, half telling, and I listened with all respect. He believed it to be true, a part of his people's history, although it is a common myth, shared by many peoples across the world. Ordinarily, that is what would have interested me, rather than pondering on the historical veracity, but now I shared some of his awe. I had never actually <u>seen</u> one of the vessels before. It was like standing in front of Noah's Ark. And it was the most extraordinary thing. At first, I thought it must be some kind of votive object, rather like those that the Egyptians buried with their pharaohs. I did not think it an actual sea-going vessel. Even so, it puzzled me mightily. There was little of the <u>ritual</u> about it. As I got closer, I realized it could, at one time, have been seaworthy. It was remarkably well preserved for the age it must have been: the skin was thick and plated, rather like rhino hide, the bones thin and hollow as if from some great bird. . .

It was the strangest thing that I had ever seen. Its structure, its design, above all the materials from which it had been fashioned, struck me as being profoundly <u>alien</u>, as if it had sailed here from some mythical time in an unknown age of the world. I knew I was in the presence of a very great mystery and that, somehow, being in this place, at this time, would shape my destiny. I also knew that I could not leave there without a piece of it. I was filled by a raging curiosity. I envied my native friend whose faith allows him to accept without question, but I am too much of a modern American, wedded to scientific proof and investigation. I stood there with every outside show of reverence, but I was determined to get a sample before I left the cave.

My companion took more peyotl buttons from his bag and ate them one by one. He invited me to join him, but this time I declined. He sat cross-legged chanting to himself and it was not long before he fell into a state of trance. I watched him for some time until I was certain that he was wandering in distant worlds, and then set about collecting my sample. I took out my knife and began to saw at the corner of a sheet of skin drooping from the hull. It was most curiously embossed, plated almost like crocodile hide, but not from any creature that I recognized. I was reminded of the fabulous Kakamakara of the Asian Indians. It proved impossible to cut and I feared my attempts would be frustrated, and then I grasped a rag of thinner stuff which was attached to a delicate spar, which looked like part of a sail. The bone split along some old fracture and a whole piece came away in my hand. I sent up swift thanks to whatever deity was smiling upon me, wrapped my "find" in an oilskin cloth and secreted it deep in my pack.

We exited much further down the cliff face, not far above the valley floor. This was the place where the first people were washed into the holy mountain. My companion pointed out from the cave's mouth and said that, although we were many miles from the sea, the wide valley before us had once been connected to the ocean. If one were to dig down, one would find sand and the shells of sea creatures, he told me. Indeed, the evidence was beneath my feet. The cave was carpeted with soft white sand, very different from the coarse red and orange riverine deposits on the valley floor. I knelt, sifting the fine grains between my fingers. Sure enough, I found tiny conical shells, bivalves as delicate as fingernails, and what looked like fragments of coral among broken pieces of larger shell. I'd always thought the great Flood stories so much holy hokum. I don't think that any more.

"Civilization"
I am now in the town of Santa Fey. We have reached what some would regard as "civilization", but beyond a plate of steak and eggs, which I consumed with gusto, and a hot bath, which I enjoyed

also, I am restless, dissatisfied. I feel as though what faith I had in anything has been shaken to the core. The place we visited scarce two days ago is there no longer. The crack in the world has closed, my friend tells me. How he knows, I do not question.

"Something has woken the Great Serpent," is all he says. "He redoubles his struggle to be free."

I am sure there is a more scientific explanation, but when I seek to explain in terms of geology, he just smiles, as if humoring a child. Certainly, we felt the 'quake here, shaking our beds, and it was not long before we heard by wire that my beloved city of San Francisco has all but been destroyed. The news saddens me greatly, but it has also made my mind up for me. I will not return. The wild charm that I loved was already disappearing; rebuilding will neaten the city further, turning it into a version of every other town.

Tomorrow we will be leaving. My companion is busy already, purchasing new supplies. When he tells me that my journey is not over, I do not think he means the paths of this world. There is no way of knowing where we are going, or if there is likely to be any kind of postal service there, so I am sending these notebooks, along with the sample I collected, to Lockwood in London with a suggestion as to whom he might contact. I'm also sending some of the peyotl buttons, in case he wants to try it for himself! Tomorrow we follow the trail going south.[21]

---

[21] Last sighting, Mexico, 1919. Presumed to have died there.

14

EXTREME UNCTION

Adam yawned. He'd found the American's notebooks absorbing. Reading them was almost like a Wild West story but more interesting because there were little drawings and field sketches, even the odd pressed flower. It made the place and the landscapes more alive for him. There was some strange stuff as well. He wondered if Lockwood ever received his parcel of bone and skin and if he ever had it tested. If so, was the explanation mundane and boring, or did the tissue belong to some unknown creature? He had a strange hollow feeling and shared Stone's sense of being on the threshold of some great mystery that he couldn't quite see. Stone had been deep within the locality that is now called Area 51. UFO territory. They were supposed to be keeping alien spacecraft there. Even aliens. Maybe that was the thing. . .

He closed the book and tried to find a way into sleep. He had to stay on his back, because of his leg, a position he never found easy, but the rhythm of his father's breathing and the unceasing regularity of the monitors meant that soon, he too, was fast asleep.

Adam woke suddenly. He lay still for a moment wondering what had disturbed him. Very little sound from outside seeped in through the double glazing. In the early hours of the morning, even the twenty-four-hour life of the hospital slowed to almost nothing. A&E might be busy, but here the lights were dimmed, the corridors quiet.

Maybe there was a difference in his father's condition. Adam listened. No, the breathing was regular and the machines sounded the same as before. So what was it? There was someone in the room with them. He was sure. He tried to keep his own breathing even. He risked opening his eyes just a crack. The door that had just been opened was sighing back. It was hard to make anything out, even though the room was not in uniform darkness. A little light filtered in from outside, and the LCD displays on the machines gave off a faint glow. There seemed to be nothing out of the ordinary. Adam was about to settle himself back into sleep again, when the curtains round the bed next to his moved, ever so slightly. Someone was easing themselves through and into the space next to his father's bed. Adam could still see nothing, but he heard the susurration of cloth against cloth.

Brother Zack eased the pillow out from under the sleeping head. The old man's mouth was half open, the slack jaw slewed sideways, his skin sallow in the green glow from the machines. He would be doing the old man a favour really, putting him out of his misery. After all, care for the dying was part of Brother Zack's ministry. He gripped the starched cotton in both hands, ready to bear down.

15

ALARM

Adam's alarm had brought the night staff running and his description of the intruder instigated a thorough search, but security staff found no strangers, no unauthorized persons. They didn't think to question the presence of a priest on Acute Ward B that held so many desperately ill people. The end often came in the early hours. A priest in a stole, on hand to administer last rites, was not an unusual sight.

Adam lay back. They didn't doubt that he'd seen an intruder, not exactly, but the sister clearly thought he might have been dreaming, or at least letting his imagination get the better of him. Anyway, it was quite safe now, so they should get some rest.

Adam and his father knew who had been in there and did not feel safe. Neither could they sleep.

"They won't try again now," Adam's father said. "It's nearly morning and there are too many people about."

He could be right, but that didn't mean Adam felt any safer.

"They'll leave it till tomorrow, or the night after,"

Abraham Black went on. "But they'll be back again. And next time, there will be no mistakes. I'm not exactly a difficult target."

Adam nodded. There were lots of ways to help a sick man to die.

"Not to worry, though," his father added after a minute or so.

"Oh," Adam enquired, "and why's that?" He didn't want to appear neurotic but attempted murder seemed a legitimate cause for concern.

"I'm going to get us out of here," his father announced.

"Oh, right. And how are you going to do that?" Adam asked.

But his question was answered by gentle snoring; the mild sedative the nurse had administered had obviously taken effect.

Adam couldn't sleep. Despite what his father said, he feared another attack. He might as well watch until morning. He put on his bedside light, opened the little case and took out the blue notebook.

There was a gap after the last page from Stone. The next section was entitled *The Great Work*, in large black letters in Lockwood's beautiful looping copperplate writing. The first entry was written straight on to the paper.

7 June, 1906
Something mysterious. . .
Another package from Stone, this time containing his promised artefact: a strange, tantalizing thing all parcelled up in one of his precious cigar boxes. Also, a couple of wizened-up little buds, which I took to be

peyotl buttons. I duly swallowed them, in the spirit of experiment, but nothing of any consequence happened, other than some rather odd dreams which were no worse than those resulting from a late-night raid on the cheese dish. I agree with him about opium,[22] but didn't find these any better, I have to confess. I much prefer a snifter of brandy and a good cigar.

I did as per instructed and took the contents (a splinter of bone and a fragment of skin) to McKendrick at the Museum of Science. The great man was, at first, more than somewhat excited. Indeed, he became extremely agitated, his face whiskers fairly vibrated and his hand glass actually shook as he subjected Stone's "find" to the most rigorous examination. Then his scrutiny turned to me. He pushed the find away from him and fixed me with his most ferocious scowl. He is a formidable-looking old chap, with a mane of white hair that grows rather wild, a hawkish nose and rather hard blue eyes that stare out from under brows deeply lined from thinking all the time. He regarded me as if I was some lowly undergraduate and was about to get a wigging for some fearful prank.

"If we didn't belong to the same club, Lockwood," he boomed at me, "I'd think you were trying to hoax me."

I could do little but exclaim and demand to know what in the bally blue blazes he meant by that.

"What is this supposed to be?" He prodded at the specimen with his pen, addressing me as though I were a schoolboy slow at his lessons.

---

[22] See previous correspondence

157

"I was rather hoping you could tell me," I answered, a little sharply. "What kind of creature did this come from?"

"Creatures, I'd say. More than one. And different species. The bones are hollow, like those of a bird. Something very big – Haast's eagle, perhaps. They are extinct, but the extinction is recent. The bones are not that difficult to get hold of. And some kind of lizard skin," he poked at a flap with the end of his pen, "probably a monitor, and big, perhaps a Komodo dragon. You've been taken for a ride here, Lockwood. Hoaxed, no doubt about it!" He looked up, blue eyes full of derision. "That's the trouble with you artistic types. Always dabbling in things that don't concern you. Leave the science to us. Half bird, half lizard?" He pushed the offending materials back towards me. "Next thing you'll be telling me it's some kind of a pterosaur!"

I could do nothing more than collect up Stone's sample and make my apologies. I left with his booming laugh ringing in my ears, wondering which was worse, to be taken for a hoaxer, or some kind of gullible fool.

I left feeling that there was a mystery contained in that battered cigar box. Furthermore, I knew that McKendrick felt it, too, but he would never admit it. I have been loath to seek a second opinion, sure that McKendrick was dining out on what a fool I was, and knowing no one would be prepared to stand up against the "great man" as he liked to think himself. Men of science are not known for their imaginations and they do not like a mystery. The sample is now an exhibit in one of my cabinets of curiosities, where it recently attracted the interest of a biologist acquaintance. He claimed to find evidence of feathers.

It remains a mystery.

Underneath Lockwood's entry his father had written the words, *Mystery no more* and pinned a cutting:

Dinosaur with fully formed feathers.

Unequivocal evidence has been found in fossils discovered in rock formations at Shangheshu, near Chaoyang, China. . .

New Science Journal, March 2002. There were a number of loose pages: carbon dating. DNA. Adam looked through them. His father must have had the material tested.

A report clipped to a cutting from a different scientific journal stated that scientists at Montana State University had obtained DNA from the soft tissue of a pterosaur specimen that had dive-bombed into a peat bog and had then been slowly turned to coal. Abraham Black had sent for a print-out. The match was almost exact.

Abraham Black had written in his fine italic script: *It is a pterosaur!*

Adam's frown deepened. How could that be?

He turned to the next page of the notebook, hoping to find more answers, but just turned up another puzzle. A letter from Stone was stuck into the book. There was no date, but this seemed to be a long time after his previous correspondence; the writing had changed considerably. It was written on notepaper from a hotel: the Belize Palace. It seemed to be about another artefact that Stone had sent to Lockwood. A crystal skull.

The Belize Palace

My Dear Lockwood,

It is a long time since any heard from me, and there is good reason for this. I have been dwelling far from any place of civilization, engaged in the difficult and arduous training needed to become a shaman. Believe me, Lockwood, when I say that this is the true way to move between different planes of existence. This is now the focus of my life, but I digress. First, I can hear you asking: How did you come by this fabulous object?

This skull came into my possession in the strangest of circumstances. I bought it from a bandit, who, in turn, had taken it from one of Pancho Villa's revolutionary soldiers, who had stolen it from the treasury of the Mexican President. The skull is supposed to have been handed from one ruler to another, as a recognition of power, going back to before the conquistadors. The Aztecs acquired it from the Maya people of what is now Guatemala. The People of the Jaguar. The skull led me to them and they have been my teachers.

They believe that the skull is old, far older than any known civilization in this part of the world. It is anatomically perfect, and would be hard to produce even now, but they believe it came from an unknown place, brought by sea, by a mysterious being and his followers. This visitor from the sea was known to the Mayans as Kukulan. DO NOT on any account show this to anyone. It is not a museum exhibit.[23] It is a living artefact, keep it around you for any

161

length of time and you will see what I mean. Besides, there are a number of howling fakes around;[24] skulls are quite the thing out here. Every joker says he's found one, but rest assured, this is the GENUINE THING and I do not want it numbered among those others.

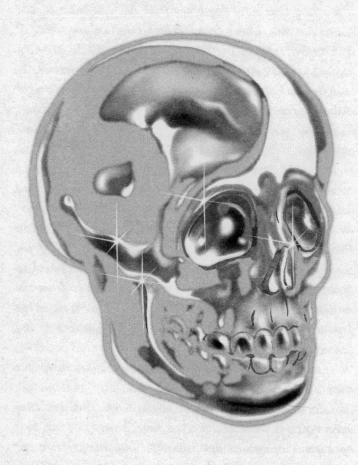

---

[23]Stone disliked museums.

[24]Possible reference to the Hodgkin-Ramen Skull, discovered British Honduras, 1924

A crystal skull! Adam had read about those, but never seen one.

The letter was unsigned. Clipped to the top of the page was a note written by his father.

Fakes? Accepted wisdom: how could ancient people have crafted such a thing? True, most don't stand up to electron-microscopic examination, however, other aspects still defy explanation. Crystal is strange stuff. And powerful. As we are only just beginning to discover: quartz crystal technology, liquid crystal technology, ruby lasers. Maybe this is just another use of the medium. One we don't understand. Lockwood saw the potential. He observed mysterious properties. He kept it in a locked cabinet. See following note.

Adam turned to the next page of the blue notebook.

All I know is that sometimes I find the skull's presence most unsettling, not in any way threatening, but so much so that I have had to cover it. There are times when I have noticed lights emanating from it. I have known it to move position within its case. At first, I suspected Mrs Abbott and her incessant dusting (although I have told her not to interfere with anything in the cases). "That queer thing? I wouldn't go near it!" was her riposte and I believe her. Thompson also swore he had not touched it. So all I can deduce is it can move of its own will. Also, although it sometimes appears as clear as water, at other times it seems filled with cotton wool. Cloudy, shot through with smoky colours, and at those times it does not do to look into the depths of it. I keep it in a closed case now.

I am willing to believe that crystals have many as yet unknown properties. I don't just mean Madame T scrying in her crystal ball, but I'm thinking about those new crystal wireless sets. Indeed, I was reading about that just the other day in a monograph entitled "Wireless, the Modern Magic Carpet" by a Mr Ralph Strange. There is much that is mysterious about them, and much more, no doubt, to be discovered.

After that was another page written by Stone, in a different ink, on paper from some hotel in Manaus. Adam wasn't sure where that was but the name sounded South American.

MANAUS REGENCY

I have to tell you, Lockwood, that the skull I have sent you has a twin, made from some dark crystal. The two are opposite in every aspect; one is clear and bright; the other is carved from shadow and gives out no light. The dark skull has to remain hidden for the protection of mankind, a task undertaken by a tribe who live deep in the Amazon basin. If it passes from them, the world will end. I'm aware that probably sounds crazy, but it is a prophecy which is taken seriously by Amerindians, from Alaska to Tierra del Fuego. And which is causing much perturbation. For this skull is being sought by a rich and ruthless man. I had been aware of his presence before, both in Central America and on the offshore islands in that region. I mean our old adversary, Buller Wesson. It is almost as if he is following me, or I him. I hear that he is journeying south. I start out tomorrow and only hope that I get to these people before he does. I intend to travel light, therefore I am entrusting my discoveries *to your safe keeping. Be careful, however, I fear that Wesson has become even more powerful, certainly more ruthless, and is making his presence felt on several planes of existence.*

Wesson again. The name jolted Adam back from where he had been drifting. How was he involved? How were all these things connected? His tired mind could make no sense in it. The next section was titled *Pages from the Lascaris.* He turned the page to find drawings of unfamiliar plants and animals, zodiac wheels strewn with strange symbols, surrounded by neat small writing in a language he didn't recognize. His tired eyes were closing. He could make even less sense of this. Enough for the moment. He shut the book and put it back in the case. It was almost morning, the hospital was stirring back to life. He didn't think anyone would come now, but he slept with the case held to his chest, just to make sure.

16

SINGER AND THE SONG

Kris had not forgotten his promise to Bram to find the girl. He'd just been subject to delays, like being knocked off his bike and getting concussion. Events beyond his control. He'd sent out enquiries via his contacts and they'd come back with a sighting. Now all he had to do was get past Mamma Celestine. Her dark brow creased into a frown when he explained, and she jutted out her bottom lip. Something that she did when she was thinking hard.

"That girl be important in some special way," she said at last. "And she be in danger. No doubting that. Added to which, a promise is a promise. But you be careful. You hear me? You had a head injury. I don' want you fighting or overtaxing yourself."

"Fighting? Don't be foolish, Mamma. Who would I be fighting?" Kris laughed, but from what he'd heard it might come to that.

"*Or* overtaxing yourself. I said that, too."

Kris promised to take it easy. "I'll have my boys with me."

She eventually let him go, with her blessing. She was as keen to find the girl as he was, but she had to do a little fussing over him and voice her concern. Kris led his posse down the steps into the tube station. Time was short. Word had come back that he was not the only one looking for her.

Zillah was at her pitch on the Underground, beyond the sight lines of the staff, just before a place where the routes to several lines met. People slowed there to check their way and were more inclined to reach into a bag or pocket for change to drop on the shawl she had spread ready.

She'd only been coming here a couple of days, but she already had regulars, prepared to throw two or three extra coins to the girl with the hair and the amazing eyes who sang in a voice that was high and clear enough to break your heart. They didn't linger long enough to catch the words, or to wonder much about the language she used when she sang. A snatch was enough to evoke pictures in the mind of another place, another time. They would carry it with them, humming through the day – a trilling refrain, fresh as a fall of rain – and wonder if she'd still be there to revive them on the long journey home.

The commuters couldn't put words to the tunes that they hummed in their heads. She sang in a language that they had never heard that she didn't even know herself. The lyrics came out in ready-made phrases, the meaning just beyond her grasp, but they cheered her in her loneliness.

Down here she was out of the weather, safe at the margins of the passing crowd. That was enough. This was her life now. Her focus had narrowed down to survival.

Her new friend, Dee, worked the upper halls. No one talked about the past, where they were from, who they had been before; each one arrived new minted. Dee had seen Zillah tussle with a couple of pimps, seen them get the worst of it.

"You're handy," she'd said as she approached her. "Got a place to stay? Need something to eat?"

That was the exact same question the two guys had asked. Zillah had kept her fighting stance.

Dee saw her wariness and laughed. She swept back long wispy hair, which was dyed pink and green and tied in places with dirty yellow ribbon made into drooping bows. Her face retained more than a hint of prettiness, but she was pale and gaunt and her grey eyes were ringed with thin violet skin that was wrinkled beyond her years.

"Don't worry, I'm not with them. Just interested, that's all. I didn't mean anything by it. Come on. I know a place, not far, it's clean and there's plenty of space. We can get something to eat on the way." She jingled the coins in her pocket. "I've had a good day."

Zillah stared at the girl, weighing up the options. Going with her could be a big mistake, but she was hungry and her legs shook with fatigue. She was sick of fending off predatory men and the loneliness was beginning to get to her. She'd always been self-sufficient, telling herself that she didn't need anybody else, but she was beginning to forget the sound of her own voice. It had not been that long, in normal terms, but each second seems like a minute, each minute like an hour, and a day is an eternity when you are on the street. She had not spoken to anyone since she left the hospital, except to spit out a warning, or make the odd monosyllabic exchange in a shop. This girl looked all right. Zillah was inclined to take her offer at face value.

"Name's Dee, by the way," the girl said now, holding out her hand as if trying to make friends with a feral cat.

"Zillah."

"That's unusual."

Zillah shrugged.

"Your real name?"

Zillah shrugged again. They went the rest of the way in silence.

Dee lived in a squat inside a run-down block of old shops that had been boarded up awaiting development.

"Sometimes there are security patrols with dogs," Dee told her. "We have to get out sharp then. But that doesn't happen often."

Dee had turned out to be a good friend. She didn't ask questions. Zillah volunteered nothing, but Dee sensed that she was not your everyday runaway. She picked up on Zillah's brittle wariness and divined that there could be people searching for her.

It was Dee who cut her hair and dyed it flame red.

"No point in hiding," Dee told her. "The harder you try and hide, easier you are to find. You're better off disguised. There. See?"

Zillah had examined the results in a broken mirror. Her hair was a bright chemical colour, somewhere between flamingo pink and scarlet. She turned her head. The cut fell in choppy, jagged points, longer at the back, coming round to just about chin length. Zillah looked through the strands of her uneven fringe. Dee had shaped her brows and outlined her eyes in kohl, making her look older. Nothing like the girl who had escaped from the hospital.

"How did you learn to do that?"

"Used to work in a salon, didn't I? When I get straight, I plan to have my own place. . ." Dee's voice tailed off. Everyone on the street had their dreams of normality. "N'er mind that," she went on, her voice tight, artificially bright. "What do you reckon?"

Zillah frowned, her initial enthusiasm dissolving into doubt. "Won't it make me stand out? I mean, hair like this? It's kind of screaming 'come and get me!'"

"Yeah, but that's the point! Who in their right mind would draw attention to themselves like that? It'll work. Trust me."

Dee was right. Zillah sang and played and agents from the Temple walked past her morning and night, never knowing that the girl they searched for so hard was metres away from them.

She was having a quiet day. There was some disruption to one of the lines which either meant crowds of people herding past, or almost no one coming down. Either way was bad for business. She kept on singing anyway, but it was hard to keep her heart in it. She was wondering whether to pack up and

170

find another pitch when the group of boys came towards her. She edged forward, shepherding the shawl with her foot. It paid to keep an eye on who was about and she could measure the passing crowd from a long way off: good givers, bad, railway staff out to bust her, those who might be after her pitch, or her money. The boys fell into the last category. She'd had trouble with gangs before. She slung her drum round to her back and dipped down to gather the shawl with the few coins she'd collected contained in its folds. She pushed this inside her half-zipped-up top and walked towards the escalators.

"Hey! Wait up!"

The shout from behind made her quicken her pace. A boy came out from the passageway in front of her, then another. She backed away, looking for a different point of exit, but the boys behind were coming up fast. She was trapped.

Zillah squared up, meaning to fight. Even though she was outnumbered, she would not give up her money without doing some damage.

"Whoa, sister! Be cool, yeah?" The smallest one stepped forward. "We don't mean you harm. . ."

"Oh yeah?" She weighed him up. He was much shorter than her, and slightly built. "I've been skanked by little shits like you before."

She made a grab for him, twisting one arm behind his back, linking her other arm around his neck. She intended to squeeze until the others backed off. She stared defiance at the gathering gang, then her eyes widened. There were others coming round the long sweep of the tunnel. The leader wore a long robe, like a priest. His companion, by contrast, was dressed in a suit. The same one that he had been wearing the last time she saw him. She was looking straight at the Advocate.

17

EXEAT

When Adam came back from physio, he was surprised to see Jethro Poutney sitting on the side of his bed. Adam knew him well. He was a familiar face around the Temple, one of the porters, always there with a ready smile, a friendly word, and not averse to turning a blind eye when boys slipped in late from an exeat. Jethro was a corrodary, a servant of the Temple, but that did not automatically condemn him. There were good guys and bad guys, even there, and Jethro was one of the good guys. His father obviously thought so because the two of them were deep in conversation.

Adam paused at the door. His first thought was that Jethro had been sent to collect him and take him back to the Temple. His second thought was that he would refuse to go.

"How are you, young man?" the porter enquired as Adam came into the room.

"I'm good," Adam replied noncommittally.

"Great stuff! See you later!" Jethro grinned and winked at them both as he went out.

Adam sat down, relieved that any confrontation had been postponed.

"How's the leg?" his father asked.

"Therapist is very pleased with me." Adam showed the lightweight plastic shell, a bit like a ski boot, that had been fitted to protect his ankle. "As long as I don't overdo it, I can walk quite easily. How come he was visiting?"

"We're old friends. Dropped by to see how we were and to bring some stuff in for you." He indicated a holdall on the boy's bed. "He's due to collect you this afternoon."

Adam nodded. It was as he expected.

"Why did he come? Why not Brother Zack?"

"Otherwise engaged, apparently."

"Well," Adam turned to look at his father, "I'm not going. I'm not leaving you on your own. Who knows what they might try, if there's no one here to protect you?"

Abraham was taken aback by Adam's fierce concern. Unaccustomed tears pricked his eyes. He was not used to anyone caring for him. The boy was little more than a child, fragile in pyjamas and robe, leg cased in plastic. They really were a pair of crocks. He trumpeted into a tissue and wiped his moustache. That would do. Now wasn't the time to give into self-pity. Age and infirmity must be getting the better of him.

"We've got to get out of here!" Adam dropped his voice to a fierce whisper. "There's no knowing what they'll try next!"

His father put his hand up to silence him as someone walked past.

174

"They want me out of bed," he said conversationally. "Not good for folk to lie about, apparently. Care to take me for a spin in that thing later?" He indicated the wheelchair by his bed. A saggy affair with small wheels, like a camping chair set on castors. "Think you're up to it?"

Adam nodded.

"Good lad."

"Are you?"

"Oh, I'm feeling much better. Far stronger. Sick of staring at these four walls."

"OK. When shall we go?"

"Now's as good a time as any." He indicated the holdall that Jethro had brought in. "You might as well get into some proper togs."

No one made any objection when Adam emerged from the room, pushing his father. In fact, the nurse on duty thought it was a good idea. It was hospital policy to get patients up and about as quickly as possible. Getting the body moving again was very important, as was external stimulation. He really was making a remarkable recovery, and a change of scenery, a little trip to the day room, a chance to interact with other patients, would do the old man a power of good.

Abraham Black was not the least interested in any of that. He'd insisted on taking his little case with him, balanced on his knees under the pink cellular blanket, and it was clear he had no intention of spending any time in the day room. He instructed Adam to go straight past it and on into one of the wide central corridors. The exits were clearly marked. Adam's heart leapt in his chest. This was not going to be some innocent, aimless perambulation. They were making their escape!

His father spoke straight into his mind: *Not too fast. Don't get excited. Don't attract attention. Look as though you know what you are doing. Taking me for treatment.*

Abraham directed him towards an exit at the back, where hospital workers and patients gathered for an illicit smoke. Jethro Poutney was there, waiting for them. Adam's first instinct was to do a reverse turn back into the hospital, but his father instructed him to keep on going straight down the ramp. *Trust him*, the voice in his head said, *it's the only way!*

Jethro took over, and as he looked just like a hospital porter, no one challenged them as he steered the chair towards the short-stay bay. He pushed the chair to the back of an unmarked 4x4. It was not the normal Temple runabout. Black, with opaque windows, it was the kind of car only used by someone from the highest rank. Jethro opened the wide back doors, reached in and pressed a button. A lift descended, holding a state-of-the-art electrically powered wheelchair. Jethro picked up Abraham, as if he weighed no more than a child, put him in the chair, and tucked a thick, plaid blanket round him. The chair went up at a touch of a button and Jethro locked the wheels in place.

"Hop in, son," he said to Adam. "Best not to hang about."

"Everything ready?" Abraham Black asked from the back.

"Ready and waiting," Jethro said without looking round.

"Right. Let's go before the bastards realize we're missing."

They left the sad little hospital chair behind with its pink blanket trailing on the ground.

Adam sat back in the deep leather seat, watching the streets, looking for signs, wondering where they were going. He hoped that Jethro was taking them off to some country retreat, as far away from the city and the Temple as it was possible to be, a place where they would be able to live free. Somewhere where they would never, never be found, but he looked out at the streets in growing alarm. He tried to alert his father, because the heavy traffic was crawling along a route he knew pretty well. The newspaper shop was where some of the older day boys got their cigarettes and the real rebels bought ganja. It had started to rain again. The words on the billboard outside were beginning to run down: *Cult Deaths Spread*. A sense of doom settled over Adam, as dark as the stone that ran along the other side of the street. Jethro had betrayed them. He sent the thought to his father as he tried to fight down his own growing panic. He received no answer. The old man had gone incommunicado. Perhaps his judgement was going also. His voice had said "*trust him*", but what if he was wrong? Jethro had operated the central locking. There was no way out. Adam closed his eyes and tried to compose himself, wondering what would happen once the tall, spiked gates of the Temple yawned open and they were taken inside. The car turned a corner into a narrow side street. The wall of the Temple ran along on the left-hand side like a sheer, dark cliff. They were heading for the back entrance. Using the front would attract too much attention. They were about to be smuggled in, like contraband goods. They would be back inside those walls any minute now.

18

UNLOOKED-FOR MEETING

It took less than a second for Zillah to make her decision. She shrugged her hood up and pulled the front of it down into a peak over her eyes. She put her hands in her pockets and hunched her shoulders, adopting the rolling gait of the others as they bunched around her. She was tall, slender, slim-hipped and lithe. She could easily pass as one of the boys. The Advocate and his henchmen hardly glanced at them as the group slouched past on their way to the platform. They jumped on the waiting train just as it was about to depart.

She sat squashed between them at the end of a carriage, not entirely sure what was going on here. If the choice was between these boys and the Advocate, there really was no contest, but what did they want with her? When the train rocked along to the next stop, she stood up ready to get off. The little one, their leader, held her arm.

"Ain't safe for you out there, sister."

"I'll take my chances." She went to pull away.

"No. I mean, it *really* ain't safe. Only one place for you now and I'm taking you there. Name's Kris."

He smiled and took her hand in a clasp of friendship. She looked into his eyes and detected no threat there. More like the opposite. He was determined to save her. She looked away. With the exception of Dee, no one had cared like that about her. Ever.

"I've got a friend," she said. "Called Dee. She'll worry."

"I'll get word, yeah?" Kris smiled. "Soon as I see you home. I'll tell her myself."

Kris delivered her to his grandma's flat, and then left to find Dee.

"Always on the move, that one." His grandmother came forward to meet her. Her Islands accent was much stronger than the street patois Kris affected, more pronounced, as if she had not been in the country that long.

"I'm Zillah," the girl offered, since Kris had not introduced them.

"Pleased to meet you, Zillah. I am Mamma Celestine."

She reached out in welcome. She was tiny, smaller than her grandson. Her hands were thin and strong. Their wrinkled skin and prominent veins showed her age, but her face was almost unlined with high cheekbones and tilted, sloe-black, almond-shaped eyes, the whites emphasized by a thin outline of kohl. Her nose was small and wide above a generous mouth, which turned up at the corners into a permanent smile. It was a beautiful face, calm and serene, but full of life.

It was a face Zillah recognized from her study of "erroneous and idolatrous beliefs". She was looking into eyes that knew everything. It was the face of a black Madonna. Human, yet divine.

In a beat of time, she was an ordinary lady again. Friendly and welcoming.

"Take the weight off your feet." She led Zillah into the living area. The room was sparsely furnished, but clean and bright.

"You must be tired. Sit down while I get you something to eat. I got beans and rice on. All right for you?"

Zillah nodded and took a seat on a wide settee strewn with colourful throws. She *was* tired. She was tempted to lean back into a nest of bright cushions and close her eyes, but she sat upright with her arms crossed, still wary. Life on the streets had taught her to take each day, each part of a day, as it comes, to assess and weigh each situation, to look for threat or advantage. That boy, Kris, had saved her. If he and his gang had not come along, the Advocate would have found her, but she was still not sure about being here. Doubts crept back. She hoped Kris could be trusted to get word to Dee, to stop her from worrying. On the street, people drifted in and out of each other's lives all the time, but Dee was a friend. A real friend. The only one that she had ever had. What was the danger here? Mamma Celestine's look was kind, even benign, but there was anxiety there, touched by fear. Zillah had seen enough in her time to know it. It was a look some of the women had in the House when a child was about to be punished and there was nothing that they could do to prevent it. It was on the face of the Madonna looking over her child. Zillah sensed something was about to happen. Perhaps she should run, get out now. The old woman would be no match for her. Zillah looked up to see her hostess gazing down, a plate of food in her hands ready to offer, her face filled with compassion. Zillah dropped her eyes, ashamed.

"Eat first," the old lady said. "Then we talk."

Zillah was hungry. She might as well get a meal out of it, she thought. The values of the street had bitten deep into her already. The food smelt good, home-cooked, and it was free.

Celestine watched as Zillah demolished a plate of jerk chicken, beans and rice, but she ate nothing herself. Zillah finished her food and pushed away the plate. The old woman sat opposite. She was wearing pale linen trousers, leather thonged sandals and a bright-coloured blouse under a long cardigan made of some natural yarn. Her hand was on the clasp that held the two sides of the loosely knitted material together. Her dark fingers traced the outline of the tapering body, stroking the wings' golden filigree. Zillah's own hand automatically went to her throat, to the talisman she wore there, threaded on a leather thong.

"I wear the same thing," Zillah said quietly. She touched the smooth, cool metal and her restless anxiety began to subside.

"May I see?" The old woman stood up and came towards her.

Zillah flipped the talisman from under her shirt. "My friend Dee made it into a pendant."

Celestine took the golden talisman up carefully. The

bee glowed against the skin of her palm. She spoke quietly, in a tone almost of reverence, as if the golden object was alive. "Tell me, child. Where did you get such a thing?" She turned it carefully, examining the surface, worn almost smooth by time. "She is very, very old."

"I was involved in a cult. I found it. . ."

Celestine patted her hand. "More like she found you. No need to tell me all the story if you don't want to, I was just interested where you find her."

Zillah ended up telling her everything, going back to what she remembered before the Children of the Sixth Dawn took her to the point where she was airlifted out. She finished with her recent encounter with the Advocate. Celestine listened without interrupting, or asking questions. When Zillah had finished, Celestine murmured, "Blessed be the Mother," and went to the kitchen to get both of them a drink. She came back with two glasses of juice.

"'Blessed be the Mother'?" Zillah asked. "What did you mean by that?"

"She save you," Celestine replied. "The bee is her sign. It signify the Hive. Many working for the good of all. The queen giving new life. Soon as you found her, she began to work. She shield you from their attention. She keep you safe. That one you call the Advocate, don't even know you there, right?"

Zillah shrugged. "I was just like all the others. Why would he notice me?"

"Because you is special." Celestine cupped the girl's face in her thin dark hands. "Believe me!" Her eyes were suddenly shiny with tears. "Blessed be! Tell me, Zillah.

What you think this Advocate want with you?"

"I'm a witness to what happened. He wants to shut me up."

Celestine shook her head. "You got a special destiny. There's something only you can do. He should have killed you while he could. You are the One. He knows that now."

Zillah recognized the truth in what she was saying. She had always known that the bee was special. That's why she had taken it in the first place. She'd risked extreme punishment in order to keep it, because holding it in her hand made her feel safe, brought her comfort in a dangerous, hostile world.

"Don't you worry." The old lady smiled. "You are safe here. Christophe will get word to your friend, Dee. Tell her you're with me. He don't lie or make a false promise. Trust him." She added, "Trust me."

"How did you know. . .?" Was she a mind reader?

"That you worried about that?" The old lady's dark eyes were veiled and enigmatic. "I know lots of things." She took Zillah's hands in hers. "May the Mother protect you, and keep you from harm."

The words were spoken like a blessing, or a ritual incantation.

Despite her doubts, Zillah bowed her head. After her time with C6D, she didn't believe much in anything, but Celestine clearly did. The Advocate would stop at nothing and he wanted her dead. A little prayer might not be wasted when she was going to need all the help that she could get.

19

11 FORFAR STREET

Adam closed his eyes, anticipating a left-hand turn into the Temple, but the car suddenly picked up speed and went straight on. Jethro took off his driver's peak cap and threw it into the back.

"Won't be needing that!"

Jethro laughed as they turned into a maze of terraced streets. Tall, narrow houses crowded the pavements and a clutter of parked vehicles made progress slow and tricky. The houses were old, some of them had shutters, and steep stone steps ran down to basements and up to front doors. Some of the houses were smartly painted and had obviously been renovated; others were scruffy, with dull peeling paintwork and dusty windows. Adam still had no idea where they were, or where they were going, and the two men said nothing, but his heart began to thud and his skin prickle with a renewed sense of relief and excitement. He had been resigned, never having defied the Order in his life, not really thinking it was possible. Now these two seemed to be doing just that without breaking sweat. What was going on?

He was just about to ask when the car took another turn, this time down a back lane. Jethro stopped in front of a pair of unimpressive wooden doors, like garage doors, only wider, the green paint peeling, the base uneven, the planks eaten with rot. He clicked an electronic device on the dashboard and the doors swung open to allow them access. He reversed the car into a surprisingly spacious backyard and the doors swung back into position. It only took a couple of seconds. Now you see it. . .

An impressive disappearing act.

"People always watch the front. Never the back," Jethro remarked as he got out of the car.

The rear doors had opened, the ramp lowering automatically. Abraham was already out and manoeuvring the wheelchair towards the house. Adam followed the two men. They both seemed to be changing before his eyes. His father had lost some of his frailty. The porter's former servility had disappeared. He held himself differently and seemed younger, physically bigger, and was walking with a definite swagger. Jethro turned back and saw him staring.

"It's the hat that does it. That and the uniform." He slumped a little in the shoulders, head forward, eyes down. "No one takes notice. Specially not that bunch of arrogant pricks." He stood straight and smiled. "It's the perfect disguise."

He took the chair up the steps to the back door and Adam followed them into the house. Jethro whisked his father away for a change of clothes and Adam went on along a wide passage. The floors were worn stone flags, the walls dark wood panelling. Gas lights flared in brackets on the walls, their bluish light diffused by pearly white glass orbs.

He found his way to the front parlour. The shuttered room was in semi-darkness, the only light coming from the fire burning in the grate. It was like stepping back in time, into another century. Something about that nagged at Adam. Something right on the rim of his consciousness.

Jethro wheeled Abraham into the room. He helped him into an armchair by the hearth and then went to add more fuel to the fire. He lit candles, and soon the room was filled with warmth and soft light.

Abraham steepled his fingers and stared into the fire. He looked completely different. Freshly shaved, and dressed in a three-piece suit of pale, soft, herringbone tweed over a cream checked shirt and a dark striped tie, he appeared younger, rather distinguished, tired rather than sick. He wore socks with a diamond pattern up the sides and shiny brown brogues on his feet. Adam guessed that he habitually dressed in this old-fashioned way. For the very first time, he felt a faint tug of memory, a stirring of recognition.

He invited Adam to take the worn leather chair opposite him.

"The house has a long and interesting history," he began. "It was owned at one time by a Dr Arnold Brume, a celebrated alchemist and associate of Robert Fludde. The site, so they say, of his secret laboratory."

"That bloke whose book I've been reading – Lockwood." Adam grinned as he finally made the association that had been nagging at the edge of his mind. "This is his house!"

"That's right." His father smiled. "When he died, he left the house to me and to Solomon Rapoport. We were to act as custodians. We had to promise to guard and protect his collection and to change nothing in the house. Jethro has been looking after the place. Apart from certain, ah, modernizations, it has remained exactly as it was."

Adam looked round at the gas light and candles and wondered what the modernizations might be.

"I was wondering. . ." Adam had many questions from his reading last night. "About the Long Room. Can I see it?"

20

THE LONG ROOM

His father waved away the attentions of Jethro Poutney and wheeled himself out of the room. An ancient Stairglide chairlift ran up the dark wood panelling. It had been there since the days of Aurel Lockwood's last infirmity. Abraham Black eyed it doubtfully.

"Does that thing still work?"

"Bit of tinkering about and it's as good as new." Jethro grinned. "Knew how to make things in them days. Hop on and I'll show you."

He pressed a button and after a few stutters the chair began to rise.

Adam followed, Jethro bringing the wheelchair.

"This is the Long Room."

Adam wheeled his father through the wide double doors and looked around. The room was exactly how he had imagined it to be. It was shuttered, just like the one downstairs. Gaslight shone and Jethro lit oil lamps. One wall was filled with tall display cabinets, fronted with glass and fitted with shining brass locks and catches, just like in an old-fashioned museum.

Bookshelves ran from floor to ceiling on three sides of the room, their length broken only by the window casements and a carved marble fireplace. They were filled with old, leather-bound volumes, their ridged spines stamped with faded gold lettering. The effect was impressive. The product of a lifetime of obsessive collecting was assembled here, perhaps more than one lifetime. It must be priceless.

Waist-high cabinets made the room into a maze of glass and mahogany. Special, precious volumes lay open, cased in glass, the thick vellum pages covered in some ancient script, the margins full of strange illustrations. Adam lifted the velvet cloth on another cabinet to uncover a long sequence of images, as bold as a cartoon strip, as bright as the day they were painted. Mayan, he guessed, or maybe Aztec. He'd done stuff on the Aztecs in school. The next case held papyri and some kind of disc: *Egyptian, Third Dynasty*; *Cretan, Linear B*. He had to lean close to read the labels, each one carefully written in Indian ink with what must have been a very fine nib, the strokes of the tiny letters thinner than a spider's leg. He pulled open one of the drawers by its recessed brass handles and found rows of pale pink clay tablets, some chipped and crumbling, others painstakingly pieced together, all crowded with tiny wedge-shaped impressions, made by a stylus. Cuneiform script. The earliest form of writing, invented by the Sumerians, as incomprehensible as bird prints.

He closed the drawer carefully and looked up. He was being watched. Eyes looked down at him from inside the glass cases. Slender, graceful figures with the heads of birds, jackals, crocodiles, regarded him with indifference. Massive, hulking, thick-lipped faces, half man, half some other creature, stared with timeless malevolence. A slim, bare-breasted female smiled at him, brandishing snakes in both hands. Another one scowled: a woman flanked by owls, with the wings of a bird and long taloned feet that seemed to hover above the backs of a pair of snarling lions.

There were gods and goddesses here, collected from all over the world, but this was different from a museum. In the ones Adam had visited, the figures were exhibits; discarded shells, faded, dusty carapaces that had long ago lost whatever power they might have contained. He sensed something else here, a carefully accumulated force. There had been method behind the collectors' obsessions. He was standing right in front of the display case now. A frieze of priests trudged for ever, hands holding offerings, eyes wide, heads inclined towards some unseen, unknowable creature. No one believed like that any more. Perhaps they should. Maybe it was wrong to dismiss such age-old power so lightly.

"Everything in the cases that you have been examining belongs to the conventional archaeology record." His father wheeled himself about. "But there is a particular method, a focus that you will not find in a conventional collection. All these things," he gestured with his hand, "the ancient writings, the depictions of gods and goddesses, come from many different traditions, but Lockwood believed that they shared a common root in a far more ancient belief system. Tell me, Adam, how long do you think civilized life on earth has existed?"

Adam shrugged, he didn't know. Not all that long, he suspected.

"A couple of thousand years?" he ventured.

"What if I told you that you were out by *ten thousand years?*" The old man gripped the arms of his chairs until his knuckles turned white. "What if I could prove it?"

I'd think you were some kind of nutball. Adam immediately tried to mask the thought.

"Of course you would." His father laughed. "That's what everyone thinks. Take a look at this," he wheeled himself over to another display case, pulled out a drawer and took out a battered brown cardboard box, well sealed with widths of shiny parcel tape. "This came the other day, according to Jethro. Open it."

Inside was a flyer:

SANDERS' MUZEUM
Something for everyone!!!
More than 10,000
astounding curiosities.

Inside this was a note wrapped round a big shiny lump of some kind of transparent stuff.

Dear Mr Black,

We met at a conference some years back. I was interested in your talk on "Fakes and Anomalies". You were kind enough to give me your card and said if I ever came across anything strange or odd, to send it on. Well, I reckon this fits the bill!

Kind regards,
Stan Sanders
Sanders' Muzeum
Old Post Office
10 East Street
Somertown
NZ

Adam turned the block over in his hands. "What is it? It looks like amber."

"Very similar," his father replied, "but not nearly so old. Ten to eleven thousand years? Amber in the making. It is ancient kauri gum from New Zealand."

"Is it rare?"

"Not particularly."

"Then what's so special about it?"

"Look inside. You see? Hold it up to the light and you will find something that shouldn't be there, see? An arrowhead. An offering maybe. Or a hunter missed his aim and hit the tree."

"What's so odd about that?"

"Nothing. Except that this gum had been in the ground for ten thousand years before any human being was supposed to have set foot on those islands. That's if you believe what you are told. So this is an anomaly. That is what I used to collect. It's like many of the artefacts in this case. All dismissed as fakes, just as I'm sure this would be."

He fished a chain of small brass keys from his pocket and unlocked a drawer in the cabinet. He took out a box. *Romeo y Julieta*, it said on the top. He flipped the lid open so that Adam could see.

This was the relic that Stone had sent to Lockwood. Adam's fingers shook as he reached in to touch the dark shard of hollow bone and the brittle piece of thin greyish skin. The surface had a raised nubbly texture and was divided into diamond patterns. Not all that spectacular, perhaps, but what about the DNA profile? Adam leant in further. His breath stirred the dusting of fine, pale sand that lay at the bottom of the box. He was looking at the skin of a pterosaur. Not a fossil, the bone was light and porous, with little holes in it; the skin was leathery, like he imagined the wing of a bat might be, but those creatures were supposed to have died out at the time of the dinosaurs. What he was looking at could change history. He stared at the contents with awe.

If anyone would believe it! His father's voice sounded in his head. *I did, though. Lockwood, too.*

"Now, come here." He was wheeling himself across

194

the room. "Look at these." He pulled out a drawer holding ancient maps and spread the charts on the top of the display cabinet. "These are Portolan maps, made by medieval Portuguese sea farers."

The maps were drawn on vellum and were very beautiful. They were incredibly detailed with tightly packed notations in tiny writing along the crinkled coast lines. There were even little pictures of people and animals. Adam could see a camel. They were not marked with lines of longitude and latitude like modern maps, but with complex webs radiating out from compass roses. Adam wasn't great at geography, but they looked pretty accurate. The Mediterranean and Black Sea coasts looked just like those in a modern atlas, or not far off.

"Hang on, isn't that Australia?" Adam turned the map round. "Surely that wasn't discovered till ages after medieval times."

"1606. First recorded European contact. Compare them with this." His father pulled out another map. This had no detail and was all out of proportion. It looked like a toddler's effort. "A typical map made of the time. By contrast, the Portolan maps are incredibly accurate, and show the coastlines of lands yet to be discovered: South America, India and Australia, in astonishing detail."

"Where did they come from?"

"No one knows for certain. They are thought to be copies of copies. Incredibly ancient, yet not equalled until the modern day. Of course, many would dismiss them as forgeries, or hoaxes. Look at this one." The vellum crackled as he pulled it out. "It was made by an admiral of the Ottoman Empire, and dated 1513. He created a world map, using various sources. One was very new, seized from a sailor who had sailed with Columbus. Others were very old, from Arabia, and from the libraries of Alexander the Great."

The map was brown with age, and the ships that sailed the oceans could have been captained by Columbus. Adam could see the opposing coasts of Africa and South America, an elephant on the mainland of one, facing what could have been a llama. Abraham Black turned the map to the bottom quadrant, tracing the coastline down to Antarctica.

"Antarctica wasn't known then, was it?"

"No, it was *Terra Incognita*. There is another, greater mystery. The coastline is shown as it would be without the ice that has covered it for millennia. And there is a notation: '*No one lands on these shores. This land is desolate, inhabited by giant serpents. Monsters created by chaos at the beginning of the world.*' The most obvious explanation is that the map is a fake, a modern forgery, but it has been authenticated as sixteenth century. The mapping of the land under the ice has been shown to be accurate."

"What other explanation could there possibly be?"

"That the original maps were made by a race of sea farers, who lived at a time when the land, or a part of it, was free of ice. An impossibly ancient civilization, lost to the historical record, but fragments of their maps remain, preserved by other sea farers, as copies of copies."

"But that's impossible. . ."

"No! The proofs are all around you! Anomalies. Artefacts, maps, manuscripts. Dismissed as forgeries and consigned to oblivion. For many years, I thought the same as you," he conceded. "Until my eyes were opened by Lockwood and Rapoport.

"Solomon Rapport was a Jew from Prague. Half his family perished in Terezin, the rest in Treblinka. He survived as a member of the *Sonderkommandos* – Special Detachments. He came here after the war searching for that which had been stolen by the Nazis. He got a job as janitor at the National Museum. That's where I met him. I caught him stealing from the Red Room: the place where anomalies are kept.

"He was looking for a particular manuscript. He came from an old and distinguished line of rabbis, scholars learned in the Kabbalah and other mysteries. They could trace their ancestry back to Moses, or so it was said. The document had been in his family for many centuries, guarded by them."

"Why would the Nazis take such a thing? I mean," Adam searched for the right words and failed to find them, "wouldn't they just destroy it?"

"Because it was held by rabbis? You'd be surprised what they saw fit to steal. They were strange people, strange and terrible, with their own interest in the arcane and the occult. The Lascaris Manuscript was written in an unknown script and regarded with very great reverence by scholars of the Kabbalah and also by the alchemists who revered the manuscript as a copy of the original version of the Emerald Tablet of Hermes Trismegistus (Hermes the Thrice Great) saved from the fire that destroyed the Great Library in Alexandria. The Emerald Tablet itself is thought to be a distillation of much older wisdom taken from the Sumerian Tablet of Destinies and the Golden Scroll of the Argonauts. With all his family dead, the sacred duty of care fell to Solomon. He fought to survive in the camps so that he could take the precious work back again. He traced the manuscript to the National Museum. It had been looted by British troops and found its way to auction. It was bought for the National Collection, but then declared fake.

"That is how it landed up in the Red Room and in my care. Solomon got a job as a janitor, just so he could be near it. He smuggled it out and spent the rest of his life trying to translate it. The manuscript was full of strange symbols, mysterious diagrams, depictions of unknown flora and fauna. The received wisdom was that it was the product of medieval fakery."

His father unlocked a drawer and took out some thick sheets of discoloured vellum.

"The originals of the copies Rapoport made in the blue notebook."

Adam leant over to see. There was a tall tree with a very thick trunk and branches sprouting from the top; a small plant with beautiful blue flowers growing on a stony ground; a thorn bush, the branches spiked with long thorns and studded with tiny white flowers shaped like stars. At first glance, the plants looked familiar. Not so the animals. These did look like they had strayed from a medieval bestiary. The pages were filled with different creatures, winged, fanged and taloned. Some with scales, others with feathers. They could be creatures from myth: dragons, gryphons, basilisks. Or they could be. . .

"Creatures we know from the fossil record?" His father grinned. "Precisely. In the Middle Ages it was known as the *Devil's Garden*, because of the depictions of strange plants and creatures. Some think it inspired Hieronymus Bosch in his visions of Hell and damnation. Solomon and Lockwood believed that the text was impossibly ancient, copied many times, like the Portolan maps, from an original that was in *the* language, the mother of all others and contained a detailed and accurate record of a lost world."

"The world of the ancient sea farers, the map makers?"

"Exactly!" He swept his arm round to take in the whole room and everything collected in it. "Taking all these evidences together, we assumed that there must have been some kind of diaspora in the deep past; a spreading out by this sea-faring people across the whole world. They took their maps and knowledge with them. Fragments from this Elder Time survived in the myths and stories, buildings and deities of other peoples from Mesopotamia to the Americas, but what this world was like, what the inhabitants were fleeing from, what they left behind them, those things were still a mystery. We knew that the Lascaris Manuscript contained this knowledge, but the key to its meaning was lost. It had always been closely guarded and passed on from father to son. In the fullness of time, Solomon would have received this knowledge, but that was not to be. All the Guardians were wiped out in the

Holocaust. Solomon had no key. Then, going through Lockwood's notebook, he found the hieroglyphs that Stone had copied from the walls of the Womb of the World. Solomon was convinced that this was the same language."

"What happened to Solomon?"

"When Lockwood died, he took what he needed from here and found lodging at a synagogue, working as the caretaker. The synagogue fell into disuse and was closed up. It was deconsecrated and the use changed. It became a carpet shop, then a nightclub. Recently, it was rescued. It is to become a museum. During the renovations they discovered Solomon's Room."

Adam is seeing through his father's eyes. He is on an upper gallery. There is building work going on below him. The smell of cement and new wood drifts up as he makes his way through an arch, partially curtained off by tattered drapery. He shoulders his way through a group of people: workmen in hard hats, passers-by come to see what all the fuss is about. News that something strange has been found has spread into the streets around. The walls are crudely painted black and purple, plastered with peeling, plastic stars: the kind that glow white in black light. There is a gap at the back. A piece of panelling has been torn out. Layers of previous use show in cream paint, under that dark green, and finally yellow-brown varnish around the crowbar marks and down the long torn edge of a door. This is where the people are clustered, peering in at something. What are they seeing? Alarm and fear run through him like alternating currents. A life frozen in a moment.

A tiny, crowded space, little more than a cupboard. One

sweeping glance is enough to take in everything. His room appears untouched, the only change a covering of fine black grit, city-grime dust and the deposits left by pigeons. The smeared windows let in little light. They are high and small, little more than skylights; one pane is cracked, a portion is missing. Pigeon guano crusts the sill and the wall, layers the top of the cheap wardrobe in squat stalagmites. A narrow iron-framed bed lies against one wall, covered in a grey army blanket rumpled up in stiffened folds. A half-eaten meal sits on the table, the food collapsed into heaps of mould spores. A pair of round-rimmed glasses lies next to it, resting on a book, the place marked with a tube ticket. Newspapers lie in tall stacks, notebooks in fallen piles. Papers curl across the floor, drifted around the legs of the chair as if spilled from the lap of a sitter who had suddenly risen. Some of them are tidemarked brown by rain, others fouled by bird droppings. Adam clenches his fists and thrusts his hands in his pockets to stop himself from gathering them up.

"Didn't even know there was a door here," one of the workmen is saying. "All been painted over. Must have been shut up ever since the synagogue closed its doors. . ."

"Must be the caretaker's place," someone supplies. "What was his name?" He turns to the old man next to him. "Solomon something. . ."

"Rapoport," Adam hears himself answer.

"That's right," an old man says. "I remember him. He was a scholar, and a tzaddik, a righteous man. He used to go round the neighbourhood, pockets full of change for those less fortunate. He must have left when the synagogue shut down."

"Door was bolted from the inside. . ." the workman's voice tails away.

There is a mystery here and he cannot explain it.

Adam steps into the room. That's when he notices. Every possible surface is covered in writing: the paper on the walls, the margins of newspapers, food wrappers, cigarette packets, tube tickets, even the piano keys are covered in tiny letters and signs. It is as if the words have spilled from the notebooks and spread everywhere. Symbols seem to dance in the air, like motes of dust in sunlight.

"So? What happened?" Adam asked his father.

"He was found under the blanket. What was left of him," his father replied. "He deliberately shut himself away, willing himself to death with a secret too terrible to release into the world. The police removed his remains, and sealed the room. I waited until they'd left, crossed the tapes, and went back for his papers and notebooks. Once he had run out of paper, he'd started to write on anything that he could find, wallpaper, bus tickets. By the end of the night, I knew the contents. I knew exactly what Solomon's book contained and could see why he would choose death rather than reveal the contents to the world. He was caught between a truth too awful to contemplate, even if any would believe it, and the certainty that there were those who would make sure his work was ridiculed, while all the time using what he had learnt for their own dreadful ends.

"The Lascaris Manuscript contained echoes of ancient beliefs that exist in the founding myths of many different cultures from all over the world. The history of a doomed Eden, an account of its devastation: the stars slewed from their places, cities destroyed, towers toppled, a whole world erased until it became a freezing wasteland dominated by cruel and terrifying Beast Gods, scaled, reptilian creatures, the ancestor gods of every nightmare daemon and deity to haunt mankind from that lost time to the present day. They were alive. They were real. The creatures died, but belief in them has survived. There are reptilian gods, dragons and serpents, in the myths of many peoples. Many religions relate versions of how these dark, chthonic creatures have been conquered: the twin pythons at Delphi slain by Apollo and wound round the caduceus; Satan spurned under man's heel; the world serpent made to swallow his own tail. So their power is contained. For the moment. But I believe the Lascaris Manuscript to be both history and prophecy. What has happened once, could happen again."

There were other parallels with Eden. Adam's naming had not been idle. The youth and the maiden, the choices they made would decide the fate of the world, as it had done long ago. Abraham said nothing to Adam about this, such knowledge now might quite overwhelm him, and he was already suffering.

Adam had suddenly had a flash of somewhere dismal, bleak and cold, filled with terrible creatures that he could sense but not quite see. The sudden vision filled him with paralysing fear and the most terrible weakness. He felt sick. His leg ached intolerably and refused to take his weight. He fell sideways, and had to steady himself against one of the cabinets.

His father watched him with concern. "Why did I not think of it before?" he said, almost to himself, and wheeled himself to a plain cabinet of polished dark wood. He selected another small brass key and fitted it into the lock. "We need all the help we can muster to face the coming storm." He took out a bundle wrapped in faded blue velvet. "Stone sent Lockwood some marvels over the years, but this is the most valuable, certainly the most beautiful."

"The crystal skull!" Adam's eyes widened.

"You read about that, too? You were busy while I was sleeping."

Abraham handled it carefully. It was heavy. A human skull carved from one single piece of clear quartz. It appeared to be anatomically correct in every detail, even down to the articulated lower jaw.

"May I touch it?"

"That's rather what I had in mind." His father smiled. "Apart from its other mysteries, it has remarkable healing properties. Put your hands on either side."

The surface was glass smooth, and not at all cold. Adam looked down into the depths of the crystal and noticed milky threads and striations. As he watched they seemed to be growing, spreading like a web, extending between his fingers like a cat's cradle. He felt a slight tingling, like a very mild electrical current, and warmth spread to all his limbs. His leg felt much easier and he was filled with calmness, a sense of well being. All the fear and tension he had been experiencing seemed to leak out of him. It really was a remarkable thing. More astonishing than all his expectations. Who had made it? How?

"Nobody knows." His father was reading his mind again. "But I believe it is a relic of the Elder Time. It is easier to dismiss such an object as a fake than admit that it could have been made by a people who had no knowledge of metal tools. Who would take a single quartz crystal, rub away at it to give it shape and form, using nothing more than sand and human hair? Who would work all the days of their lives on this one thing, lifetime after lifetime? Who knows why? Perhaps it was a form of profound meditation. Certainly, there are those that believe that all knowledge is distilled in the atoms of this crystal – of what was, what is and what will be. There is certainly the power of healing, but what else? We don't know. The skull is as mysterious to us as one of our computers would be to those people, although rather more beautiful."

Adam was an apt subject. He seemed to have a real connection to whatever forces worked within the beautifully crafted object. Abraham had never seen the skull work so quickly, or so well. They were perilously close to the abyss, but there had to be time for this. Perhaps their position was not entirely hopeless. A great deal rested on Adam. Abraham felt a slight lifting of his spirits as he watched his son.

"What happened to Stone?" Adam asked.

"Much of what happened to him is a mystery, and will probably remain so. The official story says he disappeared in Mexico in 1919 after getting mixed up in the revolution, but his correspondence with Lockwood continued well after that. He carried on travelling, continuing on his quest. All we know about his ultimate fate is that someone claiming to be Brice Ambrose Stone eventually died in a Californian asylum for the insane."

"Driven mad by what he had found out? Like Rapoport?" Adam asked. From the letters, he'd come to admire Stone's fearless sense of adventure and was sorry that such an unhappy fate awaited him.

"Perhaps."

"Do you have a picture of him?" Adam had no idea what he looked like. He wanted to see if the image that he had formed in his head in any way resembled reality.

His father opened a drawer at the base of the cabinet and took out some papers.

"Here," he said, handing Adam a photograph. "This was taken when he was in London. He might have changed in later life."

The photo was black and white, bright enough to look recent. It showed a clear-eyed, handsome man, whose gaze was diverted to the side, as if he was looking at an object that was some distance away. He was wearing a frock coat over a waistcoat. The pearl buttons of his white shirt caught the light a little bit and the bow tie he wore was skewed slightly to the left. His light-coloured hair curled to his shoulders and his full moustache was twisted up at the ends, giving a lift to his firm mouth, so he looked as if he was about to smile. It was an intelligent face, full of humour and life. Adam decided that he liked him.

"In the letter I read, he mentions Wesson again."

"Yes, Lockwood was puzzled by that. He'd rather lost track of him after the affair with the Poet and the stolen tablets came to nothing. Wesson seemed to have gone to other things: setting up some crackpot sect as a way of seducing silly debutantes. To have him pop up again, making his presence felt *on several planes of existence* was very disquieting, to say the least. Alerted by Stone, Lockwood began to collect what he called *evidences*."

Abraham Black picked up a pile of newspaper cuttings, brittle and yellowed with age and passed them to Adam.

Empire News, Sunday 15 August, 1934

A Serious Change of Spots

After a series of notorious scandals and libel cases which have marked BULLER GILPIN WESSON, self-styled "Lord of Dead Souls", forever in the nation's consciousness as the "wickedest man in the world", this newspaper has to report a serious change of spots.

Mr Wesson, also known as Master Therion and "the Great Beast", has been accused in the past of allegedly carrying out sinister ceremonies, complete with the trappings of unholy rites and black magic ceremonies involving the sacrifice of animals and the murder of babies at his self-styled Temple of Telfu in Italy. At his most recent libel case, brought against this paper, Mr Justice Anderson Montgomery observed that, during the 40 years in which he had been connected with the courts, he had never heard such appalling, hideous, dreadful, abominable stuff.

The judge will no doubt raise his eyebrows in disbelief when he reads his bête noire's latest announcement. Mr Wesson, it seems, is to turn his back on his old beliefs and is to join a religious order. The Temple Order has apparently been in existence since medieval times. Its interests used to be extensive but it is at present reduced to a small mother house in the French Pyrenees.

Wesson will be joining the Order as a novice and is said to be donating his considerable fortune (which includes extensive estates in Warwickshire) to the Order upon his acceptance.

Adam turned to Lockwood's accompanying notes.

There is method in his madness. The Order he joined has seen better days, but at one time it rivalled the Jesuits in its educational and missionary work. The Temple brothers were spread out all over the world: east to India, China and Japan, west to the New World, busily rooting out heresy, re-educating the natives, sending back the pagan texts that they found wherever they went. The brothers in Europe were just as assiduous in collecting works on alchemy, the Kabala, every kind of heresy. Their library contains a collection of proscribed texts to rival the Vatican. No wonder Wesson has reinvented himself as Brother Anslem!

"He was looking for the same thing as Lockwood and Rapoport," Adam said. Suddenly it was all beginning to make sense. "Access to a library like that must have put him on to the crystal skull! So he became Brother Anslem and then Grand Master. Clever! Hang on, though." Adam frowned and looked at the date on the newspaper he had been reading. "I can see how he became Brother Anslem and even the Grand Master, but how can he be around now?"

"More difficult to explain." It was his father's turn to frown. "There are two possible ways. One, he can project himself into, and live through, much younger men, rather as he used the Poet. It's a form of transmigration, although the host is not dead. Two, he can use his powers as shaman and adept to step outside time. When he comes back, the world will be older, but he will have stayed at the same age. Like Rip Van Winkle, or humans taken by fairies."

"So he could come back as Grand Master?"

"Yes. There's something else you ought to know. He is also the Founder of the Children of the Sixth Dawn. Same head, different branches."

"What's the connection?"

"There isn't one. On the surface. It's part of Wesson's plan. He had to have a source of gullible, willing victims. What he is preparing to attempt requires sacrifice, you see, sacrifice on a grand scale, according to the Babylonian tablet he stole."

"So he *could* still be alive to take advantage of the Cosmic Concurrence that's about to happen." Adam frowned as the pieces began to fall together.

His father nodded. "The time is coming for the Rite of Re-Generation. For the god to be born again."

"What about Stone's dark skull thing? Where does that fit in?"

Abraham Black shook his head. "He needs it for some reason, but why? I'm not sure. We have no real idea how the skulls were made. Or for what purpose. They may be extremely ancient. They may even be from this ruined world. . ."

"What would the end be like?" Adam asked, but received no direct answer, rather he felt a shift in his senses; a feeling of time and space suspended. The walls of the room they were in receded, the furnishings around him faded, as his father chose to show rather than tell him how it would be.

He is outside. It is snowing. He looks up. The pale flakes falling on his face feel hot and dry. The sun has disappeared to an orange smear in a fog of dust and ash. This is just the beginning. . .

People all around are shouting and pointing. He looks in the direction of the turned heads and gesturing hands. There is a white glow in the sky. There is no sound as yet, no explosion, just a fierce hot wind shrieking through the streets. The London Eye glows for a moment and then disappears like a smoke ring. In the City, the glass melts on 30 St Mary Axe, dripping down the fat, faceted Gherkin sides like wax down a candle. At Canary Wharf, the pyramid on top of 1 Canada Square is outlined in incandescent light; the internal framework of the building shows like a digital scan before melting into nothing. On TV screens, similar images appear from all over the world. The banner beneath the pictures unfolds. A roll-call of cities: London, Manchester, Glasgow, Edinburgh, Cardiff, Dublin, New York, Chicago, Los Angeles, San Francisco, Paris, Berlin, Tokyo, Bejing . . . the names spool out until the screens turn to cosmic snow. Stations broadcasting to the end. The screens turn black as the electricity stops. The end is suddenly finite. Buildings falling, people running, others standing, just as they are here, caught in stunned shock, staring as one might regard the loss of an arm, a leg, knowing that there is nothing to be done, that there are only seconds left in which to watch the blood flood from a wound that is fatal. The sun disappears completely as the ash storm becomes a blizzard. Street lights that are still working stutter and fizz in the blanket blackness. They fail, one after another. Darkness at noon.

"What *was* that? Some kind of terrorist attack?"

"It might help to think of it like that, although the power released will be a thousand times more than any human group could hope to unleash. There are forces moving against us. Forces led by Wesson. Forces who *want* this to happen. We must act, and act now. My 'episode' on Temple Green was not a stroke. Something happened in my head. Like a switch being thrown. I knew it would happen some time, but I didn't know when."

"Like being activated?"

"You could say that." His father gave a slight smile. "Now it's time to activate you."

"Me?"

His father nodded. "You have an important part to play, believe me, if we are to avoid Armageddon. Rapoport and Lockwood, myself as well, we were gathering materials to build a house in darkness. Now the light is on, but other things are illuminated. We find we are building on the edge of a precipice. We don't have very much time." He hesitated. He had by no means told Adam everything. He had deliberately kept certain things back from him. "We have no choice in this," he went on. "And you have a part to play. . ." He wheeled himself over to Adam and caged his son's hands with his long fingers. "Don't look at me. Look into the eyes of the skull. Now listen carefully. This is what you must do. . ."

Adam could hear his father speaking, but the words made no sense to him. He knew that what was being imparted was very important, but he found his mind wandering as if in the first stages of sleep. His eyes closed, but his hands were held fast as if bound to the slippery surface of the crystal.

Abraham kept his son's hands steady and used the medium of the crystal to instruct him. There was so little time, and what he had to impart would be too much for the boy's conscious mind. Such knowledge had pushed grown men to the edge of madness and beyond. Look at Rapoport. And poor Stone ending his life in a Californian asylum for the insane. There was no more time for questions and explanations. The task demanded nothing less than complete acceptance. Adam had to travel back to the Elder Time. Once he was there, his destiny would become clear. Abraham ached with love for his son. If the boy succeeded, they would have a lifetime together. If he failed, it would hardly matter. . .

21

CITY DAZE

They were interrupted by a loud knock on the front door, a dull thudding followed by a protracted banging. From the back of the house came the sound of glass breaking. There was less time than Black thought.

"We have visitors," Jethro spoke from the door, his voice was neutral. "Front and back."

Abraham released Adam's hands. "Find the girl."

"What girl?"

Adam felt as if he was waking from sleep. He took his fingers from the crystal.

"The girl from the hospital. The suicide-pact survivor. She may be with a boy, Christophe. His grandmother, Celestine, knows what you have to do."

"Where am I supposed to look?"

She could be anywhere. Adam looked down at his leg. It should be aching just at the thought of all that walking.

"My leg. It doesn't hurt any more."

He flexed his foot. He undid the clips on the plastic shell and flexed again. It was as if there had never been anything wrong with it. Just a bit of a twinge, that was all.

"In the city. Try the Underground system. She's itinerant. She'll be begging. You'll probably find her down there. Now go with Jethro. Quickly now. They mustn't find you here!"

Adam stood up. He only had one shoe.

Jethro held up his holdall from the hospital. "The other one's in here."

"What about you?" Adam asked as he tightened the laces.

The hammering on the door intensified. From the back came the sound of wood rending.

"No time. Jethro will show you the way."

Jethro led him down the landing, opening a door at the end of the passage which led on to a servants' staircase. The unpainted wooden stairs were worn in the centre, narrow and winding, the walls rough brick. Jethro put his fingers to his lips to indicate extreme quietness and Adam was careful to tread softly as they passed a bolted door that must have opened on to the kitchen. Through the wood panels came the sound of men's voices, heavy footsteps, grunted effort, and rending wood as the men forced their way into the downstairs passageway. The wooden stairs turned into stone steps which led down into the cellar.

The cellar had been used as a workshop at one time and Jethro went to a dusty old cream-painted sideboard that acted as a workbench and took up half the length of one wall. It was piled with shiny varnish cans and crusted paint pots. What now? Any attempt to move it would have the whole lot crashing down and it was important to make no noise. There were men standing guard outside. Adam could see their feet and trouser cuffs through the dusty, cobwebbed windows. Jethro released a catch at the side of the bench and the back panel slid out. He opened the doors at the front and indicated for Adam to crawl through. On the other side of the bench was a low alcove, arched with stone. Jethro followed, securing the doors, and sliding the panel back into place.

"That should fox 'em." He grinned. "Disappearing Lady. Oldest trick in the book." Jethro switched on a powerful torch that he took from his pocket. The archway was the entrance to a tunnel. "The house was built above the foundations of an old nunnery. The passage dates back to that time."

"What about my father?" Adam asked. "We aren't going to leave him?"

"I have to get you away from here," Jethro replied. "I have my orders." He smiled reassurance. "The old house holds a few surprises. He'll be all right, don't you worry."

The subterranean passageway was low and squat, lined with pale grey stone and barely half the height of the alcove. Jethro went first, worming his way forward. His shoulders nearly filled the space. Powdery mildew transferred to his clothes as he crawled. Adam came along behind, staring at the man's boot soles, trying not to breathe in too much green dust and listening all the time for any sign that they were being followed.

This tunnel gave on to another, taller passageway.

Other entrances opened up into darkness and Adam wondered about getting lost, but Jethro took each turn with confidence. He seemed to know his way.

Finally, they came to a set of shallow stone steps, which led up to an iron grating. Jethro indicated for Adam to stop. He mounted the steps and stood for a moment listening intently, before reaching up and lifting the heavy grating out of the way. He stuck his head into the open air and took a final look around. When he was sure that there was no one about, he beckoned Adam forward.

"Come on. Quick!"

They emerged behind a park bench. The seat was occupied, but the sleeping tenant hardly stirred as they climbed past him.

Jethro laughed. "Looks like someone's taken your dad's spot."

Adam stared at the tramp, curled up in a filthy sleeping bag. He couldn't believe his father had lived like that. They were in a churchyard, next to Temple Green Station. A stained white church reared up behind them. The Temple was close. Adam could see its forbidding stone wall.

Jethro looked over to where Portakabins and fenced-off areas showed work going on, but no sign of any workmen.

"They must be on their lunch break. Best not to hang about, though. You need to. . ."

"Aren't you coming with me?" Adam tried to keep the panic out of his voice. His only thought had been to escape; he had not considered what would happen after that.

"No." Jethro shook his head. "Need to get back to the house, see how your old fella's doing. You're on your own now, kid. Here, this should help." He found his wallet and took out some notes. "Just hope no one's watching, eh?" He handed the wad over with an embarrassed grin.

"But what. . ."

Jethro had already disappeared back down the hole like a giant white rabbit. The grating scraped back into place, leaving Adam with no idea what to do next.

The tramp reared up from his nest, his grimy paw thrust out.

Adam dodged past him, cheeks reddening. He left the churchyard and crossed the patch of mud-trampled ground with his head down, but he attracted a chorus of interest.

"Hey, pretty boy! Hey, batty boy! Over here! You want business?"

He hurried his step, careful not to look at anyone, intent on getting to the entrance to the Temple Green Underground unmolested, so he failed to see a group of boys boost themselves off the wall where they had been lounging, and prepare to follow him.

22

GOING UNDERGROUND

Adam followed the crowds down the steps into the Underground station. He bought a ticket from the machine for the inner-city zone. An image of the girl came into his head. The one from the hospital. The suicide-pact survivor. Her hair, her eyes, her face. He saw her as clear as when she was staring down at him. He had to look for her. But where? He had lived in the city as long as he could remember, but separated off within the Temple, never leaving unescorted, which made him as unfamiliar as any tourist. He could look for a lifetime and never find her. He felt the weight of it settle on his shoulders.

He bought a ticket and followed the crowds underground. He didn't know the subway all that well, but he didn't take time to study the system. There could be people after him, sent by the Temple. He didn't want to draw attention by standing about, staring at maps. He felt safer down here, anonymous in the restless surge and flow of the crowd. He'd ride the trains while he thought what to do, where to look for the girl. As he turned the corner on to the platform, the remnants of a poster caught his eye, half of it torn away.

Someone had scrawled "DON'T MISS <u>THIS</u>" across the top. Someone else had added "RIP". . .

He jumped on the train just as the doors were closing. The car was crowded. Adam moved into the centre and grabbed the bar above his head against the jolt and sway as the train clattered round the curves and bends. He found a seat after the next station and stared straight ahead like everyone else in the carriage. The man across the aisle met his eye. Adam's glance shot upwards to the route map.

The motion of the carriage was rhythmic, soothing in an odd kind of way. He let his body sway with it. He suddenly felt tired. Very tired. He would close his eyes, just for a minute, while he thought what to do.

When he woke up the car was almost empty. He looked around, wondering where all the people had gone. That's when he saw them. They were sitting bunched together right up the other end of the carriage. A group of boys, five or six of them, wearing baggy jeans and hoodies. There had been lots of people in between; that's why he hadn't noticed them before. They were noticing him, though.

They kept glancing towards him and away again. Then they would look at each other, or down at the floor. One of them would mutter something and the others would reply with soft answering chatter and glance over at him until Adam felt sure that he was the object of their observations. They might not be talking about me at all, he would try to reassure himself. I'm just being paranoid. But then they would look across and one of them would whisper while the others nodded, and all Adam's suspicions came rushing back again.

Adam looked around and picked up the newspaper discarded by the man who had been sitting opposite. They would probably get off soon. He was in no hurry; he could stay here all day if he wanted to, and that's just what he'd do. He would sit them out. The man opposite had been replaced by two others, both reading newspapers. As long as there were other people around, he'd be fine. . .

Adam focused down on his own paper.

DOOMSDAY CULT: LATEST

He turned to p.5

Reports continue to come in of deaths thought to be related to the so-called Doomsday Cult, the Children of the Sixth Dawn. Although no longer involving spectacular scenes of wholesale self-slaughter, the deaths are not over yet. In a bizarre new development, news agencies across the world report "copycat" incidents and a spate of groupthink suicide pacts thought to have been fuelled and spread by means of the Internet. Some of these victims seem to have met in chat rooms and planned their joint exits together, and several so-called "suicide bloggers" appear to have cashed in their chips.

Miracles and wonders

Some sources are linking these untimely deaths with the continuing spread of religious phenomena and wonder stories. All over the world, crowds are flocking to witness these reported miracles. The phenomena are not restricted to any one denomination or creed. Hindus are rushing to watch Lord Ganesh and Lord Shiva, the Destroyer, accept milk; a subway in Chicago has been besieged by people who have come to see an image of the Blessed Virgin Mary on a concrete wall. Crosses of light have appeared in bathrooms from Sunderland to Surbiton. Countless statues weep, while little girls cry tears of crystal and the Arabic for Allah is found in an aubergine. Giant statues have appeared in the Australian outback; white buffalo calves are born in the American Midwest and images of the Buddha emanate light. So it goes on.

Adam turned the page to:

World to End. . .

Who'd have thought it? Ancient Mayan calendars and Sumerian prophecy combine with astrology, astronomy and the latest theories of probability in Malcolm Fitzgerald's book: *Could it Happen?* Already a best-seller in America, Fitzgerald's publishers are hoping for similar success in the UK. Physicist Fitzgerald has combined ancient esoteric knowledge with the latest string theory to predict the end of the world.

Adam read through the story, his grip on the paper tightening:

And it is soon. The clock is ticking. To find out if you'll be here next year, read: *Could it Happen?* by Malcolm Fitzgerald, Streett Books, £15.99. Buy online at £12.99 and you might just have time to read it.

The paper fell from Adam's lap on to the floor. All the things his father had said, all the things he'd read, the Lockwood correspondence, it was coming true. . . He remembered that thing in America, *The Rapture*, where they stood on the tops of mountains waiting for the end, then nothing happened. What if this time it did? When was it going to kick off? The paper didn't mention it, but his father had said it would be at the old winter solstice, the twelfth of December. He'd lost track of time in hospital. He checked the top of the page. Less than a week away! He caught a flash of the vision he'd had: the fierce hot wind, the ash storm, then blackness. He felt himself begin to sweat. All these people would be dead. He suddenly felt trapped. Claustrophobic. He had to get off the train. Right now.

He stood up. They were about to enter a station. The gang of boys had moved closer and positioned themselves three on either side of him, effectively blocking his way to the doors. The train slowed. The men opposite folded their papers.

"Temple Green Station. Temple Green," a voice announced.

He'd gone round in a circle.

"Please mind the gap between the train and the platform. Mind the gap."

The boys stepped in from both sides in a pincer movement. Adam tensed. He didn't know what these boys wanted with him, but they wanted something. He had to make a break for it. He got ready to push his way through them, but he didn't need to bother. The two men who had been sitting opposite him barged the boys out of the way. Adam jumped off just as the doors were closing. He hoped that the gang would be stuck on the train, but one of them grabbed a woman's case and jammed the doors.

The automatic voice on the train squawked out a protest as Adam dodged his way to the crowded exit. He ran as fast as he could down the snaky pedestrian tunnels, heading for the escalators, taking the stairs two at a time. Three of the boys were behind him, swearing back at the people who objected to being pushed and shoved. The others took the central stairs. Adam glanced sideways. Even though those stairs were not moving, they seemed to be gaining on him. Fewer people in the way. He reached the top first, but then had to fumble in his pocket for his ticket. Some of the barriers weren't working. Queues were forming. A couple of Underground guards in fluorescent safety jackets were opening gates, nodding people through. Adam reckoned he would probably be safest with them. He risked a look back. Hooded heads were bobbing up and down, trying to spot him, but the boys were behind a solid mass of people. Adam let himself breathe again. He was nearly at the barrier now. Once he was through, he could lose himself in the crowds as they surged out of the station.

That's when he felt the hand on his shoulder. A voice spoke into his ear, very quietly. A voice he knew.

"We've been looking for you everywhere, Adam." A strong hand tightened on his upper arm, steering him away from the guards.

Adam didn't have to look round to know it was Brother Zack. He was close enough for Adam to smell the spice of the shaving cream he used and the sickly scent of the little violet sweets he chewed.

23

STRANGE MEETING

"Hey! Watch it, mate."

"Watch it yourself!"

Brother Zack looked round, scowling at the disturbance behind them. Someone pushed into him. His grip on Adam's arm tightened and two men stepped in from either side. The two from the train. How long had they been following him? A feeling of deep unease threatened to push Adam into panic. They must be everywhere, with pictures and descriptions. Whichever way he went, whatever he did, they would get him. He had a horrible, claustrophobic feeling, like he was stuck in a nightmare and couldn't wake up.

They were at the barrier now, but everyone needed a ticket or a card. Brother Zack reached one-handed into the deep pocket of his long green surplice. He cursed under his breath. He twisted to search the pocket on the other side and his grip on Adam slackened, just for a second, just long enough for Adam to feed in his own ticket. The barriers flicked back. Adam was through. The prongs shot into place before

Brother Zack could follow. He collided painfully and was pushed out of the way by the man behind him.

He cursed again and limped to the manned barrier; angered as much by the way he'd been made to look foolish, as at losing the quarry. He had men on the other side anyway. Adam could not escape. Another disturbance broke out. A group of boys came steaming through, shouting and hooting, vaulting over the out-of-order turnstiles. The guards clanged their gate locked and gave chase, charging right in front of the two men set to grab Adam. Brother Zack's cursing intensified. The boy had got away.

Adam plunged back into the labyrinthine tunnels of the station. He felt less exposed down here. He would be much too close to the Temple if he was to go out on the street. He ran down the wide underpass that connected the Underground to the mainline station. The walls here were made of thin, yellow brick, not big shiny tiles. Signs for platforms nine and ten showed above branching tunnels. If this was not really happening, maybe the wall would open and he could break through into another world, or back into his own. Either way, he had to do something. He had twisted his bad ankle some way back and his leg was hurting more now, threatening to give way on him. He remembered Brother Zack's soft sibilant whisper, the malice on his scented breath. He would love Adam to collapse and be stuck down here, waiting to be collected up and delivered back to the Temple like a parcel. The thought gave Adam the extra strength he needed. He carried on, not caring where the tunnels took him. Both sets of pursuers seemed to have disappeared, but that concern was being replaced by another worry. He was still nowhere nearer to finding the girl.

She could be anywhere. Adam felt a tug of panic and despair. The search was hopeless.

Suddenly, the boys were back, appearing as if from nowhere. There were three in front, two behind, and one descending from exposed pipes in the ceiling. Adam stopped in his tracks and backed up against the rough brick wall.

None of them said anything. Why were they after him? He had nothing. Why weren't they targeting all those tourists and commuters with mobiles and iPods?

"What do you want with me?" Adam shouted, his voice booming back at him. He stood with his back against the wall, fists balled to fight, although his legs were shaking. "I haven't *got* anything!"

"Hey! Woa!" The one who looked to be the youngest, certainly the smallest, stepped forward, hands raised in front of him, palms out, fingers spread. "Steady, steady. We don't want nothing from you, man."

"That's not what it looks like." Adam glared round, wary. The others were beginning to circle.

"You gotta come with me," the little one said. He seemed to be their leader.

"Come with you where?" Adam stared.

"To see me grandma, Mamma Celestine."

Relief made Adam laugh out loud.

"Don't go disrespecting her, know what I'm sayin'?" Kris shook his head in warning. "Don't vex me, man."

This was getting like a déjà vu thing. First the girl

yesterday, now him. Kris didn't mean to harm to them. He was trying to help them. Why didn't they believe him? If it wasn't that he'd promised Mamma Celestine, he'd leave this white boy to the priest.

"I'm not disrespecting her. My father sent me to find *you*."

Kris laughed. "You Bram's boy?"

"What's funny?"

"Nothing. He's so street and you're so. . ." Kris laughed again. "Enough chattin'. I'm Kris. These are my boys."

They fell into a phalanx around Adam, ready to march him out of there. Adam felt some of the tension leave him. These boys were on his side. He was not alone any more.

"Wait, wait, wait. There's something I have to do. Someone I have to find."

"What someone?" The smaller boy looked up at him. "Who?"

"A girl. I have to find a girl."

One of the taller members of the gang stepped closer, hood falling back. Adam recognized the girl from the hospital. He had the same feeling as then, like he'd known her before. Had known her always. Zillah half smiled at him, as though she felt the same way. He was about to ask how she got there, how she'd ended up with this gang, when their leader spoke again.

"Looks like you found her, brother." Kris grinned, noting the glance that had passed between them. "Hate to break up Friends Reunited, but we gotta go." A finger emerged from the sleeve of his silver puffa jacket as he pointed forward. "Like now. Ran, get us out of here!"

Swift footsteps sounded in front of them, answered by others, coming from the opposite direction. The tallest boy leapt for the pipe above his head and pulled himself into the crawl space. One by one, he hauled the others after him, including Adam. The last one pushed the wire caging back and wriggled away from the gap.

"They going to meet just where we was at," Kris whispered.

"Any sign?" Brother Zack's voice came up from below.

"No sign, sir."

A powerful torch briefly swept over their hiding place.

"What's up there?"

"Trunking for electrics, heating pipes and such."

"They'll have gone up there, like the little rats they resemble."

"Could be anywhere, then."

"Well, flush them out!"

"Roof won't take our weight." The railway guard spoke. "Grown man'd get stuck. There is another way."

"What's that?"

"Poison gas. They use it against rats. When the system's closed down, like."

Brother Zack hesitated, but the man with him stepped forward.

Zillah felt the sweat prickle on her palms and down her back. It was the Advocate.

"Well?" he said. "What are you waiting for? Get on to it!" He did not appear to share Brother Zack's doubts. "Close down the whole section."

"It's strong stuff," the railway man muttered. "In a

confined space. . ." He shrugged. "It ain't an exact science."

"Do it."

"They might not survive it."

The Advocate stared at him, his fleshy face impassive. "I want them in my control within the hour."

Brother Zack looked up sharply. Shouldn't they check with the New Master? The risk. . . "Our orders were. . ." he began to say, "the New Master. . ."

The words died in his mouth as the man looked back at him with eyes the colour of corroded copper.

"Orders change," he said. His voice sounded different; harsh and commanding, with a new, guttural quality. The transmigration was almost complete. There was very little left of the man known as the Advocate.

"Very well." Brother Zack instantly complied, compelled by more than the total obedience to a superior that was required by the Order. He bowed his head, but not in acquiescence. He felt the urgent need to look away from pupils that seemed to have grown long and narrow, as dark and hollow as a needle's eye.

24

GHOST STATION

They had to get out of there. And quickly. They crawled
and pulled their way along, following the tall boy, Ran. He
was long and thin and seemed to flow round bends and
tight corners like a slithering eel. It was hot and close in the
ducts, and full of choking gritty dust. Adam was altogether
less flexible and once or twice he had to fight down panic,
sure that he was stuck. Eventually they came to an outlet.
Ran went first, the others sliding after him. Adam was
aware of a sudden draught, and then felt a hot blast of air
and the shake of a train fast approaching. The passengers
blurred past him, centimetres away. Kris threw an arm
across him, flattening both of them against the wall.

"Don't get too close, man. Or you get sucked under
the wheels."

The screaming turned to a high-pitched whine as the
train rattled off round a long bend in the tunnel.

"Quick, before the next one," Ran growled. His
voice was rough, deep as a man's. "Over here."

He led them along by the side of another track. Rats
squeaked and eyed them incuriously.

"I hate them things," Kris muttered, making to stamp on a pale grey specimen which must have been as big as a cat. It scampered away towards the outlet that they had just left, its naked tail shiny and thick like pink electrical cable, slipping over the silver rails.

"How does Ran know the way?" Adam asked.

"Used to live down here, didn't he?" Kris explained. "With his dad when they had their leave to stay turned down. Knows the whole system like the back of his hand."

"Here. In here." Ran pointed to a recess in the side of the tunnel, the walls corrugated with soot.

He indicated a maintenance door, marked with a bar and the words: "EMERGENCY ONLY" and the sign of a running man. Kris nodded one of his gang forward. The biggest and strongest, the one they called Maxwell.

He forced up the bar and pushed the door open. They slipped through, one by one. He pushed the door back with a clang just as another train screamed by. They took torches from a storage bin and Ran led them along the passages used by staff for maintenance, moving them from one system to another.

They got out of the tunnel just in time. A hundred metres back up the line, the big rat lay on the track, dead before the passing train amputated its fat pink tail. Its nostrils were filled with bubbling blood; its narrow jaw stretched open, exposing long, yellow teeth in the agonizing rictus of death. It had taken precisely three minutes to die from the effects of the poison as it flooded the passages behind him.

"Due to a major incident, all services are being shut down." The loudspeaker voice penetrated every part of the system. "This is not a drill. Repeat. This is not a practice. All passengers should make their way to their nearest exit with all possible speed. Officers are on hand to aid evacuation."

"They treating this like some kind of terrorist thing." Kris looked round. "That means armed response. Guards all over. No blending in with the crowds. Ran, my man, you gotta find us a different way out."

Ran led them through to a distant platform. He jumped down on to the track, inviting the others to follow.

Adam hung back.

"How do you know it's safe?" He tried to keep the panic out of his voice. "A train could come through any time!"

"No trains, man." Ran shook his head. "You heard what they said. Runnin's been suspended."

Reluctantly, Adam jumped down, even though everything about being off the platform seemed profoundly wrong and all his instincts and senses were screaming, "Danger: Keep Out! Only crazy people jump down here! You could be smashed to pulp any minute."

"What about the electricity?" Adam hung back, eyeing the live line. "Have they shut that off?"

"Don't know, man." Max, the next in line, spat towards the thick central line and its squat, round porcelain insulators. "My advice? Don't go near it."

Away from the platform, residual lighting flickered,

giving a green, eerie light. The beams from their torches seemed swallowed by the sooty blackness. They did not need to be told to keep close together. They moved along the side of the track barely half a step behind each other. Ran touched the wall, feeling for the point where the curved metal skin turned to rough brick.

"This is it." They were maybe a hundred metres in. "Ghost station," he added by way of explanation. "Ain't used no more."

The platform had been bricked off, all except for a space in the middle. Ran trained his torch on that and nodded for them to pull themselves up and step through the gap. Everything was filthy; sooty dust lay in miniature peaks and ridges across the platform, drifted against the walls like black snow. Adam could just make out the name of the station and the directional arrows painted in yellow and brown. It was like a time-warp scene. There was even an ancient chocolate vending machine with the old price: 1/-. Here and there, ancient posters and advertisements peeled from the cream and green tiles. Ran led them down one tunnel, then another. Water dripped; stalactites hung from the ceiling. A flight of crumbling stairs led up to another level. At the top there was an empty space and even deeper blackness. The downdraught from it stirred their hair and carried the eerie whisper of distant traffic.

"The old lift shaft."

Ran skirted past it and went to a rusting metal grille. The bolt clanged back to show the bottom of a spiral staircase.

"Pace yourself," he said as he took the first steps. "It's a long way up."

They emerged in an alleyway at the side of a pizza restaurant. The boys threw their hoods back and shoved their caps into their back pockets as they joined the crowds milling down the main street. They were only just round the corner and did not want to draw the attention of the police who were out in force, mobilized to deal with the emergency at Temple Green Station.

25

THE PANIC ROOM

At one touch of a button, the glass cases turned and came back. The room had been rigged so that the cases were replaced by replicas, some smashed and cracked, all of them empty, except for the stands that had once held exhibits and faded labels curled up in fine pale dust.

Abraham Black hauled himself out of the wheelchair and left it overturned, wheels spinning. He was weak, but he could walk perfectly well. He picked up the box containing the skull. He didn't have far to go, just to the bookcase next to the fireplace. He held the box under one arm and with his left hand loosened a sequence of volumes on different shelves, pulling them out exactly halfway, and then returning them to their former position, following a pattern, seemingly random, absolutely precise. The clockwork mechanism had been put in by one of the previous owners. It was centuries old, but still in perfect working order. Any mistake in the sequence would lock the machinery and make access from this side impossible. As the last volume was returned to its place, the bookcase swung out, the solid wall slid back and Abraham Black entered the secret chamber. He pulled a sequence of brass levers and the wall and bookcase swung back again, leaving the long room empty except for the overturned chair with its spinning wheels.

"Nothing here." A voice spoke in the empty room. "Cleared the place out. Don't shout! The old man. Yeah. Wheels are still spinning on his chair. Can only just have gone. Could be, I suppose. We'll have a look for that. Thinks there might be some kind of secret panel," he said to someone with him. "Have a twiddle of them knobs on the fireplace. I'll have a butcher's at the bookcase."

Abraham Black smiled as the random movement of the books locked the door into place.

He descended a narrow flight of stairs to Arnold Brume's secret chamber. Although this was one of the oldest parts of the building, the prohibition on modern devices that applied to the rooms above did not operate here. Under Jethro's supervision, the room he was in had been refitted to the highest modern specifications and it contained everything that he might conceivably need. It had been made into what he understood was now called a panic room: soundproofed, with bullet-resistant, electromagnetic locks. It had back-up batteries and its own water supply, plenty of food (freeze-dried) and an air purification system. He had supplied himself with every comfort, even rather a good bottle of brandy, and would stay here until it was over. One way, or the other.

Abraham Black tracked the Temple goons on CCTV

for a while, eavesdropping on their conversation as they searched the Long Room. He soon lost interest in them. They would find nothing, no matter how thorough their search. He pressed a button, consigning their endeavours to a small square at the top of the screen. At the touch of another button, the screen filled with many sections, bringing images from all over the world: ice fields calving bergs the size of small countries; greyish brown flood water flowing over a drowned landscape, branching round the tops of trees and houses; a weather map showing tropical storms sweeping the southern USA; another plotting the progress of Hurricane Zenobia ripping through the Sugar Islands. A pall of smoke from forest fires was visible from space, besmirching the blue and white globe like a dirty thumb print. A volcano, beribboned with ruby lines of snaking lava, belched ash. Dusty villages lay consigned to rubble, while earthquakes rippled the ocean floor like a skein of silk.

Water, air, fire and earth. The scenes on the TV screens matched the alchemical symbols shown in faded colours on the opposite wall. This small room had been the closet of Arnold Brume, associate of the celebrated alchemist, Dr Robert Fludde. It was here that they carried on their "Great Work". This secret laboratory had been well hidden from the eyes of those who would have stolen their formula for making gold from base metal, although that was the least and most trivial of the experiments that were conducted here. Abraham Black looked up at a blank screen in front of him, and just for a moment, that former self stared back at him from under tangled, beetling brows. His hair sprung from under his apothecary's cap as unruly as frayed rope; a thick beard, streaked grey and white, hung to his chest. He gnawed at his bottom lip as he sat hunched inside his working robe, a long gown of dark green velvet, the full sleeves threadbare with wear, and the voluminous folds peppered with acid burns. The blink of an eye and the vision was banished, returning Black to who he was now. His "episode", the disturbance to his brain that had rendered him unconscious and helpless, had allowed him to glimpse who he had been, lifetime before lifetime, stretching back to the earliest time.

His gaze moved from his own image back to the scenes on the other screens. It was beginning. He undid the lock on the polished wooden box and took out the crystal skull. He unwrapped it carefully. The smooth surface felt surprisingly warm to the touch. In the eyes, twin points of light ignited. The secret of its making and the knowledge contained within it had been lost aeons ago. It had once been as clear as the clearest water, but now it was no longer pure. The crystal was fogged below the surface, striated with tiny lines. Fractures and faults were spreading through the crystal, fanning out from points deep inside. The damage had grown worse. Much, much worse. Black had been shocked when he saw it again, although he said nothing to Adam. Now, he feared even to look upon it; terrified that it might shatter. He felt the fragility under his fingers, the life pulsing, as if inside the eggshell skull of a new-born child.

The crystal would fragment when the time came,

explode into tiny pieces. He looked up at a huge stone disc, large as a cartwheel, set into the wall opposite him. Symbols set in concentric rows showed the cogs of the years meshing into each other. It showed other things besides for those with the knowledge to interpret the complex signs: the paths of the stars through the heavens, and the fates of those ruled by them, clicked together in meticulous progression. Destiny turned with tiny, absolute precision. Time by the Long Count had almost run down.

The fabric of the world was steadily being unstitched, ready to be formed into something else. Something unrecognizable, swept clean of humankind. He would stay here and lend what support he could, but ultimately all depended on the boy and the girl. The Messenger had been sent. He was taking them to the one who would guide them to their duty. Abraham Black felt the powerful tug of love and blood, even as the heavy counterweight of duty dropped through him like a stone. *It was the only way.* He felt helpless, trapped in his obligation, much as his namesake might have done as he grasped the sharp sickle knife, testing the keenness of the blade against the rasp of his thumb as he approached with dragging steps the place where his only son lay stretched on the sacrificial altar. But there was no hope of the saving angel voice from heaven; no possible equivalent of the luckless ram caught in a thicket.

There was only one chance to put things right, he told himself again. *It had to be done.* By them. Adam and the maiden. Male and female, body and soul, the divine twins of alchemy, dual aspects of one being, the chymical wedding. They had been there, in the Lascaris Manuscript's description of life in the Elder Time. Mikel and Eztar. Angel and Star. They had carried the duty with them, life after life, since then. This was the truth that had been bandaged by obscurity, the history which had been uncovered by Aurel Lockwood and Solomon Rapoport. All the evidence pointed to these two children, as true as a compass needle swings north. When the time came, they would know their duty and how to discharge it. So said the priestess, the Maman. The bee was her symbol and there was a sting. Adam, his beloved son, Mikel in the Elder World, the Chosen One, had to die by the hand of one he loved, of one who loved him. He had to die for the world to be born again.

That's what the Maman had told him. Once this was accomplished, Adam and the girl would return. But what if she was wrong? He would never see his son again. What if it was all for nothing? He turned to the shifting images of raging destruction; this was merely the beginning.

He touched a button, and the screens turned to black.

26

TEA WITH FRIENDS

"He must be in there somewhere. Don't give up!"

Brother Zack put the call on hold and studied the shifting street scenes on the monitors in front of him. The house in Forfar Street was empty, according to the men he had sent in to search it. Yet the cameras had shown no movement out of there. The surveillance team had reported nothing. Not that he had much faith in them any more. Poutney and the boy had got away from right under their noses.

"Are you still there?" he spoke into the phone again. "Check the basements and attics. We've traced a tunnel from the church. We think that's how Poutney and the boy got away." He listened for a moment. "Too narrow for his chair. Too sick to make it." He listened again, this time losing whatever little patience he had left. "He wasn't *seen* with them. So go and look *again*! Try the attic. There could be a way through to the other houses. I don't know. Evacuate the row. Say there's a bomb alert. Use your initiative!"

He folded the phone and slipped it into the pocket of

his surplice. These men were supposed to be the best of the best. Ex-MI5. Ex-SAS. They were not hired hands. There were Soldiers of the Faith in all the forces of law and order. Their belief made all the difference. No one else could be trusted. No hired men would be up to the job. Brother Zack knew all that, but at times they filled him with exasperation. They really were so stupid.

The operation at the Underground station had not gone much better. The boy had managed to slip the net. Not only that, but he'd linked up with the girl somehow. That was serious news. The two had been seen with a gang of black youths, they had been caught on camera. It was just a matter of time. The images were good. Clear. They had been sent to agents all over the city. He prepared his report. He had a different master now. The mysterious "honoured guest", the one known as the Advocate. He had taken over the Grand Master's Chamber: a circular stone crypt deep in the honeycomb of vaults that lay under the Temple. He was making it his own and had taken delivery of various pieces of electronic equipment, and a very large, very heavy crated box. Brother Zack had no idea what he was doing down there and did not enquire. Of Monsignor, the New Master, there was no sign. His rooms were deserted; his office empty. It was better not to ask questions. Curiosity was not a habit encouraged by the Order and Brother Zack remembered the Advocate's eyes. He had issued new directives. Brother Zack was now Marshal, so he was in charge of implementation. The Order ran a sophisticated network of trusted informants; the intelligence gathered by them was highly valued by government security services. Information had been passed on to them that a terrorist cell had attempted to poison the Underground system. This had been taken extremely seriously. The group had evaded capture. Their apprehension was now Priority One. City security was set at Critical.

The gang had split up almost immediately.

"No need to draw attention," Kris said.

"Do you think they know, then?" Adam was alarmed.

"Ha!" Kris laughed. The others joined in. "Where's your brain? Even if they don't know a thing, they pick us up anyway. Stop and search."

Adam and Zillah stuck with Kris and the big one called Maxwell. The others melted away from them into the crowd crossing the bridge by the Tower. Kris decided it was safest to walk and to keep off the main streets. As far as Adam could tell, they were heading south and east, but he had never been in this part of the city before.

"Where are we going?" Adam asked, more for a chance to slow down than anything, the ankle he'd twisted on his bad leg was paining him.

"To see me grandma, I told you, man!" The smaller boy grinned.

"Where does she live? How far is it?"

Kris kept up a tireless, relentless, pace that ate up the miles. Zillah had no problem keeping up, and Adam was ashamed that he did, but his ankle was really hurting now and he was limping badly. Zillah dropped back to keep pace with him and called for Kris to slow down a bit.

"Not far now," Kris called back. "Eh, Max?"

The other boy nodded and led them across a patch of litter-strewn scrubby land towards a large, sprawling housing development. The blocks were mainly low rise, four or five storeys, set at oblique angles to each other, linked by a series of concrete walkways, so it was like entering a three-dimensional maze. It would be hard to find your way out again. Impossible without Kris there to guarantee safe passage. Boys hung out at every turn and cross-cut, on every stairwell. Adam recognized one or two as members of Kris's gang. Kris nodded as he passed and exchanged a few muttered words of greeting. He touched knuckles or clasped hands as he went by them. He was well known, and respected. It was enough to veil the hostile looks that Adam was attracting. Zillah seemed a familiar face. When the boys grinned at her, and called her "sister", she gave a shy smile back. Good thing I'm with these two, Adam thought. A white boy on his own would be dead meat. No doubt about it.

Takeaway cartons and cans, cigarette butts and plastic bottles littered the zigzag twists of the dark, dank stairwells. The balconies were crusted with pigeon droppings, the narrow pathways obstructed by plastic rubbish bags and boxes full of bottles. Some of the doors were boarded; others were covered with thick metal security grilles.

Kris did not think that they had been followed. Outsiders came here rarely; a stranger would stand out a mile. Police were not seen often, and then only in numbers to carry out a raid. He had set the brothers to stand guard. The blocks acted like watch towers. If anyone suspect even set foot on the estate, they would know. Kris lived in the heart of it. Anyone looking to make trouble with him was unlikely to get that far.

"This is where me grandma live," Kris said to Adam, leading the way to a brightly painted red front door, secured behind stout wire mesh. "Fixed that myself." He took keys from a chain hanging from his belt. "Windows, too." There was a spyhole, like a fish eye, set in the centre of the door. Adam sensed a presence behind it. "It's me, Mamma," Kris shouted. "I found him. Let us in, yeah?"

Kris turned a series of keys. There was the sound of bolts being drawn back.

"Is Zillah with you?" The voice on the other side of the door sounded anxious. "Yeah, Mamma. She here, too," Kris replied.

The door opened. Kris's grandmother smiled in welcome. She was tiny, smaller than Kris, but there was a look of him about her mouth and the shape of her face. Her frame was as slim as a girl's and her face was smooth. It was hard to tell her age, except round the eyes where the skin wrinkled as she smiled.

"Glad you back safe." She reached up to embrace Zillah.

"What about me?" Kris grinned.

"You can look after yourself." She gave him a playful cuff and turned to Adam. "You must be Adam. Welcome. Welcome into my home. My name is Celestine."

Adam didn't question how she knew who he was. He just accepted that she did. Her eyes shone like moonlight on a bottomless pool that was dark and deep and full of unspoken knowledge.

"Let's get out of this draught."

Celestine pulled them into a narrow hallway with rooms going off left and right. She scolded her grandson as they went, apologizing for how he acted, how he dressed, how he spoke.

"Chill, Mamma." Kris smiled her exact same smile. "Don' stress yo'self. Ever'ting cool, hear me?"

"I tol' you! Don' talk like that. Sound like you been all your life in the Islands and you never set foot there once. You know I don't like it."

"It's black, Mamma. Street. Know what I'm sayin'?"

"You ain't in the street now, Christophe. You in my house."

"It's a flat! But all right." Kris's voice changed, losing its patois twang. "Adam? Meet my gran. This is what she's *really* like — a bossy old witch woman!"

She swatted at him and he dodged out of the way. Adam smiled. The teasing and scolding was a sign of the deep affection and regard that they had for each other. He felt a stab of envy as he followed them into the living room, feeling like he'd missed out. He simply didn't remember any kind of family life.

The room was L-shaped with a little area screened off at the end of it. Windows all along one side let panels of light on to polished wood floors strewn with bright rugs. The furniture was sparse but comfortable, covered in blankets woven with strong colours in chevron patterns and abstract shapes. The white drapes were drawn back to show a private balcony holding an array of leafy plants.

Celestine surveyed them with evident pride, looking out for a moment at the London sky.

"Hard to grow tings here. So cold and damp."

"It sunny today, Mamma!" Kris objected.

"No warmth in it!" she snapped back. "Plants need warmth or they don't grow right."

"Maybe you shouldn't try to grow stuff like bananas and pawpaws."

"Christophe?" She ignored her grandson's last comment. "Offer our guest something to drink, something to eat. Where's your manners?"

Kris hauled himself up from the chair where he had sprawled and went off to the kitchen. His voice came back.

"There's juice, Coke, or do you want tea?"

"Juice," Adam said.

"Zillah?"

"Yeah," Zillah agreed. "Fine by me."

Kris came back with the drinks. "What we got to eat?"

"Casserole in the oven. Rice on the stove."

"That OK with you?"

"Yeah." They both nodded.

Adam took a long drink. Mango and something. He couldn't help his stomach from grumbling at the thought of food. He hadn't realized he was so hungry. The day had piled event on event. He had no idea what had happened to his father. He could have been taken. He might even be dead. He had put himself in danger to get Adam away in order for him to find this girl, but now here they were, just like regular teenagers, having tea, like they'd just come home from school, or something. Adam was taken by the strangeness of it. What exactly was going to happen?

27

MIRRORS

They remained sitting at the table while Christophe cleared away the plates. He said he was going out to check on things and would be back later.

Celestine waited for the door to slam and for the flat to go quiet.

"Let's make ourselves comfortable." She invited them to join her in the living area, seating them side by side on the sofa. "You got to understand some things before we start."

Adam looked at Zillah. Start what?

"I am from the Sugar Isles," Celestine went on. "Tainos. A little island in a chain off the coast of Honduras. My people took as slaves, although not all from the same place in Africa. Different tribes, different homelands. Europeans come from France, Britain and Spain. Conquistadors from South America. The natives who live there before any of us disappear. But not all. There's a big mix on one little island. Different peoples, different languages, different faiths. But we find common threads of belief. From that come a new religion. It go by different names, but we call it Vodoun."

"*Voodoo?*" Adam asked. Zillah's eyes opened wide. That came out pretty near the top of "erroneous and idolatrous beliefs".

Celestine nodded. "That's one of the names. Don't believe what you hear. There's a lot of evil nonsense spoken by ignorant people who don't know what they are talkin' about. There is good, there is evil. Just the same in any religion. It's a mix. Like that stew. Tasted good. Yes?"

They both nodded.

"That depend on the hand doing the cooking. Too much of this, not enough of that? It taste bad. Pinch of something that shouldn't be in it, left too long on a hot day, it poison you. Does that mean that you shouldn't make stew?"

"No," Zillah said. "It just means you ought to be careful."

"That's right." Celestine smiled. "Thank you, child. You have to be careful to do harm to no one.

"We all mix with natives from the island itself. In their tradition, the islands are the remnants of a drowned world. A civilization much older than the Mayan who live on the mainland. In their story, they tell of a people who came from the sea, from a ruined land that they have to leave to start again. They bring many things with them, knowledge and wisdom. They worship a Father God, and a Mother." She grasped the bee she wore at her chest. "Their religion got a dark side, too," her face clouded, "but they know how to keep it under control. They live in peace and prosperity for many years, then the sea rose again. They move on to the mainland. Then the white man come, try to stamp out what they left behind, but a lot still there, if you care to look. A man came looking. Named Buller Wesson. . ."

Adam sat up, alerted by the name. He and Brice Ambrose Stone seemed to have followed the same path, gathering information about the past. Beside him, Zillah frowned, wondering what the Esteemed Founder had to do with all this.

"You heard of him, I see."

Zillah remembered the trunks and cases, the labels from exotic places. Maybe one of them marked a trip to the Caribbean and Celestine's island.

"But I always assumed that the Founder had shed—" she stopped herself from using the C6D terminology. "Was dead."

"No," Celestine shook her head, "he's very much alive. And he's coming back."

"Just like in the prophecy?" Zillah sat forward. "But how? And why now? All the Children are dead!"

"They have served his purpose." Celestine looked uneasy. "From what you been telling me about your Advocate, he might already be here."

"What do you mean?"

"A man like him, skilled in the black arts, knows how to take over another, live in his skin. When he wants to, when it is convenient for him."

Adam thought about his father, all that he had been told. There was a shift in the room, a difference in

251

atmosphere. He felt that they were moving towards something. Moving fast.

"Do you know my father?" he asked Celestine. "Is he all right?"

Her answer was enigmatic. "We been in contact. I know his will and intention. He's all right. At the moment. But unless we can stop this thing, none of us going to be all right. There's no time to waste. Good or bad. We got to act now."

Now it came down to it, Adam felt his mouth go dry and his stomach begin to sink with elevator swiftness. His father had primed him for this. He had not spoken a word that Adam recalled, but he knew exactly what he had to do and he was ready. Almost without thinking, he reached for Zillah's hand.

"You ready?" Celestine asked Zillah.

Zillah looked. Her black-rimmed, blue-green eyes gave her face a distinctive beauty. Opaline aquamarine, her eyes seemed to speak of distant places. Just how distant she was about to find out. Zillah nodded and clutched the bee round her neck to show that she was ready. Celestine took a deep breath. Now things would happen very quickly. She picked up a mirror from the table. It was just an ordinary, cheap, steel-framed mirror, the kind that is magnified on one side and that men use for shaving and women use for make-up. She flicked it with a finger so that it began to rotate.

"Look into it," she said.

Adam and Zillah stared, following the fleeting images that they could see as the reflective surfaces presented themselves, one side then the other. They could not catch and keep their own images; they seemed to be chasing their own faces, which made them look deeper and deeper. . .

As they stared on, so it seemed that the surface broke up into a myriad shifting, glinting facets of shining blackness, interrupted by tiny flecks of white, like static on a TV screen, except that these were whirling and turning like snowflakes falling downwards, ever downwards to lose themselves on the restless, ever moving surface of a dim, dark sea. . .

They fell back on to the sofa, and Celestine watched from the chair opposite. If the thing was going to happen, it would happen fast. The seconds ticked by and became minutes, then hours. The darkness gathered outside and Celestine rose to pull the curtains, first the inner gauzy material that reminded her of home, then the heavy outer drapes, wide stripes of rainbow colours, which she'd put up to keep out the London cold.

She returned to take up her vigil, her heart sinking deeper and deeper inside her. Something had gone wrong. If it was going to happen, it should have happened by now. The shift should be almost instantaneous. The two of them should be gone. They should not still be here, deep in trance, lying on her sofa. They should be somewhere else, tucked up in bed, leading different lives.

They lay with their hands linked. They had only just met in this life, but the love was strong between them.

Still the same problem. That is what had happened before. She would not allow doubt to infect her purpose. There was only one thing left to do. She listened for Christophe, for the scrape of his key in the locks on the door. She had hoped to spare him, but things had gone wrong already. She would have to send Christophe after them. He was the Messenger and had his own part to play in the Elder World. She did not like to put these young people in harm's way, but if this was not done, there would be no future for anyone. She sent out a prayer, for her own Christophe, for these children in her care, and all the while fear added to the heaviness weighing on her heart, lodging there like a slab of ice.

28

THE GRAND MASTER'S CHAMBER

The Advocate stood in an octagonal chamber that had been built many centuries ago as the Chapter House and meeting place for the inner circle of an Order who had shared in the knowledge and worshipped the skull. Pale cream stone lined the walls and a low bench had been carved into the eight facets of the octagon. The room was simple and carried no decoration, although the wealth of the Order was clearly displayed in the quality of the stone, the delicate architecture of the slender columns and the splayed fingers of the fan vaulting.

He walked around the room. All was in place. All was in order. He awaited the Grand Master's return, the moment when he would erupt from the deep past into the present. Already there had been passages of transmigration. The man known as the Advocate hardly existed as anything other than a convenient title and a suit of clothes, to be inhabited at will, like now. He had not *disappeared*, as such. Merely changed. The Grand Master was taking over his body, as well as his soul. To anyone who had known him, the changes would have been obvious: his face had become heavier, fleshier, a deep scar had appeared, like a hole drilled into his cheek, and he looked out with different eyes. But what did that matter? Those who had known the Advocate were all dead now. Their number included the New Master, who lay like a folded puppet, in the far corner of a dusty vault in a distant part of the undercroft. His throat torn out. The Advocate sucked at a fragment caught between his teeth. During his long wandering as Ket, priest of the Elder World, he had developed an appetite for human flesh.

The Grand Master's corporal being had rotted long ago. He was now Imago, emerging from one form into another. Soon, he would be ready to change again. Soon. He paced the room. He had journeyed far, far into the past to return with the knowledge that would unlock the secrets of the dark skull. Their *Ars Magna*, their Great Work, would come to nothing. All those centuries spent channelling the light away from darkness would be so much wasted time. From darkness they had come; to darkness they would return. The world would be reborn, transmutation would occur, was occurring now; he was the living proof. He felt the power of the beast surge through him, straining against the thin sheath of his human skin. Nothing could stop it now.

He left that room and went to another where a transparent screen showed a map of the world. Red spots pulsed, showing the principle cities on every continent. At the touch of a button an intricate geometric pattern connected them. The cities aligned along invisible lines of

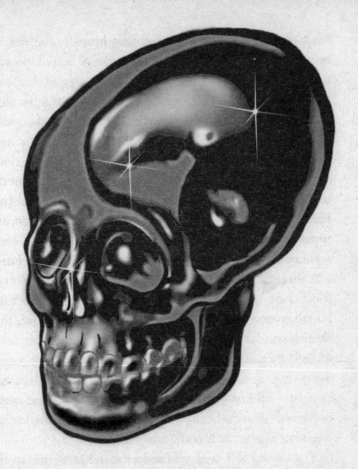

power, which, in turn, linked particular points in the landscape where the earth current flowed strong: certain hills and mounds, the place where two rivers met, the space between two bodies of water. The positioning and layout had been dictated by rules long ago forgotten, by geomancy, the lost and ancient earth magic, but cities are built on the dust of cites which have risen and fallen before them. Within the cities lay further talismans: pillars, pyramids and obelisks, placed for decoration only, their true significance long ago forgotten. These would be activated when the time came. The earth power would channel upwards into the facsimiles of Ancient Ones: dragon and cockatrice, basilisk and griffin; jaculus and wyvern that had been formed in stone and metal, quarried and mined from the earth itself. The atoms within them would become realigned. They could come *alive*! The ancient gods would wake across the world, above ground and below it. The Ouroboros, the Jörmungandr, the great serpent who circled the world, would cease biting his tail, uncurl and unleash his power across the globe. The designated time of the Concurrence was almost upon them. Everything was ready. West would meet East, the earth's magnetic field would reverse. North would become South. The knowledge within the skull of dark crystal would pass though him and complete *his* transformation, just as Lockwood's ritual tablet would wake the god whom the Chaldeans called Mimma Lemnu – All that is Evil. The basalt sarcophagus had been delivered. The clay effigy, looted by his order from the Baghdad Museum, was already in place.

Lockwood. He seemed far, far off in his memory. An image came to him now like a faded daguerreotype: hair parted in the middle, weak jaw hidden by a thin beard. And that fool of a poet, with his round glasses and lock of dark hair falling across his forehead. A handsome boy. He stood for a moment, conjuring faces. There was another. His brow creased and his face darkened. The American. When he tried to remember him, he encountered only blankness. For the first time in this incarnation, he experienced something resembling fear. He shook his head. No matter. Nothing would stop him. Certainly not a Yankee mystery man, or that lame-footed boy. . .

For a moment, he experienced another pang. That boy was important. He should have been collected. The idiot of a New Master had paid for that. The boy had been there from the beginning, his presence continuing. He'd gone under many different names: Mani, the Child of the Light; Mithras, the Living Spirit; Dionysus, the Bull-footed God of Light; Hermes; Horus; Weiland the Smith; Llew of the Ancient Britons. He'd always been a danger. And the girl. She had somehow managed to evade capture since slipping beneath the notice of the one previously known as the Advocate. And there was Black. He had comprehensively fooled the Order, posing as a down and out, and they *still* couldn't find him. He had turned out to be an adept. They should have known that and eliminated him when they had the chance. Then there was the black woman and her grandson. Ordinarily, such comprehensive incompetence would enrage him, but there was no one left to punish. Except Brother Zack. The rite needed blood and he would do nicely. He had let the boy slip through his fingers too many times. It did not do to underestimate your enemy, but his opponents were insignificant, as powerless in this world as in any other. They were an irrelevance. Whatever puny plan they were hatching would be too late. The light that they carried, always fitful at best, would soon be extinguished by the coming darkness. Their time was at an end; the hours were draining away like sand through a glass.

He turned away from the map and entered the sacrarium, the holy of holies, lit only by the red glow of a vigil light. Again, this was an octagonal room, but one facet of the octagon was taken up by a simple rectangular altar. He stepped behind this and opened the wooden door of an aumbry set into the wall. With enormous care and great reverence he removed the skull, shrouded in soft leather. Everything depended on this thing, the knowledge it contained, the power he could unleash. He let his hand stray under the velvet thin skin, touching the slippery contours, as a blind man might explore the face of a loved one.

He could *taste* the power he would soon use, like sulphur in his mouth, salts on his tongue. He stood a moment, with his eyes closed, and let out a sound somewhere between a hiss and a sigh.

On the edge of the City, a passer-by had the shock of his life. He hurried on down the Embankment, legs shaking, as far as Cleopatra's Needle, where he had to sit down. He stared straight out at the river. He did not want to look back. He had been passing the griffin which stands on its plinth, guarding the City, its front and back claws raised in the heraldic posture *sergeant*. And, now this was the weird part, he could have sworn that, as he walked past, the beast had turned its head towards him and opened a bronze-lidded eye.

29

TIME PASSING

Abraham Black stared at the calendar on the opposite wall. Stone carved, and brightly painted, it was a living, moving thing to him, operating in three dimensions, making up complex patterns, each circle turning in an opposite direction, meshing together to show the slow, inexorable passage of time. He started forward, gripping the sides of his chair, watching for the smallest of changes, the tiniest of flickers.

Nothing yet. His thoughts were with his son and the girl. A heavy duty lay upon them. Was death and sacrifice the only way? His doubts deepened. Was it possible to die in one world, but live in another? Or would Adam be dead in both as soon as the girl struck him? Would she emerge free of the taint of murder? Would either of them come back at all? What if it went wrong? What if it was all for nothing? So many questions and no answers. It made Black heart-sick to think about it. His despair took him to bleak, stony depths of utter blackness. He waited for the wave of emotion to subside and made himself focus on the tiny spirals that marked fate and destiny. He leant back in his chair. Perhaps he could find another answer there.

He began calculations, copying glyphs with a pencil, but he was making mistakes, his hand was shaking so much. He groped in one of the desk's many compartments for an eraser, but instead, his finger found a small brass key. Black frowned, turning it over in his hand. He scanned the desk. There was no lock to fit it that he could see. He looked more carefully. This was Lockwood's desk, his cabinet he liked to call it, and it was full of surprises. The edging beneath the bottom drawers seemed out of proportion, thicker than it should be in such a beautifully worked walnut piece. He felt along the veneer and sure enough, a thin panel slid away to expose a concealed drawer. Black fitted the key.

The drawer contained a thin cardboard folder tied with pink ribbon and with *The Stone Testament* written across it in Lockwood's own hand. Black blew off the layer of fine grey dust that had filtered through to its hiding place. Beneath the buff cover lay a sheaf of thin, old-fashioned onion skin typing paper.

He turned the pages over. Under his fingers, the ribbed lines of typing felt like Braille. The type was singled-spaced and travelled to the edges of each page. The print was smudged, the black ink tinged green by time. Some of the letters were uneven, showing wear on the keys, but it was still perfectly legible. He started to read.

Letter received 18 January, 1960

My Dear Mr Lockwood,

It is my duty to inform you of the sad demise of one who called himself Brice Ambrose Stone and claimed to be the man of letters who disappeared in Mexico many years ago.

Mr Stone has been a guest at this facility for some while now, and has suffered progressive ill health. He passed away peacefully last Thursday week and his last conscious wish was for certain papers to be sent to you. He extracted a solemn promise from me and I am writing to you in order to fulfil my duty.

I do, however, think you should know something about his condition, and how he came to be with us. It is a strange tale. Mr Stone was found many years ago in a Peruvian port by the crew of a whaler out of San Francisco. They discovered him on the harbour front begging and in rags. He spoke in English, and the whalers could tell by his accent that he was a countryman, although the words he babbled made no sense at all. When they asked who he was, and how he came to be there, none of the locals had any idea. Some said that he had been brought in by a fishing boat, rescued after a shipwreck; others that he had been found wandering in the hinterland, living on roots and berries. The whale men were reluctant to leave a fellow countryman in that state and, as they were on their homeward run, they brought him back to San Francisco.

Unfortunately, his experiences appear to have had a deep and lasting effect on his mental state and he was brought here for treatment. We did what we could, but his condition was chronic. In the end, we could only care for his bodily needs and make him comfortable.

I do not wish to give the impression that he was a troublesome patient. Although frequently withdrawn, and at other times absorbed in a world other than our own, he was always peaceable and generally friendly, spending much of his time helping in the library. We encourage inmates to express themselves in whatever way they can, and over the years, he worked on an account of his experiences. These are the papers that I am forwarding to you. He was a perfectionist, writing and rewriting obsessively, often destroying previous drafts.

He maintained to the last that this was a true account, but he was subject to many delusions. The powerful, mind-altering drugs that he admits to having taken, along with the privations that he subsequently suffered, almost certainly destroyed his sanity. His writings, therefore, have to be regarded as the ravings of a madman, although they do contain obvious evidence of story-telling talent.

I am sending the papers to you via the American publisher of your work. In doing so, I have fulfilled my duty to a man whom, despite his frequent delusional states, I grew to like and respect.

Make of his testimony, what you will.

Yours very sincerely,

Dr Douglas Haughton
Director
Stockton State Hospital (Formerly Insane Asylum of California at Stockton)
510 E Magnolia Street
Stockton
California

Abraham Black put aside the covering letter and turned to the testament proper. He had never read it. Never even seen it. Lockwood had said merely that Stone had died in an asylum. He had never mentioned this testimony. He must have locked it away upon receipt, mourning his friend, sorrowing at his sad end, not wanting him exposed to the judgement of others, saddened that such a fine mind had ended up wandering, lost in the twisting, labyrinthine paths of the no longer sane. Whatever his reasons, Black would never know them now.

Stone had taken strong drugs and Black distrusted the veracity of any knowledge thus obtained, but he was desperate for anything, anything that might give him hope.

He had schooled himself to believe there was no other way, but his spirit, every human feeling within him, rebelled against the idea of sacrifice. If he was sending Adam to his death . . . if he was never coming back. . . However much time Black had left would be too long for him to live with that. Again, guilt and despair threatened to overwhelm him but this time he drove them back. He unscrewed the cap on his Omas Lucens fountain pen and began to make notes in small, neat italics.

The Stone Testament

Journeys, physical and spiritual

I have been a traveler, a pilgrim, all my life: questing after truth, searching for knowledge and adventure in equal part. My desire for new experiences has taken me to many strange places. None stranger than the one I am going to tell you about now.

I had been traveling through South America, searching for the tribe who were the keepers of the fabled skull of dark crystal. I found no sign of them, apart from a few ruined huts abandoned in the forest. Fearing that Wesson had got there ahead of me, I embarked on a different journey. I had been told of a vine, used by the shamans in those parts. An extract from this particular plant, so I was informed, enabled the supplicant to fly, to move between worlds. My quest took me to a tribe in the Upper Amazon. The ingredients in the concoction they used were secret, but it was made from some species of datura, I think, mixed with ayahuasca, the vine of dead souls. Whatever the contents, it only succeeded in making me violently ill.

Sick, and sorry at heart, burdened with a terrible sense of dread and failure, I followed the turbulent dark waters of the Urubamba up into the mountains and came eventually to the mysterious city of the Incas, Machu Picchu, discovered by my old friend, Hiram Bingham. I spent some time there. That wondrous, sacred place, all hidden in that green wilderness, gave me solace and soothed my troubled spirit. From there, I moved on down the Andes, until I reached Lake Titicaca and the ruins of Tiahuanaco. There was much to learn there also, and much to wonder at, not least the great works in stone that marked the former margins of that mysterious lake. I moved further toward the coast, where I was shown great lines in the desert, left by some lost people. Everywhere I went, I was told the same legend. These great works were left by an earlier people, an advanced civilization that had existed here many thousands of years previously. This civilization had been founded by a stranger named Virococha, which means Foam of the Sea. He was described as a tall man, grey-haired and bearded, wearing a simple belted robe. He had come by ship at a time of deluge and chaos and had with him a devoted band of followers. They brought order with them, and civilization. They were scientists, magicians, engineers, and had built the roads, terraces, buildings and monuments, at which I had marveled. Later peoples had merely maintained what they had done. They had left as mysteriously as they had come, sailing north and taking their knowledge with them. In a dream, I was told to follow them.

The quickest way was by sea. I took a boat from Lima. I was the only passenger, but my berth was comfortable, the food tolerable, the captain a pleasant fellow, fond of a brandy or two and a good cigar. I spent a week or so in reasonable contentment while the vessel plied its way up the coast. Then a great storm blew up. The engine room was swamped, leaving us drifting and helpless, at the mercy of the currents. We were being taken further and further south. It got colder by the day. The radio had ceased to work. We sent up flares but saw no other craft of any kind, although whalers are frequent in those latitudes. The sea was an oily calm and fog banks enfolded us like soft, wet blankets. It was eerie, as though we sailed other seas entirely.

We were at the mercy of the sea, and she did not take pity on us. It was a clear day. The fog had lifted. The waters about us were tranquil. The sky was blue, not a cloud in it, when the mate started to shout. His voice gave way to sheer terror and it was all he could do to point dumbly with a shaking finger. Out of nowhere, a forty-foot wave was heading toward us. A great wall of green water scooped up out of a calm sea. There was nothing anyone could do. No evasive action to be taken. It hit within minutes with incredible force.

I found myself pitched from the ship. I don't even remember hitting the water. I had no sense of departure, still less of arrival. It was as though I had fallen into a great abyss. If there was no beginning, there could be no ending. I felt as though I had tumbled out of time.

I do not, therefore, remember how I came to be thrown up on that dark and dismal shore, or how I ceased to be Brice Ambrose Stone and came to be Aynegeru, the Fair One, Traveler from a Far Land, but I now believe that my coming there was no accident. It had a purpose, which will, I hope, become clear to you also as you read this account. . .

Black put down his pen. The two plants to which Stone referred, datura and ayahuasca, were highly dangerous and known to induce a catatonic state, counterfeiting death, if not death itself. These powerful substances might have broken the hinges of his mind, or Stone might actually have travelled, in some shamanistic deathlike trance, brought on by these drugs or by some other means. Everything that happened after his visit to the tribe who gave him the decoction could have been part of one long shamanistic journey which could have eventually taken him to the Elder World as Aynegeru, Traveller from a Far Land. If that was so, then Stone was an eye witness to events in the deep past. This was the testimony of one who had been there before. . .

30

THEN THERE WERE THREE

"Hey, Mamma, we got to. . ." Kris burst in and then broke off what he was about to say. "What's the matter with them two? They look dead or something!" His voice rose in panic. "What have you done to them?"

"I done nothing."

"You give 'em something?"

Celestine shook her head.

"Well, you done something!" Kris picked up Zillah's hand and let it drop back. "She's as floppy as a rag doll. Him, too." Kris's brow wrinkled. He was not believing this. "No, Mamma, not now."

"They won't come to harm. Effect is short-term. Wear off soon, I promise you. They be right as rain."

"I don't care about their come-down, Mamma." Kris tugged at his knotted hair. "We got to get them out of here!"

"Why?"

"There's guys searching the estate. They are all over the place. Look like special forces. Don't know if they are or not, but they mean business. They're tooled up with Heckler and Koch. I can't ask my guys to go against them. Only thing we can do is get them two to a safe house, and how we gonna do that if they out of it?"

"They can walk. They can hear you talk. They ain't as helpless as they look."

He looked at her, comprehension dawning. "You've made 'em. . ."

"Zombi? Nearest thing. So much nonsense said about that! Just a state of trance. Same in other faiths – don't have no trashy films made about Buddhism, though, do we?"

"Mamma, I know all about that." She was a Maman, a priestess, much revered and respected. He had no idea why she had taken this action and he did not question it. Just the timing could have been better. "They got to be moved. Like now. How long they goin' to be this way?"

She shrugged.

He thought for a moment. "Get them ready. I'll get a couple of the boys. I'll take you down to the safe place. Then see what we can do here. Got to deconstruct. Make it look empty. Get them off our backs."

"Don't break anything."

"Don't worry, Mamma. . ." He picked up the mirror on the table, making ready for the removal. He glanced at his reflection, as if checking his appearance. "That's funny," he said, spinning to the side that magnified. "I can't see my face."

Now there were three of them. She stared down at them for a moment before going outside. She beckoned to the boy who was lounging against the end of the concrete catwalk. He spoke into his phone as he came towards her, ready to summon others. They would know what to do. After that? Who knew? What will be, will be. The only thing certain was that she would be there to watch over them. Whatever happened, she would see it through. She looked at the three of them, lying side by side, and wondered where they were travelling in the Elder Time. . .

In the panic room, Black was suddenly alerted to a change in the intricate movement of the clock. The signs for the Twins and the Messenger merged and crossed. He sat forward in his seat. The wheeling symbols had noted Adam, Zillah and Kris travelling back into the past. He sent out a silent prayer to any power that might be listening, but the movement did not stop. Apart from that tiny little judder, it went on, just as it had done for century upon century. The sacrifice had not been made. Not yet anyway. Abraham Black did not know whether to rejoice or be very afraid.

Inside the crystal skull, the twin commas of the hippocampus glowed a sickly violet, like a bruise blooming deep inside the brain. They took on the hue of the skull's dark twin, as if some force had activated them. The clock responded with a flickering oscillation. A fall of dust from the ceiling powdered his hair and shoulders, as if there had been some perturbation within the earth itself. Wesson was at work. Either as Grand Master in this world, or Ket in the other. He was present in the Elder World, according to Stone, and he was growing in power, while Black was forced to sit here, unable to influence anything. He felt little rills of panic running through him. Panic room, aptly named. Despair washed over him. If he didn't decide on a course of action, it would become his tomb.

Abraham Black stared at the crystal skull. His focus had always tended towards the Lascaris Manuscript, its warnings of choices not taken, and Lockwood's Sumerian Rite, but what if he had been wrong? What if another, equally powerful talismanic object was necessary to bring the changes Wesson sought to fruition? The Dark Skull. Old World, New World, what did it matter? All these mysterious, ancient objects had come from a place the Sumerians had named the *Faraway*. And here was the testimony of one who had been there: a true account of events aeons distant. Events that could still shape the present.

Abraham Black acted swiftly. He used all his psychic force to project across time and space, as swift as thought's arrow, a message to his son in the deep past.

ELDER TIME

I

I was conducted to what I took to be the capital city: a great port set high on cliffs overlooking a deep circular bay. The city was full of fine stone buildings: some in the style of Central America or the ziggurats of Mesopotamia; others were more like the solid slab temples of Egypt before the pyramids. Such building indicated that this had once been a thriving, prosperous society, but it was clear that those times were over. Despite their privations, the people treated me with kindness.

I was put in the House of Strangers and called Aynegeru, but that was soon shortened to Ayne as I found a place in their society. I worked building boats and learnt to sail, skills that would save my life. I also took my turn in the Company, an elite body of fighting men made up entirely of foreigners, rather like the janissaries of the Ottoman Turks.

THE STONE TESTAMENT – Brice Ambrose Stone

Eztar left the House of the Mother. The End of Days was approaching. Soon the boats would be leaving. Some had left already and were lying offshore waiting for the Ativeteh. A great test was coming, the Ama, Presence of the Mother on Earth, had told her. A test for the people, a test for the Ativeteh, Wise Ruler and Mikel's father, and a test for her. Mikel was in the far North, her task was to find him, and then? She refused to think about the other test that had been set for her.

She rode through the city and all around her were signs of decay. Reeds spiked through the pavements. Grass grew in the precincts of the deserted palaces. Wild dogs snarled in the courtyard of the Red Temple of the Seers. The great carved wooden doors of the Palace of Art stood open to the wind and the weather. Tablets lay broken outside the Temple of Inscription. The dark pools on the roof of the round Tower of the Stargazers were crusted with ice.

Year on year, the cold had increased. The crops had failed, all but the hardiest animals had perished, and the people had died of disease and starvation in their hundreds, in their thousands. The Stargazers had predicted that this would happen. They kept themselves apart, marked out from other people by their dyed-red beards and large, wide open eyes emphasized by outlining charcoal. They studied the sky in the still reflecting pools night after night, until the years became centuries. Every little change in the stars was noted and recorded, the knowledge passed on from generation to generation. The heavens had altered in their courses, they reported. The constellations were scattered to different parts of the heavens or had disappeared all together, crossing the horizon for ever. The Seven Sisters no longer rose and set in their accustomed places. Blotches besmirched the face of the sun at noon and by night the sky was made light by swirling veils of colour. They were coming to the End of Days.

People reacted in unpredictable ways. Many reasoned that, for this to be happening, they must have displeased the Gods somehow; the Beast Gods, the Elder Gods who had been here since the time that the land was created. Their priests were quick to preach that the present tribulations were the result of the Gods' displeasure. They had called for more and more sacrifice and the call had been answered.

Eztar's way took her past their temple, the Place of Skulls: a huge, four-sided stone building which tapered up from its massive base in a series of steps to a flat-roof open shrine at the apex. Mikel had told her that the Beast Gods' Temple had been built to mirror the exact shape of the Sacred Mountain. Beyond the mountains lay the Forbidden Lands and the great red rock, Ha'itzilazki, the sacred home of the Beast Gods. The different places were in a line with each other, Mikel had said, one taking power from the other, all supposedly strengthened by sacrifice.

A huge, lounging human figure of polished red stone

stared out with sightless eyes from the shrine at the top of the temple, his lap drenched with blood. He was Xtal, the Old, Old One, who bore men's hearts to the Gods. He was flanked on four sides by the towering forms of the principal Beast Gods. Carved from the hardest grey speckled rock, they glared out, claws raised, teeth bared, from the cardinal points: Sigur, the Chief of All, faced north; Hortzhaganak, the Toothed One, faced south; Matxin-Salto; the Destroyer, gazed east; staring westwards was Eltlxar, Lord of the Flies. He had his great slotted eye upon her now. On the next tier down stood the lesser lords: Atzamar, Plague and Fire; Labana, Lord of Weapons and War; Otso, the Fierce One and Haize, Lord of the Wind.

Normally, Eztar would have avoided any proximity to their vile, polluting presence, but today she stared back at them, her head held high. She was a Warrior of the Mother and would show no fear. Skull racks ran along the base of the massive structure, ending each side of the central stairway. Heads in different stages of decay crowded the stone shelves. The top rack was relatively fresh, the heads' features almost recognizable through the swollen bloat; the lips only just beginning to creep back to reveal the grin of death. Further down the heads were just naked skulls with only a few tufts of dark hair adhering and patches of cracked brown skin. Some of them wore empty grins where the teeth had been removed to make masks. When the skulls were clean of all flesh they were taken and stacked inside cages. Blood silted the steps in clotted drifts. In warmer times the stench had been unendurable, the whole structure a black and buzzing mass of flies.

Sacrifice was piled on sacrifice, but still the land went on dying. The noon-day shadow on the longest day had failed to descend straight down the steps of the temple, but had fallen crooked, like a broken-backed snake. And word had come, rumours from the East, that the Gods were dying, too. They were flesh and blood, the whisper went, just like us, dependant on other great creatures for their nurture and sustenance, just as we eat sheep and cattle. And these great creatures were falling in their tracks, killed by the cold. They were not Gods at all.

Such words were shocking. A terrible heresy. Among the unbelievers was the Ativeteh, Mage King, first and wisest of the Seven.

Eztar had been there when he came to speak to the Ama.

"There is no saving the land," he had said. His face had been deeply troubled. The cheeks were hollow above his blue-stained beard; the skin around the eyes crinkled and dry, like a leaf after winter. "The only way to survive is to leave it," he'd gone on in a quiet voice as if, even here, deep in the House of the Mother, he might be overheard. "Last night I woke from sleep. It was as if a voice spoke close to my ear. 'Build boats,' the voice said. 'Fill them with those who have knowledge and wisdom, let them take useful animals, the seeds of life, all which is needful. Take ships and convey your people away from this land. On no account allow the Beast Gods to go with you, or all will perish. And beware: the End of Days is near and they will soon be upon you. Leave the Beast Gods here. Only men can build ships.' It was Patiku, Only Father," he added. "Chief among the Younger Gods."

The Ama nodded. "I heard Him, too."

"What shall we do?"

"We must obey."

"And defy the Elder Gods?"

"They are blood and bone!" the Ama declared from behind her silver mask. "They are no more gods than you or I. Boats offer the only way to leave the island and leaving is the only way to survive, for beasts or men. They will seek to prevent you, steal the boats from you, but remember the words of Patiku. For the sake of humankind, and all other creatures. The Beast Gods have to stay here. They have to die in the great cold coming. They have to perish like the trees falling. There can be no place for them anywhere on the earth."

The Ativeteh went back to the Seven, who had all agreed. If they were gods, why would they need to escape? They decided that a great fleet of ships should be built. The Sea Kings were called together; experienced captains and navigators who knew the sea roads as well as others knew the long, straight ways that criss-crossed the land. They studied their maps and divided up the world between them like sections of a fruit. Mikel, the Ativeteh's son and talented Far Seer, had been sent to the Cape of Souls to play his own part in this mission.

The work was nearly done when word spread that the Beast Gods were coming out of the Forbidden Land. They knew about the ships. Azhdarchs, great flying creatures, had been seen above the harbours. Immediately, there was talk against the Ativeteh. The old ways were not being respected. That is why the Gods were coming. Why provoke their anger? Respect and proper sacrifice might make the Gods strong again and yet save the land. Once in every lifetime, a Prince of the Blood had to take the Way of Tears up to the Sacred Mountain. Perhaps that time had come. The Ativeteh thinks only of saving his son.

As the Beast Gods approached the city, the Ativeteh returned to consult the Ama.

"The solution is simple," she told him. "They will seek to take the ships from you. You must leave before they can."

"But we are not ready!"

"Then you must play for time. Practise subterfuge upon them. Make them *think* that you are giving the ships to them, but they *must* not leave this land. They sow destruction wherever they go. They kill out of pure wantonness. Their route from the mountains is a trail of destruction. They leave nothing living along their path. You must leave now. There is great perturbation on the earth and in the heavens. The Eye of the Sea is turning."

The Ativeteh's face turned the colour of ash. Mikel would be waiting at the cape for him, as they had arranged, in a little bay of calm deep water under the great towering cliffs, but if the Eye of the Sea had awakened, then no ship would be able to land.

"I cannot abandon my own son!"

"I will put the boy under my protection."

The Ama looked at him. This would be their last

private meeting. The Beast Gods were poised to enter the city. The Ama, wearing her golden mask of ceremony, was ready to meet them in the Hall of the Ancestors. Concern about the boy could swerve him from his purpose and that could be disastrous. He was father to all the people, not just his son by blood.

"Do not worry about him, Ativeteh. Hear Her words and be comforted."

She took him into the Chamber of Oracles. Eztar waited outside, for such consultations were private. When the Ativeteh left his face was even more haggard and his beard streaked with white. He walked past her, blind to all but the Word of the Mother. The Ama beckoned Eztar forward.

"I will not be leaving on the ships." Her eyes showed like bright black beads in the bland burnished face. "I am ready to join the Ancestors, ready to go down into the darkness."

"But, Ama!" Eztar cried out in alarm. "What shall we do without—"

"Hush! And hear me! You must find Mikel at the Cape of Souls."

"And then?"

"The Mother will tell you what to do."

Eztar had followed her into the Chamber of Oracles. The voice that spoke to her there was so soft and freighted with love and honey-sweetness that Eztar wept like a little child, but the words she spoke were as bitter as the choking herb that the Seers took when they wanted to leave for another world.

Eztar passed a contingent from the Company of

Strangers. The elite corps of scouts and warriors normally bristled with pride and fighting spirit, but they were returning to the city weary and defeated, their faces gaunt, their eyes staring off into some imagined distance; even the youngest among them had been made old by what they had seen.

The Beast Gods would approach by the Ancient Way which ran in a straight line from the Sacred Mountain and came into the city by the Dark Gate. This road was also called the Way of Tears because children who were taken to the Sacred Mountain did not come back again. Once inside the city walls, the Ancient Way became the Way of Ceremony and passed through the myriad little houses that made up the Hive. The small dwellings were locked together in clumps and rows, just like the cells of a honeycomb. The Hive had once been Eztar's home. A place of colour and laughter, the little buildings kept brightly painted, the house altars and niches tended, ferns and flowers from the forest strewn round the clay figurines of the Goddess. Now, many parts of the Hive were failing: thin flanked dogs skulked in the alleys and fought over stinking carrion; deserted children wandered, wailing; the painted dwellings crumbled and dissolved back to clay. The Hive was sacred to the Mother. Her sign of the bee was everywhere, but faith in Her was failing, too, as it was in all the gods.

Eztar wore the golden bee under her tunic. The sign that she was a Warrior Priestess of the Goddess. She prayed now to the Ama for the strength to fulfil the mission assigned to her. She had wanted to witness the Beast Gods' entrance to the city, but she couldn't tarry.

She urged her pony forward. When the Beasts entered the city, she had to be far from here.

She let the Company of Strangers pass. She would have liked to know what news they had, but turned her pony to the White Gate and the road northwards. Always she could hear the voice of the Mother, roaring and whispering like the sound from a shell pressed to her ear.

"There are worse things than death, Eztar."

Eztar took the White Road out of the city. To the east, across the Plain of Agirre, the Mountains of Men ran straight north to the oceans and south as far as the eye could see. In the south, they joined the Mountains in the Sky, so called because the very tops glittered above the clouds like some heavenly kingdom. The ranges marked the border of the Forbidden Land, fabled Land of the Beasts.

As Eztar gazed eastwards, something caught her eye. The Beast Gods were nearing the city. A train of great creatures, made tiny as mice by distance, was moving in procession along the Ancient Way.

The Ativeteh returned to his preparations and did not speak to any about what the Ama had said to him, or the words that he had heard in the Chamber of Oracles. There was much to do, and quickly, if they were to cheat the Beast Gods and get the fleet away in time. And he would not leave Mikel to Her protection. He would sail north and find his son. What did the Ama know of such matters, anyway, remote in her temple with her priestesses? The Seers and Stargazers knew about the perturbations of the heavens and had said nothing about the Eye of the Sea. Neither had the Captains, and they knew the oceans as well as his commanders knew hill and forest. What if She was wrong? Perhaps *all* the gods were failing, except for Patiku, Only Father. All Merciful. He would understand a father's reluctance to leave his son. The Ativeteh would not leave Mikel to die among the Beast Gods. He would defy the Mother. If he was wrong in his judgement, Patiku would send a sign.

The Beast Gods were like the basilisk, or some creature of myth, but all the more terrifying because they were real. It was as though a species of terrible lizard which had lived aeons ago had not only survived but had changed and evolved, becoming more like men in stance and intelligence. The people called them Abere, which meant "beasts", and worshipped them as gods. They had men with them who served them. Among these priests was a face I knew.

THE STONE TESTAMENT – Brice Ambrose Stone

The Company of Strangers dismounted and took their places along the Way of Ceremony. The people around them stood with their backs turned, their hoods thrown up over their heads and their hands covering their faces. To look on the Gods was to risk being struck blind or turned to stone. Even some of the soldiers stood with their heads bowed and their eyes tight shut against any glimpse of the Beast Gods. The men from the Company of Strangers refused to turn. Ayne looked down at his companion, Iker, who stood erect, eyes straight ahead. He was not much more than a boy. His dark complexion and thickly curling hair marked him as a stranger, and he was young to be in the Janissary, but he was a fierce fighter and a skilled bowman. He was also a cheerful and entertaining companion. He was much loved by the priestesses of the Mother, having lived with them since childhood. They were rumoured to have bestowed good fortune upon him. Ayne was hoping that the luck still ran with him, for the last fight was coming and they would need it.

A hush fell like a wave, rippling down the length of the crowd. The Beast Gods were coming through the Dark Gate in a long procession, their pace measured and unhurried.

The terror that they inspired was justified. Ayne had travelled through the outlying areas; he had seen what they could do. Corpses so ripped about and mutilated that the only way to tell human from animal was by fur and hide. Many of the bodies had been dismembered; some had limbs missing, others had been completely stripped of flesh. Some of the bones showed signs of gnawing. The ground had been too hard for burial. In village after village, black smoke had billowed from funeral pyres.

Feathers, thick and glossy, shimmering with all kinds of colours, floated about them, like the cloaks their priests wore. A shift in the wind showed that the thick-shafted filaments grew out of their bluish-grey, pebbly skin. The eyes on the sides of the hideous, mask-like faces were real. A pinkish film periodically wiped up and back again. The black, slitted pupils ran vertically down the centre of their golden, amber irises and contracted or expanded to every little change of light. They walked upright on powerful, muscular legs and towered head and shoulders over the tallest man. Curved talons, like hooks on the three-toed feet, clicked on the paved stones as they walked. On each foot, the longest sickle-shaped claw curved backwards away from the ground. Their arms were well muscled and strong, and again ended in three-fingered talons of alarming length and sharpness. Bristling crests branched in twin blazes up over their heads and down their backs. The great snouts held rows of teeth like knives, the inner edges notched like worked flint. Muscles bulged at the angles of their heavy jaws. Their bite could crush bone to bloody meal.

They were a formidable force. The Gods and their entourage were followed by ranks of lesser beasts, smaller than their lords, but with the same fierce aspect and formidable teeth and claws. Behind them came a swaying procession of huge armoured creatures, stretching back into a distance lost in the clouds of dust raised by their tramping feet.

Ayne and Iker marched to the Great Hall of the Ancestors, where the Ativeteh was preparing to meet the Beast Gods. The Hall of the Ancestors was the oldest building in the city. Only there would the people feel protected, for inside its massive walls resided the Ancestors themselves: shadowy presences sitting high up in eroded niches, their faces covered by masks of gold.

The Beast Gods filed in to meet the Ativeteh and his assembled Sages. It seemed that they were intelligent. They communicated with each other in a series of clicks and hisses, the sounds they made interpreted by the priests they had brought with them.

These *were* men, although, at first sight, they could only be differentiated by their stature from the beasts that they served. They wore feathered cloaks and Beast heads, mouths agape. When the chief of them stepped forward to speak, Ayne could see his face quite clearly. Black eyes, pointed teeth and a thin-lipped grin leered out from the gaping, snarling reptilian maw. He had a deep scar like a hole in his left cheek. Ayne felt shock and recognition ripple through him. He knew that face from his own world.

The priest spoke. "I am Ket. I speak for my lords."

He looked up for a moment to the great creatures towering over him, watching the quick turns of the head, listening to the hisses and the clicking of claws.

He turned to face the council. His voice echoed round the big, open space at the centre of the massive, stone-built temple. He looked from the Ativeteh and his advisors up to the glinting masks of the Ancestors, as if all were included in his address. The slits of their eyes stared back, unmoved and impassive, as the torchlight glittered on the beaten gold that covered their faces. "We are here to accept your complete and abject surrender, or we will destroy the city and kill everyone in it, man, woman and child."

The Ativeteh stepped forward from the semicircle of Elders. He was dressed simply, as always, in a long white tunic, belted at the waist. The only sign of his office was a chain about his neck. His long black beard, stained the blue of a Seer, was threaded with silver but he was still younger than the others. He opened his mouth, as if about to speak, but was immediately interrupted.

"We are also here to take possession of the boats that you have been building. The land we share is doomed, our need to leave is as great as yours. We recognize your foresight," the priest's black eyes gleamed inside his mask, "and have come to take possession of what is ours."

No one spoke, or seemed to move as much as a muscle, but a tremor passed round those assembled. The Beast Gods were intent on taking everything and would leave them here to die.

"Very well." The Ativeteh showed no emotion. "We will have all made ready. If that is all, I must consult my captains——"

"That is not all, my lord," the beast priest's voice was soft and silky. "There is one other matter. We have been expecting an offering on the mountain. The First Born." He paused. "Your son." He looked around. "I do not see him. I understand that he is a Far Seer of rare talent. I would have expected him to be at your side."

"My son is in the North. He has a task to fulfil."

"A pity. Such an offering is as rare as the blue flowers that bloom on the Mountains of Men."

Not all the children taken to the Mountain were given up in sacrifice. The brightest, the best of them, were kept by the beasts and trained to be priests. Mikel was known to be the best Far Seer of his generation, perhaps ever; he could read the minds of men and women; he knew the secret language of birds and beasts. He was lame of foot, a mark of the young god.

"The Special Ones are valued above all others. Just as I was, brother. I thought to train him to follow on after me."

All around there was a rustle of movement, an intake of breath. Among those assembled, only a few among the Elders knew, or had made the connection, that Ket, Chief Priest to the Beast Gods, and the Ativeteh, the Ever Wise, were of the same blood.

For a moment, the brothers stared at each other. Then the Ativeteh spoke:

"Mikel will not return until after you have left on the ships. Now, as I said, my lords," he turned to address the Beast Gods, "there is much to prepare if we are to honour you. My captains and navigators are here to serve you. Even now they are supervising the loading of the ships with supplies and slaves for your use on your long journey."

III

In the far south, the Mountains in the Sky were now inaccessible, cased in ice. Glittering glaciers swept down their flanks and ice tumbled out from the valleys to spread across the plains, reaching further every year. To the north, the Eye of the Sea was turning. No one knew if these "Great Perturbations" as they were called were caused by sorcery, or were natural phenomena. Or if one had caused the other to occur.

THE STONE TESTAMENT – Brice Ambrose Stone

Mikel stared down at the Eye of the Sea as long as he dared. He knew what was wrong now. It was turning against the sun. He watched, horror churning through him like the maelstrom he was observing. That meant a great disturbance. Not just here, but everywhere in the world. The earth will turn widdershins, that is what the Stargazers had told his father, their black outlined eyes open very wide; the stars will go backwards. The earth will slew inside its skin, like a fruit inside its pith. The boy had heard their words, but he would not have believed such a thing possible, had he not seen this for himself.

The girl stood motionless behind him, fingers curled round the handle of her knife. He sat perfectly still, although the hair on his neck rose like fur and his flesh crawled and crept in anticipation of the blow that she was about to deliver. It would be hard for her to do this. They had known each other a long time. Since early childhood. They were friends. No. More than friends. Like brother and sister. They might have been more than that even. Given time. In the future. That's what his secret hope had been, but now there would be no future, because there was no more time. It was better if they both went together, he thought, as she stared past him, down into the churning vortex. They must throw themselves forward to join the spirits streaming out from the Cape of Souls.

As the girl hesitated, the lens-shaped maelstrom boiled and grew. The great swirling cauldron of water spread wider; its spiralling arms reaching far out into the three oceans, ready to catch any ships that might come within the compass of its embrace. What would that mean for the Great Fleet? Mikel watched, panic seething inside him. Was this sorcery, or some natural phenomenon? Mikel did not know. Perhaps the Mother did. She must have ordered Mikel's sacrifice to quell the perturbation. That's why the girl was here. He readied himself. It was time.

As he stood up to meet her he felt another disturbance, but this time within himself. Everything inside and outside him seemed to blur, as if time itself had begun to judder. Just for a moment, he glimpsed a place that he did not recognize. His thoughts and memories, of places and people, seemed to belong to an entirely different world. He heard a voice that he knew to be his father's, but he was speaking in a tongue that Mikel did not recognize, although he knew the meaning of the words. He inclined his head to listen. The voice was very faint, fainter by far than the diminishing echo from the departing whales. The message was coming from a remoteness in time and space, covering a distance impossible to even contemplate.

The message was clear: sacrifice was meaningless. As meaningless here as on the Sacred Mountain, as in the Temple of the Skulls. He turned to the girl behind him. Their eyes met and her fingers relaxed around the handle of the knife as she dropped it back into its scabbard. There was nothing in her mind, only emptiness. She had come to kill him, then herself. If she had failed in one thing, she would succeed in the other. He caught her hand as she moved to step past him.

"Sacrifice will not serve now," he said with quiet authority. "There is something else that we must do."

Eztar looked beyond him. The Eye of the Sea boiled below them, the whirling centre twisted tight as wrung washing. She felt a similar sickening movement inside, as though her very self was spinning, leaving an empty space which was being filled by some other. . .

"Don't look at the sea!" Mikel grasped her hand tighter. He was slightly built, even frail, but his grip was surprisingly powerful. "Help me up. It's time to go."

She took his other hand and looked into his face. His

skin was a pale nut colour, speckled as an egg; his light brown hair, thick and dense, fringed his broad forehead and clung to his head like moss. Thick strands had been plaited and twisted into ropes at the sides and back. His large hazel eyes were bright and sharp under arched brows, his mouth turning up at the corners, as though he could not help but smile. He had a sweet face, but there was something strange about it. With his wide cheekbones and pointed chin, he looked like a woodland creature, the kind that no longer existed because no one believed in them any more. She did not guard her thought from him. She was glad she did not have to kill him. He looked away quickly, as if he did not like to learn such things about himself.

He began to struggle up the rocky path that took them back to the track. The way was steep, the short grass black, brittle with frost, slippery as glass. Eztar knew better than to help him. He was skilled with the ivory-handled sticks, but still she feared that he might slip. His laboured breathing puffed like smoke into the cold air. She found his painful gait difficult to watch.

The short-legged, three-toed pony was waiting where she had tethered him. She helped Mikel to mount.

"What is this thing that we must do?" she asked as she helped him to mount.

"A message came to me. Something to do with the Ark the Mother keeps and a priest. . ." The message had been as a distant sweet bell ringing in his head, but he could not explain it to her. Instead he asked, "Did the Beast Gods come? Did they have priests with them?"

"They came, but I left before they entered the city.

They came for the ships but, Ama willing, they will be too late. There is something you must know," she paused, "especially now. Your father will defy the Oracle. He will sail north for you."

"How do you know?"

"The Ama knows all."

"But now the Eye of the Sea is turning! The ships will be caught!" He dug his heels into the pony's flank. "We must send a signal. Make for the forest. There is no time to lose!"

Eztar ran beside him. She was tall for her age, long limbed and well proportioned. Mikel admired her as he might a beautiful animal. She was as graceful as he was awkward. Her head was close to his knee. She looked up at him, her eyes the milky blue-green of glacial meltwater. Her features were strong but finely wrought, with high cheekbones, a straight nose and a finely moulded mouth and chin. She turned away from his scrutiny and he had to resist an urge to reach out and touch her shining, tightly braided, tawny hair. He had no pack, no weapons about him. He did not need weapons. She was his protection, fully armed, with a long throwing spear, a bow across her back and a quiver full of arrows. Her knife was made of the black ice that never melted and came from the Fire Mountains and was sharp enough to split hair.

These great perturbations, the dying of the land, were beyond understanding, but Mikel did not think that gods caused them, or had the power to quell them. They could not trust in gods any more. They must shape their own destiny. He was glad that they were both alive.

IV

The forest had once been a source of joy. At the Time of the Young Ferns, people would go to gather the tight green buds, the unfurling signs of new life; at the Time of Flowers, they made garlands from the bright, sweet-smelling blossoms; at the Time of Fruiting they went to gorge themselves and haul away what they could not eat to dry and preserve and bring the sweetness of summer to the Time When Nothing Grows. Now, the forest was shunned.

THE STONE TESTAMENT – Brice Ambrose Stone

The trees should be growing strong, lush and green, or flame tipped, as they always had been, the colours ever changing, like the sea. But first the rain had come, and now the cold. The flowers had fallen before fruiting; pods and cones lay shrivelled. The fern trees had shed their foliage; the few remaining leaves were brownish black, stripped to skeletons, drooping down from trunks that were nothing but broken stumps. The great palms had lost their crowns and stood naked as poles thrust into the ground. Bare trees strode away, rank on rank, as far as the eye could see, sweeping like a grey ghost army up to a distant ridge, their branches linked in delicate tracery, their cracked trunks bleached and creaking, as if they could fall at any minute. The wind stirred the boughs and set them clashing against each other. The sound they made was like the death knell of the forest. Needles and the tough, splayed, knuckle-shaped leaves of the bakah tree lay drifted between the trunks, or caught in spiders' webs, which drooped between the boughs like fallen shrouds.

When they reached the tallest tree, Mikel called a halt. What he was about to do was fitting. But first, he must ask forgiveness.

This great Lord of The Forest was venerated and worshipped as the living symbol of the axis on which the world turned. He was the object of pilgrimage, his enormous trunk tied about with bright plaited threads, garlanded with flowers, the trees around hung with bells and prayer wheels. His roots reached down into the hollow hills, his branches soared upwards into the heavens. He seemed as strong as ever, towering over the rest of the forest, his girth greater than the linked arms of many men. But all the small plants who gained sustenance from him lay dead at his feet. High above, his branches were bare of leaves. They rose, naked as horns, and he looked down almost with a human face while the silvery skin of his great trunk wept great gouts of gum. There were no fresh offerings. The garlands had withered; the threads had lost their colour. All around, his sons and daughters, the last of these great trees, were dead or dying, their leaves fallen. Some stood stark, others lay across each other, or leant in a last embrace, roots exposed, torn up from the ground.

Eztar beat on the small drum she carried and sang the Song of the Forest as Mikel took a piece of jade, carved in a green curl, like the tight bud on an unfurling fern, a symbol of life renewing itself, although all around the ferns lay black and dead on the ground. He reached up and stuck it deep into a gout of gum, as was the custom. Eztar cut a braid from her hair, threaded with shells and shiny beetle thoraxes, and did the same. They both stepped back, heads bowed in prayer. The Lord of the Forest wept his rolling amber tears and they shared in his sorrow at what was lost, and what was to come.

"Father of the Forest, forgive what I do now," Mikel muttered and when he looked up there were tears in his own eyes.

He stood in silent veneration, before holding up a wetted finger to find the direction of the wind. It was blowing from the sea now, steadily inland.

"Get out your sparkstriker," he said to Eztar. "The ones you use to make fire."

She took out her flints and the silver grey chip from the star stone while Mikel scraped up leaves with his sticks, heaping them at the base of the tree at the points where the weeping gum had collected.

"Strike fire. Here and here."

The gum would burn quickly. The tree was dry, the

wood cracking. It would go up like a torch. Taken by the strong, steady wind, the flames would leap to the trees nearby, which were all equally dry and resinous. The wind would take the flames away from them, up to the ridge that acted as the great watershed. If they went in the opposite direction, they could descend the cliffs and find safety on the shore.

"It will be visible from a great distance in all directions."

Mikel stepped back, from the wavering heat that was already scorching him.

"It will serve as a warning for our ships to change course."

Mikel and Eztar fled before a wall of fire. The wind blew the worst of it away from them, snatching the flames up and hurling them inland, but running tongues snaked through the undergrowth and swirling crosswinds eddied the blaze in unpredictable directions. Embers flew and sparks burst from exploding trunks and branches, frizzing their hair and peppering their clothes. The smoke made the pony panicky and skittish. Eztar held his rein tightly to stop him from bolting, but he knew the way. He instinctively found the quickest route to the sea. It was a relief to see the wide sands stretching away: the long expanse of Eternity Bay.

Eztar found a path and guided the pony down to the firm grey sands. Near the towering cliffs sparks still showered down upon them, so they moved out further to where the dry loose sand skimmed along the crusted surface like snaking lengths of fine-spun yarn and the sea roared to shore.

Mikel had not spoken since they left the forest.

It was the dark time of year; the sun would soon fall towards the distant rim of the horizon. Low-lying banks of white mist were rolling in from the sea. Eztar pulled her cloak closer. Without the sun, the cold would be biting. They had to find somewhere to camp and soon. Inland, the fire was dying back, although smuts still whirled out on the eddying wind like black snow. The cliffs would provide shelter. She chose a good place, a narrow fissure in the cliff, and tethered the pony by laying a rock across his reins. Mikel sat on a mat she laid for him and made no attempt to help her as she gathered driftwood and built a fire. There was no shortage of fuel. It was as if whole forests had tumbled into the sea.

The dry salt-soaked wood caught quickly and burnt with flaring spurts of green and purple flame. She prepared meal cakes, putting them on flat stones to bake.

The boy sat, cross-legged, staring out to sea.

"What are you thinking?" she asked him.

"I'm thinking about my father," he answered. "Because he is thinking about me."

V

There was only one way to the harbour: a narrow, cobbled street with great stone ashlars rising on either side. Down this way, the last of the people poured. Priests and priestesses from the temples, healers and scholars. The map makers and Stargazers were already on board. Time was short, and they all knew it, but there was no panic among them, just a frantic sense of purpose. They worked like ants together, or bees in the Hive of the Mother. The loading had begun.

THE STONE TESTAMENT – Brice Ambrose Stone

Out in the harbour, the high-prowed vessels rode low in the water, for each carried far more than their normal quota of passengers and cargo. The loading had begun before the Beast Gods reached the city. The subterfuge played upon them had bought precious time for the task to be completed, but the trick had not held. Even now the terrifying creatures were pouring down the narrow ways towards the harbour, held back only by the brave Janissaries – and there were precious few of them.

Every ship was captained by a Sea King and carried a compliment of navigators, Stargazers and builders, so that, even if the ships were separated from each other, blown by the winds, taken by ocean currents, each vessel contained the elements needed to start anew. No one knew how long they would be journeying, or where they would come to shore, but every person had been given a sack containing the sacred seeds, so wherever they landed there would be a new planting and life would continue.

The bulk of the fleet lay offshore. They were riding the waves, waiting to see the great blue Eye outlined in black that marked the prow of the Ativeteh's vessel. The captains were growing increasingly uneasy. They did not understand the delay. Few would want to leave without the Ativeteh, but some had already raised their sails. They could tarry no longer. From the ships, they watched the battle raging. They had to leave before the beasts reached the shore.

The Janissary would fight to the last man to buy the ships time to get away. The last of the ships had been loaded, the Ativeteh had boarded, when the alarum sounded within the Beast God precinct. The huge durak drum, made from the stretched skin of an azhdarch wing, boomed out over the city, speaking of deception and treachery. Within moments the beasts and their priests were pouring down the steps of their temple like dark smoke. They were joined by other creatures summoned by the drum from outside the city walls. The beasts swarmed towards the harbour, killing as they went. The city resounded with the screams of men and the deep-throated roars of the beasts.

The Janissary retreated before them to the cobbled way that wound down the steep-sided cliff to the harbour. The way was called the Gut because it was so narrow and twisting. This was where they would make their last stand. The great walls on either side had been built by the Ancients. Ashlars, great stone blocks many feet thick, were fitted so closely that it was impossible to feed a leaf between one and another. Much of their knowledge had been lost down the ages, but not all.

The Captain of the Janissary had a few surprises. As soon as the first rank of beasts entered the narrow way, one great vessel of oil after another was poured down on them from above. Torches followed. Roars of alarm turned into shrill screams as drenched feathers and robes flared. Bright balls of flames tumbled backwards in agonized blindness, igniting those behind them. Smoke billowed up, bringing with it the sickening stench of burnt feathers and roasting flesh.

"There are more coming!" a lookout shouted.

Further cohorts of beasts were issuing from the city. While his soldiers readied more missiles to rain upon them, the Captain jumped down and began pacing the outside of the wall. He beckoned for Ayne to follow him.

"What are you doing?" he asked.

"I'm counting," the Captain replied. "I joined as a young lad, Iker's age or less. The old Captain told me about these walls. They were built by the Ancients to defend the city from invasion from the sea, or to cover an escape like this one. They have a secret. There's a key stone in each wall. Remove it and the whole lot will fall. Hey! Young 'un!" he called up to Iker. "You got sharp eyes. Come 'ere!"

Iker dropped down to join them.

"What am I looking for?" Iker looked up. The wall was made of hundreds of stones, thousands. The task seemed hopeless.

"About halfway down." The Captain was counting. "The wall is a thousand and one paces. The stone is shaped like that." The Captain raised his forefingers to make a T shape.

"I see it!" Iker pointed. "There it is! There are even faint footholds leading up to it."

"Two of you. Get up there!" The Captain shouted out commands. "All but two watchmen down from the wall!" He turned to Ayne. "Take a few and go round. There should be a twin on the other side."

"It's moving!" The shout came down.

"There's one here, too!" Ayne called back from the other side of the opposite wall.

"Good! Good!" The Captain rubbed his hands. "Now we bide our time."

The key stones slid out as if they had been greased with butter. They heard them tumble and crash and a thin screech as they fell among the massed ranks that were now pouring down to the harbour. The beasts surged on, oblivious, trampling on their crushed companions. The janissaries looked at each other, despair seeping back. Only the key stones had fallen. What were a few rocks? Another rock fell, and then another. The great ashlars began shifting with a slow groan that rapidly turned into the terrible screech and grind of stone upon stone. The men standing outside the walls were showered with flying chips and choked by grit and dust. They leapt away as the whole edifice began falling inwards upon itself. That first screech was joined by the cries of many. Then the cacophony of shrieking groans was lost, drowned by the crash of rock upon rock.

There was silence all along the whole length of the wall.

The Captain led them, clambering up and over the chaos of tumbled stones. The way to the port was completely filled up. There was no sign of life under the huge fallen blocks. No sign of anything at all.

"Go to the Temple of the Mother." The Captain put his hand on Iker's shoulder. "I know you're anxious to see how she fares. Give our thanks and ask her blessing. I release you from the oath you made when you joined the Company."

No need for the lad to die needlessly, for this would delay the beasts only. The advanced guard were crushed under the great stones, but others would come after. Lesser beasts, fast and nimble, behind them great lumbering monsters, while all the time, azhdarchs flew in the sky.

While his Janissary fought so bravely for him to get away, the Ativeteh loitered on the shore. He stood in the prow of his ship, staring straight ahead, seeing nothing, blinded by sorrow for the loss of his most precious son. He should be here, by his side, as they had planned. The others could sail west, but he would go north. Perhaps the girl had not reached him. She would not know of the bay they had chosen for their meeting place. Mikel could be there waiting for him. He would defy the Mother. Prove her oracle false.

He could hear the hiss of her voice like sand blowing across the desert floor. The Mother could be kind and loving, but there were other aspects to her: she could be cruel, ruthless in the protection of her children. That is why she was sometimes shown with the face of a woman and the body of a lioness.

Mikel had to die. That is what she had told him. The warrior sent to find him would be his assassin.

Easy for her to say. She was not a parent.

All men are my children, Ativeteh. Remember your duty. All men are your sons.

He did not care what she had told him. He did not care that he was letting love blind him. He was a man as well as Ativeteh. Perhaps there was another way. He would wait for a sign from Patiku. Wait, even though the Beast Gods' monstrous armoured creatures might be wading through the water towards him and azhdarchs flew above dropping rocks.

He was so lost in his thoughts that he did not hear the Captain hail him, or see the sailors waving and pointing.

"Sir!" the Captain shouted. "Look there!"

The Ativeteh raised his eyes. In the west, the sun was falling towards the horizon, but the eastern rim of the world was fringed with red as though lit by a fiery dawn. Black smoke billowed up into the sky. The forest was on fire. This was the sign. Patiku, Only Father, had spared his son, and sent a warning by him. Mikel had fired the forest to show where the danger lay. The Eye of the Sea *was* turning. He had created a beacon that his father must heed. Do not go north.

The Ativeteh ordered the Captain to raise the anchor stone and the signal to be sent. The conch shell bellowed in notes high and low over the water. The ships moved all together, like pieces on a gaming board, as the Captains adjusted the angle of their sails and set course for the west. The oarsmen bent to their task. The ships were leaving at last. His duty was to his people and their survival, but his heart still lay heavy in his chest. He was abandoning his son to a world where the Beast Gods now ruled, but a spark of hope had been ignited. They would not meet in this life again, but Mikel was alive.

He sent a quick prayer to the young god that Mikel most resembled, marked by him from birth, the bull-footed one, both blessed and cursed. He asked him to watch over his son and shut his ears, heart and mind to the whisper of the Mother:

If he leaves, so will the beasts.

As the slender vessels met the deep swell of the open ocean, the sails filled and the oarsmen found their rhythm. From here, they would spread all over the globe, taking their knowledge with them. The voyage of the Sea Kings had begun.

From a lookout point, high above the city, what was left of the Janissary heard the angry cry of the beasts, their howls of frustration at being thwarted, and they let out a ragged cheer.

"The Ativeteh's ship has left shore," the Captain addressed them. "Thank you, friends and comrades, you fought hard and well." He looked around at his diminished band, their faces masks of black soot and white stone dust, streaked with rivulets of sweat and blood. "For me, it is not over. While I have breath I will fight them. You may come with me if you will, but I release you from the oaths you made when you joined the Company of Strangers. It is every man for himself."

He made a line in the dust at his feet and every one of them stepped over it. All except Ayne.

"I will join you," Ayne said. "But first, I want to find Iker."

"Until later, then," the Captain clasped Ayne's hand in the manner of the Janissaries. "The city has many hiding places. Look to the high towers. Go well, my brother. Go well."

VI

They had other, more civilized gods. Prominent
among them was a matriarchal goddess figure
called the Ama. Her priestess was believed to
be an avatar, the presence of the goddess on
earth. Her rites resembled the Eleusinian
Mysteries of Ancient Greece and she was
believed to have oracular powers. Her worship
was carried on in implacable opposition to the
more primitive worship of the Elder Gods, with
their demand for human sacrifice and blood.

THE STONE TESTAMENT – Brice Ambrose Stone

Iker followed the wall back to the city. There was the
smell of smoke on the wind and a glow in the sky to the
north, as if the forest was on fire. Out at sea, the ships
were leaving, sailing westwards, tiny black flecks against
the great red orb of the setting sun.

The streets of the city seemed deserted, but he
approached the Temple of the Mother with caution. He

was on his guard, looking out for prowling beasts, or other assailants, so was entirely unaware that he was being watched.

Ket, the beast priest, observed from a safe distance as the exhausted boy came nearer. He was returning to the Mother for succour, his kind always did, and the Great Whore was still there, Ket was certain. One of her priestesses had told him, after a certain amount of persuasion. The sound of fighting, thinned by distance, carried from the harbour. Ket left fighting to others. There was no point now, anyway. The fleet had got away. It was just beasts satisfying their blood lust. He had other matters more pressing than killing for killing's sake. The Temple of the Goddess was a labyrinthine warren of tunnels and passages with who knew what traps and hazards. If he was to get inside, and get out again, he would need a guide.

Iker came in his armour, trailing weapons. All instruments of warfare were banned inside Her precinct, but today it did not matter. The palace was deserted. If the Ama had left, if she had gone with the ships, then truly all was lost. If she remained, then she would know what to do.

He had been sad to part with Ayne. He was the truest friend that anyone could have. He was tall, with long pale hair and eyes the colour of the sky. He allowed the hair on his upper lip to grow, which was most unusual. Most men shaved there and grew beards that fringed chin and jaw. Ayne was brave and strong, an excellent soldier. He had a weapon made from star stone: the heavy, dull grey rock used to make fire. The blade could cut through bone. Star stone was rare. There was not enough of it to make any more knives like his, but Ayne had collected as much as he could to fashion arrow heads. Each member of the Janissary carried one special arrow in his quiver, fletched in red and white to distinguish it from its flint-tipped neighbours.

Iker entered the Precinct of the Mother. It was the End of Days. The bundled reeds that counted the years had been broken, thrown to the winds, scattered like so much chaff. The calendar stones lay in fragments on the floor. The perpetual fire had been extinguished, never to be reignited. The fires had been doused recently; an acrid mix of charcoal and incense still hung heavy in the air. The priestesses must have been among the very last to leave.

The Palace of the Mother, Temple of the Goddess, was old and plain, a circular, domed structure made from massive blocks of pink stone. The entrance was a narrow gap between huge stone lintels which had been sculpted into the fiercest aspect of the Mother, lion haunched and bird clawed. Iker sparked life into a blackened torch and stepped into the darkness. Inside, passages curled around themselves, like a maze, leading to three round chambers. The first was dedicated to the younger aspect of the Mother. She stood in a niche in the wall, hissing snakes clutched to her bare breasts. The chamber was empty. He followed the curving passages round to the next room. The Mother lay resting on her side: heavy and voluptuous, ready to give birth. There was no one here either, so he went on to the smallest room. The Painted Chamber. Lit by the gutter of his flickering torch, images of the Mother, arms raised, legs splayed, a repeated shape, hardly recognizable as a woman at all, moved in a perpetual dance round the room. The domed ceiling was covered in a honeycomb pattern which turned into rows of stiff-armed spirals where the roof curved down to the walls. The Ama was still here, somewhere, he could sense her living presence. He took the Stairway of Seven Steps and entered a labyrinthine mass of tunnels cut into the living rock.

Long before he had served in the Janissary, he had been taken into the temple by the Ama herself. He had been found floating in a tiny boat, adrift on the endless sea. He had been very small and remembered nothing of the time before he was cast afloat on the ocean. It seemed that his first memory was of a great painted eye looking down at him. It was painted on the slender prow of a great sea-going vessel which rode easily on the waves as it towered above his tiny craft. They had found him floating far from any shore, but could tell by his hair and the colour of his skin that he belonged to the people of the Burnt Lands. He had tried to hide from the men coming down the rope ladders, and had used what little strength he had left to resist them, but he had been plucked away from the old man who had accompanied him and taken on board the bigger ship. No one knew how he had survived. His companion had been dead for many days, little more than a skin-covered skeleton, desiccated by the sun and wind. They had no way of knowing the rites of his people, so they had laid his guardian curled up, according to their own fashion, wrapped in a sail. They had fired the boat, soaking the inside with oil and casting lighted brands down into it. He had watched it until it had become a little spark on the water to be swallowed in the purple shades of night as darkness began to fall.

He should have entered the House of Strangers, but because he had been so young, he had been put into the care of the priestesses in the Temple of the Mother. His dark skin and curly hair marked him as different; his ready smile made him a favourite with the priestesses, who treated him like a pet, or a mascot. He was even allowed into the place of the Ama. She was dark skinned, like him, and pronounced that the scar pattern on his cheek marked him as having royal blood. She named him Iker Erregin, Messenger, Prince of the House of Strangers, and allowed him into her inner sanctum. The Chamber of the Oracles.

The room was small and circular, carved from the living rock. The walls and ceiling were stained red with ochre. There were no designs here, no decoration of any kind. Two niches were cut deep into the far wall. The higher one contained the sacred Ark of polished bone. It was the colour of aged ivory and covered in carvings and strange markings. It was never handled by anyone, other than the Mother. It was rumoured to contain the Dark One, a skull carved from some livid crystal, the tenebrous twin of the Skull of Light kept by the Ativeteh. To touch it meant death. The lower niche gaped open like a wide mouth. Iker went over to it and spoke the summoning.

"Ama, Mother, come to me."

His own voice came back to him, booming and hollow. The last time he spoke here, there had been no echo. He must be a man now.

He stood quiet, waiting for her answer in the silence. Sometimes, the Ama spoke straight into his mind. She was speaking to him now, but her words were faint.

"You have come, my little one," her voice whispered to him, like the wind fluting through the crevices in the rocks.

She emerged from the shadows, gliding towards him like one of the wall paintings come to life. She wore her gold mask. Two slits for eyes, a single stroke for a nose, a slashed opening where the mouth would be. The merest suggestion of a face.

"I have come. . ." He bowed. "I thought you might be gone, left with your priestesses."

"No, little one. My place is here. But I have one last duty to perform and you can help me."

"Anything, Mother. What do you want me to do?"

"Come. Come with me." She moved towards the sacred Ark. "Take this down from its place."

Iker was reluctant, knowing its reputation. The Ama laughed softly.

"You will not be harmed."

Reassured, Iker reached up, dislodging the dust of centuries, and handed her the dome-shaped casket.

She held the Ark between her thin hands. The box hinged in the centre to reveal a skull crafted from some dark, glittering stone. Like, but not like, the Skulls of Light, which had gone with the ships and contained the wisdom of the people. Those were made of clear crystal; the shape was rounded and human. This was different. The brain case was elongated, the big eye orbits dished and shallow, the nasal cavities large and flaring, the jaw long and the teeth pointed. It looked as if it could be the skull of a beast.

"Something worse, I'm afraid," the Ama answered his unasked question. "This skull, the Dark One, is both man *and* beast. An abomination created by the Ancient Ones before the Ancestors ever came to these shores."

"What happened to them? The Ancient Ones?"

"They tried to wake the world serpent and the knowledge they unleashed destroyed them. Just as it is doing now. Great perturbations occur when men think that they can become as gods. Sorcery is *Pa*, forbidden for good reason, but I fear that such practice has lived on in the lodges of the beast priests who dwelt with their masters on Ha'itzilazki. There was no contact between them and us for many lives of men, so that it has not mattered, but one has come who seeks the knowledge locked within the dark skull of how to join the power of beast and man together; to be both at the same time. Ket, the beast priest, has steeped himself in sorcery. With this," her dark hand curled round the hideous elongated skull, "who knows what he could do? He has already found a way of stirring the sleeping serpent; that is why the land is freezing and the Eye of the Sea is turning around the Cape of Souls. Mikel was sent to quell it so that the ships could pass."

"How could he do that?"

"By sacrificing himself."

"Sacrifice?" Iker was astonished. The Mother shunned sacrifice.

"The Mother abhors the bloody plethora of the Place of Skulls, but Mikel has the marks of the Young God on him. Sometimes it is necessary for such a one to die for the good of all others. It has happened before. It will happen again. But the sacrifice was not made. The Eye is turning and the Ativeteh refuses to heed the Mother's warning. . ."

Iker realized that the Ama had not been outside. "Mikel sent a sign," he said. "He fired the forest. The ships are sailing westwards."

The Ama raised her arms in the sign of the Mother. "Blessed be. Perhaps all is not lost." She closed the box. "For the good of all mankind, the Dark One will go with me into the darkness. Iker, you are my Messenger, tell Aynegeru the Fair One, Traveller from a Far Land, for he has searched long, travelling across time to secure it. Tell him that it is safe with me."

"Not so, Old One. Not so." The man's voice echoed, harsh and hollow, as he advanced across the chamber. "You have had it for too long. It is time to hand it on. To me."

"Ket. Servant to the Beasts." The Ama's gold mask turned towards him. "I am old, as you say, and ready to go down on my last journey. Only the Mother endures. She will find others to do her work. None of us can escape destiny. Even you. Even me. Your beasts will die, as their kind have everywhere else in the world.

319

There are many paths, priest, but only one bourn from which none will return."

"The time for oracles is over, old woman. Save what breath you have left."

He stepped forward to meet her. In his hand he carried his chosen weapon: the sharp, curved, toe claw of the beast. He tore the golden disguise from her face and threw it aside. Her dark, bright eyes were the only sparks of life in another mask of wrinkled, grey flesh, withered like a wizened fruit. Her head was bare, apart from a few whitish wisps of hair. The face of the Ama was that of a crone who had lived long beyond her span of years.

Tell the Traveller, little Messenger. This is why he came here. He must succeed where I have failed.

Ket swept the claw in from the side, wielding it like a scythe, and her last words ended in a gargling welter of blood.

As Iker melted away into the darkness, he caught her dying thought:

Find Mikel. Tell him this: Even if it cost him his own life, no beast is to leave this land.

The boy fled through the temple, biting back sobs, choking on the salt from his tears. He was swift footed and small. Even if Ket came after him, he was heavily built and hampered by his feathered cloak. Iker could get into places that the man couldn't reach. Besides, there were many nooks where he could hide. The House of the Mother was a honeycomb and he knew it better than anyone. He'd spent half his childhood getting lost in here; the other half finding a way out. He took himself to a distant gallery and sat down there. The Ama called him her Messenger. Her last words rang in his head. He must find Ayne. He must find Mikel. Already he was failing her. Fresh tears ran down his face. He could not make himself move from here. Life was worth nothing without the Ama.

Ayne watched from the shadows as Ket emerged. He started forward, and then he stopped himself. He had no idea what had happened to Iker in there, but the priest was looking mighty pleased with himself. He held his arms tightly to his chest, as if holding something to him. Ayne watched with impatience. He wanted him out of the way, so he could go and search for the boy, but Ket showed no sign of moving. Ayne watched him with the loathing that only a deep-seated and ancient enmity could bring. Why was he standing there, hugging himself, grinning his shark's grin? Ayne was trying to work out what he could be doing, when Ket started up a strange hooting, nasal kind of whistle.

His strange hollering attracted answering calls. Round the corner came a pack of carrion eaters, scarcely knee high, with narrow ribcages, wide bellies and long whippy tails. The men in the Jannisary called them Naxar, their word for scavenger, and by the look of their bloody muzzles they had been busy among the corpses that now littered the city. Their skin was green with patches of vivid colour and a straggle of oily, iridescent feathers hung from their backs and clung to their chests. They loped on long scaly legs; their snaky necks and heads naked of feathers, like vultures. Their narrow jaws were full of needle teeth that could remove a triangular section of flesh at one bite. Their arms were small and puny looking, but each hand had three long, sharp, curving claws. They looked about them with large eyes that were accustomed to darkness. Their wide, elongated nostrils flared wide. They hunted by scent and they hunted in packs. Despite their ungainly, ugly appearance they were extremely intelligent creatures. They looked up at Ket, heads cocked on one side as if listening to instructions, and then went streaming into the temple. Ket grinned as he went on his way, still hugging himself as if he held some precious thing to his chest.

Ayne drew his bowie knife as he followed the Beast Gods' little cousins into the Mother's compound. They were scavengers, but not averse to fresh meat and, given what they normally fed on, the slightest graze from those sharp teeth would be toxic. He had to find Iker before they did.

VII

I believe we are born again, life after life, as the
Buddhists do. I believe we can travel between
worlds, as shamans hold.

THE STONE TESTAMENT – Brice Ambrose Stone

The mist was creeping close. It would soon be all
around them. Eztar left Mikel to his leave-taking and
went to collect shellfish from the shore and gather more
branches for the fire. When she came back, she set
clams to cook among the embers and filled leather cups
with water and a sprinkling of herbs, dropping in red-
hot stones to make an infusion.

Mikel ate what he was given, but still did not speak.
Eztar sang to him, filling the silence with songs they
both knew, rapping on her little drum as if the soft low
beat could keep the surrounding darkness at bay and her
high, clear voice could lighten his mood.

"I heard my father's voice," he said at last.

"From the departing ships?"

"No." Mikel shook his head. "Before that. When I was at the Cape of Souls. It came mingled with the song of the departing whales, but from a much greater distance." He spread his arms to take in the curve of the darkening horizon, the infinity of stars that shone above them. "I believe the message was true, but I do not fully understand it."

Eztar listened as he told her how the voice had countermanded the need for sacrifice, and placed another task upon him. There was a shift in the heavy burden of guilt she had carried with her ever since she had disobeyed the Mother. She drew in the sand, a plan of the city, showing walls and towers surrounding little square buildings, open plazas and palaces and, at the centre, the round Temple of the Mother.

"The thing that you seek is kept in the Chamber of Oracles," she said.

"How do you know?"

"I've seen it there many times. It is kept in a niche on the wall."

"Perhaps the Ama has taken it on the ships?"

"No." Eztar shook her head. "She will not be leaving. She told me."

"We must go to her. She'll know what all this means. She will know what I must do."

Mikel made to rise, but Eztar shook her head. "It is too dangerous to journey in the darkness and, besides, your leg is hurting. You must rest."

He hated to show weakness, but his hand instinctively strayed to his knee, his aching ankle. "How do you know?"

"I know."

Eztar opened her healing pouch and took out a little leather bag. She shook out thin flint blades, worked to very fine needle points. She found the blue striations on his knee and ankle and pushed the points home to open the channels and relieve the pain. Mikel grimaced, but nodded his thanks. She packed the needles away. He needed deeper treatment, but that was all she could do for now.

They slept curled up together against the cold, wrapped in a brightly patterned blanket made from the soft belly fur of the creatures that roamed the high mountains. Eztar drew Mikel to her. He allowed her to cradle him, like a little brother, like a mother would her child.

31

DECONSTRUCTION

Celestine kept watch, her whole body stilled, her ageless face expressionless, as though cast in bronze, or carved from ebony. She felt as though she had been travelling with them and was slow to comprehend what was happening when loud and urgent knocking roused her. The children slept on without stirring when she went to the door.

She undid the bolts and turned the keys in the locks to find Kris's friends Ran and Max outside, hopping from foot to foot.

"Gotta go, Mamma," Ran said.

Celestine looked out over the balcony. It was fully dark now. Unmarked vans were fanning out across the estate.

Max gently guided her back into the balcony's shadow. "Don't wanna go too near the edge, or they catch you on CCTV."

She looked up at him. "Is everything ready?"

"Sure." He grinned down at her. "Place is perfect. No one lived there for a long time. Plus they been through that block already. Ain't exactly five star, know what I'm sayin'?"

"That don' matter." She put her hand on his arm. "Just as long as it is safe."

"Safe, Mamma," Ran said. "Safe as we can make it. Now, let's go."

She took them into her flat.

"They can hear you," she said. "And they can walk OK. They need guiding, though. They don' see too well."

"We'll go get help." Max and Ran loped off.

"You seen anything like that?" Max said as they went down the stairs.

Ran shook his head. They knew Celestine's Islands reputation, but this was a strange business.

While they were gone, Celestine spoke words of summoning, whispering to each of them, one at a time. She picked up what she needed. When the boys came back, she was ready.

Some of the gang stayed in the flat to close it up, while others took Kris, Adam and Zillah down the stairs one at a time. Kris was the smallest, so they rolled him up in a rug and Ran carried him over his shoulder. They put Zillah in a wheelchair, as though she was going out with a carer. Two of them put their arms round Adam's shoulders and walked him, laughing and joking, chatting in a high-spirited manner, but not loud enough to attract attention, as though they had all had a few too many drinks, or were stoned, and he was a little the worse for wear.

They got them up the stairs and stopped outside a

boarded-up, burnt-out crack house. Ran undid the grilles, pushed back the plywood and took them in, one at a time.

"Told you it wasn't much," he said, almost apologizing as he helped Celestine in through the gaping hole where the door had been. He wanted to ask what she was doing with the mirror she was carrying, but the expression on her face made him think better of it.

Celestine looked around. "It'll do," she said.

"I fixed you a little lamp." He held up a camping lantern. "Don' use it, though, 'less you got no choice. There's water in that bag, plus crisps, fruit and that. But I'm going to have to lock you in here. Got to make it look like no one's home."

"Go ahead." She nodded. "We'll be fine."

The boys had laid sleeping bags against the wall.

"Don't lay 'em down," Celestine insisted. "I want 'em sitting up."

Lying down, they looked uncomfortably like they were dead.

"You OK now?"

Celestine nodded.

"Be back when it's clear."

The boy went out. Celestine heard him manoeuvre the plywood back and screw down the grilles. The place stank of burnt wood and melted plastic and was dank from water pumped in to put out the fire. The walls were blackened with scorch marks reaching halfway across the ceiling. The floor was a litter of melted bottles, the remains of syringes, warped spoons and scraps of foil turned bronze by heat. Celestine looked away with distaste and settled herself in the little folding garden chair that one of the boys had put in there for her. From outside came the sound of van doors banging open and heavy boots hitting concrete. Men shouted orders, while dogs on short leashes snarled and barked.

"Hope they don't do damage to my front door," she thought as she made ready to continue her vigil.

In her own flat, the boys worked hard and fast to remove all signs of recent activity. They emptied the fridge, turned off the utilities, spread junk mail and papers on the mat, reversed the motor on the vacuum cleaner to blow a thin layer of dust over all the surfaces. The neighbours, who had no liking for the authorities, had all been primed to say that they didn't know where the Baptistes were, or that the old lady and her grandson had gone away for an indefinite stay, probably back to the Islands. Rent was paid up, but no one knew when they would be coming back.

VIII

Being strangers, the Janissary was our family. We were a band of brothers. A cry for help could never be ignored, even if to answer it meant certain death.

THE STONE TESTAMENT – Brice Ambrose Stone

Iker woke suddenly. He must have fallen asleep for a little space, exhausted by his grief. He had dreamt and been comforted, because the Mother had been there with him, but now he felt her loss even more keenly and began to grieve anew. Then a noise, close to him, dried the tears from his eyes. Out in the darkness, he could hear a kind of chittering, followed by the slithering, skitter of clawed feet on stone. He groped in the darkness, feeling for the torch that had become extinguished. His fingers touched the sticky, resinous top of it and he reached in his pouch for his sparkstriker. This slight movement brought an instant silence followed by a low, throaty hissing, as if he was surrounded by a crowd of snakes. With shaking hands, he struck flint and stone together, praying he wouldn't drop either one. The resulting spark was reflected back to him from many eyes. They were close and drawing closer, and when they moved, they all moved together. Iker struck again and again, sending prayer after prayer to the Mother. His prayers were answered. The torch flared to reveal a tight circle of green, smooth-skinned creatures, mouths agape to show their sharp little teeth. He was sitting on the floor and their heads were on a level with his. Their eyes showed ruby red for a moment, then their wide pupils contracted sharply and they began to hiss, moving their heads from side to side, discomforted by the sudden brightness.

"Don't like that, do you?"

Iker's voice rang out as he sprang to his feet and swept the torch around. He lunged out, then retreated. It was important to keep his back against the wall. He shouted again, loud in the confined space, and was answered by a distant, delayed echo. The creatures looked about, confused. They didn't like the sudden noise any more than the flames. They began to fall back, with an angry squeaking, but they did not go away. They grew quiet and stood, just outside his reach, watching. They were patient animals. They seemed to know that the torch would not last for ever. They kept their eyes on the sputtering flame, which was already dying. Every time the light dimmed a little, they took a step closer. Iker yelled and lunged at them, sweeping the torch in a ribbon of fire, but each time the action was a little less effective. They were closing the circle round him. As soon as the light went, they would be upon him, biting and tearing. Within minutes his carcass would be stripped to the bone.

Ayne took a torch from the racks in the precinct and lit it to see the last of the green monsters disappearing into one of the passages that led away from the public areas. He had to be careful, this place was a labyrinth and if he got lost here, he was done for, but they were not hard to track. He hung well back, shielding the light, but they obviously had no sense of being followed; they were noisy little creatures and he followed their excited high-pitched calls and chatter deep underground. Their big eyes gave them excellent night vision and they had an inbuilt sense for the traps that had been set up to protect this place. They filed carefully past gaping chasms and dodged round great stone obstacles that fell in their way. Ayne kept as close as he dared, he had not realized that some of the passages were booby trapped, but the Naxar did not look back. They kept up the same pace all the time and it was a fast one.

They seemed to know exactly where they were going, but sometimes even they had to stop at a confluence of tunnels and take a moment to decide which one to follow. They all started at once, and stopped the same way, like a choreographed dance troupe. In other circumstances the effect would be comical, but there was nothing amusing about the prospect of being stuck down here in the pitch-darkness with a pack of ravenous carrion eaters.

Suddenly all sound stopped and Ayne's own steps faltered. He stopped to listen. Nothing. No sign of them. It was as if the ground had opened and swallowed them. He took a few steps forward, holding the torch up for maximum light. There was a tunnel, low and narrow, branching off sharply to the right. He put his head in, listening for them ahead of him, when he heard a shout. A human voice, high and light, a fluting mixture of terror and anger. A boy's voice, not long broken. Ayne's pulse surged. It was Iker. He'd found him. There it was again: the battle cry of the Janissary. Only uttered in extremis, when all hope is gone: *Vaa na! Vaa na! To me! To me!* To shout out like that, knowing no one was there. It was the last cry of despair.

Ayne bellowed the answering call: *Immer! Immer! I arrive! I arrive!* and plunged into the rounded tunnel, which twisted and turned as though bored through the living rock by some monstrous worm. At times, Ayne was bent double; his wide shoulders almost filled the cramped space. Every now and then he stopped to listen. The strange whirrs and chitters of the creatures were louder, but Iker's shouts were weaker. Ayne hurried on, not knowing if the boy had been injured or if the fight was going out of him. All alone down here, surrounded by those loathsome creatures, it would be easy to lose heart. He shouted encouragement: *Hold on! Hold on!*

Iker's torch sputtered fitfully, the resinous gum that fuelled it almost spent. The creatures edged closer, sensing the end was near. Iker grasped the dying torch in both hands, ready to use it as a club and gathered his strength for one last shout, but the creatures were already turning away from him, their hearing being more acute than his. The next time the yell came, he heard it. The answering cry of the Janissary.

It was Ayne. He had come for him. Relief flowed through Iker, threatening to undo him, but he could not afford to relax yet. It would not do to drop his guard now. The creatures could rush him and bring him down in a heartbeat.

Ayne doused his own torch and moved with swift stealth towards the tiny spark of light. The tunnel widened out into a small round chamber. Feeble as the flame was, the sweep of the boy's torch described fantastic shapes on the walls and ceiling, making the Naxar creatures appear as big as their noble cousins. They had turned back to Iker and were bobbing their heads and shifting from side to side as though intent on hypnotizing their prey. Ayne drew his knife and crept as close as he dared.

The attack took the Naxar by surprise. Iker leapt forward with a loud shout and used the last spark of his torch to drive the creatures towards Ayne. They fell back, squawking in enraged confusion and Ayne loped off two heads with one stroke of his big knife. He plunged the blade into the throat of another and skewered a fourth in the soft hollow where scrawny neck met the hard breastbone. The headless bodies continued to run and stagger like fowl, spraying hot blood all over their fellows. The Naxar were not fussy creatures and they were hungry. Maddened by the smell of the warm blood, they fell upon the dead and dying, snapping out great chunks of flesh, ripping into the soft bellies with their long, sharp claws, tearing out the steaming innards with a furious shaking of heads.

Snarling fights broke out as the creatures bickered over the carcasses and fell on each other. Ayne grabbed Iker and they fled back down the tunnels away from the spreading carnage.

Iker followed Ayne out into the night. There were no lamps lit. The torches were dead and black in their niches, yet the sky was lurid with fire, the air thickened by smoke. From a distance came the screams of men and trumpeting, bellowing roars which were not human at all. The Beast Gods were exacting their revenge on those left by the departing ships, rampaging through the city, killing as they went.

Ayne and Iker moved cautiously. There were other threats in the streets, besides the beasts. Not everyone had left on the boats. Some thought the Council's decision premature and had stayed true to the belief that the Beast Gods would save them. Others had been unlucky in the selection that had taken place to decide who would leave and who would stay. Criminals and those judged unworthy had been deliberately left behind. The deserted city meant rich pickings. Houses, temples, palaces all lay empty and people had been allowed to take very little on to the ships. What they had left was there for the taking: gold, silver, jewellery, clothes, wine, beer, fine foods, the buildings themselves.

"If they can avoid the beasts, they can live like kings," Ayne said as they walked past drunken people spilling from rich houses, furniture and clothing strewn about. "Until it all runs out."

"What will happen then?" Iker asked.

"The God knows," Ayne answered.

Freezing and starving, the furniture they were stealing would go for firewood, and they would be fighting over the last handful of grain left in the city. Iker shuddered. That was before they started eating each other.

"Not a very pleasant prospect," Ayne said, following his thought. "It won't be long before those killed by the beasts will be counted as lucky."

They moved through the Hive. There was no sign of trouble here, little sign of life at all. Before them, the great White Gate lay open. They slipped through unchallenged; there was no one left to close it at curfew or guard it now.

Once they were out of the city, Iker judged it safe to tell Ayne about what had happened in the Chamber of Oracles. Ayne bowed his head in real sorrow to hear of the passing of the Ama and out of respect for her. When Iker spoke her dying words, Ayne bowed his head further.

So that was the precious thing that Ket held cradled to his chest.

"It is my duty," he muttered. "It is why I came here."

"How will you get it away from him? What if he has taken it to the Place of Skulls? It would be death to follow him there." Iker shook his head. "It is an impossible task that the Ama sets for you: to do something she herself could not do!"

"We will find a way. In good time. The ships have left; Ket will not be going anywhere just yet. Meanwhile, we will do what is possible." He put an arm round Iker. "The Mother instructed you also, Messenger. You must carry her words to Mikel." He paused for a moment, his hand on the boy's shoulder. "Perhaps it is all one."

Mikel was somewhere in the north, so they took the White Way out of the city. The road was paved with white pebbles which showed bright, catching the moon and starlight even on the darkest night, and served as a guide for the spirits of the departed, heading for the Cape of Souls. The road had a neglected air and was in a poor state of repair. There were potholes everywhere. Some had been filled with dirt and grey river grit; they showed in the pale surface like pits in teeth.

There were hardly any settlements out here. The causewayed track passed across countryside that was wild and uncultivated, a poor, stony landscape of tawny heath land, dwarf spiny shrubs, and clumps of dark, needle-leafed trees. The Plains of Agirre spread out around them, flat and featureless. After dawn, Ayne called a halt. They broke their fast in silence, chewing dried goat meat and filling their water skins from an icy stream.

"Hear that?" Ayne asked.

"Hear what?" Iker listened and heard only silence.

"That's what I mean. No sign of animals anywhere and no birds singing." He rinsed his mouth and spat. "I don't like it. I don't like it at all."

Ayne decided to scout about, examine the countryside around, but he found nothing suspicious, no sign of the beasts, anyway. It did not occur to him to look up into the sky.

The silence spread as they continued their journey across the bleak plain. Even though the azhdarchs flew high, their passing did not go unnoticed by the birds and lesser creatures on the ground.

IX

These people put great store by the symbolism and meaning contained within dreams. They went to the Red Temple of the Seers to have their dreams interpreted. They were then recorded and kept in archives that went back for centuries.

THE STONE TESTAMENT – Brice Ambrose Stone

Eztar was dreaming. She heard the Mother softly speaking. She seemed to be calling from an impossibly long distance, like the voice Mikel had heard, and Eztar glimpsed things that were utterly unfamiliar, but the Mother's tone was so gentle and loving that Eztar wept. Tears coursed down her sleeping face. It must mean forgiveness. Her conscious mind could accept Mikel's reasoning, the rightness of his decision not to go through with the sacrifice at the Cape of Souls, but in her heart she felt excluded from the warmth of the Mother's love, the light of her kindness. In the dream, she was comforted.

The Mother's voice was replaced by Mikel's. He was shaking her.

"Wake up, Eztar! Eztar, wake up!"

She woke to find Mikel bending over her, his breath white in the freezing air. The dream was still there. What did it mean? Seers were also Dream Diviners. She would ask Mikel.

The sky was light in the east, but the sun had yet to rise above the high cliffs, so the beach was all in shadow.

"I had a strange dream," Mikel said, his face pale in the grey of the coming day.

Eztar looked at him in surprise. "I did, too. I was going to ask you about it."

"I dreamt of the Mother," he said.

"I did, too," Eztar replied, but what he had to tell her drove her own dream from her head, and all the comfort that she had gained from it fled.

"I dreamt I was in the Chamber of Oracles," he said. "I've never seen it in life, but now I could see it plain. The niche in the wall was empty."

"What of the Ama?"

Mikel shook his head. "I don't know. I could not feel her presence." He looked at the girl, his gentle face stricken. "I fear something terrible has happened, Eztar."

They broke camp. The cliff above them was sheer. Eztar decided that the quickest way would be to follow the beach until a mass of great tumbling rocks made further progress impossible, then they would climb the cliffs to head inland.

To the south, a shape appeared, small as a fleck of

black ash against the growing brilliance of the sky. It seemed to be following the coastline, as if hunting the tidal margins, looking for carrion, or small marine creatures. It flew high, so its size was hard to gauge, but as it came nearer, it took on the distinct crescent shape of an azhdarch. A close examination would have told the observer that the flying creature was much bigger than a bird, but Mikel and Eztar were too busy with their thoughts to look up at the sky.

Four others had been sent to fly over plain and forest, covering every arm's length of land from the city to the cape and back again. If the king's son was dead, they had orders to bring back his body. If he was alive, they were to report his position to Ket.

Eztar and Mikel toiled up the steep, twisting narrow path that traversed the crumbling cliff face, while showers of earth, stones and pebbles cascaded and bounced down to the black, restless sea. Eztar led the pony, while Mikel held on to his tail. Progress was slow and it was noon before they reached the top. They were keen to travel on as fast as possible, but this was wild country of tall thorn scrub with few clear paths. It was possible to get lost for days, but luckily they found traces of the Old Way, which followed the coast round to the city.

The way had been used, time out of mind, by goat herders who brought their animals here to graze on the kalaama bushes, whose little grey leaves were supposed to give the meat a distinctive tang. The herders had disappeared, but wild goats still nibbled at the withered foliage and dried stems. The thorn had powerful medicinal qualities and the air still held the distinctive, sharp scent. Healers had been frequent visitors here. And beekeepers. The blossom had long since fallen, never to flower again, but bees had loved the small white flowers which gave the thorn its name, *Star of the Mother*. Kaalama honey had healing properties and was highly prized.

They journeyed on until the light was failing. They would not get to the city that night. Eztar shot a young kid and set Mikel to skin it and prepare it for roasting while she went to see what else she could find. She came back with a bag of withered leaves and her hands full of honeycombs. The bees were all dead. The wax was thick, but there was honey inside. Mikel munched through the chunk she gave him, swallowing it wax and all. He had never tasted such sweetness. Eztar spread some of the honey on to the roasting kid, sprinkled the carcass with herbs, and then wrapped the rest of the combs in oilskin to add to their supplies.

They ate well for the first time in days. Eztar infused leaves, sweetening the brew with honey, and they sat and watched the sun fall into a welter of crimson. The sky darkened from pale to darker blue and Mikel looked for the stars that he knew. He spent a long time studying every part of the heavens. Even though they were no longer fixed in their rightful places, he took comfort from the familiar shapes described in the sky. In the south, the Serpent writhed much higher from the western horizon; the Cross, with its two bright

Pointers, Kalaofic and Kaladim, had moved nearer to the centre of the sky, next to where the Hive clustered round the single brilliance of Anama, the Queen. To the north, the Warrior sprawled, falling towards the horizon. Mikel spoke the names of the stars that described his outline: Luga and Gelas, the points of his shoulders; Oris, curled like a fist on the clasp of his cloak; Gimel, Mira and Kalagirel, the red star, the jewels on his belt; Tusca, Xtan, and Vulpec, the sandals on his feet and the tip of his sword. On the opposite side of the sky, the Fish Hook dangled from the bright eye of Vorcas. The cold air seemed to bring the stars nearer and as they thickened against the deepening blue of the zenith, Mikel looked for the rivers of darkness that ran through their brightness and made out the shape of Kalasagitzl, the Giant Azhdarch, stooping for his prey.

X

The Abere were matched in the air by terrible
flying creatures, called azhdarchs. These huge
winged monsters resembled the dragons of
legend. They did not breathe fire, but if I were
to say that some species of pterosaur had
survived almost to the modern age, I would
undoubtedly be dismissed as some kind of
fabulist.

THE STONE TESTAMENT – Brice Ambrose Stone

Ket, High Priest to the Beast Gods, stood on the flat,
square roof of the Place of Skulls and watched the
sunset. He looked to the north and west, studying the
horizon intently, then he brought up the flute that he
wore round his neck and began to play. The instrument
was long and thin, made from the curved bone of an
azhdarch wing. He blew, covering the stops with his
thick fingers. As he did so, he wove from side to side in
time with the song and his face moved and puckered as

if he was in sympathy with the emotions that the song was expressing, although the instrument made no sound, or no sound within the range of human hearing. Every so often, he would cease playing to stare at the horizon, and then he would take up his flute again.

He set his flute aside. Dark shapes had appeared as small specks against the last of the light draining into the west. Gradually, five crescent shapes became more distinct, flying in a blunt arrow. As they approached the Place of Skulls, four of the creatures peeled off to the left and right and remained in dancing formation, while the largest, a female, landed on the platform next to Ket.

She folded her wide wings, one extremely long articulated finger turning them up and back like sails. She rested her weight on much shorter digits, not much bigger than the spread of a man's hand. She inclined her head towards Ket, her mouth slightly agape; her long, narrow jaws were fringed with a row of small, very sharp teeth.

"Come to me, come!" Ket crooned. "My pretty, pretty one!"

He went towards her, offering bleeding gobbets of flesh. She listened to his whispering and her third lid slowly furled back to reveal a round-pupilled, milky blue eye surrounded by scarlet and purple creased and pebbled skin. He bent forward and whispered. She heard him and clashed her beak together, once, twice, moving her head from side to side. The priest stood, all his attention focused upon her. Then he nodded.

"You have done well, my great one, my pretty."

Ket praised her good work and offered her more flesh from the gore-filled leather bucket that he carried with him. She had found Mikel and the girl. They would be collected without delay. Her flight had also reported a man and a boy wandering across the plain. The young one was small, dark with fuzzy hair. Iker and another. Escaped the Naxar, had he? This time he was unlikely to be so lucky. The azhdarch inclined her head once again. One bite would take his hand from his wrist, but she allowed Ket to touch the smooth surface of the bright yellow crest that ran from the top of her head and tapered down between the triangular slots of her nostrils. Ket stroked her shoulder, combing his fingers through the thick pelt of fine, dark filaments, soft and long, a cross between down and fur. The man and the boy would be her reward. Then he stood back as she took off in a great flapping motion to join her sisters wheeling above. They scattered across the city, to find a suitable roost for the night. Ket left the platform and descended by narrow steps into the depths of the ziggurat. He would report to Sigur and the hunting party would leave immediately. The azhdarchs did not hunt at night, but the great beasts most certainly did.

XI

Beast Gods was an apt name for them. I was reminded in turns of dragons, gryphons, of Quetzalcoatl the plumed Serpent, of Satan in the Garden, of the Great Beast of Revelations, of every foul thing that had stalked mankind since time began. But these creatures were flesh and blood.

THE STONE TESTAMENT – Brice Ambrose Stone

They lay prone in the pre-dawn semi-darkness, pinned by the neck to the ground, each held by a great caging claw. Struggling was pointless. It was impossible to even glance upwards. Talons as sharp as needles curled in to prick at the pulsing skin. They sensed the great and powerful creatures towering above them. Their strange, musky scent was all about them and they could hear the heaving snorts of their breath. They both knew that they lay in the grip of the gods and that the slightest move would mean death.

The pony was dead already, stripped to the bone. The ribs gleamed white and bloody, caging the blackened mess that spilled on to the ground. They both lay still, wondering when the same fate would fall upon them. Mikel closed his eyes and concentrated on a series of whirrs and clicks coming from above him. He sighed his relief. They were to be released. Claws hooked into cloth instead of flesh and hauled them to their feet.

The boy stared in awe, dwarfed by the great creatures towering over him. It was as if the bright-painted stone effigies that marched along the temple friezes had come alive. Snorting breath plumed from the nostrils set at the sides of their long scaled snouts, and the feathers adorning their skin fluttered and ruffled in the rising wind. He closed his own eyes against them, but their terrible regard stayed in his mind. He could still see the round bulge of golden amber bisected by long black slitted pupils, as devoid of light and life as the ocean depths.

Behind the signals that passed between them he could hear their thoughts.

Be careful. The boy is subtle.

He glanced up, as if one of them had spoken.

Don't let them know you can understand!

The girl's thought came to him and he dropped his eyes away from them.

He judged the one who had spoken to be their priest. He was much smaller in stature than any of the beasts, but he was listened to, respected, even treated with deference. A human face lay behind the great gaping jaws with their fearsome curved teeth. Everyone knew that not all the children who went to the Mountain were taken in sacrifice. The most talented were kept and trained for this bizarre priesthood. It was the fate that Mikel had always dreaded. If he had gone to the Mountain, he would have been taken for a priest, but he would rather die on the stone altar, have his beating heart cut out, or feel the rocks pile up on him, slowly crushing the life out of him, than be a man inside a great feathered skin.

Ket, in his turn, regretted the waste of such enormous ability. He turned his brooding gaze upon the boy. Ket had already had to guard his thought against him. He had the true talent and would have made the perfect apprentice, not just in this world, but in the one where Ket belonged. There he was again, using his thought like a lance, probing for the weak spot in his armour. Ket smiled. The boy might be of use to him yet.

Is he the one? the tallest of the Beasts asked. *The Ativeteh's son?*

Yes, my Lord Sigur.

So this was Sigur. Chief of the Beast Gods. Despite himself, even though he didn't believe in them any more, Mikel started to shiver.

And the girl? What about her, Ket? Do you want her killed?

Not for the moment. The man shrugged. *We may find a use for her. . .* He was trying to sound indifferent, but his black eyes gleamed coppery in his fleshy face as he looked at Eztar.

Mikel felt anger surge inside him. How dare he offer her insult? This man. This *Ket* should be punished. . .

Then he smothered the feeling as quickly as it had ignited. What was the point when he could do nothing?

They were taken. No one even bothered to secure them. They were pushed into line, and the creatures turned back to the city.

Sigur was with his trusted band: Hortzhaganak, the Toothed One; Haize, Lord of the Wind; Otso, the Fierce One; Labana, Lord of Weapons and War; Eltlxar, Lord of the Flies. The other lords had been left to mop up any remaining resistance in the city. Sigur kept up a cruel pace; he wanted to get back as soon as possible, now that they had secured the boy.

Mikel was near the end of his strength.

"I don't know what you want with us," Eztar spoke to Ket, the priest. She could not keep the hostility and contempt out of her face. "But you will have to carry him if you want to keep him alive."

So Sigur scooped up the boy and carried him. Mikel was not afraid. His leg had been paining him cruelly and he was relieved to ride, even in the arms of a beast. Besides, he wanted to study their captors more closely. They were all of the same kind, but they differed in small ways, just like humans do. Eltlxar was leaner, his snout more pointed; Labana had a thinner jaw; Hortzhaganak had more pronounced crests on his head and back. Mikel began learning their characteristics. He thought it was important to differentiate between them, to know who they were.

They were obviously intelligent. They communicated in turns of the head, clicks of the claws, grunts and soft hooting whistles, but every sound and movement carried meaning. Sometimes there was no sound, no movements, just fluid lines of thought that merged and divided like currents in a river. They are better at that than us, Mikel thought, with something approaching admiration. He was also awed by their physical strength. Any human would be puny in comparison. He had been plucked from the ground like a toddling child. He tentatively smoothed the long, floating filaments that wrapped themselves around him like an extra coat and looked over Sigur's shoulder at the beasts following. They possessed a great and terrible beauty. It was easy to see how they could be worshipped as gods.

The feathers were not like those of a bird with a central shaft and barbs on either side. They hung down like a great undulating cloak made of long, fine strands that changed colour when they moved. Sigur's feathers shimmered with rich purple, turquoise and blue. Others were more drab, but even they could change colour: grey brown took on a pinkish shimmer, or turned pale green as they moved. Exltlar's feathers were very dark: the black on his back shone a bright, deep hue of greenish blue, like a beetle's wing case, or the thorax of the blowfly for which he was named. Mikel guessed that the feathers gave good camouflage in light or shade, useful in almost any terrain. Their skin had an odd quality which also intrigued him. It was not tough and dry, but smooth and pliant, pebbled rather than scaly, made up of many shades, like different layers of coloured wax melted over one another. He wondered if they might even be able to change the colour at will.

Three long, curving claws held him steady in a

curling grip. The talons were dark and shiny, like horn. One claw on each foot was raised and flexed back, to keep it from damage, keep the point needle sharp.

Men lose control of their bodies merely by looking at us, the thought came straight into the boy's mind, *yet you are not afraid. Why not?*

You could kill me at any moment, Mikel replied, *yet you carry me in your arms like a baby. I may feel fear when the time comes, but at the moment, I'm safe.*

The beast's mind was silent for a while.

And the girl?

She is a Warrior of the Mother. She is not afraid, either. To her you are an enemy. She will kill you if she can.

The creature cocked his head to one side as he looked at the girl with an amber, slitted eye. Then he opened his mouth. Strings of saliva stretched between rows of great curving teeth; bleached strands of shredded flesh were caught between the fangs. Mikel flinched as a gust of foul air escaped in a harsh, wheezing creak. The beast's reaction surprised the boy. He had not thought them capable of laughter.

Eztar watched him. Mikel had a way of putting worries behind him, living in the moment, but she did not have that skill. Thoughts of the Mother, fear for her, filled Eztar's mind. Her own guilt had returned and churned inside her like the Eye of the Sea.

"We cannot worry until we get to the city," Mikel had said. "Now we have to concentrate on staying alive."

There was wisdom in that. She made herself think about killing the beasts instead. That was something she understood. You knew where you were with such an enemy. You could work out ways to fight them. Her fingers itched on her knife hilt. She watched the way that they walked, loping along with their wide toes spread. A thick tendon took the tension of their springing gait, standing out like a taut rope above the heel. She could imagine her blade entering just below where the leg muscle narrowed, imagine it slicing through, separating bone from sinew. She saw the great creature crash to the ground, writhe there helpless, while the thick muscle ravelled up the leg like a bunched sleeve.

She smiled at the satisfying image. That was the way to deal with *them*. But the man who served them, he was a different matter. He was flesh and blood, of that she was certain, but there was something about him. Something strange and alien. He could snare her with a net of sorcery before her fingers could even grip the handle of her knife.

As if summoned by her thought, Ket appeared at her side. Away from the beasts he served, she could see that he was a big man. She could not see his face clearly because of the mask he wore, but what she could see was fleshy and heavy featured. One cheek was marked with a deep, round scar, as if it had been pierced at one time, and there was a pronounced cleft in his bulbous chin. His eyes were large; very dark, almost black, and set in hammocks of fat. His lips were thin, which made his smile like a knife slash. His teeth were filed to points to resemble his masters', marking him as their priest. He was dishonest, the smile said, dangerous, not to be trusted. Loyal only to himself.

"You don't like me, then?" He gave his razor grin,

making her feel stupid. She must remember to guard her thought.

"No," she replied. "No one likes your kind. You should have died at the Place of Sacrifice."

"Maybe." He shrugged and grinned again. "What would you have done?"

"Died! Gone for sacrifice!"

"Dead is dead. What's the point of that?"

"Honour. It would be the only *honourable* thing to do."

"I don't believe you. It's not a pretty death, you know. You'd change your mind as soon as they began piling the stones over your face. What would these say to you?"

He threw back his cloak. He carried a bundle of some sort slung round his chest. He thrust this aside to show her a necklace made from little hands and withered hearts taken from sacrificed children.

Shock and disgust showed in her face, but she shook her head. "I would still choose death."

"No, you would not." His black eyes gleamed with triumph. "Haven't you made just that choice already, and recently?" He dropped his cloak back again. "Don't lie to Ket. He knows everything."

Her long stride and firm step faltered. She had betrayed the Mother. He felt the guilt well up in her and savoured her shame like a succulent fruit.

"I was a Seer, remember, as talented in my time as the one who now rides with Sigur. And I am older, so I see more. If you want to hide your guilt, don't worry at it like a tongue going to a rotten tooth. Your disobedience has brought him to me. To see one with his talents die needlessly! It would have grieved me. You have delivered him into my hands. I must thank you for that."

He watched her walk away from him. So young, so passionate, a true Warrior of the Goddess. And beautiful. Shame to waste her on a crippled boy. She wore the Great Whore's bee talisman, clenched in her fist to ward off evil. Much good it would do her now, not with Ket on the prowl. He smiled to himself. It was going to be a pleasure to pull off *her* wings. In this world and the other, he would be in need of a consort and successor. He had them both now. All he had to do was find a way off this cursed island. He had ideas about that. He hugged the box he carried to him and felt energy and power surge through him. The skull inside it was already beginning to whisper its secrets and the boy was part of it.

XII

Intelligent and cunning, tireless and powerful, the beasts were pack hunters. With each member many times stronger than a man and tuned to the others by almost preternatural senses, they were, quite possibly, the most effective predators that the world has ever seen.

THE STONE TESTAMENT – Brice Ambrose Stone

To the east, the mountains stood in serrated relief against the brightness of the rising sun. Light flooded the upper land and brought a little warmth after the bone-chilling coldness of the night. They were still some way from the city when Sigur signalled a halt on the edge of a tall bluff, high above the plain. He put Mikel down and the other beasts moved forward to flank him. They stood in a line, their great bodies perfectly balanced, long snouted heads craning forward, some scanning the flat land that stretched out before them, others studying the sky. Ket approached his master, as if to intervene, perhaps to counsel against delay, but his intervention was met with a snarl and a roar of impatience. The priest was obviously discomforted. His impatience was matched by Eztar's. She was in an agony to get back to the city. What was the delay?

"They are beasts," he said with a shrug. "They like to hunt."

"Hunt what?" Mikel asked.

"Azhdarchs! See?" Eztar whispered to Mikel. "Coming from the south."

Mikel could just see the little dark specks flying in formation, coming from the direction of the city.

"What are they looking at down there?" he asked.

"I don't know." Eztar craned forward; her eyes were sharp, but the grey, featureless expanse of desiccated, dusty shrub, barren rocks and sand seemed empty, devoid of any movement or life. "They have better sight than us."

Sigur signalled to his band. They moved swiftly, jumping and bounding down the boulder- and scree-strewn face of the cliff, leaping from rock to rock with sure-footed confidence. At the base of the slope, they formed a line behind Sigur and set off across the flat expanse of the plain. Even though they stood half the height again as a man, they were quick, light on their feet, running up on their toes, their long legs covering the ground effortlessly. They ran with their whole body pitched forward, their short arms tucked in, or spread out to manoeuvre. They ran with feathers streaming down their backs and trailing from their shoulders, so their arms looked almost like wings. They ran with their tails stuck out and stiff for balance and quickness of turning. Every now and then, one would stop, scan the land with his large eyes and lash his tail: thick at the base, tapering to a fine tip, thin as a whip. This signalled a change in direction. Another would leap up in the air, jumping to twice his own height to secure a better view. They fanned out across the land, each falling into his assigned position within the pack. They moved with incredible swiftness across the terrain.

The azhdarchs flew high, covering the ground between the city and the plain. They located their prey easily – the sparse scrub of the open plain provided poor cover – and took up position, fanning out to cover the flanks, signalling with their wings and movements of the head to make sure there could be no escape. The leader turned. She would mount the attack, coming in fast with no warning.

Ayne and Iker were taken by surprise. They were just breaking camp when they heard a harsh cry from above, followed by another. Then the scream of wind across folded wings was all around them. They had not expected attack from the skies.

"Down!" Ayne shouted. "Get down!"

Iker threw himself flat on the ground, avoiding the sideways swipe of the heavy bill and head meant to break his neck. He rolled over and over to where his weapons lay while the swooping creature climbed and banked, turning for another approach. Ayne got into a crouch and prepared to run, but their attacker was not alone. More of the creatures were turning in readiness to fly in from different directions.

The first azhdarch sent him sprawling. The open beak with its razor teeth sliced through his sheepskin coat, tearing his shoulder to the bone. There was another, following after. Ayne eased his bowie knife from its scabbard and rolled over. A stone blade would be useless, but with this he could slash the exposed underbelly, or sever the stretched windpipe. He waited. Powerful wings beat above him. His hand tightened around the hilt. He would take one with him that was for sure.

The azhdarch was flying in low. Ayne lay prone as the dark crescent-shaped shadow wavered towards him over the ground. The creature's beak was open, talons extended to seize and disembowel. Iker nocked his prized red and white fletched arrow and drew his bow. He rolled on to his back and let fly. The arrow caught the azhdarch under the wing. The wound inflicted was not mortal, but the steel tip bit deep enough to make the creature swerve in its deadly trajectory.

The wounded azhdarch sheered off, the wing on her injured side dipping as she joined her sisters. Iker notched another arrow, but Ayne lay motionless, blood from his wounded shoulder soaking the ground. The flying creatures circled lower, all their attention focused down. They were more wary now, but the end was inevitable. Iker drew his bow in readiness, knowing that his flint-tipped arrow would barely penetrate the tough azhdarch skin. The two of them stood about as much chance of surviving as mice under the wings of stooping owls.

The azhdarchs were moving in to claim their reward. The prey was small and puny, hardly enough for all of them, but it was alive, an increasingly rare prize. The others deferred to their leader, banking to left and right, wheeling away for their own incoming flight.

She seemed to have recovered, as if the arrow in her side had been no more than a pinprick. Her wing dipping only slightly as she came in low to the ground, talons extended, jaws agape for another scything bite. She focused on the bigger, wounded one, while her companions moved simultaneously to attack the smaller prey from two directions at once. They came in for the kill, so intent on their purpose that they failed to notice a sudden disturbance below them as they skimmed over the low scrub.

Sigur signalled the hunting party to scatter in a grouping that matched the flight pattern of the azhdarchs. They crouched, poised and motionless. The dappled skin on their necks and faces had dulled to their surroundings; their feathers drab against the dun-coloured plain. Sigur counted the approaching wing beats and he looked up, gauging the distance as the leader of the azhdarchs passed over him. Then he leapt. The long curved finger claws shot out; needle-sharp points dug deep into each side of the long neck. The powerful talons tore into the throat, cutting though the arteries, tearing out the windpipe, so the flying creature tumbled from the air in a gasping, wheezing, gargling welter of foam-flecked blood. Sigur swung up with his feet. The large central toe claws snapped forward, flicking in an arc to clamp into the underside of the chest. A quick downwards thrust of the legs tore out the ribcage and the soft underbelly until there was nothing left but an empty body cavity. He rolled out as the creature flopped to the ground. He stood up, licking the blood and sweet flesh from his claws. This was their preferred way to kill.

The other flying creatures, which had been coming in on their own low trajectories, were dispatched just as quickly. Ayne and Iker lay a little way off from the killing site. They stayed motionless, eyes closed. They had heard the harsh clamour of cries, sensed the intense violence going on around them, but some deep instinct held them still.

Ayne risked a glance round. Alert to the slightest motion, any kind of sound, the great creatures ceased what they were doing. Their heads turned as one. Ayne felt their focused attention swing towards him in a concentrated beam. He shut his eyes tight again. They had merely substituted one form of death for another. That was all. The beasts were coming, although it was impossible to tell how near they were getting; for such large creatures they were light of foot. Iker lay a little way off. He hoped that the boy had made his peace with whatever god he worshipped. Ayne hadn't prayed in a long time. As he took leave of his life, he saw what had brought him here: Lockwood in his study, the Indian guide on his spotted pony, the crystal skull, the boat of bone and skin. Finally he saw Wesson, sitting in a Paris café, deep in conversation, and as he was now, the Priest Ket, grinning his triumph through the jaws of his beast mask. Then all thought fled and from somewhere deep inside the words came back to him: *Our Father who art in Heaven*, as he heard the soft exhalation and felt the warm, blood-scented breath pass like mist across his face.

XIII

At the moment when I thought death was upon me, I saw everything with absolute clarity. When I found that I'd been spared, it could have only been for a reason and that had to do with Wesson. I had to take that dark thing from him and wipe him from this earth.

THE STONE TESTAMENT – Brice Ambrose Stone

Sigur opened his great blood-stained maw in a long, deep-throated roar. Thin threads and gobbets of flesh trailed from his gaping jaws. The skin of his face and neck was flushed deep crimson. On his head and down his back, twin ridges stood erect in bristling turquoise crests. The flowing filaments on his chest gleamed and rippled iridescent purple in puffed-out display.

He stood with his arms raised in the air. A body lay draped there. A human shape.

He laid the inert form on the ground.

Eztar stooped down. It was a man with pale skin and

long golden hair. He must be from the House of Strangers. Eztar thought she recognized him from somewhere. He was not dead but had fainted from loss of blood. The flesh on his shoulder had been slashed to the bone and the edges of the wound were already swollen and angry with infection.

"Go and get my bag," she said to Mikel. "And boil some water."

Her travelling stock of medicines was small, but she had honey and she had collected a big bag of the healing leaves from the kalaama thorn.

"There is another with them." Mikel pointed. A boy was coming into camp, escorted by two of Sigur's lieutenants. He looked halfway to manhood, Mikel's age, maybe less. Small, slightly built, like Mikel, but dark skinned. So they were both from the House of Strangers.

"Do you know him?" Mikel asked.

Eztar nodded. "His name is Iker. I've seen him in the precincts of the Ama. He was favoured by Her."

The boy came and squatted down next to the man, regarding him as tenderly as any son might a father. "Can you help him?"

"I'll do what I can."

"I am Iker." He held his hand out to her.

"I know you from the House of the Mother. I am Eztar. And this is. . ."

"I know," Iker bowed his head and touched his forehead in deference, "Lord Mikel, the Ativeteh."

"Just Mikel will do." Mikel was embarrassed by the other boy's deference. "And I'm not Ativeteh while my father lives."

"Your father has left the land," Iker raised his eyes to him. "You are ruler now."

Mikel gave a grim laugh. "Let's hope my people have few expectations." This line of talk was making him uncomfortable. "Who is your friend?" he asked to change the subject.

"This is Ayne. Short for Aynegeru."

At the sound of his name, the man stirred and opened his eyes.

Eztar gave him a decoction of bitter leaves to dull the pain, but he hardly murmured as she cleaned the wound, sewed the edges together and bound his shoulder tightly with strips of cloth.

"Ativeteh!"

Mikel started round at the name, as though his father had miraculously appeared, but then he realized that the boy was addressing him.

"I told you not to call me that. My name is Mikel."

"Mikel," Iker corrected himself. "I have a message from the Mother."

Mikel put a finger to his lips. "Do not tell me yet," he said and limped away before the boy could say more.

A message from the Mother would be important and something he wouldn't want Ket to know. The beast priest was a talented Seer, an expert at snooping into minds, even Mikel was not immune from his intrusion. Ket had been regarding them with some curiosity but now he turned and went with a number of the beasts in the direction of the kill site. Mikel followed. He had never seen one of the great flying creatures close to before, and he wanted to do a bit of snooping of his own.

The azhdarchs lay sprawled, their big heads flung back, long necks twisted like rope, claws flexed in a dying rictus. Their thick, dark pelts were already dusty with death; the long, fine filaments flew about in the constant wind to expose the grey pimpled flesh underneath. Their eyes were sunk into circular, wrinkled depressions, glazed bulges under the scarlet and purple skin.

The beasts were soon busy removing the wings under Ket's direction. Mikel was intrigued. What did they want with them? Other things puzzled him. Why were the azhdarchs so far out of their territory? Why had Sigur attacked them when the azhdarch traditionally served the Abere? And why had he saved the man and the boy? The beasts killed so easily, and with such pleasure. Mikel would have expected them to have ripped off the heads of the humans and be tossing them back and forth like balls in the ball court.

Mikel felt a sudden intrusion, like a low jeering laugh at his train of thought. He started round to find Ket standing behind him. He had not heard or been aware of him. He raised his eyebrows in surprise.

"Sigur likes to hunt. The flying creatures are the rarest and most formidable of all opponents. To pluck such a creature out of the air takes strength, skill and perfect timing. They are of little use any more as spies and sentinels."

"Why did he spare the man and the boy?"

The priest shrugged and his face soured. "Who can read the mind of a god? Why don't you ask him?"

"What do you want with the wings?"

The priest's face soured further. "Not for you to know," he said as he walked off to supervise the work.

Mikel watched as the beasts hauled away their trophies. The slender bones were like delicate spars. When the membranous skin was stretched taut between them, the triangular limbs were very like sails. . .

He limped after the priest. Ket waited for him and smiled. The boy had guessed his intention. He was quick. Ket admired that. And he would be useful. He knew the sea roads. His powers were great and such a one could easily be subverted. Given time. He was Ket's nephew, after all. He could see himself in the boy. He would make an admirable apprentice and successor. Hadn't he already disobeyed the command of the Mother? If he had been taken to the Mountain, as he should have been, Ket would have taken him to undergo the training. Ket grinned to himself at the rightness of things. It was clearly Mikel's fate to follow him. And the girl? Ket's admiration of her had been growing. Her beauty, her grace, even her fierceness. A Warrior Priestess of the Mother, Ket would find other uses for her and would enjoy doing so. The others? The man and the boy? They were expendable.

Mikel watched him, watching him. Ket had hidden his mind, but Mikel was more talented than the priest knew. He caught all of his thought without appearing to do so. What he learnt filled him with anger and indignation, but he was careful to give away nothing. He kept his face as much of a mask as the priest's gaping jaws and filled his mind with new thoughts. Boats of bones and skin.

"An ingenious idea," he said, "but you will need someone to build them. Ayne, the man the beasts have just captured, is skilled in that. I remember seeing him when I visited the boatyards with my father. He was working with the shipmaster. Of course, once they are built, you will need someone who knows the sea roads."

Ket laughed. "You want me to take you with me?"

"Certainly! I can show you where to go by the sun, moon and stars and from what the whales told me. I have much to learn from you, Uncle. I have always wanted to study the forbidden arts, to know the secrets of sorcery and the ancient magic of the earth. You can teach me. We will need someone who can sail, though; I have no knowledge of that." He paused as if deep in thought. "The boy, Iker, he was born a sailor. Story has it that he sailed a boat from the Burnt Lands when he was only a child."

Mikel limped along, eager to share his ideas with the priest. By the time they returned to camp, he had set the bait. Whether Ket would take it was a different matter.

XIV

I woke with a renewed sense of purpose but also with the knowledge that I was not alone in my endeavor. We made a strange quartet and appeared, on the surface, to pose little threat to the forces ranged against us, but perhaps the weak could inherit the world, or at least save it from destruction.

THE STONE TESTAMENT – Brice Ambrose Stone

As soon as he got back to the camp, Mikel could see something was wrong. Eztar's face was as pale as ashes. She did not weep, but when she spoke, she could not keep the emotion out of her voice.

"Your vision was correct," she said slowly, her voice deep and husky. "Something happened in the Chamber of Oracles. Iker has grievous news. The Ama is dead."

She turned away, while Iker told him what he had witnessed.

"And Ket has this dark skull?" Mikel asked; that explained the beast priest's sudden ingenuity.

Iker nodded.

"He keeps it in the bundle he wears slung round his neck." Eztar turned back to them.

"How do you know?" Mikel asked.

"I don't know for certain," she replied. "But it is clearly something precious. He has it with him always."

"It will be hard to take, then." Mikel frowned.

"Not if we cut his throat!"

"How do we do that, Eztar?" Mikel shook his head. "He is surrounded by beasts most of the time, and even if you found him alone, he is a Seer of uncommon talent. His senses would detect any of you at twenty paces. I might get close enough, but I am no warrior. He would overpower me. We will have to find another way."

"How?" Eztar asked.

"I don't know yet, do I?" Mikel's mild eyes flared with impatience. "I'll think of something."

Eztar was no longer listening. The grievous news of the Ama came back to her, eclipsing all other thoughts.

Mikel turned to Iker. "You said she gave you a message for me."

"Yes. She said: 'Even if it cost him his own life, no beast is to leave this land.'"

Mikel let the boy run off to see to his friend. The man was sitting up now. He looked pale but was regaining at least some of his strength. Which was good. If he could not walk, the beasts would leave him here. Their mercy did not extend very far. Eztar was a skilled healer, a true Warrior of the Mother. Those who kill can cure. He turned his mind to the Mother's words to him. No beast was to leave the land, even at the cost of his own life. He could see the wisdom behind Her words but he would go along with Ket's plan. It offered their only hope of leaving. If the beasts came with them, so be it. When the time came, he would find a way to obey her but he would decide when and how. He was Ativeteh now.

Mikel rode with Sigur. There was something he wanted to know and this might be his last chance to talk with the Beast Lord.

"Why did you save the man and the boy?" he asked him.

"I have no love for any of your kind," Sigur said. "Do not mistake me. But Ket is different. He was like one of us. Like a brother. But he has changed of late and I no longer trust him. I saved them because Ket wanted them dead."

When they neared the city, Sigur set him down and the beasts went on ahead. Mikel followed with the others, deep in thought. Eztar would speak to no one, she walked arms folded, head sunk in misery. Ayne could walk with Iker's help, but he was weak, so their progress was slow. The beasts were some way ahead, under the city walls, when Sigur's deep roar rang out and they saw him fall.

He lay on his side, and at first, they could not see what was wrong with him. A vitreous ichor leaked from one eye. An arrow showed, buried up to its fletching of red and white feathers. Shot from a Janissary bow. The point had entered the brain. He died where he lay.

Mikel felt a kind of sadness as he looked down at the great body. He was an enemy, but he had been a magnificent creature. Mikel had admired his strength and power. He could not bear him any malice. What he did was in his nature. He was a beast and could not do otherwise. Mikel had come to respect him.

The beasts had no such sentiment. They attacked the corpse of their fallen lord. They flayed off the feathers and skin, under Ket's direction, to make a new cloak for him, and then began their feasting. Mikel turned away, sickened as the first among them took his portion. He reached in to wrench the great heart steaming from the carcass and held it up for all to see, the gore streaming down his arms. They had a new leader: Eltlxar, Lord of the Flies.

XV

"I am a Stranger," I said. "A shape-shifter. A sorcerer. A trickster. A walker between worlds. Where I come from, such people are called shamans, and there is another of our number here."

"Time runs differently," I told them. "If it runs at all."

THE STONE TESTAMENT – Brice Ambrose Stone

The assassins were hunted down. The steps of the temple ran afresh with human blood.

Mikel led them to the Hall of the Ancestors. They moved with wary care as their weapons had been taken from them, but beasts and men kept their distance. The Hall of the Ancestors was thick with venerable spirits. Men regarded it with deep superstition; even the beasts disliked the atmosphere. The air was full of strange, eerie noises that sounded like voices and the Ancestors themselves, resplendent in rich garments and masks of gold, looked down from shadowy arches and niches set high in the walls.

Ayne wondered at the noise around them.

"It is just the wind blowing through vents in the upper galleries." Mikel smiled. "The Ancestors turned to dust ages past. Even if they *were* here, since our world is threatened with utter ruin, surely they would want to help us and not do us harm."

They were sitting round a fire that Iker had built in the middle of the hall. Smoke drifted up to become lost in the darkness. They were dwarfed by the place, like robbers in a cave. The only light was made by the flicker of flames.

Mikel listened in silence while Ayne told his story, which ended with the attack of the azhdarchs on the Plains of Agirre.

"But who *are* you?" Mikel asked when he had finished his tale. "Why are you here?"

There was something about this man, Ayne. Although Mikel had only seen him once before today, and then from afar, he felt as though he knew him somehow. . .

"I am a stranger. But you know that." Ayne dropped his voice. "I am also a shape-shifter. A sorcerer. A trickster. A walker between worlds. Where I come from, such people are called shamans, and there is another of our number here."

"Ket!" Iker supplied.

Ayne nodded.

"Did you know him? In your world?" Iker asked.

"Yes."

"Does he know who *you* are?"

"I think that he suspects something, but can't quite decide what it is. I'm not like other people, but then no one is in the House of Strangers." He gave a low laugh. "We're famous for it. Besides, I'm a good enough shaman to hide myself from him."

"Don't be so sure." Mikel frowned. "He is clever and dangerous."

The man nodded. "More dangerous than you know."

"How long has he been here?" Mikel asked.

The man shook his head. "There is no way of knowing. All I know is that I was following him in my world and I found myself in yours, more by accident than design on my part. His transit here might not have been so random."

"You mean he came for a purpose?"

Ayne nodded.

"To get the skull?"

"No, I don't think so. Not exactly. The skull exists in my world, too. He came to secure the know-how to unlock the skull and to make sure it comes through. If it is destroyed now, it cannot survive in future time."

There was something about what Ayne was saying that made Mikel feel light-headed.

"I don't understand how he got here," Iker said. "You, either."

"There is a space between death and life when a person can walk between worlds. I took a potion to bring on this state."

"Like the herbs the Seers use?" Mikel asked.

"Something like."

Mikel fell silent. He remembered the voice he'd heard at the Cape of Souls. The feeling he'd had of being in this place and another. He shivered.

"What's the matter?" Ayne looked at him. "Are you cold?"

"No. We have an expression, 'a bird flew over my grave'."

Ayne gave a grim smile. "We say something similar."

"I've been watching him," Mikel said. "Sometimes he sits rapt. I've tried seeing into his mind then and it's like a sealed room. No way in, or out, but nobody there."

"That is when he's travelling," Ayne said.

"Maybe we could seize the skull when he's like that." Iker leant forward.

"In the Place of the Skulls? With beasts all around him? We must think of a different way." Mikel turned to Ayne. "Is it possible to be in the two worlds at the same time?"

"For him, maybe." Ayne shook his head again. "Not for me. I don't know how I got here, so here I stay."

Iker's brow creased. To be in one world and another. . . He remembered the strange dreams he'd had as he hid from Ket in the Temple of the Mother. "I don't understand," he said.

"Why would you? I don't understand myself." Ayne sighed. "Time runs differently and can't be measured. If it runs at all." He took a charred stick from the margins of the fire. "This is one place in time. Your place." He drew a shape like an island. He stood up and disappeared into the shadows that filled the rest of the hall. "The man you know as Ket and I, we are from another place." His voice came echoing back. "This place here. Imagine the earth heaves and all this part of the floor falls away. Then——"

"The circles end up next to each other," Mikel supplied.

"Exactly." Ayne came back and sat, legs crossed. "Maybe something like that happens in space and time."

"If Ket is from your time," Mikel pointed to the wall lost in the darkness, "how did he get here?" He put his finger into the island on the floor.

"I don't know, like I said," Ayne shrugged, "any more than I know how I got here myself."

"No." Mikel shook his head. "I mean with the beasts. The priests are taken as children. Any other human would be killed."

The man shrugged again. "He is here because what he wants is here. He must have taken someone's place. A cuckoo in the nest."

"A what?"

"It's a kind of bird . . . never mind."

Mikel nodded. He thought he knew what Ayne meant. He'd suspected that something wasn't quite right with Ket, as if he'd taken over the shell of another. Like those little crabs you see on the shore.

"But wouldn't the Beast Gods notice?" Iker asked.

"Not necessarily. Ket wears that mask for one thing; maybe they see that, not the face beneath. And perhaps they see differently. Like some kinds of lizards, which they closely resemble. Excellent distance vision, but not so good with near things. And beyond big, small, man, woman, perhaps we all look the same to them. Who knows?"

"Perhaps they already *have* noticed, Sigur at least." Mikel told them what the Beast Lord had told him.

"Now Sigur is dead."

"But that was the work of the Janissary!" Iker objected.

"Even so," Mikel looked at him, "the gambling pieces fall in Ket's favour. We are all strangers really, I suppose," he said, after a while, his mind jumping to something else. "We have been here for many lives of man, but that is not long, not long at all. We are still newcomers compared with the beasts and the ones who came before."

"The Ama spoke to me of the Ancients," Iker said quietly. "In her last moments. How this had been their place originally."

"Yes," Mikel said. "They left their great buildings and their knowledge: calendars, maps of the earth and the heavens, ways of treating the sick and the well. We inherited much from them, including the skulls of crystal."

"She said they overreached themselves, releasing power over which they had no control. That is why they died out."

"Then we came after them," Mikel spoke quietly, almost to himself. Much that had always puzzled him was now making sense. "We brought new gods with us: Ama, the Mother; Patiku, Only Father; Ti'ana, the Son, the Bull-footed One; Ti'una, Maiden and Daughter. But the Beast Gods were here before."

"I don't follow. . ." Ayne shook his head.

"The beasts were here with their priests. Or their priests were here with them. Those that were taken to serve them carried on a form of the ancient wisdom. There would be continuity. Never broken." He paused to gather his thoughts. "The Skulls of Light have revealed some of their secrets: the arts of seeing, and of healing, but even the greatest sages do not know everything about them. The dark skull contained different knowledge. That which is hidden. *Pa*. Forbidden."

"Sorcery," Ayne supplied.

"Exactly!" Mikel spread his hands. "And the ancient earth magic."

"Geomancy?" Ayne frowned.

Mikel nodded. "If that is what you call it. The Ancients disappear. Who knows where? And we come along. The worship of the Beast Gods goes on. They are placated by yearly sacrifices, but the practice of magic is forbidden. The Ancients might have disappeared, but their priests had not gone anywhere, had they? They stayed with their masters, safe in the interior, their knowledge never lost, continuing, untouched by changing times. Their priesthood constantly renewed, their wisdom passed on to newcomers saved from sacrifice."

"They had the knowledge, but we had the skull. They were kept apart. Until now."

"Again, the pieces fall in Ket's favour," Ayne said.

"Not for much longer," Mikel said.

"What do you intend to do?" Iker looked from one to the other. "Kill Ket and smash the skull?"

"That would be one plan, but no." Mikel shook his

head. "We need Ket to get off the island. We will go with him."

"Get off the island!" Iker's eyes widened. "But if he leaves, the beasts will, and the Mother said——"

"I know what she said," Mikel interrupted him, "but we have to survive."

"How does he mean to leave?" Ayne asked.

"He intends to build ships."

"What from?" Ayne gave a harsh laugh. "There's scarcely enough useful wood to make a child's dugout and the forest trees are fallen and rotten."

"He does not intend to use wood. The boats are to be made from bone and skin. He's got it all worked out. The hides from their giant prey animals will form the skin of the hull. The hides will be tough and waterproof and the plated ones could protect the gunwales and the prow where the risk of collision is likely to be greater. The skins will overlap each other and be sewn together with sinew. Rib bones will form the internal struts of the craft. The sails will be made from azhdarch wings, which are extraordinarily thin, but pliable and very strong. The bones are hollow, which will make the craft very light."

Ayne shook his head. "Ingenious stuff."

Mikel hugged his knees to him. "Too clever for him, I suspect. The skull is already speaking to him, telling him what to do."

"There's one flaw in his plan." Ayne chewed the end of his moustache. "I'd wager that neither beasts nor priests know how to build boats or sail 'em. I doubt they can even swim."

"You can build them," Mikel smiled, "using whoever is left in the city to help you. Ket has already agreed."

"I can think of something better. . ." Iker said, his voice a whisper, as if the shadows gathered around could hear him. "We should leave without them. As soon as one boat is built, we steal it away. *They* will be left here, as the Mother intended, to die of the cold. The ice will creep over the land, burying beasts, priests, skulls, everything many soundings deep, and both of you will have fulfilled your obligation to her."

"You just might have something!" Ayne's drawn face, creased with tiredness and pain, relaxed into a smile.

Mikel nodded. "The best ideas are the simplest kind."

32

RAID

Celestine had been dreaming, travelling with them in the Elder Time. She felt the sharp pain of their anguish and sorrow. The passing of a sister. She sat in the darkness of the empty flat, and rocked herself, tears streaming down her face. She was living through the moment as fresh as if it had happened right there and then.

A hammering from the door roused her to the present time and place. Her hands ached from where she had gripped the metal arms of the plastic garden chair. She did not stir from her seat. This place was supposed to be empty. No light showing. Perhaps they would go away. The knocking intensified, accompanied by shouting.

"Anyone in there? Open up!"

The banging changed. The dull thud of a hand-held ram bar sounded down the narrow corridor and echoed through the empty rooms. Her eyes flicked to the three of them propped against the wall. None of them stirred and there was no time to move them, no place further for them to go. She went over and laid them out flat, covering them lightly with a blanket. She was back in her seat when the rending of wood and metal told her that the men had broken through.

Boot-shod feet thumped on the bare concrete. Doors banged back as voices roared, "Secure! Secure!"

She was in the last room to be searched. The door hit the wall, showering rotten plaster, and she turned to face the glaring light from a powerful torch. Her presence gave the guard a fright. She heard the soft snick as he flicked back the safety catch on his gun. His face was cased in a black wool balaclava, but she heard the distinct quality of his accent as he asked her, "What you doing here in the dark?" His voice marked him as a generation away from the Sugar Isles, maybe two.

"No 'lectricity," she replied. "Not supposed to be here anyway." Her voice was querulous, soft with fear and pleading. "Don' tell no one. They send me back."

He caught the glint of her big, dark eyes in the strong torchlight, and then swept the beam round the room.

"What's over there in the corner?"

"Just me bed and t'ing."

He was about to go over to investigate, when she stepped in front of him. He looked down at her.

"Get out of the way," he began to say, but her eyes held him. Next minute he was walking to the door.

"Secure!" he yelled as he entered the passageway.

"Thought I heard you talkin'," one of the others said to him.

"Radio," he said and touched his earpiece.

When all was quietness, Mamma Celestine folded

the blanket back from the faces of her charges and sat
down again to continue her vigil.

Across the city, Abraham Black watched the wheels
turning. He watched with the quiet fascination of one
who never thought that the moment would actually
come. The elaborate glyphs which marked the different
counts were coming into alignment. In turn, they were
about to mesh with the glyphs representing the
movements of the planets through the constellations.
They would meet where the mouth of the celestial
serpent swallows the golden smiling face of the sun
god. The latter marked an extremely unusual alignment
between the galactic and solar planes. The Cosmic
Concurrence was due to happen the day after
tomorrow. The waiting was nearly over. Centuries had
come down to years, the years to months, the months
to weeks and days. Now it was the turn of the hours and
minutes to slip away like so many grains of sand.

Was it too late? He had no way of knowing how time
ran in the Elder World, but it was running out here. If
the dark skull was destroyed, then there was hope, but
if it was not? All he could do was wait and nurse his
doubts and fear.

In the Temple, the Advocate had no such doubts and
misgivings. The preparations were almost finished. The
skull stood delicately balanced on the ancient stone
altar, pivoting on two points located on the underside of

the base. It floated there, as if suspended in the air. A source beneath it directed a steady light up through the zygomatic arches into the skull's interior, where a ribbon prism deflected the light through tiny tunnels to suffuse the whole skull with a deep purple glow. The eye sockets were concave lenses. The rays directed outwards cut through the semi-darkness as thin and intensely luminous as twin laser beams.

At the time of the Concurrence, the moon, Venus and the other planets would stream out in a line from a sun that was nearing the exact centre of the galaxy. At noon on the winter solstice the sun's elliptic would cross the galactic plane at a point that the Mayans called Xibalba Be, the Road to the Underworld. The Grand Master would walk this road and return through the dark rift in time and space, carrying the last secrets of the dark skull with him. He would emerge from this great cross in time and, at that joyous moment, he and the Advocate would become one. The first part of the Great Transformation would be completed. The Grand Master would be accompanied by the Youth and the Maiden. The Advocate expected the present fleshly forms of Adam Black and the girl called Zillah to be delivered to him within the hour. Their location had been pinpointed to a small area on some run-down estate. He had men searching every inch of every dwelling. It was merely a matter of collecting them and eliminating their guardian. Then the rite could begin.

The blood sacrifice had already been carried out. The body of the young man known as Brother Zack lay sprawled on the floor. The seven Chosen would enter and take their places in the wall niches, readying themselves for a day and a night of ritual and prayer. All over the world others like them would be gathering, in designated meeting places. The places of power. At the pre-ordained time and hour, the Grand Master would take the place of the effigy in the sarcophagus of Mimma Lemnu. The twin beams of light from the skull would begin to pulse and direct themselves towards the basalt coffin. The Grand Master would repeat the ritual words while this world ended in fire and flood, and the next one dawned. This would complete the second and final part of the Great Transformation when all trace of Wesson, Grand Master and Esteemed Founder, and his willing vessel the Advocate, would disappear to be reborn as the god, Mimma Lemnu.

XVI

To kill the priest would doom us to stay there for ever. The irony was not lost on me: our only hope was to go along with Ket's plan.

THE STONE TESTAMENT – Brice Ambrose Stone

Ket looked down from the Place of Skulls and dreamt and schemed. The city lay in ruin, but Mikel's father and his people had brought this on themselves. The rebellion of the Ativeteh had been a very major upset to his plans. He could hardly control the anger surging inside him. Their duty, first and always, was to their gods. To take the ships to save themselves, abandoning their own deities, was a heinous, blasphemous act, for which they would pay, not just now, but in the future. These coastal dwellers were ship builders and seafarers; they had taken their boats and their skills with them. He had to get off this cursed island and take the skull with him, or all his plans for the End Time would come to nothing. He simply would not exist there. Neither would the skull.

Or if it did, if it somehow survived into the future, it would just be a useless lump of rock. He looked down at the dark crystal. Intricately made and beautifully crafted, without his knowledge it would be a priest's trick, made to nod on a stick, or a toy in some magician's study: a party piece, a talking point. The skull pulsed under his fingers, responding to his touch. There was a mind there, a powerful consciousness working for its own survival. The skull had already given him the answer. It was telling him what to do.

Mikel looked down from the Eye of the Ancestors, a vantage point high in the walls of the hall. Ayne had been summoned to see Ket. Mikel was watching for his return. Below him, lines of beasts were trudging from the interior, carrying boat-building materials: piles of hides and great curved rib bones balanced like cages on their heads and shoulders. Mikel looked up at the sky, trying to work out how long Ayne had been gone, but there was no sun. The day seemed to be over before it had really begun. Great banks of clouds were forming, sullen grey with a hint of sulphur. There was a salty smell in the air and a piercing wind. Mikel felt pressure behind his eyes as if icy fingers gripped his temples. Always a sign that snow was coming. Already, a few feathery flakes were falling, sifting down past the entrance to the temple, swirling white against the gathering darkness of the sky.

As the snow thickened and the sky gave up the last of the light, Ayne returned.

"What did he want?" Mikel hardly gave him time to knock the snow from his cloak.

"It is what you said. He wants me to build a boat. Just one. I guess he wants to see if the idea will work. . ."

Ayne left Mikel deep in thought. Why just build one? He suspected the reason for that. It was getting colder. When he exhaled, his breath plumed in the air. It had snowed today. Ice was collecting out in the bay. There was not time to build a fleet of ships. But one? How long would that take? A week? Two? If Ket was planning on leaving, it would be soon, and he would be alone. There would be no room for Beast Gods. He would still need a crew and navigator, or he would not even get out of the harbour. When he was ready to depart, they would either go with him, or steal the boat before he could leave.

All the people who were left in the city were herded to the Place of Skulls to learn their fate.

Ket came forward to address them. His hands rested on a domed ivory chest that stood on the red stone lap of Xtal, the Old, Old One.

"I speak on behalf of Eltlxar, Lord of the Flies, Chief of the Beast Gods."

Ket stepped back to make way for his new master. He smiled behind his mask, pleased by the change in leadership. It was not of his doing, but he could not have planned it better. Sigur had begun to suspect him and the Beast Lord was unpredictable, difficult to control. For a beast he was tender hearted. He had spared the man and the boy and, as far as he was capable, even seemed to care for Mikel. Eltlxar served Ket's purposes far better. All beasts were cruel, but he was the cruellest of them all.

Eltlxar stepped forward and stared down at the gathered crowd with his amber slitted eyes. He was leaner than Sigur had been, and younger. His snout was longer and marked on both sides by twin ridges of short, stiff black quills. His mottled skin was striped in shades of grey and his feathers shimmered the iridescent blowfly blue-black, one reason for his soubriquet. The other was his love of carrion.

The other lords gathered around him. The assembly stared up in stunned awe.

Ket spoke. "Lord Eltlxar has decreed that all will be taken off the island. In boats that you will build for that purpose."

A sigh passed through those assembled, like wind through grass. Many assumed that they had been brought here for sacrifice, although providing slave labour for the beasts and their priests might yet prove a death sentence to all but the very few.

"We will make boats to take us all away from this place," Ket repeated. "Now go back to your dwellings. You will be told what to do."

The bones and skin were delivered to the empty boat halls, where the tall ships had originally been built. Here the skins were stretched on frames and scraped of fat and flesh. The fat was rendered down and then worked back into the hides to make them supple. Smoke from the fires helped to cure the raw skins.

Meanwhile, Ayne worked on his boat. He had to admire the idea. The bones were easy to shape and work. The sinews, plaited together, made a good alternative to rope. The azhdarch wings made excellent sails. Iker worked with him and the boat began to take shape. It was enough to lift the spirits. His shoulder was better, that girl really was some kind of healer, and Ayne liked using his hands. The design was working, and he liked that. He was even happy, in a strange kind of way. As bizarre as Ket's plan was, he began to believe that it might just work.

The Beast Lords were rarely seen. They disliked the cold and had retreated deep into the ziggurat, their artificial mountain, to go into semi-hibernation. The lesser of their kind continued to toil, bringing bones, skins, azhdarch wings for boats that would never be built. The columns crossing the plain were joined by others, struggling through the snow, battered by the wind, holding things close to their chests: younglings, hatchlings and eggs cradled to their feathered breasts. The skull cages inside the Place of Skulls were cleared. The eggs were stacked there on nests of feathers. They plucked the down from their own bodies to keep the eggs warm.

XVII

What a strange craft this would have seemed
to any watcher from the shore.

THE STONE TESTAMENT – Brice Ambrose Stone

Ayne worked night and day. In two weeks, the boat was
finished. He told them to meet him on the shoreline
and bring their bundles. He had loaded supplies and
everything would be ready.

They went down to the narrow strip of grey shaly
beach in the dim half-light before dawn. A low mist
extended over the water. It would aid their escape. Ayne
was already there and Eztar went on to help him drag the
boat down to the sea. Mikel followed ahead of Iker, who
was carrying the bags of seeds that he insisted that they
take with them. Not to be eaten on any account.

"For the Ama," he had told them. "So that wherever
we land there will be a new planting and life will go on."

Their own land was dead. That was certain. Nothing
would grow there again.

Mikel turned when he reached the base of the cliff. The other boy should have been right behind him, but there was no sign of him.

"Iker!" he called.

The boat was in the water. Mikel looked down to Ayne beckoning and struggling to keep the craft steady. They must hurry or they would miss the tide. Suddenly, the man's eyes went wide. Eztar's hand went to the empty scabbard she still wore at her side.

"You didn't think to leave without us," Ket's voice sounded harsh against the quiet lapping of the water.

He came down the path towards Mikel and he had a companion. Eltlxar, the Lord of the Flies. He held Iker in his grip. The boy's neck as slender as a stem in the great curling talons.

"We are coming with you. Any resistance. . ." He looked to the beast. The needle end of the claw punctured the skin and a rivulet of blood flowed down Iker's throat. "Quickly now. It is time to depart."

Eltlxar half carried Iker, half threw him into the boat and then climbed in himself. He had several pouches about him made from soft skin, padded with down. He laid them carefully under one of the storage awnings.

"Nobody is to touch or go near them," Ket said. "He carries his progeny with him."

Ayne shoved the boat out further to where the tide would take it and leapt over the side. The beast would be useful. He was big and very strong. He could row them out to the deeper water, where the current would take over and the wind would fill the sails. Ayne looked around. They would have to be on guard at all times.

Their usefulness was probably limited. Once they were set on course, Ket would be keen to dispose of unwanted passengers.

The boat was a strange-looking vessel, but it seemed to float well enough, even when fully loaded. Ayne took the steering oar while Iker managed the sails. Everyone had to do something. Eltlxar took up position as oarsman. His feathers rippled with changing colours as he made ready to paddle with the great scapula of some slaughtered prey creature. Eztar and Mikel took up oars on the other side. Only Ket refused to do anything but stand at the prow, cradling the Ark to him as if it contained something living.

There was a heavy, opaque quality to the blue-green water that heaved in wide, slow ripples under the covering mist. Mikel half expected the boat to be stuck solid, but the long, narrow craft began to nose its way cautiously out from the shore towards the open sea. Ayne's forehead creased in concentration as the oarsmen bent to their work.

"Slowly, slowly!" he shouted while Iker leant over the prow, ready to call out what he saw. The bay was deep, but there was ice floating on the surface, which made the manoeuvre dangerous.

As they laboured further from the shore, Mikel glanced back at the uneven outline of the city that ran along the edge of the tall, dark cliffs. The walls and towers, squat roofs and hulking ziggurats appeared to be melting away, to become indistinguishable from the natural formations of the landscape itself.

He turned away from the land and stared at the reflection of the hull moving through the gelid water: a variegated skin of different hues and textures, brown, yellow, green, stripes of black, patches of red and blue. He ran a hand over the side, plated and armoured with lumps and spikes, as rough as a palmful of pebbles in some places, in others as smooth as a snake. It was as if they were taking all those doomed animals with them. There could be nothing like it on all the wide ocean, or ever would be. He looked towards the open sea. He hadn't forgotten his promise to the Mother. You couldn't miss it. No, it would be impossible to miss.

They were nearing the mouth of the harbour. The water was very deep here and had taken on an oily darkness, like lamp black. Dazzling ice floes floated on the surface. At last, the craft surged forward to meet the swell of the Southern Ocean. Their voyage had begun.

Ket sat in the body of the boat now. He seemed rapt, beyond communication. He hummed as he caressed the box, hugging it to his chest. He had escaped! Now he was ready for the next stage with all the knowledge secure within this bone casing, to change shape, to wake the sleeping world serpent, to become a god. With the strength of the beast coupled with his human cunning, who could stand against him? None! He was ready to conquer new worlds.

Ket crooned on, but Mikel would not allow his shaman voice to enter his consciousness. Once they were beyond the Cape of Souls, he would sing his own song.

XVIII

So we were locked together, each one's survival depending on another, enemy and friend alike. I sailed the boat as best I could and trusted to Mikel and his song.

THE STONE TESTAMENT – Brice Ambrose Stone

Mikel received no answer until they were far out from land. Ayne and Iker were clever sailors; Iker caught the wind and Ayne kept the boat where the current was strong. They passed far west of the Cape of Souls, to avoid the disturbance, and navigated a way through the ice floes floating up from the south. They sailed from one day into another, but Mikel did not change his position, nor did he stop his song.

At dawn on the third day, when light was leaking from the horizon, streaking the grey sea orange and yellow, Eztar looked for Mikel. She found his dark shape still at the prow. She had done as he'd instructed, all was ready, but still he had not moved. Or eaten, or slept, or drunk anything, as far as she could tell. He had not even risen to relieve himself. He was in some kind of trance.

Suddenly, he moved. He gave a nod and a half smile, and then he unfolded his limbs. He rose to his feet and immediately staggered. He would have fallen had Eztar not moved to his side. He stood for a moment to regain his balance and then he waved her away.

"Is everything ready?"

She nodded. He lay down on an inflated water skin next to Iker. Eztar and Mikel settled themselves and pretended to be sleeping, holding the swollen skin tight as if it was a pillow.

"When?" Eztar whispered.

Mikel smiled. "Not long now."

He made the signal and Ayne lashed the steering oar and settled in the stern, his arms round a water skin. Ket remained rapt, his mind elsewhere; Eltlxar appeared to be dozing. No one else could hear anything, apart from the slap and surge of the waves against the side of the vessel, but to Mikel the noise was getting louder and louder until it bordered on the unbearable. He wanted to put his hands over his ears, but knew that would not block out the excruciating sound.

Suddenly it stopped.

The whale, half submerged, hit the vessel with its huge blunt head. The light craft spun in the water as if it had been fashioned from leaves. Mikel and the others were braced for the blow, but the beast and his priest were caught unawares. It was over as quickly as it had begun. The enormous creature ploughed on, the long, smooth grey back furrowing the restless waves, while the boat came to a halt and ceased its spin. Ket and Eltlxar were on their feet, trying to see what had happened, when the vessel was caught by the twin flukes of the diving whale's great tail.

The boat was flipped clean out of the water and turned over to land empty of crew and passengers. Everyone had fallen into the ocean. Eztar clutched on to her water skin, a purely reflex action. Eltlxar and the priest were not so lucky. They had nothing to hold on to and neither of them could swim. Weighed down by their heavy cloaks and waterlogged feathers, they sank beneath the waves like stones.

The whale surfaced again and began pushing the righted craft, gently this time, until it was near enough for those on the surface to abandon their bobbing skins and climb back on board. Much of the cargo was still safely strapped in place. There were even dry clothes. Mikel leant against the side, weak with relief.

He didn't know how much longer they would survive on these vast cold seas, whether they would ever see land again, or complete their journey, but as far as he was concerned that didn't matter. The beasts' time was over. They had not escaped the island. He helped Eztar drag the eggs out from where Eltlxar had stowed them. The eggs were big: a forearm's length, at least. They cracked the thick, pitted shells and tipped the contents over the side: yellow and brown yolk sacs streaked with red and little balled-up bundles of grey flesh.

Ket bobbed in the waves, brought to the surface by

the ivory box strapped to his chest. The boat had righted itself. He shucked off his heavy, sodden, feather cloak and began to paddle. The vessel was not too far away.

Nobody on board noticed his approach. They were too concerned with their own survival: changing their clothes and coaxing a fire in the stone-built hearth. There was a splash. The back of the boat bobbed and lurched. Mikel sent a message of thanks, assuming that the movement marked the whale's farewell.

Iker let out a shout. Ket was trying to climb into the boat. Ayne freed an oar and hit him across the side of the head. The priest still clung on, despite the heavy blow. Ayne threw the oar aside and attacked him with his bare hands. The flimsy craft tipped and rocked. The others stood frozen as the men fought; any movement towards them would have had them all overboard. All they could do was look on in horror as the two went over the side, locked together.

They sank beneath the waves, still clutching each other's throats. Ket's grip slowly loosened. He released the casket and watched it bob away from him. His eyes rolled to show the whites and his body fell away, sinking down into the deep as the spirit passed out of him. The Ark would not sink with his empty shell of a body, but would float away across the ocean. The precious skull would find its way to shore, where it would be guarded and looked after, age after age, until his own time came round and he would take it back again, for now he knew its secret.

33

STRANGER IN A STRANGE LAND

I watched him float away, bubbles streaming from his mouth, his white face a blurred shimmer in the deep, blue green waters. I surfaced and looked about me, but could see no sign of my companions in their small vessel. A swell had started, which meant I could not see much beyond this wave and the next. I found myself all alone in that vast cold ocean, but the instinct to survive is great in all of us. I wrapped my arms round a piece of passing jetsam and used it as a float. It was a while before I realized that I was hanging on to Ket's coveted Ark. I thought it safe in Davey Jones's locker, along with its owner. Now, it was all that kept me from a watery grave. What devil's irony lay in that? Even so, I knew where my duty lay. With numbed and fumbling fingers I prised open the catch that secured the lid and emptied the hateful contents into the depths. I watched the skull fall away from me, swallowed quickly by the sea. From darkness it had come; to darkness it was returning. I closed the lid before the thing could ship too much water and managed to stay afloat long enough to clutch on to one of the spare sails that had fallen from our queer little ship. Fragile but strong, it had unfurled itself and, bowed to a convex shape by its framework of bone, it was light enough to float by itself. With the last of my strength, I hauled myself up and fell back on to my strange coracle. I stared up at the sky. Ribbons of cloud were scudding past preternaturally fast, it seemed to me, and I lay there thinking of Lockwood and the little vessels that he had described plying the rivers of his beloved Gwalia under restless skies. I did not know what would happen to me. I did not expect to live, and did not much care if I did. My job was done.

THE STONE TESTAMENT – Brice Ambrose Stone

Abraham Black's eyes kept closing. He could hardly focus as he read to the end of the manuscript that lay on his lap. He loosened his dark striped tie, undid the top button on his tattersal-check shirt and unbuttoned the waistcoat of his pale herringbone tweed suit. He was not really dressed for hospital visiting and it was hot and airless in here. He supposed they had to keep it like this for the patients, and the windows only opened a fraction. Health and Safety reasons, no doubt, but the policy made the place uncomfortable for the able-bodied and fully clothed. The roses were drooping, he noticed. They hardly lasted a moment. Catherine would have to replace them. She insisted that there be fresh yellow roses in the room at all times.

He would have liked to get up, stretch his legs, get some fresh air, a coffee, anything to help him stay awake, there was nothing in here except tepid water in a plastic jug, but Abraham Black remained at his station. He couldn't go yet, whatever the temptation. His son had been brought in to rectify a minor abnormality in his foot. An overnight stay merely, but something had gone wrong during the routine operation. Adam had been in a coma ever since.

Abraham Black had promised to stay until his wife got back. Where was Catherine? He took his watch from his waistcoat pocket. She should have been here to relieve him at least ten minutes ago. His eyes went back to the manuscript. Enough for today. The story was almost finished. He flipped open the lid of the little leather case that lay at his feet, ready to put the papers back inside. It had belonged to Aurel Lockwood; he'd bought it at auction. He liked to keep the notebook and the Stone Testament in that. It seemed appropriate. An affectation, almost a superstition. He was superstitious about some things, especially about his work. Pens, objects associated with it, took on an almost talismanic significance. Even attaché cases. His superstitions extended to other things, too. He'd been reading to Adam, sitting here every day, reading from Lockwood's blue notebook: the correspondence, the Lascaris Manuscript, the Stone Testament, all of it really. He was nearly at the end of the Testament and he'd told himself. . .

Well, never mind what he'd told himself. It was stupid, like a child avoiding the cracks on the pavement, or counting the number of cars on his way to school. How could his son's recovery depend on finishing a story? He used to do it in the dim and distant. Counting things. Odds. Evens. Did it really make a difference? He couldn't even remember now which was good and which was bad. Catherine was probably right. What he was doing was pointless. He sighed, gathering the loose papers carefully. If he did drift off, the whole lot could end up on the floor and it would be the devil of a job to put them in order.

His wife looked through the little porthole of a window before coming into the room. The doors were cushioned with plastic sheeting and made no noise. She rubbed her hands with antiseptic gel from the dispenser on the wall and came in as quietly as she could. Both sleeping. Father and son. She listened to her husband's light, even snoring and the slightly longer more laboured pauses that came from the regulator that controlled the breathing of the boy in the bed.

For a moment she found herself holding her own breath. Then she went towards her husband, hand out to wake him. She swept back her long red hair and looked over his shoulder at the papers on his lap.

I have no recollection of how I came to be deposited upon that dark and dismal shore. . .

Was it really suitable? she wondered. But then, it wasn't as though Adam had heard a word of it, so what did it matter? She immediately scolded herself for being so negative. The doctors had said that any kind of stimulation could be helpful. The TV was left on and they had been encouraged to read to him, talk to him about anything, and even sing. Others came in to help out, to take some of the burden, but it was a strain to think of things to say when there was never any response. Abe had begun reading his research to him. Distinctly odd, given his area of interest, but better than sitting in silence, listening to the machines.

She shook her husband's shoulder and he started awake.

"Have I missed something? Has anything happened?"

She shook her head.

"Sorry." He wiped a hand over his face. "I must have dropped off."

He looked tired; the skin beneath his eyes was dark with fatigue and crinkled like tissue paper. And old. What had happened to Adam had aged him. His face was gaunt, he was thinner than ever, the back of his hand splotched with liver spots.

"Go and get a coffee," she said as she took his place. "And make sure you have something to eat," she added, although she knew he would not.

He couldn't breathe. He was choking. The boat must have capsized again, tipping them all into the water, just like Ayne and Ket. He opened his eyes and, for a

403

moment, he couldn't see. There was darkness all around. He must have sunk deep under the water. He thrashed around, no longer sure which was up and which was down. Then he saw light shining above him. All he had to do was struggle towards it. That was all he had to do. . .

Catherine was paralysed, just for a second. After so many days of utter stillness, he was thrashing about in the bed like a salmon. Then she hit the button and the room was full of people. They removed the ventilator to allow him to breathe normally, and checked all the other machines. All his vital signs were much stronger. Adam looked around, bewildered, his eyes dilated, trying to focus on what was happening around him. His mind was miles behind, unable to make sense of anything. He coughed and struggled to sit up, but the effort was too much. He fell backwards while a doctor with an ophthalmoscope peered into one eye, and then the other. Catherine looked on, sidelined by the medical staff, unable to think of anything except: "He's alive!" All this time she'd not thought it was Adam in the bed at all. Now her son was back, and not only that, he was awake! She did not even notice the tears running down her face.

"Where's your husband?" the nurse asked, touching her on the arm.

Catherine shook her head. She could not take her eyes off the bed.

"He probably went for a coffee." The nurse answered her own question. "I'll go and find him. He should be here."

The nurse left. Catherine wanted them all to be gone. She wanted to be alone with her son.

"Little sips of water." The auxiliary handed her a plastic cup. "He's still being hydrated intravenously, so not too much."

Catherine went over to the bed to help Adam sit up. He had lost muscle weight and seemed light in her arms, like he was a little boy again. He coughed and she helped him drink. He took the water gratefully, before turning to speak to her. His voice was a whisper, faint and hoarse from the tube that had been lodged in his throat.

"Who are you?" he said.

34

REUNION

A man came in. He was tall and thin, clean shaven and dressed in an old-fashioned way in a pale brown tweed suit with a waistcoat over a cream checked shirt and dark tie. His shiny brogue shoes squeaked a little as he walked over to the bed. He stood looking down, the hair flopping forward, nearly all grey, but still with a trace of fairness at the sides. He swept it back out of his eyes, a characteristic gesture.

"Hello, old mate," he said.

The tears in the corners of his grey eyes spilled as he blinked, finding their own way down his furrowed face. One splashed hot on Adam's hand.

This man reminded him of someone, but Adam couldn't quite place who it was.

"He might be a little confused," the consultant was talking about him as though he wasn't there. "It's normal."

Adam closed his eyes. He felt impossibly tired. His

406

head was filled with jumbled memories and strange images. None of them appeared to belong to the person he was now. He wished they would all just go away.

"Yes, sleep," someone was saying. "Best thing for him."

The door closed with a swish. Adam had his wish.

He was in a side ward with a glass wall between him and the corridor. The glass was frosted, so the shapes outside were fuzzy and distorted. He could see outlines: the couple who said they were his mother and father, talking to the consultant. Adam pulled the sheet up to his chin. He thought maybe he would go to sleep, although that could be dangerous. What if he went to sleep and couldn't get back again? On the other hand, it might take him back to a life that was more real to him than this one.

Which *was* real, anyway? This place, or the one he felt that he had just left? Fragments of memory were coming back to him, like a kind of déjà vu. But what about these people? They must be his parents, but he couldn't recall. . . He closed his eyes, trying to keep back tears of fear and frustration. His memory of the other place was melting away, like snow on a spring day. Soon he would be nowhere.

New voices outside roused him. Some kind of argument was going on.

"Chill, yeah? Just wanna see him for a minute. I won't do nothing."

The door swung open. A boy came in without waiting for a reply.

"Hey, man! How ya doin?" His braided hair fell free

as he threw back his hood. The dark face broke into a wide smile.

Adam smiled back. It made his face hurt, but he knew this boy.

"You been out a long time." The boy came over to the bed and clasped his hand, careful not to dislodge the drip there. "Good to see you back."

"How long?" Adam asked, his voice still hoarse. He coughed to clear his throat. That hurt. The boy looked uncertain.

"Hey, take it easy. You want me to call a nurse, or something?"

"No." Adam shook his head. They would all be in there, fussing. The boy would be thrown out and he really needed to talk to him. He was the only one he felt he could trust to tell him what had been happening. "Just give me some water."

"Don't want none of this hospital stuff. Warm piss recycled, I swear." He poured water from a plastic bottle, beads of cold still on it. "Here. Got it from a machine outside."

Adam gulped it down gratefully; it felt cool and clean, soothing to his throat.

"How long have I been out?"

The boy sat in the chair by the bed, stretching out his legs.

"Don' know exactly but a while. It won't be long till Christmas."

For the first time Adam noticed the cards on his board, carol-singing penguins and skateboarding Santas, and the decorations strung down the corridor. A sudden anxiety, close to panic, welled up inside him. December. The solstice. It meant something. But when he tried to recall just what, the thought slipped away like a fish in a stream.

"They. . ." the boy went on, then stopped, not knowing whether to say the next thing. "Good to see you made it through."

"I know it sounds stupid," Adam's voice was low. "But do I know you? I feel as though I do."

"I'm Kris. I was in here, too. I got knocked off my bike." He laughed. "Stupid really. Stupid thing to happen." He threw back his long dreads to show where his head had been shaved. "Head injuries. I was out, too. Not as long as you."

"But do I know you from somewhere else?"

"Maybe." The boy changed his position, leaning forward. He cocked his head to one side; the beads braided into his hair clicked together. "Maybe you do."

"When," Adam started to ask him, "when you were 'out'. Did you dream at all? Did you dream that you were somewhere else?"

"Hmm." The other boy looked at him. "Maybe. It's all kind of faded. So I can't be sure. I didn't tell no one, 'case they thought me crazy and kept me longer. 'Cept me grandma. I told her."

"Your grandma?"

"Yeah, she's down the hall, chattin' with your parents."

"What did she say?"

"She's wise, you get me? She knows stuff. She says, she says," he stood up and began to walk about, suddenly restless, "it's hard to explain. Maybe she'll tell you herself one day. Hey!" He picked up the manuscript that Adam's father had left on the table. "This is one cool story. He's been reading this to you. Your dad. He's, er, he's," he hesitated, as if he couldn't quite find the right words to describe him, "he's lots of things, but he's certainly one clever dude. Working in the museum, and that. He was telling me. It's real. Think I might check it out." He furled the papers, then let the edges flick through his fingers, one by one. "I been in here when he's been reading to you. Not just this, other stuff, too. An old book he's been working on." He went over to the window and didn't say anything for a while. When he turned back, his face was serious, his voice low and conspiratorial. "It's all there, y' know. What I dreamt, what you dreamt." He dropped his voice even lower. "They thought this Stone guy was crazy, too."

Adam's head flooded with questions. He couldn't decide which to ask first. He got to ask none of them, because just then a nurse came in.

"What are you doing here? Out!" she ordered, but Kris was already ambling towards the door.

"Hey! No!" Adam pushed himself up off the bed. "Stay!"

"Steady!" The nurse pushed him down again. "That's enough excitement for today. I want you to take these." She held out pills in a little cup.

"What are they for?"

"To help you sleep."

"But I've been sleeping!" Adam was almost shouting. "I don't want to sleep again."

He looked up into the nurse's face. There was something about her that was familiar. He remembered her from before, whenever "before" was.

"I won't take them unless you tell me something," he said.

She sighed, hoping he wasn't going to be too difficult. When they woke up, they were usually confused, yes, but docile. He wasn't acting true to type at all. She put down the container of pills and busied herself about his bed.

"What do you want to know?"

"What happened to me, for a start-off."

"You came in for a routine operation on your leg. Something went wrong in the operating theatre, with the anaesthetic. An equipment malfunction led to a critical incident. . ."

"What does that mean?"

"Your brain was deprived of oxygen and. . ."

"I almost died?"

"Yeah." She nodded. "A bit blunt, but that just about sums it up. Now," she was beginning to bustle about him again, "let's. . ."

"No. There's something else I need to know. You were looking after me on the day of the operation. I remember."

"That's right!" she said, her voice full of false brightness. Sometimes memory loss could be a problem. Any recall should be encouraged. "You remember!"

Adam nodded. More things were coming back to him. "There was a girl. . ."

"A girl? What girl?"

"She'd been brought in because of that mass poisoning. We talked about her."

"Mass poisoning?" Her puzzled frown deepened. He was going "off" again.

"Yes! All these people! They killed themselves. They belonged to a religious movement." His sluggish brain fought to remember the name. "Children of the Something . . . Sixth Dawn! We talked about that and all!"

"Like Heaven's Gate?"

"Yes," Adam said, although he'd never heard of that.

"No," she shook her head. "I would *definitely* have remembered. Especially now."

"Why especially now?"

"The world is supposed to end tomorrow. Some special date or other. Been all over the papers. And the telly. My friend Judith is ever so worried. She really believes it! She was even going to have the cat put down. I told her it was a load of baloney."

The solstice was nearly upon them. The Cosmic Concurrence. It wasn't a joke, he was about to tell her, but what was the point? She'd probably think he was delusional, or like that doctor said, confused. Besides, what could he do about it? His earlier anxiety was replaced by a weary fatalism. What would be, would be.

"Now. Let's get you settled." She was bustling round him now. "No Children of the Sixth Whatever. No girl."

"No girl at all?" He collapsed back, all the fight gone out of him. He looked as if he was about to cry.

She shook her head. Tears sparkled in his eyes. He blinked rapidly to get rid of them, and then looked back through lashes clumped with wet.

"Wait, now," she said. "There *was* a girl. Bit older than you." She handed him a tissue. "Brought in near the same time. Maybe it's her you're thinking about. Collapsed on the street. An illegal, living rough, not looking after herself. She was in a bad way for a bit, couldn't decide what was wrong with her. Low blood count. Right as rain now, though. She had to stay for a while for them to sort out what to do with her. She came in to see you a couple of times."

"What did she look like?"

"Tall. Very good-looking. Beautiful, really. Tawny hair. The most amazing eyes. Like that Afghan girl on the poster. She was from Uzbekistan, or somewhere, that part of the world."

"What happened to her?"

"That black kid you were just talking to? His grandma took her in. Lovely woman. So kind. She's been another one of your visitors. Her and the boy, been in almost every day. The girl's probably still with her. It'll take 'em a good while to decide if she can stay, or not. Now come on." She rattled the pills in their cup. "Get these down you. A good sleep will make you feel better."

He did not resist her. He took them quietly. He wanted to sleep now. He had woken to a nightmare. It was the only way back.

In the space between waking and sleeping, he knew what would happen, but the drugs made it impossible to struggle back to consciousness.

He was back at the beginning. Snow swirled all around him, allowing only glimpses of the black glitter he knew to be the sea.

He heard her approach: the soft, light footfall behind him, and he heard the knife loosen in its scabbard, but he did not flinch or turn. He sat, facing forward, waiting. The knife would not leave the scabbard. She would fall past him, and continue to fall down and down, as graceful as a diving bird, for when had she ever done anything less than gracefully? And she would be swallowed by the Eye of the Sea. The Eye of the Sea would stop in its turning. The waters would calm and he would climb down, painfully, with limping slowness, to a small cove shaped like half a moon.

The water here is deep, protected from the open sea by jutting cliffs. He will wait with his cloak wrapped around him, wait for the ships to come and get him. A day, perhaps two will go by and then he will be reunited with his father, just as they had always planned it before the Beast Gods came and changed everything. They will sail away as day closes, off across the oceans, leaving this cursed land for ever, guided by the stars and the song of the whales.

"Come," she whispers the word in his ear. "We must do this together. Come." She pulls him to his feet. "Come."

She takes his hand in hers. Grips it hard. Something bites into his palm, making her grip painful. "Do not be afraid," she says, although he knows that she is. They are standing right on the edge of the cliff now.

"We will fly." She holds their linked arms up in salutation to the Goddess. "We will fly like birds."

She brings down her arm, his with it. That is the sign. It is time. He should plunge like the birds' diving, go down into the darkness like the whales' sounding, into the cold that will go on for infinity, but he has no sense of falling, just a feeling of incredible lightness, as if he is a downy feather and can float on the wind for ever.

Below him, a boat bobs up out of the whirling chaos of water and the Eye ceases in its turning. The water is calm, as glassy smooth as a dark mirror. An odd-shaped ship is skimming across the surface, as if propelled by some miracle wind. Three passengers stand at the prow. It is a moment within a moment, like a message inside a bottle, for then he is with them, Eztar on one side, Iker on the other. Ianna, sister star, light bringer, shines in the brightening sky and the sun is emerging like a great pearl through banks of white mist and bars of grey cloud. They laugh and put their arms round each other, their voices rising together, for this is a new day dawning and they are the children of the morning star and this is their song.

35

RAVINGS OF A MADMAN

He wakes to his mother and father both in the room together. His father is slightly turned from him. He has been reading to her:

I did know what would happen to me. I did not expect to live, and did not care if I did. My job was done.

"The last sentence is handwritten." He held up the page for her to see. "'*What had begun so long ago, is finished now. How can such things be?*' 'Ravings of a mad man'," he went on, "that's what the accompanying letter said."

"From what you say, they were both as mad as each other. Him and the other one. What's his name?"

"Lockwood," her husband supplies as he goes back to the page.

"That's it." She laughs softly, as if at a private joke. Then she falls silent and touches her husband's arm to gain his attention. She nods towards the bed where their son is awake. Her eyes become wary, full of fear that he still will not recognize them. They brim with tears and her lips tremble. She does not trust herself to speak.

His father turns quickly, spilling the pages of the manuscript, almost turning his chair over in his haste to get to his feet. His grey eyes are as wide as his wife's. His mouth opens, as if to say something, then closes as if he can't find words either. His lined face is creased still further. . .

"Mum? Dad?"

Their faces clear. They look years younger. It is amazing the changes that joy brings with it.

They are at his bedside now, looking down at him. They still have not said anything, just touched him, his arm, his cheek.

"How do you feel?" his father asks at last.

"All right." He smiles up at them. "I feel all right."

"Natural sleep. That's what you needed." His mother squeezes his hand and he winces.

"Except. . ."

"Except what?"

"Except my hand. My hand hurts."

He opens his fingers to show them. The red mark, in the shape of a bee, showed like a brand in the centre of his hand. Then suddenly, tears are falling. To his horror, he finds himself sobbing. He begins to tell them the story of everything that happened in the Elder Time. It's the only way he knows to keep it with him, keep it alive. He has to tell it quickly, because it is fading already. Every episode disappears as he speaks it, like footprints erased by the incoming tide.

He falls back on to his pillow after he has finished and feels nothing. Merely empty. There is a long silence and then his mother speaks.

"All that stuff you read to him. I knew it wasn't a good idea."

His father listens in silence to her criticism, her condemnation.

"Human beings will always find the story," he says simply. "They find their own place in a narrative formed from what they hear, what they see, what is read to them, even their own dreams. He used what I was reading to find his way back to us." He looked to the bright thin line of the monitor, for so long the only sign that Adam was still attached to life. "Like Ariadne's Thread. Who knows what would have happened without it? It might just have saved his sanity."

It might have saved more than that. The words come directly into his head. Adam opens his eyes and sees his father looking down at him. His grey eyes are full of knowledge and a kind of satisfaction. In that moment, Adam knows what truth is and what is fiction. His father puts a finger to his lips and touches his son's forehead in a kind of benediction. They will not speak of this again.

36
AFTERWORD

Not far from the hospital, in what used to be known as the Temple area of the city, a sudden wind blows across one of the many building sites and stirs a thin layer of fine powder, twisting it up into eddying spirals. This dark material is all that remains of that distillation of everything evil, every black art made into crystal. The particles hang in the air, a sparkle and glitter of deep amethyst purple, before they drift back down again and become lost in the lesser dust.

ACKNOWLEDGEMENTS

Ambrose Bierce, *Can Such Things Be?*, published 1893 in New York by The Cassell Publishing Company.

Stephen W Hawking, *A Brief History of Time: From the Big Bang to Black Holes*, published 1988, by Bantam Press, a division of Transworld Publishing, now part of Random House Group, Ltd. By permission, Bantam Press.

Arthur Machen, "The White People" from *The House of Souls*, published 1906 by E Grant Richards (copyright © Arthur Machen, 1906). By permission, AM Heath & Co Ltd.

I would also like to thank the many people who took an interest in and helped me with this project. Terry, as always; Janet and Cenfyn Hopkin; Judith Smith; Ismay Barwell, Jeff Thomas and Jenny Vial in New Zealand; Dick Leith for his help with languages; Jackie D'Arcy for her advice about acupuncture and my editor, Kirsten Skidmore, for being there at the beginning and at the end. . .

I hope any omissions will be forgiven.

To learn more about *The Stone Testament*, go to:

www.celiarees.com/stonetestament

or visit my web site: www.celiarees.com